PIT GUARD

The Tanner's Boy

Robert E Kreig

Whitekeep Books

Book Cover Design by Dee Dee Book Covers [www.deedeebookcovers.com]

Character Design Illustrated by Yves Münch [https://www.yvesmuenchart.com]

Edited by Sally Odgers [www.affordablemanuscriptassessments.com]

ISBN Print Version: 978-0-6453846-7-3

ISBN eBook Version: 978-0-6453846-8-0

Published by Whitekeep Books.

www.whitekeepbooks.com

www.robertekreig.com

First Printing, 2023

For our dad, Robert.

Our father.
Our friend.
Taken too soon.
We miss you.

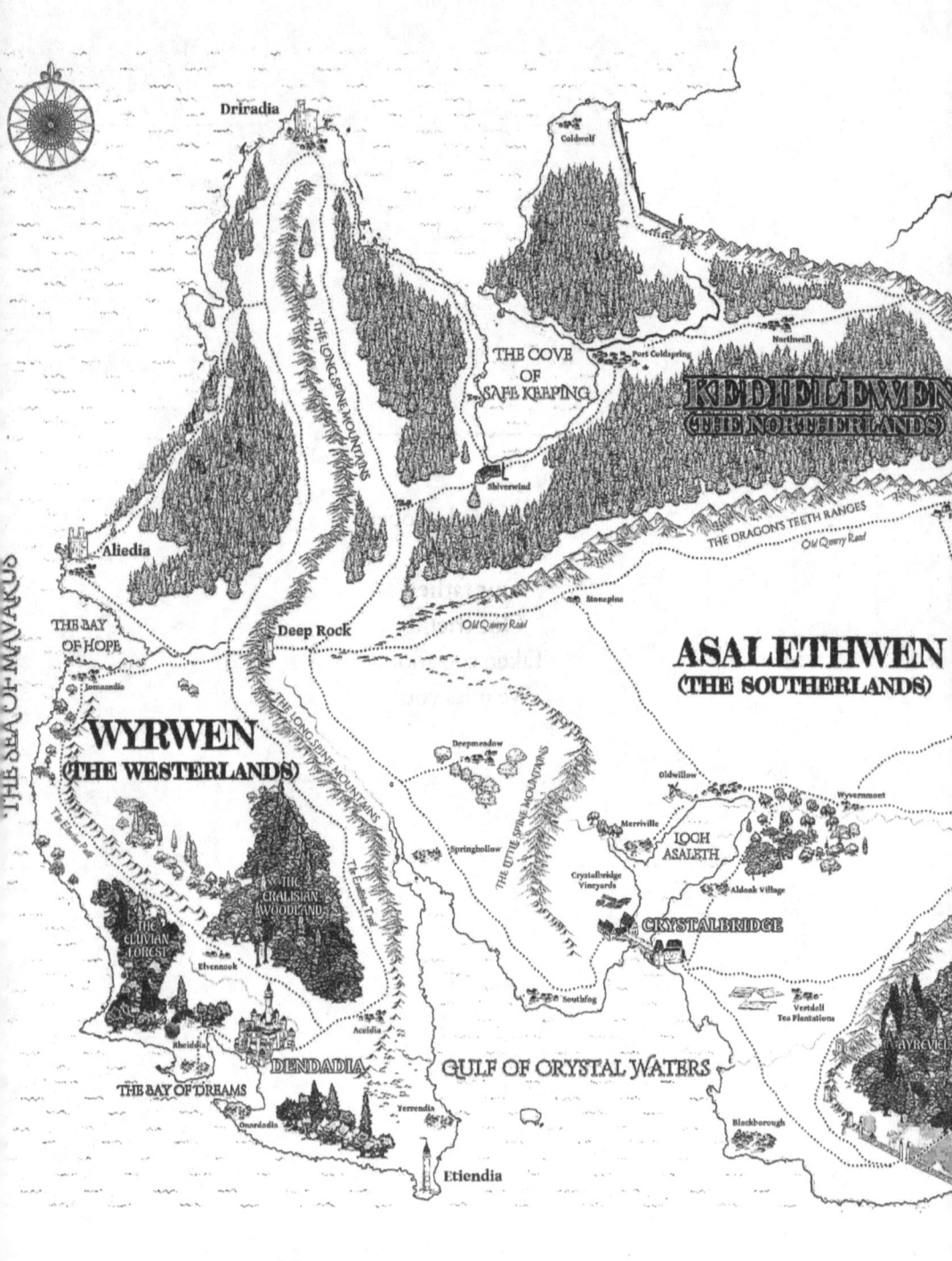

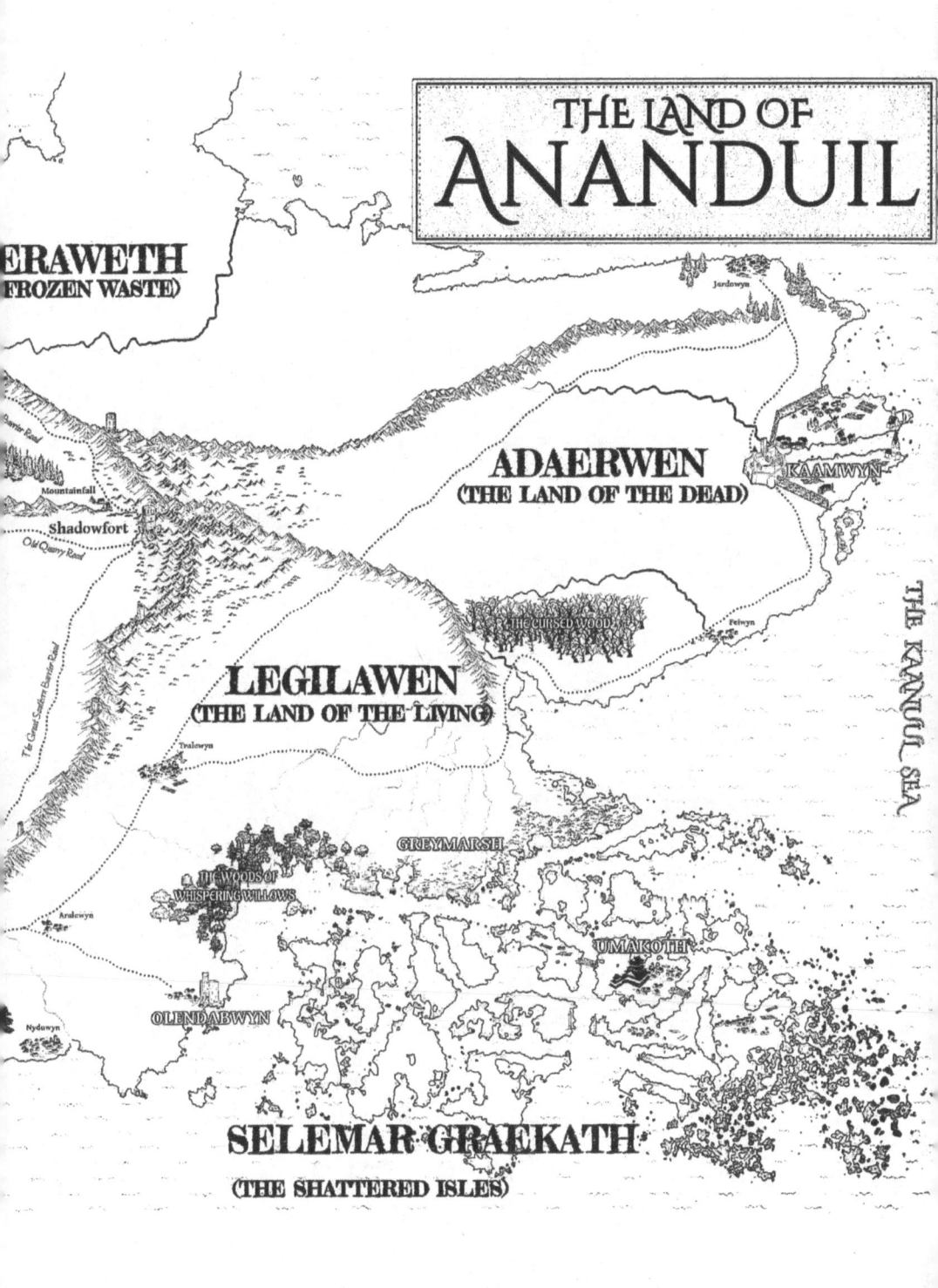

THE LAND OF ANANDUIL

ERAWETH
(FROZEN WASTE)

Jardewyn

ADAERWEN
(THE LAND OF THE DEAD)

KAAMWYN

Mountainfall

Shadowfort

THE CURSED WOOD

Feiwyn

THE KAANUUL SEA

LEGILAWEN
(THE LAND OF THE LIVING)

Tralewyn

GREYMARSH

THE WOODS OF
WHISPERING WILLOWS

U'MAKOTEI

Aradewyn

Nyduwyn

OLENDABWYN

SELEMAR GRAEKATH

(THE SHATTERED ISLES)

Once Upon A Time...

Prologue

———◆○◆———

D ROPLETS GLISTENED LIKE DIAMONDS in the pale moonlight, clinging tightly to wildflower stalks and spiderwebs stretching between the reaching arms of the deep wood trees. A soft breeze filtered through the limbs, shaking away some droplets, diamonds falling with coloured leaves to the damp ground below.

Dusty flecks of white flittered onto the branches as ominous clouds moved to cover the silver fingernail-shaped sliver hanging in the sky.

The jewels dangling upon the wildflowers and webs vanished, giving way to a bitter and beautiful intruder.

Snow.

A loon cried from deep in the woods.

A wolf replied.

A man screamed.

"Help me," he cried into the darkness, clinging desperately to the trunk of a gnarled, ancient oak. His fingers clawed at the bark, blood trickling from broken nails.

Mud, grit, and filth gripped his naked, wiry form. Grazes and small wounds adorned his body. Blood had spilled over his arms and legs, streaking through the filth clinging to his skin. Leaf litter from the forest floor attached itself to him, giving him the appearance of something not quite human. He attempted to step forward, stumbling, limping, reaching into the darkness for the next tree to lean against. His knees buckled, and he fell awkwardly onto his front, smashing his member against something hard, hidden in the blackness. A fresh pain filled his loins and expanded into his stomach and spine.

He looked to the sky for deliverance. The silver glow of the moon fought to pierce the cloud cover, to no avail.

"Gods help me," he muttered with sincere desperation. His beard twisted, now knotted and matted with fresh grime, slapping against his neck as he spoke.

The world spun about him. Branches reached over like twisted arms and fingers, closing upon him, stretching, and grasping, stretching and grasping.

He blubbered something unintelligible as he crawled away as quickly as he could.

A sudden, sinister whisper in his ear made him freeze in place.

He stopped breathing.

He tensed every muscle in his body.

His fingers felt numb, and a strange pain throbbed in his hands and feet. His groin ached, continuing to send a pulsating pang deep into his stomach. It took every ounce of strength he had to not move.

"Javanakhan," whispered a vile voice. He felt the warmth of her breath against his ear. His head swam in circles, disorientating him momentarily.

Instinctively, he reached out towards the sound.

Nothing.

"Javanakhan," it said again. A dizzy sensation overwhelmed him.

He saw nothing but trees. Twisting, reaching trees. Grasping, clawing, gnarled branches with talon-like fingers.

"What have you done to me, witch?" he called, wiping his eyes with the back of his hand.

"Javanakhan," the voice wheezed. Warm breath struck the back of his neck.

Unsteady and swaying back and forth upon his knees, he knew he needed to escape.

A knot tightened in his stomach as he forced himself to his feet. Within moments, he was running as fast as his wounded body could.

A shrill cackle filled the air, echoing about him, growing deeper and louder with each step he took, turning into disturbing, mocking laughter.

"Help me," he cried again, pressing the palms of his hands to his ears. It didn't help.

The laughter seemed to emanate from inside his own head.

Something, demented and twisted in form, scurried from behind a shrub to his left. A white flash crawling on all four limbs, bent oddly yet unmistakably human. A woman.

He lowered his hands from his ears and turned to look.

Nothing.

An illusion the witch conjured, he thought.

The laughter subsided to a deep, guttural chuckle as he picked up the pace and continued his escape.

The strange form scuttered to his right.

Again, he turned and saw nothing.

"Help me, please gods, help me," he muttered.

The world appeared to swell and contract, distorting and contorting around him. Another trick of the witch, he surmised as he reached out with his hands so as not to run into a tree, attempting to navigate through the visual deception.

"A pox on your stew," he cried, tears streaming down his cheeks. "A pox on you."

"Javanakhan," she whispered again, as if right beside him.

Her breath panted steadily against his cheek.

Slowly, he turned his giddy head, hoping to see nothing.

Dark, empty eye sockets stared back. A hideous face of jaundiced, shrivelled skin grimaced menacingly, revealing crooked, yellow teeth and dark, splotchy gums.

The witch opened her mouth and unfurled an unnaturally long tongue. Strands of thick, greenish phlegm stretched away as she sluggishly dragged it across his lips.

His throat tightened.

His stomach grumbled noisily.

He felt immense revulsion and terror sweep over him.

With a shriek, he ran. His feet stumbled over exposed roots and loose stones as wet leaf clutter fastened to his legs. The world swayed and rocked like a vessel upon a tumultuous ocean. It took every ounce of control he had to keep himself upright.

He glanced over his shoulder to see she had gone, vanished into the blackness of the night.

Limping, hobbling, moving as fast as he could, he ventured deeper and deeper into the woods.

His chest burned.

It hurt to breathe.

His stomach bubbled.

An uncontrollable urge to bring up the contents of his guts was sudden and overwhelming.

Falling to his knees, the man vomited. A thick, grey, and black mixture streamed onto the ground before him, steaming in the frosty air.

He stared at it for what seemed the longest time.

It appeared to swim with movement. Worms, maggots, and slugs writhed among pulsating chunks of unnameable things.

He wasn't sure if this was real or just part of the illusion.

"By the gods," he burped, rising to his feet again.

He started forward, unable to take his eyes from the swirling mess he made on the forest floor, and stumbled, hitting his head against a low branch of a thick tree. A terrible pain spread over his forehead as a warm flowing sensation spilled over his left eye and down to his chin.

Resting his hand against the trunk of the tree, he lifted himself again. He tried to move forward, only to have one of his feet slip in the mud while the other became tangled in the twisted tree roots protruding from the ground.

He fell onto his back and felt something pop along his spine. The pain was excruciating. An agonising roar bellowed from his lungs. Tears streamed down his face.

With everything he had left, he tried to move his legs, but they didn't respond.

Knowing she was nearby, lurking out of sight, hidden in the darkness was all the encouragement he needed. He had to get away.

With his legs not able to move, he tried reaching for something to hold on to; something to grasp and help with dragging himself out of the woods.

His fingers dug into leaf litter, dirt, and grime. Eventually, his grasp found something hard and twisted near his waist.

Tree roots.

Carefully, he tried to roll onto his stomach.

A sharp pain shot through his back, along his spine and into his shoulders. His foot, still caught in the roots, held him in place.

It was over.

He closed his eyes and sobbed silently, lying on the forest floor, surrounded by darkness, alone.

Alone.

"Javanakhan," she whispered.

He opened his eyes and peered up at the swirling trunks of the surrounding trees, towards the sky where the inky clouds parted enough to allow a thin beam of moonlight through again. He felt lightheaded, vulnerable.

The grotesque, slender figure perched on a thick branch, far above the ground, smiling balefully upon him. Her long, white hair swayed gently in the breeze.

She stared with hollow sockets, slowly cocking her head as if considering him in some macabre manner. She widened her grin, revealing her yellow teeth and blackened gums.

Her taut, sallow, naked flesh flexed as she scampered a little farther along the branch like a spider, positioning herself directly above him.

Without warning, she leaped from the tree limb, her feet landing in the mud on either side of his waist.

"Javanakhan," she whispered again. His head pulsated with the sound of her voice. Her breasts drooped flat against her chest, reaching down to her stomach. The creases in her skin deepened as she lowered herself upon him.

She appeared old. Ancient.

His stomach turned, bubbled, and he vomited the black and grey sludge again, all over his own chest, neck, and cheeks.

The witch bent lower and lapped at the filth before scooping it with her misshapen fingers and stuffing it into her mouth with a soft cackle.

The sight was sickly.

He felt the urge to vomit again.

"By the god..." he said.

Before he could get the rest of his words out, the witch struck his face hard with her palm, pushing his nose and upper jaw deep into his skull with a sickening, wet crunch.

The last of his breath vanished as vapour into the air as she stood over him. With a vice-like grip, the witch grasped his ankle and pulled him away, snapping the roots tangled around his foot. She dragged him effortlessly by one hand, back the way he had come.

Slowly, with each step, the witch's form changed. Yellowish skin filled to a silky, smooth white complexion. Her white hair transformed into dark, luscious locks. Chipped nails became rejuvenated. The monstrosity gradually vanished to give way to the appearance of a young, beautiful woman.

The snow fell more steadily.

She called out, mimicking the cry of a loon.

A wolf howled a mournful cry far in the distance.

PART ONE

Müqin, sì

Chapter One

———◆◇◆———

H IS BONES ACHED FROM the cold. Age did that. The weather added to the pain.

The fire helped a little, warming his skin against the elements. The thick undergarments and tunic he wore under his dented and stained armour soaked the fire's heat in, held it there against his flesh and gave some comfort. But still, his bones ached.

He felt compassion for his steed, a colt with a grey caparison covering its black hide from shoulders to knees. Tethered to a nearby tree with plenty of slack, it had moved closer to the small hearth to take its share of the warmth. The woodlands about them offered some protection from the wind and falling snow, but nothing thwarted the pervading cold.

The old man leaned forward, scratched his silver beard, lifting himself slightly from his seat on the fallen tree so he could turn the rabbit cooking over the flames. The fire spat as juice from inside the carcase spilled onto the glowing embers.

The wolf resting by his feet growled softly, flashing her large yellow eyes in the direction of the road. The highway lay a scant distance away from the campsite, through a tangle of pine trees and shrubs, barely visible as the last light of the day faded.

"Quiet, girl," the old man murmured, shooting a quick glance in the same direction. "Control yourself. I promised, didn't I?"

He sat back upon the fallen tree, adjusting the long sheath on his left hip and the dagger strapped to his right. Reaching down, he stroked the wolf's ear. She licked his boot softly in reply.

Soft thuds resonated from the road, hoofbeats of horses plodding slowly southward. The sound of men's voices followed. The old man couldn't hear the words, but he sensed the tone.

They spotted his fire.

The wolf raised her head, locking eyes with the old man. He gave her a knowing look.

"Well, hello there," a deep, cheerful voice called from the road. The horses started towards the campsite, weaving slowly through the pines towards the old man's position. "Mind if we share your fire for a bit?"

He counted nine hooded riders. The glint of pommels and blade guards reflected firelight as they drew closer.

"Not at all," the old man offered, gesturing a hand to the hearth. "Just don't expect much in the way of food."

"I see a fat coney there," another wheezed, lowering his hood to reveal an old, frayed biggins resting upon his head. Dirt stained his face so the old man couldn't determine where the feeble excuse of a beard began or ended. The wheezing rider smiled, exposing blackened teeth.

"That's for me and my friend here," the old man replied.

"You'd put a dog before the needs of a starving man?"

The old man looked to the rider's paunchy belly.

"This is no dog," he answered. "This is her kill. She's just sharing it with me. And you look far from starving."

The wolf bared her teeth at the wheezing rider.

The nine riders pulled their horses to a stop.

"Are we going to be safe if we dismount?" the cheery one asked, his voice filled with concern.

"As long as you respect your hosts," said the old man.

"We eat the dried meat from our packs," the rider told the others.

"Come on, Barkley." Wheezer gestured to the rabbit. "It's been almost a week since we had something cooked for us."

"You're just having a baby cry because you've almost eaten all your stash, fatty," said another rider, dismounting from his saddle.

"Shut up," the other spat back before turning his attention back to Barkley. "Come on," he pleaded.

"We're guests," Barkley answered as he tethered his steed to a tree. He lowered his hood to expose a short-cropped head and a clean face devoid of facial hair. "Do what is asked of you."

Barkley approached the fire with his riding companions trailing closely, pausing momentarily to gain reassurance of the old man's permission to sit by the flames with a gesture of his hand. The old man replied in kind.

"So," Barkley started as he lowered himself to the ground across the way from his host, reaching into his waist bag to retrieve a short ribbon of dried meat. "What brings you this far north? Or are you going south?"

"North," the old man answered. "And work brings me here."

"Work?" Barkley smiled, biting off a portion of meat. "Not much work in these parts. Me and this lot were made redundant from the millers in Driradia. We're making our way south to find work. The landlords aren't hiring any farmer's hands. Winter's almost over, but the ground is too hard to plough yet, they say. And looking at you, I wouldn't think you were a farmer or farmer's hand."

"Not with all that nice armour," added another, who bore a scar across his forehead.

"No," the old man replied, standing to take the rabbit from the flames. The wolf licked her lips. "Not a farmer."

"I bet that nice armour would be worth a bit," Scarface put in, eyeing the intricate detailing etched into the breastplate. A wreath of twisted thorns adorned with roses in bloom, surrounded four faceless women standing bolt upright, shoulder to shoulder. The women, shrouded in hooded cloaks, each rested their hands upon the pommels with the point at their feet. "Even with all them dings. Bit of a polish, and you could trade it in for a nice bag of coin. Could buy you and your dog some nicer meat than that coney there."

"Perhaps," the old man said, tearing a hind leg from the rabbit. He peeled the flesh from the bone before placing the steaming meat in front of the wolf. She devoured it instantly as he tossed the leg bones into the fire. "But she isn't a dog."

"Wolf then," the other replied, shaking his head with a roll of his eyes.

The old man tore the other hind leg from the rabbit and rested the remains on the log next to him before chomping into the portion.

"So," Barkley said with a grin. "What are you? A knight?"

"No," the old man answered, his mouth full of meat.

"But you saw battle," Barkley pointed to a prominent dent on the breastplate.

"Mmm." The other nodded.

"You fought in the War of Six, I bet." The cheery visitor laughed.

"I did."

"Well, well, well," gushed Barkley. "A proper warrior. Where did you fight?"

"All across Asalethwen and into Legilawen," the old man replied, tossing more bones into the fire.

"You must have seen amazing things," Barkley said, sounding like an excited child.

"I put the noose around Amalith's neck," he said, locking eyes with Barkley.

A lengthy silence followed. All nine men stared at the old man, expressing a mixture of disbelief and awe.

"You?"

He nodded.

"That would make you one of The First," said Barkley with a hint of fear in his voice.

"The First?" Wheezer asked. "The First what?"

"Oh, come on, fatty," said Scarface. "You must know the stories."

"This, Francis," Barkley said to wheezer, "is one of The First Pit Guards if his words are to be believed."

Wheezer sized the old man up.

"Horseshit," he said, and chuckled.

"I knew that armour looked familiar," said Scarface. "It's worth more than a simple bag of coin. We'd need a cart to haul the gold we could trade this lot in for."

The old man smiled.

Barkley stood to his feet and pulled his sword from its sheath.

"Why are you this far north, old man?" his voice was shaky and low.

The old man stood to his feet and looked at each of the nine men carefully.

"I know none of you are going south for work," the old man replied. "I can tell you haven't done a day's hard labour in your life. You're all bottom of the barrel scum."

"You don't know who you're talking to," Barkley growled.

"You're Bald Barkley," said the old man. "Although you're not really bald, are you? At least, not on top of your head. They say you can't grow a beard. The whores say you can't grow hair down there, like most men can." He pointed to the other man's crotch.

"And you," he gestured to Scarface. "You're Derrik Gord. The scar on your head gives you away. How did you get it? Oh, yes. Your sister hit you with a fire poker when you were fifteen, after she wouldn't let you under her skirt.

"You," the old man focused his attention upon Wheezer before Scarface could react. "You're Francis the Foul. Your beautiful smile gave you away. They say no purse of any size will contain enough coin for any whore to bed with you. That's saying a great deal considering the quality of whore in these parts."

The old man pulled his sword free, letting it sing a metallic note as it cleared the sheath. The wolf rose to her feet and bared her teeth with a low growl.

"You other men all have names too, I suppose," the old man said. "But it is these three that the magistrates have warrants for."

"Warrants?" Barkley sneered. "For robbing rich travellers who can spare more coin than any of us will ever see in a lifetime."

"These warrants aren't for thieving or being highwaymen," he continued. "They're for the rape and murder of women and children in that Elvish town north of Aliedia about three months back."

"Elvish town!" Wheezer guffawed. "Elves aren't even people. You," he pointed to the old man with his sword. "You even told us you hanged one."

"I put a noose around his neck, is what I said," the old man corrected. "And he was my enemy during a time of war. What you did to those people is unforgivable."

"You were waiting for us," Barkley stated. "Sitting out here, waiting for us."

The old man nodded.

"Nine of us," Scarface put in. "One of you."

"Warrants are for you three only," said the old man. "Magistrates have promised more coin for the rest of you."

Scarface shook his head.

"Fuck it," he huffed, running forward with his sword stretched out in front.

The old man moved his attention to Barkley as the wolf leaped over the fire to snare Scarface by the throat. Swords clashed loudly as Barkley and the old man duelled.

The wolf took one of the other riders down within moments. Strings of flesh dangled from her teeth as the torn necks of her victims spread blood across the snow-covered ground.

Wheezer lunged towards the old man, hoping to stab him in the back as he focused his attention on Bald Barkley. The wolf wasn't having any of that. She turned away from the remaining five guests and bolted for Francis the Foul.

With a leap, she knocked her target to the ground and clamped her enormous jaws over wheezer's face, drawing blood. He screamed, shouting into her open mouth, seeing nothing but teeth.

"Bitch," he called. "Fucking bitch."

She shook her head violently, tearing the skin on either side of his face, piercing to the bone. He let go of his sword, lying on his back where he tried to push her away. She was too heavy for him.

The taste of his own blood filled his mouth. His screams turned to a gargle as he inhaled and started to choke.

The wolf let him go. He felt a slight reprieve, but it was fleeting. She tore into his throat viciously before leaping away to her next victim.

The old man blocked a heavy blow from Barkley, who had noticed the wolf's handiwork. As she toppled another of his men, he realised his chances of survival were plummeting.

With Barkley distracted, the old man struck him in the thigh with his blade. The wound was deep.

Barkley fell to the ground.

He had underestimated the old man.

"You were meant to be an easy target," said the thief as he blocked another blow from the old man.

"You were the easiest target I ever confronted," the other replied, striking again.

Barkley looked around and saw all of his men lying on the ground. It happened so quickly. One moment, they were all standing. Now they lay in the snow. Blood bubbled from the eight victims' necks as the wolf slowly made her way back to the old man's side.

She licked her lips and locked her big yellow eyes upon Barkley.

"You don't need to kill me," he pleaded in desperation, tossing his sword aside towards the fire. "Turn me in alive. I must be worth more to the magistrates alive?"

The old man shook his head.

"They want you dead," he answered.

Tears streaked down Barkley's face.

"The leg would probably do it," he offered, gesturing to the wound that the old man inflicted. "At least drag me closer to the fire where I can die a little warmer."

"Not up to me," the old man told the other, sheathing his sword. Barkley offered a confused look as the wolf stepped forward. "I promised her."

"Promised?" asked Barkley, as the wolf lowered her muzzle to his neck. Her fiery breath fell over his neck. "What do you mean promised?"

The old man smiled as he reached for the roasted rabbit resting on the log.

"I told you," he said, tearing off a portion of flesh from the ribs with his fingers. "It's her kill. She's just sharing it with me."

Chapter Two

———◆◇◆———

A GENTLE DRIFT OF snow fell upon the thatched roofs of clustered huts by the water's edge. Fishing vessels creaked softly, their mooring ropes stretching tightly as the tide ebbed tenderly beneath the long, wide pier.

Lamplights flickered in the darkness, hung upon iron hooks on tall poles throughout the hamlet. Warm firelight illuminated windows as dwellers cosied in for the frosty night ahead.

On the outskirts of the township, a small distance away near the edge of the woods, two small timber huts faced one another. Between them, set farther back, stood a small stable and a workshop. The workshop, attached to the side of the stable, consisted of a thatched roof held up by thick poles. It had no walls. Three wooden benches sat within its confines, as well as an iron stove with a giant pile of firewood to one side.

Animal skins hung from lines under the shelter, swaying leisurely as a light breeze made its way through the structure. Timber frames held more skins, stretched fast to dry. A crude sign hanging by chains from a crossbeam on the shelter's edge announced the purpose of this place;

"TANNER."

Two bearded burly men, two boys and a woman sat on chairs surrounding a fire pit neatly positioned between the two huts.

"I think it's time for bed," said the woman, glancing up from her sewing to the two boys.

The boys responded with looks of disappointment.

"Not before a story," said the younger of the two.

"Yes, Mama," the older agreed. "We can't go without a story."

She shook her head with a smile.

"I would expect this from Jörgen," she replied, nodding to the younger boy. "But you're almost thirteen. I don't know many thirteen-year-old boys who still like bedtime stories."

"I still like bedtime stories," said one of the burly men sitting on the opposite side of the fire from them. His beard reflected a deep red in the firelight.

"Thank you, Ibore," she offered with a scowl.

"You're welcome, Letitia." He smiled. "So, what story will you tell, Raulin? A scary tale, or an adventure romp with knights and dragons? Maybe a love story? I hear they're Arnald's favourite." He shot the older boy a knowing look.

Arnald appeared shocked, glaring back at his uncle with wide eyes.

"Ew." The younger boy screwed his face up in disgust. "Love stories are the worst."

"All right," the other man grumbled, running his fingers through his black beard. "One story. A true story."

As their mama sat by the fire, darning another hole in the younger boy's trousers, their baba leaned back in his chair, stroking his thick black beard. Both boys listened intently as he began the nightly ritual of telling.

"There's no better place for telling stories than by a warm fire, my boys," he began.

"The flames dance over crackling logs, dressed in shrouds of yellow, orange and red. They spin and leap to the sound of their own music and songs, hissing and spitting as they turn the timber black. And, if you look closely, deep into the flames, you can almost see what it is the teller of stories is weaving with the words they speak."

"Ooh, here we go," growled Ibore, leaning forward in his seat.

"Long before the time of the Pit Guards, the entire world suffered through a period of turmoil, dread, and terror.

"The lands far to the west, across The Sea of Mavar'us, bore the weight of

20

The Realm Wars. King rose against king. Army against army. They battled from one side of the continent to the other and back again for many, many years until all the kings were dead and those left standing no longer remembered what they fought for.

"Soldiers returned to their homes. Farmers went back to their crops and livestock. Merchants reopened their stalls and began trading again. A multitude of families mourned for those who didn't come back home.

"Although all the kings were dead, along with thousands of their subjects, life plodded on and, mostly, the lands far to the west remained unnamed.

"During this time, the land of Ananduil, the very land where we live, weathered its own share of torment; a great war fought in all six provinces."

"The War of Six," Jörgen interjected.

"Ay, The War of Six," his baba agreed. "The Elvish King Amalith of Legilawen, the land of the living, joined forces with the Pirate Emperor Morsel Sho'sar of Selemar Graekath, the Shattered Isles, along with the Witch Queen Akasha Miroslava of Adaerwen, the Land of the Dead. Their union held only one purpose. To conquer the provinces west of The Barrier Mountains and force all into subjugation."

"Subjugation?" asked Jörgen. "What's that?"

"When everyone is controlled by someone else," Arnald replied, annoyed by the interruption. "Now, shhh!"

"Not willing to fall into slavery," continued Raulin, "the people of Dendadia mustered an army made up of the finest warriors from the remaining three provinces. Elves, trolls, sorceresses, and men left their homes and marched together, converging upon an ancient ruin called Shadowfort.

"There, the great land war began.

"Meanwhile, ships from Selemar Graekath sailed along the southern coast of Ananduil to The Gulf of Crystal Waters, where they met the Dendadian navy. The Pirate Emperor left the safety of Umakoth, his fortress among the Shattered Isles, to lead the assault himself. The battle raged for days, through wild tempests and gargantuan waves." Raulin, the boys' father, raised his arms to mimic a tall swell in the ocean.

"Many of the crew members from Dendadia sank into The Gulf of

Crystal Waters along with their ships as the days and nights dragged out through relentless battle. Resources waned. Food stores and water barrels ran out of supply. The powder kegs grew low in number.

"The crew of the Dendadian ships prayed to the four gods to protect them. The Pirate Emperor and his men scoffed at the clouds, proclaimed lordship over the water and cursed the wind." He paused and raised a finger, leaning closer to his boys as if to make a point.

"That's when the gods intervened."

He clapped his hands loudly, causing the others to jump in their seats. Letitia clasped a hand to her heart.

"Lightning from a monstrous storm struck the Umakothi vessels first, sending the Pirate Emperor and his most trusted crew members to the bottom of The Gulf of Crystal Waters. One by one, the storm destroyed the remaining warships from Selemar Graekath. As the screams of drowning men reached the ears of the Dendadian crew members, they offered cheers of victory, gratitude, and songs of praise to the four gods.

"On land, the war spilled into the plains of Asalethwen, the Southerlands. So much blood spilled that it stained the grass red for as far as the eye could see and soaked into the soil, turning the ground to slush. Hundreds of thousands died there."

"I'm not sure this is a suitable story for the boys to hear before bed," Letitia offered.

"No, no..." Ibore waved his hand at her. "He's getting to the good part."

"The Witch Queen Akasha used her trickery to manipulate and warp the minds of warriors allied with Dendadia," Raulin continued. "Some turned on each other, slaughtering hundreds of their own, thinking friend was foe. The Elvish King Amalith used this to his advantage and thinned his enemies' numbers to almost half their size, slaughtering them during their delusion."

"Delusion?" asked Jörgen.

"When you see something that isn't really there," Arnald answered.

"With so little opposition on the battlefield," their baba carried on, "the Witch Queen commanded half of her forces to come north into Kedielewen, the Northerlands.

"Our homelands.

"Despite our inherent ferocity, the Witch Queen's soldiers were too many to repel. All of our finest warriors were south of The Dragon's Teeth Ranges, fighting on the plains of Asalethwen. Only the elderly, the women and younglings like you remained behind to defend our lands.

"The man-wolves reached the forest dwellers at the feet of the mountains where The Dragon's Teeth meet The Great Northern Barrier. They tore the families in those tiny settlements to shreds while they slept and feasted upon them. A few survived their wounds, scratches, and bites from the animals that attacked. They shared their tales of survival to those in the next village, who passed the word to the township of Northwell. Eventually, the word of the Witch Queen's invasion reached all in Kedielewen.

"Alas, by the time they mustered a force and marched south to confront the enemy, it was too late for the survivors of the man-wolves' attack. By the next moon, they succumbed to their wounds and turned into the same kind of beasts that consumed their friends and families. We killed most, hacking them into small pieces. But some escaped.

"Even now, when the moon is high and we hear a wolf cry in the woods, we wonder if it could be one of them lurking out there."

Feeling a chill run along his spine, Jörgen turned his head and peered into the dark woods behind the stable. Silhouettes of looming pine trees against the night sky suddenly appeared frightening. He wondered what might creep among them, lower to the ground, watching from the shadows.

"You said *we*," Arnald chimed in. "*We killed most.*"

"Aye," his baba nodded. "I did."

"We were there," Ibore added. "Your father and I. Go on Raulin."

"When the mustered forces reached the villages along Kedielewen's southern border, it wasn't long before they encountered men and other fell creatures sent by the Witch Queen—things that crawled on many legs; things that walked like men but were not; things that flew on wings like those of bats. Things I do not know the names of, nor do I wish to know.

"Akasha remained in the south, fighting the bulk of the Dendadian allies, focusing her attention there. In her stead, she sent two of her neophytes..." he looked to Jörgen, knowing he was about to ask what that meant, and added, "apprentices, to command the northern attack. These were an enchantress named Elene, and a necromancer named Lycia.

"Elene was young and very beautiful with long black hair and unnaturally deep, green eyes. She could turn many an old man and a callow boy to her wiles. With her soothing voice, soft words and mesmerising stare, she would have her prey eating out of her palm like a love-crazed pup.

"She would manipulate that love-crazed pup into doing whatever she desired from bed with her to slaughter everyone in an encampment. It was a game for her and we were the toys.

"Lycia was nowhere near as subtle as Elene. She was hunched, twisted, a vile creature to look upon and cruel. She commanded a garrison of witless men, infested with the skull-worms of Greymarsh.

"The skull-worms are long, thin, slimy things that would bore into a man's head and breed inside his brain. There, they would grow fat, eating the soft tissue inside the man's skull, all the while controlling his movements, making him eat and drink whatever was available in the marshlands to keep the body alive as they stretched along his spine to feast upon the juices of the nervous system.

"Eventually, the worms would colonise the other organs of the body too and eat the poor victim from the inside out. They would abandon their dead home and return to the marsh, where they would wait patiently for their next victim to stumble upon them.

"But the skull-worms dwelling in Lycia's garrison grew beyond that stage. They were so large one could see them moving beneath the pale flesh of their habitat. Some even dangled and twisted from mouths, ears, nostrils and emptied eye sockets as the witless men marched."

"The boys are going to have night terrors," Letitia complained.

"Oh, yes." Ibore chuckled excitedly. He waved a hand at his brother. "Go on, go on."

"During the fighting, some worms fell to the ground where they died and shrivelled almost immediately. It would seem that Kedielewen, with all the snow and frost, is a little too cold for some creatures to thrive. The skull-worms need the warmth of the Greymarsh or the flesh of living men.

"This gave the norther-men a tactical advantage of sorts. We drew the witless men into the deep snow on the open fields near Northwell. There, we cut the garrison down and the worms left to die in the cold.

"But the neophytes' victories along the border were far more numerous than those of the norther-men. Too many villages burned throughout the forests. Too many of our people bled to death in their homes.

"The women took to prayer when news of the man-wolves' attack had reached the monasteries in Northwell and Port Coldspring, inviting the gods to intervene then. It wasn't long before a mandate to pray and make offerings sent from the temple in Shiverwind reached all corners of Kedielewen.

"Only after the defeat of the witless men, almost a year later, when all the villages in the woodland burned, did the gods hear us.

"I was there to see it myself, along with your Uncle Ibore," he gestured to the red-bearded man across the fire from him. Both boys looked at their uncle, who was nodding and smiling enthusiastically. "I wouldn't have believed it to be true if I wasn't and could not tell you so if I hadn't been not yet a man by age, but no longer a boy with gratitude to battle.

"A large gathering of men pushed the bulk of the Witch Queen's forces back to the feet of the mountains. We couldn't vanquish the creatures of the air, except with an occasional arrow or blade edge when the beasts flew low enough. The creepers and crawlers on land, however, fled back through the forest, some retreating over the mountains, back towards the Land of the Dead.

"The neophytes stood atop a ledge overlooking the battle, where The Dragon's Teeth met The Great Northern Barrier, cursing and using their magic to strike the cowardly beasts withdrawing away from the fight.

"Without warning, the ground opened beneath Elene and Lycia. An entire mountain upon which they stood cracked like an egg and slid away in a column of dust that filled the sky. The earth shook so violently beneath our feet, I thought we were all about to die.

"But we didn't.

"The dust spread over us, covering the snow and the trees with a thick coat of dirt and powder. We could hear a multitude screaming among the terrible roar of the ground, churning like the ocean where the neophytes once stood.

"My hope that it was the sound of enemy soldiers and not the cries of people I knew. Days passed before the dust cloud settled. When it did, we saw a mere pile of rubble where a mountain once stood. The Witch Queen's neophytes, along with their armies, were nowhere to be seen. Either they clambered over The Barrier Mountains back into Adaerwen, or it buried them beneath the ground where The Great Northern Barrier Road now twists through the fallen mountain's remains to Shadowfort.

"By the time the norther-men made it to Shadowfort, the war in the south had moved from Asalethwen, over The Great Southern Barrier Mountains and into Legilawen. The Elvish King Amalith was in full retreat. His only living ally, the Witch Queen Akasha Miroslava, had abandoned him after the defeat of her neophytes, possibly back to her throne within the walled realm of Kaamwyn.

"She's still alive?" Jörgen queried.

"We don't know," Ibore replied. "Maybe she died on the battlefield. But no one ever found her remains."

"What of the Elvish King?" asked Arnald.

"Amalith never received the chance to return to his home in Olendabwyn. For three months, the allied forces of Dendadia gave chase and encircled the Elvish King, trapping him in the Woods of Whispering Willows, only a few hundred leagues north of his palace.

"After his generals surrendered, sick of all the fighting, they handed Amalith over to the commanders of the Dendadian forces for trial. There wasn't one.

"Your uncle and I witnessed the hanging. They built no gallows. Just a rope slung over a branch of a tree by the sea. There, a king died. His body was tossed into the water afterwards for the sharks to feed upon.

"Very fitting," Ibore added.

"After many celebrations," said Raulin, continuing the story. "Dendadia sent envoys to the eastern provinces; Adaerwen, Legilawen and Selemar Graekath. With treaties signed in all major towns and cities of all lands, except for Kaamwyn, the walled empire, trade opened with Dendadian garrisons established in all major municipalities east of the Great Barrier Mountains.

"As a measure to give thanks to the gods for their direct intervention upon the sea to the south, where the Pirate King drowned, and the mountains to the north, where the ground swallowed the two neophytes, the civic council and priests of Dendadia established the Pit Guard to protect the shrines and temples dedicated to the four gods throughout all the land. They gave this most honourable position to those who could prove their abilities in the arena pits in all the large towns and cities across Ananduil. The best of those fighters became Pit Guards. They would post the best of the Pit Guards at the temple in Dendadia, the largest and grandest temple dedicated to the four gods anywhere.

"It has lavish gardens with plants and flowers from all over the known world. There are grand auditoriums where people come from all over to hear priests and priestesses speak. The temple itself reaches into the sky, carved into a towering wall of white rock. And four giant pillars, shaped like cloaked women, hold the roof of the entrance open as they watch over the immense city of Dendadia below. Or so I'm told."

"You've never seen it?" asked Jörgen.

"No," his baba replied. "Perhaps one day you'll see it. Or at least live long enough to make promises to wives of your own that you'll take them there one day, just like I do with your mother," he said, finishing the telling. He offered his wife an apologetic smile. She responded with a smile and a shake of her head.

"Now, I think that might be enough storytelling for one night," he told his sons. The younger one whined softly. "We should let the flames rest. Their music and singing have softened. It's time for them to put their yellow, orange and red shrouds away and time for you to close your eyes and sleep, my boys." He rose to his feet and gestured for them to move. "Off to bed with you."

Chapter Three

───◆───

"**D**O YOU THINK THE Witch Queen will ever return, Baba?" the younger of two boys asked as he climbed onto the bed. His elder brother was already beneath the covers beside him, sliding deeper beneath the thick blankets as he mashed his pillow with his head to even out the clumped feathers inside.

"Who can say?" his father replied. "No one has seen her since the end of the war. Either she's dead or in hiding."

"In Kaamwyn," the younger added.

"Perhaps." His father lifted the blankets so that the boy could slide beneath them. "I wouldn't bother with thinking about her, Jörgen. She's gone. Her apprentices are buried far beneath the ground where a mountain once stood. Everyone knows a witch has limited power without her coven to support her."

Jörgen pictured the mountain tumbling and the great dust cloud his father had spoken of in his story.

"Did you see them?" he asked.

"Hmm?" His father folded the blankets down just low enough for the boy's head to be in the open.

"The two neol-fight?"

"Neophytes." The man chuckled softly. "It means learner. Well, learners," he corrected himself.

"Did you see them fall?"

"Well..." his father shrugged. "They were a long way from me, and on much higher ground. I can't see how they could have escaped in time."

"But they could have."

"They've been gone a very long time," the man reassured him. "A very long time. If they were still lurking about, Dendadia would have news of it and sent their best soldiers to make rid of them once and for all."

"Would they send the Pit Guards to kill the neol...?"

"Neophytes," his father corrected him. "Possibly. They give the Pit Guards assignments occasionally. And they can give each Pit Guard a garrison of his own to command in some situations."

Jörgen looked from his father to the ceiling and smiled. He watched shadows dance and sway against the underside of the thatched roof, cast by flickering candlelight striking the dark timber crossbeams above the bed. Visions of grand armies and swords clashing filled his mind. He saw heroes clothed in crisp silver armour, brandishing the eagle insignia of Dendadia on their breasts. In his mind, they protected the innocent people of all lands, like those in his tiny village; and vanquished evil enemies like things that crawled on many legs; things that walked like men but were not; things that flew on wings like those of bats. Things like man-wolves, witless men, dragons and witches.

"I will be a Pit Guard one day," Jörgen announced.

"You're too little, Jörgen." The elder boy laughed.

Jörgen offered his brother a disapproving look.

"He won't always be," their father said. His voice rumbled like soft thunder through his thick, dark beard. With his thick elk skin draped over his shoulders, his appearance reminded Jörgen of a bear.

"I'm eight," the boy told his brother. "When I get to your age, I'll be as big as the tallest trees of the forest."

"You can't even tan a skin," the other snickered as he slid under the covers and turned away to face the wall. "That's why all your skins are floorings for all the huts in the village."

"Arnald!" his father growled.

"No, you're right, brother. I can't tan a skin," Jörgen agreed. "But at least all my kills with the bow are always one shot through the head. Yours are always in the stomach where the shit sack is. And it explodes all over the fine pelt, staining it brown and black. So, the skins of your kills are only good for wiping our arses with."

"You little runt," Arnald spat, spinning around like a flash to attack his brother.

"Baba!" Jörgen called to his father, trying not to burst out laughing. In an instant, their father's hand was upon the elder boy's shoulder, preventing the intended strike for the younger.

"Both of you settle down," he growled softly. "You should be sleeping, not fighting."

The boys lowered themselves to their pillows, watching one another intensely. "Each of us has a set of skills meant for only ourselves. Arnald, your brother is good with a bow. He is better than any man I have ever known, and yet he is only young. You are not good with a bow—"

"Ha!" Jörgen let out.

"Shuttup," the older brother spat.

"You're not good with a bow," their father continued, offering the younger a stern look. "But you are a great tanner. Even better than me. Your skins are highly sought at the markets in Shiverwind and seek a higher price than mine or your uncle's.

"As it is, you make a perfect pair," he continued. "Arnald's kills are the skins you tanned, Jörgen."

"But they lie upon floors throughout the village," the younger boy replied, sounding disappointed.

"We need floor coverings." His father smiled. "May the gods strike me down if we don't." He turned his attention to the older boy. "And your skins that fetch a higher price than mine and your uncle's, well, they are all from the kills Jörgen made with his bow. You have both been working together as partners, helping one another, and you didn't even realise it. You should be proud of one another."

Arnald and Jörgen sat in silence as they considered their father's words. Arnald cracked first, leaning over to his little brother to wrap his arms around Jörgen's shoulders.

"I'm sorry for what I said," the elder boy offered. "You are a skilled hunter and I know you would make an excellent Pit Guard."

"There, that's it," their father whispered. "That's how it should be between brothers. And what of you, Jörgen? Do you have anything to say to Arnald?"

"I'm sorry too, brother," the younger replied with a wry grin. "Sorry, you can't shoot a bow for shit."

With that, Jörgen leaped out of bed and darted behind his father for cover. Arnald was right on his heels. His fists balled tightly, and his face turned red with anger.

With a shake of his head, the boys' father turned and flung Jörgen onto the bed with his left hand and pushed Arnald back onto the bed with his right.

"I've had enough," he barked as he stamped out through the door, slamming it shut behind him. "Stay in there."

"Baba? Baba?" called Jörgen from within. But the cries went unheeded.

Their father returned to the table by the fireplace. There, his wife waited with a steaming mug of tea for him.

"Your stories excite them too much, Raulin," she said as something in the boys' room thudded against the wall.

"I know," he nodded, trying not to laugh.

"You're smirking," she said, sliding the mug closer to him. "What is it?"

"That little one of ours, Letitia," he grinned. "He's got a mouth on him. It'll get him into trouble one day if he can't control it."

"He didn't take after me," she said defensively.

"Nor me," he added. "He's one of a kind."

Another thud against the wall drew her attention away from her husband.

"I'll go see," she said, standing. He quickly grabbed her wrist and pulled her to his lap, almost knocking his mug.

"Let them wear themselves out," he whispered into her ear. "Stay here with me."

Chapter Four

<hr />

J ÖRGEN SCAMPERED BETWEEN THE rows of tents on a large clearing by the edge of the township, ducking under the stiff guy ropes pegged into the ground, leaping over assorted stock and small crates of bric-à-brac stashed out of the way, ready for selling at the festival markets. The access was tight, even for someone as small as he. Carefully, he manoeuvred through the thin passage, avoiding anything he regarded as an obstacle. Skilfully, he twisted around poles, ducked under support lines and leaped over baskets of cloth, tarpaulins of many colours and annoyed adults who flared their nostrils at the boy. All the while, Jörgen laughed and laughed.

He laughed, noticing the four older boys chasing him were not as nimble as he. They tripped and stumbled clumsily over everything in their path. Adults cursed them loudly as flung bric-à-brac tumbled in all directions. Tents fell as the older boys' careless feet plucked ropes from the ground.

The older boys were not more than a year or two older than Jörgen. They towered a good head and shoulders above the young absconder, who thought there must be a great deal of growing after turning eight years old. Arnald, his elder brother, was almost thirteen and stood taller than the four on his heels. Much taller.

Jörgen wondered if growing so big hurt much. He hoped not, for otherwise, he might just have to stay the size he was.

"I will beat you for what you said, Jörgen," a beady-eyed, angry boy screamed. The boy's face was red, and his lips peeled back into a snarl. His stringy blond hair streamed over his shoulders as he reached out to grab the young escapee.

Being small, Jörgen thought, brings some advantages.

He slid gracefully under a low trestle table where an old lady had set out an assortment of fine linen. This would not have been a successful action on his part if he had been any larger. He lifted himself from his slide, jumping to his feet just in time to leap over a patch of sodden ground where horses and carts busily traversed during the morning. He heard a clamour and crash behind him, before a tirade of foul language spewed from the old lady's mouth.

The four older boys had knocked over the table, bearing fine linen, sending the cloths into the patch of damp ground.

"Stop right there, boys," he heard a burly man with a thick, red beard holler. It was Uncle Ibore. "This nonsense needs to cease, now."

The boys reluctantly complied, shifting their gazes to the man, then to the ground. The blond, red-faced lad stared angrily after Jörgen with beady little eyes. Jörgen slowed to a walk, turning to observe and make sure he was safe.

Ibore and the old lady focused their attention on the four older boys. The adults had not noticed Jörgen. Or so he thought, until the angry boy gave away his position.

"I'll find you later, Jörgen," called the angry boy.

"No, you won't," he answered.

"You'll answer for what you said," the angry boy added.

"But it's true." Jörgen laughed. "Your sister has the arse of a seal. Or is it walrus? Everyone says so." He cheekily pointed to all the surrounding people, who were setting up for the festival, before nodding to the angry boy.

"I will hurt you," the angry boy growled, setting to chase the young troublemaker again.

Suddenly, an enormous set of pincer-like fingers bit down upon his ear.

"You're going to apologise to Omma Gerthney for what you did to her stall," said Ibore. "Then you and your friends will clean this mess up and help her with her stall today. If you don't, I'll tell all the stall keepers that it was you who knocked those tents down and trashed their belongings. And when your fathers find out... Well, let's hope it doesn't come to that. What do you say?"

The boys nodded reluctantly, turning to the old lady, before they chorused, "sorry, Omma Gerthney."

Jörgen smiled and started on his way, walking confidently with his head held high.

"Boy," Ibore called after him.

Jörgen stooped in his tracks. The colour left his face, and his smile sank.

"Turn and face me, boy."

He turned to see the man approaching. His stomach tightened, and he felt his legs shake.

"Yes, Uncle Ibore," Jörgen said sheepishly.

"Those lads are bigger and stronger than you," the burly man said in a soft, commanding, but comforting voice. "You're just lucky you can move quickly. But that won't always be so. You'll grow up too, and if you continue to be cocky and mouth off the way you always do, one day someone will teach you a lesson you will regret. Do you understand?"

"Yes, Uncle Ibore." The boy nodded sheepishly. His countenance changed slightly. "But what if I don't want to grow up?"

Ibore offered a warm grin.

"Some things you just cannot control, boy," the burly man replied. "Now tell me, what put you in this unpleasant situation?"

Jörgen looked away towards the fishing boats docked along the piers. He felt embarrassed by his actions and hesitated with his answer.

"Jörgen?" Ibore pressed, crouching to the boy's eye level as he gently placed his forefinger and thumb on the lad's chin before guiding his face towards his own.

"I told Gren that his sister has a fat arse, like a seal."

The burly man smiled and nodded.

"I suppose Gren didn't like you saying that about his sister, hmm?"

"No," Jörgen answered.

"And his friends were angry about what you said?"

"So, it would seem." The boy nodded.

Ibore chuckled. Jörgen gave him a perplexed look.

"What's so funny?"

"I suppose, to someone like you, Gertrude's rear end appears a little large compared to others her age," Ibore responded. "Though she is anything but fat, Jörgen. She's growing up, maybe a little faster than the other girls. The boys have noticed this and they... Well, they like what they see."

"Even Gren?" Jörgen appeared disgusted. "He likes his sister's fat arse?"

Ibore let out a loud chuckle.

"No," he answered. "Probably not Gren. But others his age and a little older."

Jörgen shook his head in disbelief.

"Older boys like girls' arses?" He continued to shake his head and look to the ground. "I never want to grow up."

"I sometimes wish for that, too," Ibore said, rising to his feet. "But you'd best get used to Gertrude being around. And, if you said anything about her to her face, it would be best if you apologised to her."

"Why?"

"Because your brother and her are becoming friendly," the burly man told him, rubbing his enormous hand through the lad's black hair.

"What?" Jörgen looked at his uncle, surprised.

"They're sitting together on the end of the pier," Ibore whispered, crouching near to Jörgen's ear. "They're sneaking kisses when they think no one is looking."

Jörgen felt his body tense.

"Does Baba and Mama know?"

Ibore nodded.

"I think there may be another wedding in the wind." He smiled.

"No," Jörgen protested. "He's only twelve."

"About to turn thirteen," his uncle reminded him. "Your baba and mama were promised to one another when he was twelve and she was still eleven. They married when they both turned fifteen."

"No," the lad said again, quickly turning to run towards the pier.

Ibore laughed out loud before slowly following the boy onto the boardwalk.

The tall lampposts lined either side of the pier, adorned with streamers and bunting that zig-zagged above pedestrians' heads like colourful vines. Wildflowers and banners decorated the fishing boats moored to the wide jetty. There, the crewmen of each vessel gathered to play an assortment of instruments and sing songs of life on the sea. Some struck frame drums and timbrels as others strummed gitterns, harps, and lutes.

Sunset marked the impending start of the festival. But here, on the dock, in the early morning sun, the celebrations were well underway.

Jörgen ducked and weaved his way through people who had gathered to listen, sing along and dance. The smell of wine and rum grew ther as he passed by each boat, fading a little between the vessels. He didn't like the aroma. Something about it made him feel queasier and queasier as he scurried by each of the docked crafts. He was thankful when the smell of rotting baitfish wafted past his nostrils, emitting from the barrels stacked on smaller side jetties extending from the main pier.

He passed sixteen vessels, eight on either side of the boardwalk. The crewmen stretched the boats' fishing nets along the yardarms. After cleaning them, young ladies decorated them with more wildflowers and ribbons.

Colour draped everything in sight.

Jörgen pushed through the last of the people gathered near the musical fishing boats towards the end of the pier. There, he saw Arnald and Gertrude sitting on the boardwalk's edge with their backs to him, their feet dangling over the side several feet above the water. Arnald had his arm around the girl's shoulders. She leaned into him, resting her head on his shoulder.

The young boy thought of how easy it would be to race quietly up behind them and push them both off the edge. A smile crept upon his face as he imagined the splash.

He turned to see his uncle weaving slowly through the gathered people near the fishing vessels. His smile quickly vanished as he realised what trouble he would be in for if he followed his urges. Instead, he approached the young couple gingerly, not wanting to upset his brother or uncle.

"Oh, hello, Arnald," he announced, trying to sound innocent but coming across puckish. "And Gertrude. My, you look lovely in that dress."

It was a dirty brown set of sewn together rags she always wore. Jörgen guessed it was something her mother made for her when she was younger, to which she added length and girth as the girl grew.

And grew and grew, Jörgen thought as he looked to her seated posterior.

The young couple turned and eyed the boy suspiciously.

"What do you want?" Arnald asked.

"I just wanted to say hello," replied Jörgen. He saw the burly form of his uncle appear in the corner of his eye. "And I want to apologise," he added.

"Apologise?" his brother inquired, rising to his feet. He helped Gertrude up from the boardwalk. She brushed her blonde hair away from her eyes, offering an expression similar to what her younger brother had offered Jörgen only moments before. Only, along with anger, she displayed distrust and weariness.

"To Gertrude." Jörgen waved his hand towards the girl.

"To me?" she queried with scepticism.

"Yes." He looked to his uncle for support.

Ibore nodded and gently patted the boy on the back.

"Go on, lad," he murmured.

"I want to apologise for saying things about you I shouldn't have said."

"Like what?" she asked.

Arnald shot her a cautionary look.

"Don't ask," he whispered. But it was too late.

"That you have a fat arse," Jörgen blurted.

Her jaw dropped, and her eyes widened in disbelief.

"Uncle Ibore said it's not true," the boy continued. "He says you're growing up quicker than other girls your age and that many other boys Arnald's age like your arse, but I don't know about things like that."

"Jörgen!" Arnald growled. "Stop."

"I mean, I told your brother it was like that of a seal or walrus," said Jörgen, holding back the urge to laugh. "I could have said cow or horse. I don't know if that would have been better or worse. But Uncle Ibore says you and Arnald might be promised to each other soon, and that means you will get married and have babies. That would make me an uncle, then. I should try to be nicer to you."

Gertrude continued to stare, dumbstruck and clearly offended.

"So, I am sorry for saying you have a fat arse like a seal or walrus," Jörgen finished with a broad smile. "Forgive me?"

"I am going to kill you," Arnald promised his brother.

A sturdy grip squeezed down upon his forearm before he was pulled away from Arnald and Gertrude, back along the boardwalk.

"I think you've said enough for today," Ibore grumbled. "Time to take you to your mama so she can talk some sense into you."

"She won't talk," Jörgen protested. "She'll beat me silly."

"After that show, you deserve it," his uncle replied.

"Wait," the boy called as he almost tripped as he turned to look back towards the end of the pier.

"You've done enough damage. Leave your brother be for the rest of the day."

"Wait, I see something," Jörgen persisted.

"You can't bargain your way out of this, laddie," replied Ibore.

"Look!" Jörgen pointed. "Just look."

"Uncle Ibore," Arnald called. He was peering out into the open water. "I see it, too."

The burly man stopped in his tracks and turned. "See what?"

"A ship," Jörgen answered.

"A ship?" Ibore let the boy go to retrace his steps and approach the elder sibling.

"I see nothing," Gertrude said, shielding her face from the sun with her arm and following Arnald's gaze with her eyes.

"I don't know what it is," the older boy admitted. He pointed directly out from the pier. "But it's there. Something dark on the horizon."

Ibore looked for a long time.

"You're sure?" he asked.

"Yes," Arnald answered. "It's there."

"It's a ship," Jörgen insisted with some frustration.

The burly man took a deep breath. He still couldn't see anything out there. He squinted and put his hand to his brow.

Eventually, he shook his head.

"I'll take your word for it, boys," he conceded. "You've got younger and better eyes than I. Probably just a merchant heading to Port Coldspring."

"Can you see Port Coldspring from out there?" Gertrude asked. "I would have thought you would need to be farther away."

"You're right." Ibore nodded. "If you can see them on the horizon here, they're way off course. Tides and winds can do that."

"Maybe they're coming here," Jörgen put in.

His uncle grinned. "I doubt it. There's not much to see here."

"The best pelts in all of Kedielewen," added Jörgen.

Ibore laughed and scruffed the top of the boy's head with his fingers.

"Aye. That we do, laddie," Ibore smiled. He then took Jörgen by the arm again, reminding the boy of the trouble he had caused. "Now, let's go and see your mama."

Chapter Five

R AULIN CLIMBED THE TALL timber ladder to the platform of the eastern tower. It stood upon the shore's edge, by the wide pier, offering a commanding view of the township's rooftops with smoking chimney stacks and the broad expanse of glasslike water.

"Hard to know where the sky begins and the water ends," Raulin huffed, as he clambered onto the platform and peered out to the view.

"Especially on a day like today," replied a lean man, standing in the shade of the thatched roof, holding a long spyglass to his eye.

Raulin nodded slowly, breathing out a long vaporous huff as he pulled his thick cloak about himself. With no clouds about, the expanse of water and sky appeared as one.

"What can you see, Hjalmar?"

"Your boys have good sight," the other answered. "There is a ship out there. Very far away. Just resting on the horizon."

Raulin stepped to Hjalmar's side, placing his hands on the guardrail lining the platform's edge. He squinted, scanning the thin line where the water met the sky, or at least he thought so.

"Does it bear any colours?"

"I can't tell," Hjalmar answered, offering the spyglass to the burly man. "How those lads could tell there was a ship out there is quite bewildering, to say the least."

"Only one of them could see that it was a ship," Raulin said, taking the telescope and raising it to his eye. "My younger one, Jörgen. My elder boy could just tell there was something out there but not what it was."

"Even so," the lean man said, "they must both have good eyes in their heads." Hjalmar pointed to the furthest fishing vessel moored on the pier. "Follow the mast of Einar's boat, straight up and a little to the right. You'll see…"

"Got it," Raulin acknowledged. A tiny, black blob floated in the middle of his view. He would have dismissed it as a mere smudge on the lens had it not moved slightly as he corrected his stance. "How can you tell it's a ship?"

"I see better than you," replied Hjalmar.

"Yes, you do." The burly man smiled, handing the spyglass back to its owner. "That's why you're up here freezing your balls off in the breeze and I'm going back down there to eat rabbit stew."

"Get a runner to bring some up here," the lean man put in as Raulin lowered himself to the ladder. "And don't forget Ebbe in the south tower and Einar in the north tower. They might like some too."

"I'll do that," the burly man growled as he started climbing down. "And it's the other way around. Einar's in the south tower. Ebbe is in the north tower."

"Are you certain?" Hjalmar called back.

"Does it matter?" Raulin replied. "They both look the same. Their own mother can't tell them apart."

Hjalmar laughed out loud before returning his attention to the cove.

Raulin kept his gaze upon the water, looking into the distance where he had seen the dark spot on the spyglass. There was nothing there for his stare to lock onto, and the distant object he knew to be out there sat so far away it posed no immediate threat. Yet, his stomach felt a tense uneasiness as he turned his face to the gathering of people in the large clearing near the edge of the township.

An enormous bonfire, shaped to resemble a shrine, stood in the centre of the open space. It had four timber pillars, set in a wide square and crudely fashioned from the trunks of pine trees. A poor excuse of a thatched roof made from pine branches rested on top. As Raulin looked on, a few men crammed chocks of timber and pinecones inside the confines of the pillars, filling the space from ground to roof.

Children clustered around the minstrels and marionette performers on the field as their parents spent their coins at the market stalls set up around the edges.

"There's a breeze coming from out there." Hjalmar gestured to the water with his chin. "It will be a chilly night, I think."

Raulin couldn't feel anything, let alone see a single sign of any wind blowing against a leaf or hanging fabric. "Are you certain?"

The other nodded.

"Just a small breeze," he replied. "Nothing to worry about."

Returning to the ground, Raulin followed a path leading away from the watchtower to the stalls lining the edge of the field. There, he found Letitia rummaging through exotic fabrics of many colours and patterns set up on a trestle table. Approaching from behind, he wrapped his arms around her waist and kissed her cheek.

"How much debt am I in for these fine Dendadian fabrics, my love?" he whispered into her ear, moving his hand to feel the hessian bag slung over her shoulder, hanging by her hip.

"Nothing." She smiled. "I've bartered my wildflower jams away for everything in there."

"All of your jams?" He nuzzled her ear. "How disappointing! What am I to have on my toast in the morning?"

"Not here." She giggled.

He bit her lobe gently. "Why not?"

"Dirty man." She shot a quick look around to see if anyone noticed. "The boys are preoccupied. Arnald is on the pier with Gertrude, and Jörgen is off causing trouble somewhere. Help me take this bag home."

A broad smile stretched across his face.

"Dirty woman," he responded.

She took his hand and led him along the path, away from the stalls. Several village folks greeted them along their way, offering handshakes, waves and the occasional knowing nod from an elder or two.

"We can't be too long," Letitia said as she opened the door to the house.

"We're expected to attend the night celebration."

"Fuck the night celebration," he answered, following her into their home.

She giggled again.

He peered back out the door, past the village to the vast expanse of water. An unsettling feeling stabbed him in the stomach.

"Come on," she whispered, dropping her bag on the floor.

He closed the door, quickly forgetting about everything outside.

At least, for the moment.

Chapter Six

HJALMAR PULLED HIS THICK cloak tighter. The breeze grew stronger, sweeping across the water and into his face, biting his skin with its icy touch.

A quick glance down to the world below showed him that the people on the ground didn't feel the chill as much as he did on top of the tower. They continued to barter goods, dance to music and drink while children ran about like feral beasts.

A deep crimson veil stretched over the sky as the sun disappeared below the mountains behind him. He peered to the southern tower at the edge of the village, where Ebbe or Einar held a spyglass to his eye, pointing it to the cove. Hjalmar shook his head slowly.

You won't see shit in this light.

He turned his attention to the water, focusing on the area where he saw the ship earlier. It was dark out there and appeared glassy; a crystal-clear reflection of the sky.

The ship, if it lingered in place, hid among the deepening colours floating on the surface. While the villagers lit tall lamps lining the edge of the field, the ship remained dark.

Perhaps it moved on, he surmised. Moved on to Port Coldspring or Shiverwind.

Still, an uneasy feeling gripped his stomach as he kept his eyes on the water far into the cove. He couldn't help feeling that, as he watched the water, the water watched him as well.

———◦———

Arnald held Gertrude's hand, interlacing his fingers with hers. She rested her head on his shoulder as they sat together on a log near a bonfire where a band of minstrels played vibrant music. People clapped and danced along while others drank and danced... if it could be called dancing.

Gertrude watched the band, swaying slightly in time with the rhythm, keeping herself against him. Arnald, however, couldn't take his eyes away from his brother, who mocked the drunken dancers. He spun when they spun, stomped his feet when they stomped their feet, swayed when they swayed and fell over when they did. Some cheered the lad, others laughed, but Arnald felt embarrassed.

"Let's dance," Gertrude whispered in his ear.

"My brother is behaving like an idiot," he said, not registering her words instantly. "What?"

"Let's dance," she repeated. "Forget your brother. He'll always be this way. He needs to be the centre of attention. Let him. Meanwhile, we dance."

He smiled. She was right.

Jörgen was Jörgen, and Jörgen was an idiot at the best of times.

"All right," said Arnald, rising to his feet. He reached his hand out to Gertrude. "Let's dance."

She took his hand and, together; they moved onto the open ground, closer to the minstrels where others linked arms, jumping and twirling to the music. The sound of the lute, tambourine, flutes and bagpipe filled his ears and vibrated through his body as he pulled Gertrude close, placing his hands on her waist. She laughed excitedly, putting her hands on his shoulders as they danced, copying other couples nearby.

There wasn't any structure to the movements, just plain fun, moving this way and that. Before long, he laughed too.

Jörgen noticed the two of them. He started towards the young couple, continuing his drunken caper from one side of the dance area to the other, only to stop dead in his tracks a few paces from them. His eyes grew large with fear, as he saw his father standing off to the side of the minstrels.

Raulin stood tall, scowling at the boy. With a slow shake of his head, he let Jörgen know he'd be in trouble if he took one more step towards Arnald and Gertrude.

Jörgen swallowed hard, bit his lip and nodded to his father. With that, the lad turned on his heels and resumed mocking the drunken dancers, who desperately tried to not spill their drinks while twirling.

After a moment, the music stopped. The dancers stopped dancing, responding with a cheer or a whistle, applauding the minstrels for their efforts.

"People," a cloaked man called, moving before the musicians. "People, it's time."

"Time for what, Priest?" hollered a drunken dancer. "Not time to go home, surely. I'm in need of more ale and a fine woman to bed."

"Best not let your wife hear that, Gustus," the priest replied with a smile.

"She already has," shouted an angry woman at the edge of the dance area.

Those gathered nearby laughed.

"You're in the shit now, Gustus," someone yelled through the din.

"All right. All right!" The priest chuckled, signalling everyone to settle down with a gesture of his hands. "It's time to light the shrine of the four. The sun has gone, and the stars are twinkling in the sky. The rising moon signifies a new beginning to the harvest year. Let us hope the winter's end is quick, and spring brings an abundance of new life with it."

As he spoke, four men dipped torches onto the bonfire before making their way to the makeshift shrine standing in the middle of the field.

"Let us thank the gods for the year we had," the priest continued. "And for the year to come."

"For the year we had," everyone repeated. "For the year to come."

With that, the four men set the shrine ablaze.

Gertrude kissed Arnald on the cheek.

"I think I should be with my parents," she whispered in his ear. He nodded, letting go of her hand as she started away. "I'll meet with you after."

"All right." He smiled.

He quickly located Jörgen and placed a hand on the boy's shoulder.

"Come on," he whispered, gesturing to their parents at the edge of the dance area with his head.

The boys stood by their parents, watching the shrine crumble in the flames. Once in a while, something big would topple, sending an explosion of embers into the air. Several people gasped in response.

"Why do we burn the gods?" Jörgen asked, keeping his voice low.

"It's symbolic," Letitia, his mother, answered. "We aren't really burning the gods. The gods can't be burned."

"But why do we burn them?" the boy asked again. "I know they're not the real gods, but I don't understand why we burn them."

"So, we won't forget," she told him. "Do you remember the Festival of the Four last year?"

"Yes." Jörgen nodded.

"And the year before?"

He nodded again.

"How about you, Arnald?" she queried. "Do you remember?"

"Yes," the older boy replied.

"How many of these festivals do you remember?"

"I don't know," he said. "At least since I was three or four."

"I can remember them since I was six," she smiled. "Every one of them is a happy memory. Even before I understood what the festival represented."

A large piece of the shrine toppled and splashed into the flames with a loud crack.

"This represents the conclusion of one harvest year," she continued, "and the beginning of a new one. We set up these stalls to barter and share our skills and goods we made during the year behind us. We dance to welcome the year ahead. We burn the shrine to remember all the things we gained and lost and hope to gain. Everything we have, once had and will have exists within the hands of The Four. Life, Earth, Sky and Death. Nothing that is, can be without them."

Jörgen scrunched his nose and shook his head.

"I still don't understand why we burn the gods," he mumbled.

"You'll remember this next year." Raulin, his father smiled, ruffling the youngling's hair with his big hand.

"And you'll be told the same thing then as you were now." Arnald snickered. Jörgen shot him a disapproving look. "Because you're an idiot," the elder boy finished.

The shrine burned down to embers. Some gathered by the smouldering remains to watch the last of the flames die away. Among them, were Raulin's family and several others still drinking. Gertrude returned, and Arnald held her beneath his cloak to keep her warm while Jörgen stood between his father and mother with his uncle just off to the side a few paces away.

"More ale," a man grunted, holding out an empty mug.

"No more ale," Ibore replied. "Not tonight."

"There has got to be more ale," the other remarked. "I saw barrels of the stuff on the pier."

"Not all of that is for tonight. If you drink it all now, you'll have none until the next supply ship. And that's not for another three months."

"Sometime during spring," Gustus put in.

"That's a long time between drinks," the man acknowledged. He stared at the flames for a while, wobbling back and forth before chuckling to himself.

"What's so funny?" asked Gustus.

"Do you remember that time in Northwell when that soldier from Dendadia challenged you to a drinking game?"

Gustus snickered. "Yeah. Yeah."

"What happened?" Jörgen queried.

"This doesn't sound like a story for a child," Letitia interjected.

"No, no. It's all right," the man slurred as he swayed drunkenly. "It's quite all right. I'll stop before I get to the part with the whores."

"Morus," Raulin barked.

"Sorry," the other replied, pressing a finger to his lips. "No whore talk."

"What happened?" Jörgen repeated.

"Well," Morus started as he reached a hand out to Gustus to keep himself balanced. "We were returning from the place where the mountain fell, after seeing the witches swallowed by the ground. On our way, we stopped at Northwell with many different people from many different places, and we all got drunk at a tavern there. It was a celebration. The witches were dead, you know. That was a big thing. Anyway, the next day most of us were too sick to travel, so we stayed. During the day, this soldier said he could out-drink any of us northerners and challenged any of us to a drinking game. So, Gustus accepted."

"Was he a Pit Guard?" asked Jörgen.

"What?" Morus looked at the boy quizzically. "No. Just a fucking soldier in the army. There weren't any Pit Guards, yet. Not proper ones, anyway. No, this soldier was just a low-life piece of shit in a big army."

"Oh." The boy appeared disappointed.

"Just listen to the story, laddie," Ibore whispered.

"So," continued Morus. "Gustus gets into the ear of the innkeeper and lets him know about the challenge. They make an arrangement and set up the competition for that night. Now, the thing to remember is, we were really hungover from the previous night and none of us wanted a repeat of that the next morning. We really wanted to get home. But the challenge had been accepted and so the game must be played. The innkeeper dug out a barrel of long-fermented ale sitting in his cellar and marked it with a cross. He got another barrel from the night before, still about half-full, and marked it with a single line before topping it up with water."

"Why did he do that?" Jörgen questioned. "Wouldn't that make the ale weak?"

"Exactly." Morus smiled, touching the side of his nose with his finger. "So, when the soldier and Gustus sat across the table from each other, the innkeeper served them the drinks himself."

The boy laughed, pointing a finger at Gustus. "Giving the long-fermented ale to the soldier to make him drunk and the weak ale to you so you could win the game."

"Wrong," Morus barked, almost falling over. Gustus was quick to keep the other on his feet. "The fucking innkeeper forgot which barrel was which and mixed them up. Gustus became so violently ill, he threw up all over the soldier and the table and the floor. By the gods, it was the funniest thing."

Those gathered laughed out loud. All except Jörgen, who glanced at his uncle and father.

"So," he said. "You didn't go to the Woods of Whispering Willows?"

"Unfortunately, no," Gustus answered. "Both Morus and I were injured in battle. I argued our case to go with your father and uncle, but those in command wouldn't have it. Oh, how I wished to be there when Amalith swung from that tree."

"Enough stories for one night," Letitia said. "Time for bed. You too, Arnald. It's beyond time you should walk Gertrude home."

"Yes, Mama." Arnald nodded before turning his attention to the girl. "Come on."

"I'll tell you about the man-wolf I killed on the road to Shiverwind another time," Morus told Jörgen.

"You killed a man-wolf?" the lad asked, all wide-eyed and excited.

"Aye," the other replied. "Big fucker, too. Claws the size of your..."

"Another time," Letitia interrupted.

"Sorry," the other said bashfully.

"But Mama," Jörgen complained. "He killed a man-wolf."

"Time for bed," she said, taking him by the arm to lead him away.

"A big fucker, too," the boy persisted.

"Bed!" she snapped.

Raulin smiled and nodded to the gathering.

"Good night," he said before following his wife. He glanced at his brother.

"I'll stay awhile," Ibore said with a wave, eyeing a young lady standing across the fire from him. "I'll check on Hjalmar and the twins before I retire for the night."

"Take some food to them," Raulin told him. "I'm sure others have already done so, but they'll appreciate it."

"Will do," he replied. "Good night."

"Good night."

With one hand on the waist of a young lady and his other carrying a platter of steaming chicken, Ibore carefully made his way to the tower. Several times he caught himself before he stumbled, making the lass giggle.

"You're so drunk!" She laughed.

"Shhh," he hissed, pulling his arm from her waist to place a finger to his lips. "Don't tell anyone. I've got a reputation to keep."

"Is taking me home for the night part of that reputation?"

"No way," he said. "If your father found out, he'd have my ball sack for a purse."

"Not if you made an honest woman out of me," she said.

"Aye." He grinned. "I could do that. But I best get this chicken to Hjalmar first." Ibore peered up the ladder to the platform far above. "Oy," he called. "Hjalmar. I bought some chicken. Are you hungry?"

Ibore waited for an answer. None came.

"Hjalmar," he called again. "Are you sleeping?"

"Maybe he left for a piss," the woman put in.

"No, he'd just piss off the side," Ibore replied before calling again. "Hjalmar. Wake up."

"Hjalmar," the young lady echoed. She giggled.

"Here." Ibore handed the platter of steaming chicken to her.

"What are you doing?"

"I'm going up there to take a look," he answered, starting up the ladder.

"You'll get yourself killed," she told him as he carefully climbed.

"Hjalmar," he called again as he neared the top. "I'm coming up. You best be dead or dying. Because, if this is some joke, I'm going to kill you."

He regretted his words immediately as he lifted himself onto the platform.

Hjalmar sat slumped against the guardrail wall to the side of the tower, an arrow shaft sticking from his right eye.

Ibore stood dumbfounded for what seemed an eternity, soaking in the sight before him. Dark, glistening blood trickled down Hjalmar's cheek, vanishing into his beard.

"What's happening?" the young lady called out.

Snapping back to reality, Ibore called out. "Alahr—"

An arrow shot into his mouth and pierced through the back of his head. He toppled backwards, off the side of the platform and down, watching the rungs of the ladder pass by. He landed with a loud crunch that seemed to resonate throughout his body.

Good shot, he thought as he peered at the shaft sticking from his mouth. Ibore tried to retrieve it, but his arms wouldn't cooperate. He tried to sit up and stand, but his legs wouldn't move.

From nearby, he heard the lass scream. Another arrow shot from the darkness suddenly silenced her.

I hope, someone heard her.

She fell next to him, spilling the steaming chicken across his chest. White vapour rose from the meat into the chilly air.

His mouth and nose filled with liquid, blocking his sense of smell. But the taste of blood became overwhelming.

Ibore closed his eyes as the hastened footfalls of many passed by, heading towards the village.

I hope someone heard.

Chapter Seven

⟨⬥⟩

R AULIN WOKE SUDDENLY.

His heart pounded noisily in his ears. He felt as if someone had stirred him from a deep slumber.

Letitia slept soundly beside him, curled on her side, deep under the covers. Whatever had woken him, it wasn't her. He lowered himself to his pillow and closed his eyes.

"Baba?" a soft whisper questioned from the door. It opened slowly with an awkward creak to reveal Jörgen standing in the passage between bedrooms. "Ma-ma?"

"What is it, boy?" Raulin murmured.

"I heard something," he replied with a slight hint of fear in his voice.

Raulin thought this to be particularly unusual and found himself fully awake, and aware.

"What did you hear?" he asked, sitting on the edge of the bed, reaching his hands out to his son.

Jörgen immediately moved into his father's embrace.

"I heard someone scream," the boy answered.

"Might be a bird," said Raulin, dismissing the news.

"It wasn't a bird," Jörgen told him. "It sounded like a woman."

"When?"

"Just now," said the boy.

"Perhaps it is just someone still celebrating," Raulin guessed as he wondered if the scream Jörgen referred to had woken him moments earlier. "We had a very late night, and it won't be long until morning comes. You should try to get some sleep, son."

He took Jörgen's hand and led him to the boys' bedroom, where he saw Arnald sleeping soundly.

"It didn't sound like a *happy* scream," the boy said as he crawled onto his bed.

"A *happy* scream?"

"I've heard people scream when they are happy," Jörgen explained. "Like, when people jump off the end of the pier in summer, or when Uncle Ibore tickles one of the ladies he takes home sometimes."

"Tickles?" Raulin smiled.

"I asked him," said the boy. "He told me they play tickle games all night until they fall asleep."

"That sounds about right." His father smiled. "Lay down and close your eyes. Forget about the screa—"

A high-pitched squeal resonated from outside, followed immediately by another. And another.

Pigs, thought Raulin, as he dashed to the window. Pulling back the curtain, he saw a farmhouse farther down the road ablaze and two men slaughtering penned pigs with long, thin blades.

"Jörgen, Arnald, get dressed," he barked.

"Hmmph," Arnald groaned, rolling onto his other side.

Jörgen instantly acted, slipping into his clothes he'd discarded earlier on the floor when they returned home after the festivities.

"Get up, Arnald!" The younger boy slapped his brother's shoulder.

"What?" the older lad groaned, looking about confusedly.

"Baba said get dressed."

"And grab your bows," their father added. "We're under attack."

As Arnald lifted himself out of bed, Jörgen reached for his bow and quiver resting against the wall.

"Are we going to fight them?" he asked.

"Not you," Raulin told him. "You're going to hide with your brother in the woods. You'll go to where I left the empty buckets and tapping gear. Take cover under the bushes there and wait until I come and get you."

"All right," Jörgen said, clearly disappointed.

Arnald stumbled in the darkness as he slipped his boots on.

"Who's attacking us?" he asked, not fully comprehending the situation.

"I don't know," his father replied, returning to his own bedroom. "Letitia. Get up."

Like Arnald, she groaned as her body protested the instruction.

"Get up, now," he barked.

She sat upright in a flash, shocked at the tone in his voice and frightened by what might make him behave in such a way.

"What is it?" she asked, suddenly aware.

"The village is being attacked," he informed her as he retrieved his sword, wrapped in a wolf-skin sheath, from a large wooden trunk at the foot of the bed. "Get dressed and take the boys to the tapping equipment. They know where it is."

She dressed as she watched him sling the sword over his shoulders and onto his back.

"Fetch me my..." she started.

Already a step ahead of her, he tossed a smaller sheathed sword onto the bed before he retrieved a bow and quiver resting against the wall.

"Take my bow," he said, holding the archery equipment out to her. He then nodded to the sword as she slung it over her shoulders. "Try to save the close combat for the last resort. With luck, you won't need to use that thing."

"Shoot first," she said, taking the bow and arrows. "Stab later. You taught me well, Raulin. You don't need to worry."

He frowned and nodded.

"You ready, boys?" he called softly.

"Aye," Arnald replied.

"Good." Raulin went to them and placed a hand on each of their shoulders. "Go with your mother and hide. Do not come back out until I come and get you myself. Do you understand?"

"What about Gertrude?" asked Arnald. "Should we get her, too?"

"No time, son," his father explained. "I'm sure her parents will look after her. Right now, you need to do what I say."

"Yes, Baba," the boy replied, tearing up.

Raulin wanted so much to promise Gertrude would be fine, that everything would be fine, but the squealing pigs, the burning farmhouse and the possibility of people trapped inside told him not to make promises he might not keep.

He turned and kissed Letitia hard on the lips.

"You come back to me," she commanded.

He nodded.

"Go," he instructed them. "Stay in the shadows."

The family ran from the house. Raulin watched his wife and children make a dash past the workshop and into the darkness of the woods before turning his attention to his brother's hut.

"Ibore?" He thudded softly against the door, keeping his voice low. "Ibore, are you there?"

There was no response.

A shrill scream echoed from the village. Turning, Raulin saw flames rising from several rooftops. Without hesitation, he pulled his sword free and raced towards the farmhouse, where two men continued to slaughter the pigs.

The first didn't realise what happened until after the blade jabbed through his back and out through his belly. He dropped to his knees and spat harsh words Raulin didn't understand.

The second man spun on his heels and raised his thin sword above his head before charging. Raulin blocked the attack with his own and kicked the man hard in the knee. A loud snap erupted from the man's leg before he fell to the ground. Raulin pierced the man through the neck, driving the blade deep into the body.

With both pig killers dead, Raulin peered at the burning farmhouse. He knew none inside survived.

Another scream from the village caught his attention. He saw several figures moving about between huts and houses. Women, children and men were being cut down by marauders with thin blades or shot with arrows. He couldn't kill them all. There were too many.

Where's Ibore?

Farther along the road, away from the village, he saw movement. Darkly clad figures moved towards the forest.

With a quick glance about, seeing that none had noticed him, he made a dash towards them. As he closed the distance, he recognised them as Gertrude, and her brother Gren, draped in blankets. Both of them were bawling their eyes out, keeping as quiet as they could. Upon hearing Raulin's approach, Gertrude produced a short carving knife.

"It's all right," he told them. "It's me. Where are your parents?"

"They... they," she started. Her breaths turned to moans as she tried to force the words. "They killed Baba. Th-they forced Ma-ma to..."

Raulin understood.

"It's all right," he said, placing his hand on her shoulder. "You'll come with me. This way. Quietly."

He turned to lead them towards the woods, towards his family.

A sharp pain jabbed him in the small of his back, and he toppled to the ground.

Gertrude let out a piercing scream.

"Gertrude!" Arnald gasped as he crouched low behind a thick shrub.

"Stay here," Letitia whispered before racing off into the darkness.

"Where are you going?" he called softly, too scared to raise his head to peer towards the source of the sound or to where his mother ran.

"It's all right," Jörgen told him. "She'll find Baba and Gertrude. And we'll all be together again."

The din of more cries and screams filled the air, echoing through the surrounding trees. It sounded as if the attack was all around them.

Arnald lowered himself onto the ground and curled into a ball to cry. Jörgen placed a gentle hand on his brother's back before rising to his feet, risking a look back at the village.

It appeared as one enormous bonfire.

Everything burned.

———◆———

Letitia loaded her bow as she ran towards the road. She saw her husband lying on the ground with an arrow sticking from his back. Her stomach tightened into a knot. But she didn't have time to grieve.

Next to Raulin, lying with a shaft sticking from his chest, was the boy, Gren. His beady eyes stared lifelessly at the moon high in the night sky.

Anger filled her senses when her eyes fell upon Gertrude. The girl lay on her back, struggling against a marauder trying to force his way between her legs. His hand pressed against her mouth as he struggled to lower his pants, wiggling his hips to push himself between her knees as he laughed.

Seeing his bow and quiver lying on the ground a few paces away, Letitia seized the moment. She shot a bolt straight into the top of his head.

He slumped onto Gertrude, who let out a sound of fear, relief and sadness all at the same time. Letitia ran to the girl, rolled the man off, and helped her to her feet.

"You're all right now," she said, wrapping her arms around Gertrude. "We must go."

The girl nodded as Letitia took her hand and started away.

They moved a little way from the roadside, towards the woods, closing the gap between themselves and the tree line.

"Arnald waits for you there," Letitia whispered, hoping her words helped, knowing they didn't.

Suddenly, Gertrude fell. Turning to help her to her feet again, Letitia realised the girl had not simply tripped.

Two shafts stuck in the back of Gertrude's head.

Letitia stared, bewildered.

A soft whistle broke the silence as an arrow shot into her shoulder. She dropped her bow onto the ground.

Two men appeared from the other side of the road. They casually crossed the ground, speaking words she didn't know. One of them pulled his thin sword from his back with one hand, pointing to her as he spoke before grabbing his crotch.

She understood the message and pulled her blade from its sheath. Her shoulder, still bearing the shaft, throbbed as she tried to hold the sword in both hands.

The man charged and swung his blade down hard. She blocked his attack but felt the hit shudder through her body, causing her shoulder to explode in pain.

He struck again and again. Each blow sent a sharp, unbearable pain into the same place.

Eventually, it became too much, and she dropped the sword onto the ground before falling to her side.

The marauder dug his blade into her ribs, deep enough to pierce her organs but not kill immediately. Letitia let out an agonising cry as he retrieved his blade.

Stay hidden, boys, she silently pleaded, placing her thoughts upon Arnald and Jörgen.

The marauder signalled to the other man. *You first.* The second man placed his bow and sword on the ground and unlaced his trousers.

The first marauder lowered himself behind Letitia, placing her head in his lap and his blade to her throat. He chuckled as the second revealed himself. So did Letitia, out of spite.

"So small!" She laughed.

"Hey," the second barked angrily, glancing at himself before slapping her across the face.

THWACK!

An arrow lodged into his temple, sending him onto his side.

The first marauder hollered something. Letitia then noticed several others not too far from where she lay. They were all making their way towards her position as the first marauder stood up.

He looked at a patch of land near the Tanner shack. She followed his stare and saw Jörgen with his bow levelled at the man.

"Jörgen, run," she screamed.

The boy stood his ground and pulled back on the bowstring.

The marauder glanced at the woman and back to the boy. With a grimace, he plunged his sword deep into Letitia's chest.

"Müqin, sì," he slurred, glaring at the boy.

Jörgen roared as he let the arrow fly. It ploughed through the marauder's forehead and lodged deep in his skull. The boy turned to see others approaching. He quickly loaded his bow again and fired at the nearest man, hitting him square in the chest. As he loaded his next arrow, he peered over at his mother.

She watched him with lifeless eyes.

He released the string and hit one attacker in the stomach.

A poor shot, he thought. But he found it hard to aim with tears in his eyes.

The attacker fell to his knees momentarily before snapping the shaft off and continuing towards the boy.

Jörgen released another arrow into the man, hitting him in the neck.

Better.

The man fell face-first onto the ground, forcing the shaft through so it stuck point up out the back.

Turning, Jörgen loaded another arrow onto the string. While he focused all his attention on that one attacker, several others had closed in. Five of them were within a few paces of taking him.

He fired, knowing his target would die from a chest wound at such proximity. He didn't know if he could take out the other five closing on him.

He loaded another shaft, pointed, and fired. This one fell within spitting distance.

Jörgen took another shaft from the quiver and placed it on the string, pointed and fired. A man fell right next to the boy's feet.

He reached for another arrow, only to be grabbed by a large attacker's hands and lifted from the ground. The attacker turned the boy around violently to grip him by the ankles.

As the large man swung him by his feet, Jörgen felt the pit of his stomach fall. He knew what was coming.

With everything he had left, he let out one last roar.

"Fuck you all!"

Arnald silently bawled as he watched the marauder smash his brother into the ground over and over again. Each hit onto the earth emitted a loud thud and sickening crunch. Jörgen's arms flailed like those of a rag doll being swung around by a child.

The sting of bile filled his throat.

The large man flung the little boy's body aside, watching the lad cartwheel through the air until he landed on top of his mother. The other men gathering around gave a cheer.

Arnald felt as if something gave him a great kick in the stomach. He buckled over and threw up before slinking back to the ground as the men turned to walk away, back to the burning village.

PART TWO

The Lazy Traveller

Chapter One

ARNALD COULDN'T MOVE. HE had been in place for what seemed an eternity.

The attackers had revisited the roadside, where his family rested, several times. He surmised they came back for their dead and to rummage through the buildings nearby.

He wanted to run, but his body froze in place as he listened to the men ransack his home. They shouted and laughed, noisily smashing windows and furniture. He could hear their words, but not understand them as they moved back onto open ground.

Lying on his side with his knees tucked tightly into his body, he looked up to the trees where he saw a faint orange glow illuminating the snow-covered branches gradually grow brighter as the men set fire to the house.

He listened as they moved away, continuing to laugh and talk. Even after their voices faded, and he heard them no more, he still couldn't move.

Shivering, afraid and tired, he stayed in place and cried.

Silence swallowed him, except for the sound of fire and the chattering of his teeth.

After some time, the judgemental, condemning voices in his head started shouting as the faces of those he loved passed through his mind.

Baba is dead, one hollered.

Mama is dead, called another.

Gertrude, your beloved, is dead.

Jörgen, your little brother, faced them on his own. Your little brother died fighting. And what did you do?

"Shut up," he whispered, squeezing his eyes shut tight and pressing his hands to his ears. It was a pointless gesture as the voices were all his.

You lay down and cried, shouted a voice. *That's what you did. You lay down and cried.*

Coward, they all shouted at once. A tremendous, thunderous chorus. *Coward! Coward! Coward!*

"Shut up," he pleaded.

The chanting continued, sounding almost like a twisted song.

Coward!

Coward!

Coward!

His sobs turned into uncontrollable bawling. He wrapped his arms around his knees, trying so desperately to shrink into nothingness. A sudden desire, a wish, to die in the place of everyone else, filled his thoughts.

Too late, a voice taunted.

Too late, coward!

His soft breaths turned into long moans as every ounce of internal pain he felt tightened its grasp.

The sound of birds singing brought him to his senses. He opened his eyes to see the early light of the day spread over the scenery about him. The pungent scent of smoke filled his nostrils as he lifted himself to his feet, briefly forgetting about the marauders.

Seeing the burned and broken village in the morning light reminded him of the attack. Smoke continued to billow from places. Several skeletal structures of buildings' frames stood charred, while others lay crumbled in heaped embers and ash. Surprisingly, a few appeared to stand untouched, saved from the flames.

From his position, a short distance beyond the tree line and crouching behind his father's equipment, Arnald peered about the devastation and couldn't find anyone moving about.

His eyes fell to where his mother and brother rested. Jörgen's body lay, twisted, contorted, unnaturally across his mother's stomach.

Arnald felt his mouth turn downwards, his chin quiver, as tears spilled over his cheeks. He wiped them on the back of his sleeve, smearing mucus dribbling from his nose over the fabric. Gingerly, as if each step mattered, he moved from his hiding place and onto open ground. Glancing about, he kept a watchful eye out for any marauders still lingering about.

Then, he saw Gertrude, lying face down in the snow, two shafts sticking from the back of her head. His body shook uncontrollably as he slowly stepped towards her. His vision blurred as tears welled again.

Stop crying, a voice hissed.

He tried, but he couldn't comply. He fell onto his knees beside her and placed his hand on her back, wishing she'd wake up.

At that moment, he realised he was truly alone.

All alone.

Coward.

Carefully, Arnald tried to roll her over. The arrow shafts contacted the ground, causing her head to get stuck in place as the rest of the body moved.

A knot tightened in his stomach as he wept uncontrollably. He tightened his hand around one shaft and tugged. It was lodged deep and took some effort to remove it. A sudden, sharp and loud cry fell from his lips as he dropped the arrow to the ground before reaching for the other, still protruding from her head.

It felt harder to move and took more of his strength to dislodge it. Some blood spattered onto his hand and shirt sleeve. For some reason, the sight of it made him feel worse than he already did. He lifted her, cradling her in his arms, placing his head next to hers in an awkward embrace.

"I'm so sorry," he whispered.

Coward, she replied in his mind.

"I'm so sorry," he repeated. "I'm so sorry."

He stayed there with her in his arms for some time. The sun was high in the sky before he moved again. Believing he'd finished crying, or at the least couldn't physically cry any more, he lowered Gertrude gently to the ground and stood up. He lifted his arm to wipe his face clean on his sleeve but stopped short when he saw her blood there.

It didn't feel right. To do so would be desecration.

He used his other sleeve instead.

Turning to his home, crumbled, and still burning, he noticed the workshop stood untouched. The TANNER sign swung loosely by one chain and part of the thatched roof showed scars of charring. The stove and firewood still sat in place while the rest of the workshop's equipment sat tossed and broken. Uncle Ibore's hut showed no sign of damage, save for the busted door. Arnald surmised the interior would be a mess.

Uncle Ibore?

Arnald glanced about. He saw his mother and brother. His father lay a short distance away, but he couldn't see his uncle. He turned to the village and knew Ibore was there, somewhere.

A great deal of work needed to be done, and there was no one to help him.

Forcing back the tears and swallowing the building lump in his throat, Arnald made for the workshop to retrieve a tarp.

———◈———

The work was arduous.

Using the tarp, Arnald dragged the bodies of Gren, Gertrude, and his family to a portion of ground near his burning house. His father was the most difficult to move. Placing him on the tarp was hard enough on its own. Dragging the large man from the road to the house took all his strength and a great deal of time. Still, Arnald believed his family should be together.

Arnald carried his father's and mother's weapons to the workshop and placed the swords on a bench near the stove. The bows and quivers he hung upon hooks on the large pylons holding the roof up.

He considered taking Gertrude and Gren back to their own hut, to place them with their father and mother. But Gertrude was to be his wife, making Gren his brother, too. At least, that's how he saw it.

After building a pyre of sorts with some of the firewood, nothing more than a large, low campfire, he placed the bodies on top as best he could.

While Raulin was the heaviest, Jörgen proved the most difficult to position with so many of his bones shattered. No matter what Arnald did, moving the boy's arm a little this way or that, turning his foot, his brother didn't look right. Eventually, he just had to accept his efforts as sufficient.

Gertrude was the hardest emotionally. A deep ache spread from his heart to his entire body as he lowered her onto the chocks of timber. He thought of how uncomfortable she would be, resting on the splintery wood, but her eyes remained closed. She continued to sleep without complaining.

Just sleeping.

He then carefully put more firewood over them, effectively burying his family with timber.

It was anything but what anyone could regard as a traditional parting, but it was the best he could do. He took a piece of burning timber from his home and lit the pyre.

He couldn't think of the words spoken at such times. Instead, he touched the bloodstain on his sleeve and thought of her.

Somehow, his body found more tears to shed as he watched the pyre burn.

Arnald lit a fire in the stove and retrieved a freshly slaughtered pig from the farmhouse, dragging it along the road on his tarp. Using the pulley system his father and uncle set up, he hoisted the animal so he could begin the disgusting task of butchering.

He placed a large wooden tub under the carcase, as his father taught him, ready to catch the intestines as they fell. Gripping a knife in his hand, he pressed the point of the blade to the pig's belly.

His eye caught the stain on his shirt, causing him to stop.

He didn't want to accidentally mix pig's blood with hers. So, he placed the knife on the bench next to his father's and mother's swords before entering his uncle's hut.

Before long, he changed out of his shirt and into one of his uncle's. It was too large for him, but he tucked it into his trousers and rolled up the sleeves so it felt comfortable to wear.

Returning to the pig, he took up the knife again and sliced it into the flesh.

He didn't feel hungry, but knew he had to eat.

After such a hard day, his body showed signs of fatigue. Sitting on a bench in the workshop, he forced down a few mouthfuls of fried pork, sizzling directly on the stovetop.

Fierce guilt overwhelmed him as he realised only he ate anything tonight. He looked to the smouldering remains of the village, his house, and the pyre.

Coward, she said.

"I'm so sorry," he whispered, lowering his head in his hands.

After repairing the door as well as he could, reattaching the hinges with a hammer and reusing the bent nails busted from the frame by marauders, Arnald climbed into his uncle's bed.

The condemning voices increased their tormenting. He could hear all of them at once. Not just with his voice, but his mother, father, brother. The entire village. The loudest of all was Gertrude.

Coward.

You let us die.

You should have died, too.

He closed his eyes and saw his brother's twisted, broken body.

You should die.

You should die.

His father and uncle shared a disapproving expression.

PIT GUARD

You should die, coward.
Die, coward!
His mother offered an angry scowl.
Die, coward!
Die!
And then he saw Gertrude's sleeping face.
Die!
Die!

Chapter Two

H E DIDN'T KNOW HOW long he had slept. It could have been hours or minutes. But when he opened his eyes, he was wide awake.

Darkness still prevailed outside, and he did not know how long he needed to wait for the sun to rise, so he got out of bed and dressed in his uncle's shirt again. He looked at his tunic hanging over the back of a chair near the bed. The dark stain of Gertrude's blood appeared black in the dim light spilling from the fireplace.

The sound of a dull bell made him start.

Arnald moved to the window and peered outside.

Nothing.

Tink-Tok!

The noise came from outside, just beyond his range of vision. He looked about for a weapon, realising he left his father's and mother's swords in the workshop.

Stupid!

His heart felt as if it would burst from his chest.

Surely, his uncle kept his sword stashed in here somewhere, unless the marauders took it.

Tink-Tok! Tink-Tok!

The sound was just outside and closing.

Tink-Tok!

Too close.

No time to look for Ibore's sword, and there was no sign of his bow anywhere.

Tink-Tok!

With nothing to use for a weapon, he opened the door.

It turned its head to look at him before bleating loudly.

A goat.

A fucking goat.

"Hey!" Arnald whispered, stepping delicately through the doorway.

The goat moved away slowly, warily. The little bell emitted its sound with each step.

Tink-Tok! Tink-Tok! Tink-Tok! Tink-Tok! Tink!

"It's all right," the boy murmured, continuing to move cautiously towards the animal. "Come on."

It let out a long bleat and took a step towards him.

"That's it." He reached out his hand and rubbed his fingers together, realising just how silly he might look to someone watching. The goat took another step and another.

"Come on," Arnald urged the beast. Gradually, the space between them closed, and he grabbed the collar around the goat's neck. With a gentle pull, Arnald led the animal into the hut. It followed him without protesting, almost as if it wanted to go with him.

Once inside, he closed the door, shutting the cold outside. He examined the goat in the firelight, petting it as he checked for wounds.

"So, you're a girl," he said as he squeezed one of its teats. Milk dribbled over his hand and onto the floor. "That'll be the first job of the day, I suppose. Milking you."

The goat lowered itself to the floor in front of the fireplace.

"All right, then," Arnald said before climbing onto the bed. "That seems like a good idea."

He positioned himself on his side to watch the goat fall asleep. After a while, as his focus moved to the flames, his eyes felt heavy, and he drifted off.

Tink-Tok!

He woke to see the goat standing inches away from his face. His heart jerked when he saw a part of his shirt hanging on the back of the chair sticking out of the animal's mouth.

"No," he barked, suddenly on his feet and taking the garment from the beast. Quickly, he looked the shirt over and saw Gertrude remained there. A wet patch of goat saliva had soaked into the shirttail, however.

Relieved, Arnald plonked himself onto the bed. The goat stared at him quizzically before bleating.

Using his teeth, the boy undid the stitching of the sleeve at the shoulder. Carefully, he removed the section from the bulk of the shirt. He wrapped the stained sleeve around his forearm several times, like a bandage, before tossing the rest of the shirt to the goat.

"There," he said. "Go ahead and eat it."

The animal didn't hesitate, lifting the garment in its mouth.

"You're hungry," the boy acknowledged. "I don't suppose you like pig."

The goat stared at him, chewing the shirt contently.

"The second job of the day," Arnald said. "Finding you some food."

He looked to the window and saw a faint light in the sky. The morning had arrived.

With his boots on and his thick cloak pulled around him, Arnald went outside, leading the goat to the workshop. There, the boy found a long length of rope and tethered the animal to one pylon. After some rummaging, he uncovered a pail and got to milking the beast. He had almost half-filled the bucket before she couldn't give any more.

"Good work, he told her, scratching the top of her head. She snorted, continuing to chew what remained of his shirt.

"Right then," he said, lifting the pail to carry it to the hut. "Now, to find you some food."

Before long, he set off for the charred farmhouse.

Passing the slaughtered pigs and the still-smoking hut, he found a barrow tilted on its side near a small snow-covered mound. After correcting the barrow by placing it upright, he put his attention on the large mound, kicking at its base with his feet.

It moved strangely, causing the snow to shift on top and slide down around his feet. He immediately bent and hooked his fingers under the hidden tarp and lifted it. Some stones holding the tarp in place rolled aside, disappearing in the heaped snow.

Straw.

Arnald used his hands to dig into the straw, drawing out scoops to dump into the barrow. With the barrow full, he placed the tarp back in place and pushed the wheeled cart home.

"I'll look for more things for you to eat when I go into the village," he told the goat as he heaped the straw near the pylon where he had tethered her. "I need to find Uncle Ibore and bring him home."

What about all the other bodies you will find? Gertrude's voice said.

He looked dolefully at the stained sleeve wrapped around his arm.

"I don't know," he told her.

Pushing the barrow through the village, Arnald collected what he considered useful items from among the rubble. He discovered several sacks of flour stashed in a pantry of one untouched hut and a small keg of fresh water in another. Scattered about on the ground, he found potatoes, carrots and apples. Some appeared crushed during the attack, but there was enough to last him a while if he stored them correctly.

Stopping at the pier, he hoped to find fish, or anything on the boats he could use. Unfortunately, all the vessels sat on the bottom of the cove, burned and broken. He found some netting made from thin rope, too coarse for catching fish. Gathering it up, he considered using it to make a temporary pen for the goat, at least until he found something better.

There weren't many bodies in the mess. Most of the people's remains lay charred among the burned shells of huts. The few he found rested on the outskirts of the village, a short distance from any structure and usually with an arrow shaft or two sticking from them. The sight of one woman lying on her stomach reminded him of Gertrude.

A lump built in his throat, and a tear welled in his eye.

He pushed the pain deep down and pressed on, making a mental note to return and take care of all of them later in the day.

Arnald passed a house with the front left corner burned away, exposing the interior, which bore the scars of fire on its walls. But when he moved to the back, the structure appeared untouched. A small chicken coop, standing about waist-high, rested against the exterior wall. They had killed several birds.

Stomped to death by the looks.

Eight more clucked and scratched at the snow not too far away.

He lifted the lid of the coop and counted nine unbroken eggs. Arnald moved a few things around in the barrow to make room for them. Carefully, he positioned them between two flour sacks before glancing at the chickens.

"I'll be back for you later," he promised them.

He started along a thin road that led from the pier to the field where the festival took place, closing upon the eastern tower overlooking the cove. As he approached, he discovered five bags of oats, a loaf of bread, and a pile of firewood in another hut. He piled the oats by the door of the hut as they couldn't fit in his barrow, ate the bread, and stared at the firewood. As he left, he patted the bags of oats, inwardly promising to return for them.

Arnald pushed his laden barrow farther along the path where he saw two more bodies lying at the tower's base; one woman and one man.

It took him a moment to realise the man was his uncle. Even then, he needed to get closer to be certain.

As the knot tightened in his stomach, he looked at his uncle's twisted form. A sudden image of Jörgen flashed through his mind.

"You must have fallen," Arnald whispered, peering up at the top of the tower. "Are there others up there?"

He moved his gaze to the southern tower, adding another mental note to check the towers later in the day as well.

———◆———

It took a while, but he got quite a lot done in such a short time.

The goat had a corner of the workshop to itself, now hedged in by the netting Arnald found on the pier. He threw some straw on the ground and piled some more at one side of the temporary pen with a bucket of water he collected from the village's well.

He returned to the village for the chicken coop, using the barrow to carry it home, where he placed it against the wall of his uncle's house by the door. The next trip saw the bags of oats brought back. Next, he carried Ibore home.

Arnald thought it a little undignified for his uncle, but it was the best he could do. He placed Ibore on a layer of firewood chocks next to where he had burned his father.

By then, the sun was high in the sky, and he still had much to do.

Returning to the village, he rounded up all eight chickens and put them in a hessian sack. They protested noisily, squawking, and flapping their wings as he lifted them by their feet to drop them into the bag. It wasn't long before he set them free on the ground outside his uncle's house, tossing some oats on the ground near the coop. They ran about at first, settling quickly after spying the food lying about.

Taking the barrow, Arnald ventured to the farmhouse to collect a load of straw. He carried it to the house where he found the oats and dumped it on the floor before returning to the mound to collect more. After seven trips to and from the farmhouse, he covered the entire floor space of the hut with straw. He then spread the chocks of firewood from the pile inside, onto the straw.

Afterwards, he began the hard task of collecting bodies, starting with the young lady he found near his uncle at the base of the tower. After climbing the tower, he discovered Hjalmar slumped to one side. With great effort, Arnald rolled the man off the edge. The terrible crunch as Hjalmar hit the ground made Arnald wince.

Eventually, he collected Ebbe and Einar from the north and south towers using the same method. Each of the men was stuck with so many arrows, the boy left them in rather than plucking them out, as he did with his own family before burning them on the pyre.

There's no time, he told himself. *And there's so much to do.*

By the end, he counted seventeen bodies. Among them were five little children as small as, and smaller than, his brother. He wanted to cry for them, but he couldn't. He believed he already cried so much, there were no tears left in him.

Using a flintstone from the workshop, he ignited the hut, leaving with his barrow to let it burn.

The sun touched the tips of the mountains to the west. Night approached.

Arnald took the flintstone and set fire to his uncle's pyre.

He watched the flames take hold before returning to the workshop. There, he stoked the fire in the stove, shaved some meat from the pig still hanging from the rafters, and cooked it on the stovetop.

———◦———

After he had his fill, Arnald checked on the goat. It lay curled upon the ground, sleeping soundly. He noticed the chickens had retired to the confines of their little coop as the flames subsided over his uncle's remains.

He turned to position the bags of oats on a bench, taking them off the ground. The area beneath the workshop roof remained dry, but there was always a chance of rain or snow drifting in and soaking the earth.

With the five sacks piled neatly next to his father's and mother's weapons, he bent to lift a sack of flour, intending to start a new pile next to the oats.

A deep growl made him freeze in place.

Fear gripped him tightly, realising the source of the sound stood right behind him.

Slowly, he took his hands away from the sack of flour and reached for the closest item to defend himself; his mother's sword.

The growl intensified as he gripped the pommel.

"I wouldn't do that, son," a man's voice called from farther away.

Too late. Arnald turned to face the snarling demon with the sword in his hand.

He saw giant white teeth and angry yellow eyes glaring back at him.

A monstrous wolf.

"Put the sword down," said the voice. Arnald quickly glanced to the source and saw a man in armour riding a horse and leading two others. "She doesn't want to hurt you. She wants some of that meat you've got hanging there."

Arnald hesitated. His arms shook and his legs felt weak.

"If she wanted you dead, she would've killed you already," the man told him. "Just put the sword down."

The wolf tilted its head slightly, as if spurring Arnald for a fight.

The boy nodded and dropped the sword.

Coward, hissed Gertrude.

The beast's demeanour changed instantly. It licked its lips and moved slowly past Arnald to the pig hanging from the rafters.

"Wait," the man called to her. She glanced at him, then back to the pig before plonking herself onto her rump.

Arnald didn't know where to look. He turned his head to the man, to the wolf and back again several times, too afraid to move.

"What happened here, lad?" the man asked, lowering himself from his horse. "Where is everyone?"

"Dead," Arnald spat. "All of them."

"Not all," the other replied, bending down to retrieve the sword by the boy's feet. He turned it around in his hand, admiring the blade. "Nice. Yours?"

"My mother's," the boy answered, eyeing the newcomer suspiciously.

The man turned the sword to hold it by the blade, pointing the pommel at the boy. Arnald took it and lowered it by his side.

"Best put it with the other one there before she thinks you intend to attack me with it," he said.

He complied, sliding the blade onto the bench.

"So," the man started. "How about some of that pig for the bitch and me? And some straw for the horses— if you can spare it? I'd like to set up camp for the night. Can I claim this spot here?" He pointed to some ground near the workshop.

"You're not here to kill me?" Arnald asked, distrustfully.

"Kill you?" the man furrowed his brow. "Boy, don't you recognise this armour?"

Arnald scanned the breastplate. It showed four women holding long swords pointed down to their feet. He shook his head.

"Best I introduce myself, then," said the man. "My name is Osman Steigauf. I am one of The First. A Temple Guard of Dendadia. Pit Guard, if you prefer."

Chapter Three

"A PIT GUARD?" ARNALD whispered. He stared at the dented and stained armour, shaking his head in disbelief. He recalled his father's tale of the War of Six and the men who guarded the Temple of Four in Dendadia. Jörgen swore he would be a Pit Guard when he grew up.

When he grew up.

Arnald fought back his tears

"That's right." Steigauf nodded.

"My brother wanted to be a Pit Guard."

The soldier looked at the boy apologetically.

"I'm so sorry, laddie," he said.

Arnald glared at the man angrily.

"If you were here—"

"They probably would have killed me, too," said Steigauf. "How is it you survived?"

Unable to hold the tears back, Arnald let them roll over his cheeks.

"I hid," he admitted. "I was frightened. So, I hid like a coward while my whole family died."

Steigauf nodded, placing a comforting hand on the boy's shoulder.

"There's nothing I can say to ease this," the soldier told him. "You lived, and they died. Beating yourself up about it will not help you."

"I watched them kill my brother," he snapped. "My little brother. He fought them and they swung him by his feet and smashed him into the ground over and over and over."

The soldier stood tall.

"He fought them?"

Arnald nodded.

"And you hid?"

The boy nodded again.

"Your brother, how old was he?" asked Steigauf.

"Eight," Arnald answered.

"And you are, what? Twelve?" He looked the boy up and down as if measuring him.

"Almost thirteen."

"Almost thirteen," the soldier repeated.

Steigauf moved to the pig carcase and shaved a piece off the hind leg with his dagger. He tossed the portion to the wolf, who caught it in her jaws. The soldier cut another sliver of meat away and carried it to the stovetop.

"No offence, lad," he said, placing the pork onto the hotplate where it softly sizzled. "Your brother was stupid, and you were wise."

Arnald scowled at the man.

"You didn't know him," the boy growled.

"I understand your anger," Steigauf told him. "I do. But, your brother, being so young, didn't appreciate danger the same way you do. He was too young to understand and so he ran into a fight without thinking. I'm sure you thought he was brave, but how many times did his bravado bring him to trouble?"

Arnald softened his features, remembering many times Jörgen found trouble just by confronting bigger boys for sport.

"See," the soldier said as he pointed to the boy with his dagger before using it to flip the portion of meat over on the stovetop. "You know him. I don't. But I've known many like him. I'm sure he would have made a fine soldier with training. Perhaps, he'd even have made it as a Pit Guard. Although, it's not bravado that makes men into Pit Guards. It's this."

He tapped the flat edge of the dagger against his head before lifting the meat with the tip of the blade to bite a piece off.

"Ooh! Hot!" he huffed before chewing the morsel and swallowing. "You might think you're a coward because you hid, or because you let your fear control you. But, by the looks of your village, there must have been a great number of attackers. What else could you do? Hide or die. I think you chose wisely."

He blew on the meat before shoving the rest of what stuck on his dagger into his mouth.

"Did you see anything during the attack?" the Pit Guard asked. "Did you see a uniform? What about weapons? Did they perhaps say anything you can recall?"

Arnald furrowed his brow and looked to the ground, searching his memory. He saw Jörgen's broken body.

"Müqin, sì," Arnald whispered.

"What?" asked the soldier. "What did you say?"

"Müqin, sì," the boy repeated. "They carried thin blades and one of them said Müqin, sì."

"Selemar Graekath," the warrior growled.

"What?"

"The Shattered Isles, laddie," Osman replied. "A long way to come to pillage one township. My bet is they've attacked other places along their way. They could be anywhere, now. Perhaps somewhere else in the Cove of Safe Keeping or running out to the Sea of Mavar'us as we speak."

"So, they get away with this?"

"I am sorry for your loss, laddie," Steigauf said, returning to carve more meat away from the carcase. The wolf licked her lips expectantly. "I truly am."

The wolf didn't have to wait long before he threw another portion her way.

The soldier returned to the stovetop and cooked another chunk.

"You want some?" he asked the boy.

"I've eaten," Arnald answered, wiping his eyes on his cloak.

Steigauf looked past the boy to the village, noting some smoke rising from a building closer to the shore.

"You light that?" he asked, his mouth full of pig.

"Burning the dead," the boy replied.

Steigauf nodded thoughtfully as he looked at the makeshift pen for the goat and the pig hanging from the rafters.

"You've been busy," said the soldier. "Most people would have curled up in their beds and waited for days before doing all of this. Or they might have just left."

"I didn't know what else to do." Arnald lowered himself to the ground to sit cross-legged. He placed his head in his hands, his elbows on his knees.

"You did well, laddie." Steigauf smiled. "Exceptional work. Unfortunately, I can't leave you here on your own."

Arnald looked at the Pit Guard questioningly.

"For your safety," the soldier clarified. "I'll take you with me to Shiverwind. I know the magistrate there. We'll let him know what happened here and he can send word to Dendadia."

"And they'll go after these men from the Shattered Isles?"

"I can't promise something like that," said the Pit Guard. "We'll go the day after tomorrow."

Arnald peered at the wolf. She lowered herself prostrate onto the ground, resting her head on her front legs before closing her eyes.

"You should sleep inside," the boy offered. "You could take the bed. I can put my uncle's..." he paused and reconsidered his words. "I can put my bedding on the floor and sleep there. Your wolf can come in too."

"She's not mine," Steigauf informed the boy. "We just travel together. You don't want her to eat your goat. Do you?"

"What?"

"That's why you offered for her to sleep inside, isn't it?"

Arnald nodded bashfully.

The Pit Guard grinned.

"We'll be fine out here," said the soldier, looking at the wrapping on the boy's arm. "But thank you all the same. Did you hurt yourself?"

Arnald glanced at the stained sleeve.

"No," he answered. "It's just something to help me remember. All I have left of her."

"Your girl?"

"Gertrude," Arnald replied. "We were promised."

"And you had to..."

Arnald gestured to the ash pile near the remains of his family's home.

"I put my father, mother and brother there also," he told the soldier. "I put her brother near her and my uncle next to my father."

"Her mother and father?"

"In there somewhere," Arnald gestured to the village. "I couldn't find them. But I know they're in there."

Steigauf nodded understandingly, as he lifted the boy's mother's sword and placed it carefully into its sheath before lowering it delicately onto the bench. The act appeared almost ritualistic, respectful.

The soldier lowered himself upon a small stool next to the bench, causing the armour to clink softly. The wolf opened her eyes momentarily and glanced at the soldier before closing them again.

"Why did you come here?" Arnald asked.

The Pit Guard pointed to the two horses tied to his.

"I hoped to sell those to a farmer or two who might need a plough pulled or something like that." He smiled.

"You sell horses?"

"No." Steigauf chuckled. "Not really. I hunt men and collect bounties."

"You hunt men?"

"Criminals, law-breakers, thieves and murderers," he explained. "Men who have warrants issued against them. I recently came upon these horses after delivering their previous owners to the magistrate in Driradia. I sold all their horses, except for these two."

"Why not these?" Arnald turned to examine the animals. "What's wrong with them?"

"Absolutely nothing," the soldier replied. "With the exception that two of the foulest men to have lived rode the poor things, at least, according to many living in the lands on the other side of those mountains."

"So, you thought you'd try your luck on this side?"

"See?" Steigauf grinned. "I told you, you're wise."

<hr/>

After helping the Pit Guard with his horses, penning them in with the goat and fetching more straw from the stack at the farmhouse, and buckets of water from the well, Arnald considered retiring for the night. The only problem was, he didn't know this man well enough to trust him.

They sat and talked well into the night, mostly old war stories the old man shared with the young listener. Arnald's eyes grew heavier and heavier with each new tale. He stifled his yawns, trying desperately to hide his weariness from the other. As Steigauf spoke about a bar fight he took part in, the boy's head lowered to his chest. He quickly recovered.

"Am I boring you, boy?" the soldier asked.

"No," Arnald told him truthfully. The soldier told captivating stories.

"You're tired," the other said with a nod. "But you're trying to stay awake. You're not sure about me yet. Are you?"

The boy shrugged.

"I understand." Steigauf smiled. "If I had been through what you went through at your age, I'd be a little distrusting towards newcomers, too. Look..." He stood up. The sound of his armour clinking aroused the sleeping wolf. She yawned and peered at the soldier. "It's all right, girl." He waved a hand at her, at which she lowered her head and closed her eyes again. The Pit Guard lifted the sheathed swords from the bench. "Take these inside with you. You shouldn't leave them out here to be weathered upon. Keep them sheathed, sleep with them, whatever makes you comfortable. The truth is, if I wanted to take from you and hurt you, I would've done so already."

Arnald lifted himself from the ground and took the swords. The sudden weight on his arms almost caused him to fall.

"You need to take care of them," Steigauf told him. "They're remnants of your family. Heirlooms, as they say. I'll teach you how to use a whetstone if you don't know how to already."

"I know," Arnald replied. "My father made me sharpen all the carving knives for skinning."

"I bet you're good at it too," the soldier said, leaning on the bench. "Skinning, I mean."

The boy nodded.

"My father said I was a better tanner than my brother," he replied with a hint of sadness in his voice. "Better than my father and uncle, too. He said my skins sold for the highest prices in the markets."

"You're a hard worker, then?" the Pit Guard asked.

"I guess so." Arnald nodded.

"You are," the other replied. "Look at how much you accomplished today. On your own. It's no wonder why you're so tired. You need to sleep, lad. You need to recover."

He nodded.

"Then, off to bed with you," Steigauf commanded. "Sleep. With your permission, I'd like to cook some more of this pig in the morning, and maybe some eggs for breakfast, and more for the journey ahead."

Arnald nodded again.

"Good." The Pit Guard grinned, "I'll see you in the morning, then. Goodnight."

"Goodnight," Arnald replied, turning to make his way to his uncle's hut. Upon opening the door, he turned to see Steigauf removing a vambrace from his forearm. He looked at the old soldier curiously.

"I don't wear this while I sleep, lad," the man informed him. "Go to bed. I'll see you in the morning."

The boy moved inside and latched the door closed behind him. He placed the swords on the far side of the bed, near to the wall before turning to stoke the fire and place a few chocks onto the flames.

Climbing into bed and pulling the covers over himself, he considered how much sleep he'd get with a strange man just outside the door.

Not much, he supposed.

Chapter Four

———◆———

ARNALD TOOK CAREFUL AIM, directing his bow and arrow at the stag. He crouched low, his back resting on the trunk of a pine tree, his knees almost touching the earth.

"Take your time," Jörgen whispered from behind him. "Breathe out, like Baba said."

The older boy slowly exhaled, held his breath, and checked his aim.

He released the arrow and watched it arc through the air to stick into a tree behind the stag's head.

The beast bolted into the woods and out of view.

"How?" Jörgen asked, frustrated. "How could you hit the tree? The deer's head was in the way. Did the arrow twist as it flew? Did it go in one ear and out the other?"

"I don't know," Arnald answered, standing up. "I don't know."

"You're cursed." The younger boy pointed at his brother. "The gods do not see you fit to kill with a bow. That's it."

"I can't shoot," Arnald said, walking to the tree his arrow stuck into. "That's all. You're much better than I am."

"That's true," Jörgen replied, sounding haughty. "I'm better than you at many things. Shooting, running, swimming."

Arnald wrapped his fingers around the shaft of the arrow and pulled.

"You know what else I can do better than you?" the younger brother asked.

"What's that?" Arnald said, placing the arrow in his quiver before glancing over at his brother.

"This," Jörgen said, lying on the ground. His body was twisted, beaten and bloody.

Arnald sat upright and placed his hand over his heart. It felt as if it tried to burst from his chest. His breathing felt short, rapid. He looked around the room, darting his eyes about until they fell on the low flames in the fireplace across the room.

He wasn't out hunting with his brother.

Slowly, he gained control of his breathing, and his heart slowed to a regular pulse. Lowering back to his pillow, he lay awake staring at the ceiling, too afraid to close his eyes. Jörgen waited there to remind him of what happened and to torture him with more condemnation.

If not Jörgen, then his mother or father. Perhaps his uncle would appear to execrate him for using the hut. Or worse, she would arise to whisper in his ear that one detestable word he couldn't escape.

Coward.

He touched the sleeve wrapped around his arm.

"It's not her," he whispered. The faces of his family flashed through his mind. "It's not them."

After dressing himself, Arnald went outside. It was still dark, and the boy expected to see the soldier asleep.

"Good morning," the Pit Guard called. "You're up early. Did you shit the bed?"

"Wha...?" Arnald furrowed his brow before realising the man's remark was a poor attempt at humour.

Steigauf had on his tunic and cloak, leaving his armour in a neat pile

94

on his bedroll next to his equipment he'd taken from his horses' backs the previous night.

"Ah, good morning."

Steigauf pointed to a pale of milk on the workbench.

"I've milked your goat. She produced quite a lot. Is this always the case, or does she have younglings to feed?"

The boy heard the sizzle and smelled the inviting aroma of pork cooking on the stovetop. He saw a pot of boiling water next to the frying meat.

"I don't know," Arnald answered, approaching the other. The watchful wolf kept a wary eye on him as he drew near. "She appeared yesterday."

"Probably scared and lonely," Steigauf said. "Funny thing about animals like goats and horses. They run away from you when you go near them, but they want to be near you at the same time. Very odd." He turned and pointed to the chicken coop. "I hope I didn't wake you when I gathered a few eggs. There are still more to be collected. Good layers, those ones. It'll be a shame to slaughter them."

"Slaughter?" Arnald felt his stomach drop.

"We can't leave them when we go, laddie," the soldier explained. "It would be cruel to them. Like your goat there, they rely on people as much as we rely on them. The kindest thing to do is to kill them. I know that sounds backwards, but they'll die a terrible death without us to feed them and to take care of them. A fox or wolf could get to them."

"What about the goat?" the boy entreated. "Should we slaughter her, too?"

"Actually, I'm thinking we could take her and sell her in Shiverwind," Steigauf said. "You'll certainly get a bit of coin for her. She's young and, well, just look at how much milk is in that bucket."

Arnald glanced at the chicken coop leaning against his uncle's hut.

"Couldn't we sell the chickens?"

"I'd doubt it," the other replied. "Chickens are easy to come by. Besides, I don't intend to leave them."

The boy shot him a quizzical look.

"What do you mean?"

"I'm going to roast them," said Steigauf. "Shiverwind is almost a week's journey from here. Maybe a little longer with this goat in tow. It'll be slow going. We'll need food, and you have plenty here. Chickens are good eating. We'll cook up some more of this pig and carve up some more meat from one or two of those other ones lying in that yard over there." The soldier pointed to the farmhouse along the road. "After that, I intend to take a look around your village to see what I can take."

"Take?"

Steigauf offered him an apologetic look.

"Listen, laddie," he said. "The people of this place won't need anything left lying about. If there is anything I think is useful, I'd like to use it. If there is anything of value, I'd like to sell it. That said, I'll share any profit I make with you. Half, half. All right?"

Arnald nodded understandingly but couldn't help feeling offended at the same time.

"I'll take the barrow with us," he offered.

"Good boy," Steigauf smiled. "Now, how about some pork and eggs? If you've got a mug for yourself, I can make us some tea using this boiling water and maybe a little milk, if you like that kind of thing?"

"Tea?" Arnald questioned. "I don't have any tea. Any my mama kept burned with our house."

"I've got tea," the Pit Guard explained, stepping over to his equipment to fish a small leather pouch and a tin cup from his saddlebags. "All the way from Vertdell, the best tea in all of Ananduil."

<hr>

After a hearty breakfast, Steigauf and the wolf took the barrow to the farmhouse, where he recovered two pigs. The job took two trips, one for each hog, both a tremendous effort. The soldier struggled with the first carcass, a sow roughly his size. Its legs and head bounced and almost scraped the ground as he pushed the barrow to the workshop. The second proved a little easier, being about half the size of the first. However, the Pit Guard couldn't help but wonder how the boy had managed to cart and hoist the pig hanging from the rafters on his own.

Meanwhile, Arnald started a fire on the open ground between the workshop and his uncle's hut, where he constructed three small spits using wood chocks and short iron rods, about the length of his arm, found in the workshop. He then set to killing the chickens, laying their necks over another chock of timber before removing their heads with a hatchet.

"That'll have to do us," the Pit Guard said upon his return.

"Only two pigs?" Arnald questioned the old soldier. The swine jostled and wriggled as Steigauf wheeled the barrow by. "Why not all?"

"Because first, I can't push that much weight," the other explained. "There are three more pigs down there. Second, these two are the only ones that have most of their useful meat intact. The others were hacked to pieces and their intestines have seeped into places. Disgusting!"

Arnald took a headless bird, sat on the step of his uncle's hut, and plucked feathers.

"It should be enough," he said. "A week to Shiverwind, you said. We've got all these chickens and pork. We'll have enough for there and back."

"You forgot one thing, laddie." The soldier gestured to the wolf as he pushed the barrow into the workshop. "She eats quite a bit, and I'm not about to let her starve. She might be lucky enough to catch something for herself, but the climate up here in the northlands keeps prey on the move, in search of something to eat. It's rare to see a large thing like a deer or elk when you're on the road."

The boy nodded. His father, uncle and brother hunted in the woods, away from the village and people. The deer and elk never ventured near the roadside.

"Plenty of rabbits, though," the soldier put in, moving a second pulley and tackle system next to the carcase hanging from the rafters, ready to hoist another in place. "Should I hoist both, or do one at a time?"

"One at a time," the boy answered. "I don't think that beam will take much more weight after you lift one of those pigs up there."

"Yeah," Steigauf said, examining the timber beam stretching from one side of the structure to the other. "Exactly what I was thinking. This is going to take some time, then."

"Not as long if you take that one down and put it on a workbench," Arnald said, placing the chicken on the step and getting to his feet. He pointed to the carcase they had carved meat from. "I'll clear a space."

Soon, the two swine taken from the farmhouse swung from the rafters with their bellies open and their intestines sitting in a tub on the ground beneath them. The wolf eyed the grotesque mess with a hungry glare, licking her lips anxiously.

"What?" the Pit Guard asked her. She let out a soft whine, bobbing her head to the tub. "You want to eat that shit?"

She licked her lips again, edging towards the discarded, slimy organs.

"Will she really eat it?" Arnald asked, continuing to pluck chickens.

"Yeah." Steigauf frowned. "Waste not, want not. Besides, she would eat the stomach out of anything she caught in the wild before eating anything else."

"The softest place," the boy said. "Also, the easiest to penetrate."

"Well," the Pit Guard remarked. "There's more of that wisdom. Who told you that? Your father?"

"Uncle Ibore," he answered, gesturing with his thumb to the hut behind him. "He tried to teach me how to hunt. I was a poor student."

"I'll teach you a few things on the way to Shiverwind," Steigauf told him as he carved into a forelimb of one of the hanging animals. "It won't be life-changing stuff. But it might be enough to help you get by. With your permission, of course."

Arnald nodded, placing a freshly plucked bird next to another he'd completed.

"You're good at that," the soldier observed. "Quick. Perhaps you're meant to be a cook?"

"Plucking chickens, carving animals, skinning, tanning and hiding away like a coward." The boy frowned.

"What's that?" the old man asked, placing the forelimb on the bench.

"All the things I'm good at," Arnald replied.

Steigauf turned to face the boy, about to speak some words to ease the pain he sensed in the lad's voice. Instead, the soft whimper of the wolf interrupted him. She continued to stare at the tub of innards.

"All right, then," he growled at the animal before looking over at the boy again. "Come help me take this outside so she can eat it away from us."

"She can eat it there," Arnald replied. "Can't she?"

"You know what pigs' intestines smell like, laddie?" questioned the soldier. "Pig shit. Come, help me."

Chapter Five

I T TOOK MOST OF the day to cook all eight chickens and all portions of the two swine, plus the leftover parts of the first Arnald originally fetched from the farmhouse. During that time, the soldier bundled straw from the heap while the boy prepared his uncle's equipment for travelling. He found a bedroll, tin cup, a foldable tripod for cooking, a small pot for boiling water and a little frying pan stashed under his uncle's bed. There, he also discovered his uncle's sword, encased in a leather sheath, and wrapped in wolf's skin.

It looked just like his father's and mother's; a simple two-edged blade with a straight guard, leather grip, and round pommel. It bore no insignia or markings.

"It looks as if it would do the job it is intended for," Steigauf noted upon examining the sword. "Like the others... you should keep them. Heirlooms, remember?"

Arnald nodded.

"I don't know if I would ever get any use out of them," the boy told the old soldier. "But I will keep them. Something to remember them by."

"What have you got of your brother's?" the Pit Guard asked as he tied some twine around some neatly bundled straw, as thick as his torso.

"Nothing," the boy answered, sounding upset.

"What about that?" Steigauf pointed to a bow hanging on a pylon. "Isn't one of those his?"

"Yes," Arnald answered. "But it's too small for me."

"Then, his quiver," the soldier suggested, struggling as he slid a large hessian bag over the bundled straw. "Pack it with arrows and choose a bow. I'm going to teach you to shoot, or at least try to."

With that, Arnald lifted Jörgen's quiver from the hook and loaded it with all the arrows from other cases hanging nearby. He chose his father's bow, wrapped with black cow's hide around the grip.

"I might teach you how to fight with all three swords, too," Steigauf said as he bundled another bunch of straw together.

"You can't fight with three swords," Arnald replied with a smile.

"No?"

"You've only got one sword." The boy gestured with the bow as he carried it to his uncle's hut.

"Here, yes," the soldier replied. "But I have another five swords in my house."

"In Dendadia?" Arnald asked, entering the hut to place the bow and loaded quiver on a pile of things he intended to take with him.

"Dendadia, no," Steigauf answered. "My home is Wyvernmont, laddie."

"Where's that?" questioned the boy as he emerged from the hut.

"Where's that?" the Pit Guard repeated, considering how to explain where anything was to a boy who had not ventured outside of his village. "If Vertdell is far, far to the south, and we're far, far to the north, Wyvernmont is closer to Vertdell and only a little farther to the north from it. But still far...if that makes sense."

"No," Arnald told him. "But I'll take your word for it that it's far to the south from here. Just not as far as Vertdell."

"Good enough," Steigauf replied, wrapping a piece of twine around the straw.

"Is that where you're heading?" the boy asked, placing a cloth on the bench to wrap a chicken.

"Yes," the other replied, peering at what the boy did. "Is that clean? The cloth?"

"I took it from my uncle's collection," Arnald told him. "By what standards do you call *clean*?"

Steigauf nodded.

"To answer your question," the old soldier said, tying the twine off. "Yes, I'm going back to Wyvernmont to live out my days. But I'm taking the long way."

"The long way?"

"I travelled north from Dendadia, along the Eluvian path to Jomaandia to swim in the Bay of Hope," he began. "I then followed the coast to Aliedia, where I started my hunt for the former owners of those two horses there. I found them about a week later, on my way to Driradia. I then took them to Driradia and took payment for my services and a few horses."

"Except for those two," Arnald added.

"Except for those two," the soldier repeated. "I then came south along the coast road to see the Bay of Safe Keeping again, one last time."

"And you found me."

"And I found you," the Pit Guard said.

"Where to next?" the boy asked, wrapping another bird in a cloth.

"Shiverwind obviously," Steigauf replied. "South to Deep Rock, then Springhollow, Southfog. I think I'll take another swim there in the Gulf of Crystal Waters. We'll see. Then, I'll go north to Crystalbridge, cross the bridge, and go north to Aldoak Village and on to Wyvernmont."

"The long way." Arnald smiled.

"The long way," the soldier agreed.

With all things prepared and put away, they left the loading and packing of the horses for the next morning. The sun was beginning its descent and Steigauf still wanted to explore the village before nightfall.

They walked together along the road to the southern edge of the village; the wolf, the man and the boy pushing the barrow. The scent of smoke and ash remained thick in the air. They turned left, towards the southern tower, and made their way towards the shoreline.

"Here," the soldier said, guiding the boy to the water's edge. "See these marks?"

Arnald looked to three deep furrows dug into the mud.

"Boats came ashore here," he offered.

"Three long boats," Steigauf added. "This is where your attackers landed. Three longboats give me the impression they sailed into the cove onboard a large vessel. Possibly a galleon or frigate. Maybe two."

"I saw one ship out there," the boy said.

"A long way out, though," the Pit Guard clarified.

"Barely a blot on the horizon."

Steigauf stood to his full height and stared across the expanse of water while the wolf sniffed at a rut left by a longboat.

"You can't see across to the other side from here," the soldier uttered to himself. "It's an ocean to cross from here to Port Coldspring. Maybe two days of sailing. Maybe more." He scratched his chin as he stared at the cove.

The wolf moved to the boy's side and sniffed his hand. Arnald stiffened out of fear. The wolf stood almost as tall as he and could easily knock him to the ground.

Two gulps, he thought. And I'll be dinner done.

"She wants you to rub her ears," Steigauf told him. "She's starting to trust you."

Arnald peered at the man, then to the wolf. She nuzzled his arm gently. Timidly, the boy wrapped his hand around the wolf's ear and rubbed. She tilted her head towards him, emitting a low groan.

"She likes that," the Pit Guard said. "You've just made a new best friend."

"Does she have a name?" Arnald asked, feeling more confident, scratching gently around the base of the animal's ear.

"No name," said Steigauf. He continued to scan the cove. "How about you?"

"Sorry?" The boy shot the soldier a quizzical look.

"A name?" the old man asked. "Do you have one?"

"Arnald," he answered immediately. "I apologise for not telling you earlier. I thought I..."

"No apology needed, laddie," said Steigauf, waving a dismissive hand. "I didn't want to ask or press you until you were ready. But my curiosity grew impatient, and I needed to know."

"I should have said so," Arnald replied, moving his hand across to the

104

wolf's other ear. "I just forgot."

"Understandable with everything that has happened," the soldier said, turning to face him. "Let's continue into the village, Arnald. I'd like to visit the blacksmith, if you have one here."

Arnald returned to pushing the barrow. The wolf whined a small protest before plodding behind the boy.

"There's not much left," Arnald told the old man. "I didn't really take a good look, but most of the workshop is burned away.

"Iron is a little hard to burn," the Pit Guard replied. "Could be something useful in there, or something of value. It's worth a look."

Arnald peered into the water as he walked.

"What are you thinking?" he asked the old man.

"Thinking?"

"When you looked out to the cove," the boy expanded. "You scratched your chin and said something about sailing to Coldspring."

"Oh that..." The other nodded. "I was considering if the attackers came from one boat or more. You told me you saw only one on the horizon. But there might have been more out of view, beyond your range of view." Steigauf pointed out to the cove. "Coldspring is right over there. It would take a day or two to sail across to the other side. You can't see it from here, but it's there. These attackers could have more boats sitting in deeper waters, half a day's sailing from here. For all we know, an entire armada might have been out there."

"Or one ship with three longboats," Arnald put in.

"Precisely." The Pit Guard nodded. "We'll never know. But I can't help wondering."

"Are we still at war with the Shattered Isles?" the boy asked, steering the barrow around some obstacles on the path as they moved into the village.

"No," the soldier answered. "But relations with them aren't the best. Let's just say I wouldn't call them friendly."

"Where would they go after this?"

Steigauf looked at the boy curiously.

"You plan to go after them?" he asked. "You want revenge?"

Arnald frowned and shook his head.

"I hope I never see them again." His mind flashed to the big man flinging his little brother around.

The soldier considered the boy for a moment.

"They'll sail north and steer well wide of any land," the old man explained. "They won't want to be spied by the watchers at Driradia or Aliedia as they move south on the Sea of Mavar'us. So, they'll stay well west of the coast. When they eventually turn east to sail home, it will be far to the south of Dendadia and the watchtower of Etiendia."

"They'll get away with everything they did," the boy muttered.

"Possibly," Steigauf told him honestly. "That doesn't mean we don't report it to the magistrate and Sheriff of Shiverwind when we get there, and demand a message be sent to Dendadia. Our own navy takes pride and pleasure in hunting unwelcome visitors."

Arnald stopped and lowered the barrow. The soldier furrowed his brow, wondering if the sudden pause was because of something he said.

"What's the matter?"

"This is it." The boy gestured to a stone building with its roof burned away, exposing charred rafters and beams inside.

The blacksmith's shop was practically gone.

"All right," Steigauf huffed, stepping into the remains of the workshop. "Let's see what we can find."

───────◆───────

The scavenger hunt provided nothing more than a large iron pale filled with arrowheads. As the boy and man ate fried pork, they stared at the newly gained bucket.

"If we had some dowel," the soldier remarked.

"What?" the boy asked. "You'd teach me to make arrows?"

"No," Steigauf answered. "Do you know how to make arrows?"

"No." The boy shook his head. "Do you?"

"No," the Pit Guard answered. "I usually purchase mine from a smithy or huntsman."

Arnald nodded.

"As did we."

"I guess we could sell it all to the smithy in Shiverwind." The old man bit a sizeable chunk of meat from the portion he held in his hands.

"Or ask him to use them to make arrows for us," the boy suggested.

Steigauf grimaced.

"Truthfully, Arnald, I'm not much of a bowman," he admitted. "I can aim and shoot, but I'm not good with a moving target. My strength lies with the blade. Unless you suddenly become a wizard with archery, I can't see the point in keeping these things. I'm tempted to just leave them here. Deadweight and all."

The boy stared at the bucket of arrowheads as he chewed a large morsel of pork.

"We take them to Shiverwind," he told the soldier. "Might as well see if we can get something for them."

"All right," the Pit Guard agreed. "But you carry them on your horse."

Chapter Six

———◆———

A RNALD WOKE WITH A start.

His heart raced, beating loudly in his ears. Looking at the fireplace, he tried recalling what brought him from his sleep. He couldn't remember if it had been the image of Jörgen's misshapen body or Gertrude's dead stare boring into his soul as she taunted him again, or perhaps something worse and more horrifying.

Coward, her voice spat from far away.

He touched the stained cloth on his arm, hoping she'd forgive him one day.

With a long inhalation, he pushed the thought away, not really wanting to know what terrors had stirred him awake. A glance at the window told him it was still dark outside. He wasn't sure if morning had come or if it was still late in the night. Either way, he didn't want to go back to sleep.

He dressed, folded his blanket as small and tight as he could before placing it into a hessian bag barely large enough to fit it into. After placing it with the collection of equipment he intended to take with him, he carefully opened the door, trying not to make a sound so as not to arouse the soldier and the wolf sleeping outside. It was a silly gesture on his part; he realised. The noises of the world outside were much louder than a door opening. Still, he proceeded with care as he pulled the door on its hinges.

Steigauf stood by the stove in the workshop, frying more ham and boiling eggs. The wolf offered a soft whine as she turned to face the boy, alerting the soldier to his emergence from the hut.

"Good morning," he said without turning. "Breakfast? I'm cooking as much of that pig as I can before we leave. I think it might turn if we take it with us, being that it has been hanging up there for how long?"

"Two days," Arnald answered. "No, three. Maybe four. I forget."

Steigauf turned to face him momentarily.

"It's all blending together, isn't it?"

The boy nodded.

"Don't worry, laddie," the old soldier offered. "It becomes a little easier with time. Even the nightmares don't seem as bad after a while."

Arnald frowned as he nodded.

"So, breakfast, then?"

"All right," the boy replied before pointing to the corner of the hut. "I just need to..."

The Pit Guard furrowed his brow, then seemed to understand.

"Go right ahead," he said. "This'll be a while." The wolf started after the boy as he rounded the corner of the hut. "No," Steigauf told her. "Leave him with some privacy."

She sat in place, watching the boy vanish from sight.

Arnald moved to the rear of the hut, undoing the cords of his trousers as he walked. Feeling the release on his bladder as he urinated against the wall, he closed his eyes and let out a long exhalation.

The sound of a footfall caused him to stop midstream. He looked towards the forest for the source of the sound and saw nothing. Another noise, like that of something stepping closer, made him freeze in place. Fear gripped him as he stood with his cock in his hand, unable to piss, unable to move.

A beast moved from the shadows of the tree line into view, followed by three others of its kind.

Wolves.

They each lowered their heads and growled as they edged slowly towards the boy. They appeared smaller than Steigauf's wolf, but not any less menacing.

"Os.., Os..," he whimpered, trying to call for the Pit Guard. His voice was a mere breath. He kept trying to call, "Osman. Osman."

The wolves edged closer and closer, fanning out to surround him.

"Osman," Arnald called with all his might, managing only a whisper.

Closing, closing, the wolves narrowed the gap between themselves and their prey. Arnald felt his bladder open involuntarily, spilling a fresh stream of urine over the wall of the hut.

"Osman," he whispered, feeling a tear roll down his cheek, his voice vanishing in the air as vapour.

The wolf farthest to the boy's left circled behind him and picked up its pace.

Arnald closed his eyes, believing this was it for him. As the beast lunged, he prepared to die.

A sudden loud growl followed by a ruckus exploded behind him. He opened his eyes to see Steigauf's wolf tearing the throat of the smaller wolf open with one violent shake of her head. She dropped the dead animal, blood dripping from her bared fangs, before she turned her attention to the remaining three intruders. Glaring at them with her yellow eyes, she offered a deep growl, stepping towards them, hackles raised.

They replied in kind, moving together to attack.

From nowhere, Steigauf appeared, sticking his sword deep into the side of the wolf farthest to the right. It yelped, turned to snap at the old soldier before falling on its side. The Pit Guard hacked the beast again, chopping his blade through ribs and tissue.

The sudden appearance frightened the remaining two wolves. They quickly turned and fled for the forest. Both Steigauf and the wolf gave a short chase, the man yelling profanities as they neared the tree line.

Upon returning to Arnald, he asked, "Are you all right, laddie?"

The boy nodded, shaken by the experience. The old soldier glanced down at Arnald's trousers.

"I think you're done," he told the boy. "I think you can put that thing away, now."

Arnald snapped back to reality and looked down at his member, still grasped in his fingers. Quickly, he stuffed it back into his pants and tied the cords together.

"Sorry," he said to the soldier as he cried.

"No apology needed," Steigauf replied. "That was quite frightening."

Arnald nodded as he wiped his eyes on his cloak sleeve.

"Thank you," he said, looking at the soldier.

"You're welcome," the Pit Guard replied. "But you should thank her. She wanted to follow you. She must've known they were coming."

"She saved me," Arnald said, before petting the wolf on the head. She responded by licking his face.

"I told you; she likes you." The soldier smiled. "Now, how about breakfast?"

<hr />

After breakfast, Steigauf and Arnald packed the horses for the journey. The boy selected the white horse to ride upon, therefore the tan horse became their packhorse and bore most of the heavier and bulkier equipment. It carried the bundles of straw, several leather bags from the workshop stores packed with swine meat and chickens, as well as a well-wrapped bucket of arrowheads Arnald managed to stash among the equipment.

Everything else needed to fit on the riding horses. With help from the Pit Guard, Arnald packed his bedroll, camping equipment, three swords, bow and quiver on his charger.

Steigauf dragged the last of the hanging pig's remains onto the ground, near the crumpled and burned remains of the boy's house. He nodded to the wolf, gesturing to the carcase.

"Eat it up, if you want," the soldier offered.

The wolf replied with a deep whine and turned her nose to the road.

"She doesn't want it?" asked Arnald.

"She's had her fill," Steigauf replied. "She's ready to move on."

Before long, they set off, heading south along the road for Shiverwind. The boy's gaze fell on the dead wolves lying behind the hut.

"They may come back for the pig," the Pit Guard remarked. "Perhaps with more. I hope they won't follow us. But the scent of the meat we carry could draw them."

The boy moved his gaze to the slain animals, to the she-wolf and back again.

"Why are they smaller than her?" Arnald asked, watching the wolf trotting alongside him. She moved off to the side of the road to sniff the ground before re-joining her travelling companions.

"I think it's more that she is bigger," Steigauf replied, peering at the expanse of water on their left, the sun shimmering on its surface. "To be honest, I don't know why. I guess we could ask why some people are taller and others shorter? They just are. Her parents might have been of good breeding. She could be a freak of nature."

As they rode, Arnald turned now and then to see his home growing smaller in the distance, feeling his heart sink more and more with each step his steed took.

"Maybe you'll come back someday," Steigauf said, turning to peer at the remains of the village. He admitted inwardly, the place looked pretty, except for blackened skeletal frames of huts that continued to stream smoke in places. But the forest by the water's edge, even with the blasted snow covering everything, was something to behold.

The boy, on the other hand, saw the place he burned his family, a place of pain and terrible memory, and nothing more. He frowned as a small part of him mourned for them, but a larger piece of him felt relieved to be moving on. Rolling up the sleeve of his cloak and shirt, he looked at the stained cloth wrapped around his forearm.

"I don't believe I shall ever return," he told the old soldier. He rolled his sleeve down and touched his mother's sword, sheathed, and strapped to the saddle by his right leg. "I have all the memories I want to take from this place. There's nothing left for me here."

The old man nodded thoughtfully.

"Then, on to new beginnings, we go," the Pit Guard said.

Trotting ahead of the riders, the wolf sniffed the road here and there. She moved on, maintaining the distance between herself and the horses, occasionally looking back as if making sure the soldier and boy kept up.

"What if those wolves return?" Arnald questioned. "What do we do?"

"We'll deal with that when or if that happens," the Pit Guard replied.

"How will we know if they come back?"

"Watch her," the soldier instructed him. "She'll let us know if there is any danger. She'll let us know if there's any food worth killing, too. She might even kill for us."

Arnald looked at the old man, wide-eyed.

"She kills for you?" he inquired. "What, like, deer and rabbit?"

Steigauf watched the she-wolf zigzag across the road. His mind flashed to the night when he and the wolf took down Bald Barkley and his band of murderers.

"Like deer and rabbit, yeah," the Pit Guard agreed.

Chapter Seven

E VERY ONCE IN A while, the goat paused to look about, only to have its neck yanked by the rope tied to the back of the packhorse if it lingered too long. Arnald thought it was amusing, smiling to himself as he watched the goat trot up to the packhorse, increasing the slack in the rope, before stopping again to look about, repeating the whole thing over and over again.

"Silly goat," he muttered under his breath.

"What's that?" Steigauf queried.

"Nothing," the boy answered. "Just talking to myself."

"What about?" the soldier asked. Admittedly, they had been riding in silence for a long time. The sun was high in the sky and Arnald felt the small pains of hunger setting in. A conversation was probably long overdue.

"The goat," he replied.

The old man turned in his saddle to see the little beast receive another hard tug from the rope.

"Mmm." Steigauf nodded. "Goats aren't the quickest of learners. She'll work it out soon enough. A sore neck is a good persuader. You hungry?"

"A little," the boy answered.

"Me too," the soldier said, looking into the sky. "It's past midday. What say we pull to the side of the road and break open one of those chickens?"

Sitting upon a rocky outcropping that jutted into the water from the shoreline, the two travelling companions sat to eat chicken. Arnald looked to the south to see water stretch on as far as he could see.

"How far until we see where the shore turns towards the east?" he asked.

"You've never been to Shiverwind?" queried the old soldier.

"I've never left our village before this morning," the boy replied.

"Well..." Steigauf wiped his mouth on his sleeve. "You're about to see many strange things, I should say. The way people behave out here in the world might be different to what you're used to seeing in your little village. There are good people and bad people, and sometimes they're the same people. You'd best keep your wits about you."

"And which are you?"

"Sorry?" the Pit Guard asked.

"Which are you?" Arnald replied, tearing some breast meat from the bird. "Good, bad or both?"

"A little of everything, I suppose," Steigauf answered. "I guess it depends on your perspective. Some might say I'm good. Others, like the former owners of those horses, might say I'm bad. Some, like those I collect payment from when hunting wanted men, might think me a little of both."

Arnald chewed while he mused on the old man's words before swallowing.

"I think you're good," he said.

"What makes you say so?"

"You helped me," the boy pointed out. "You saved me from the wolves. You're taking me to Shiverwind. You could have easily left me to starve and die back there."

"I don't think you would have starved, Arnald," Steigauf said, wrapping the remaining chicken back in the cloth before stashing it into a saddlebag. "I think you're clever enough to find a way to survive."

"The wolves would have got to me today if you weren't there."

The Pit Guard shook his head.

"I think they would've moved on, or not have even shown up if I hadn't come along," he said. "Who knows?"

"Still," the boy said, standing up, peering to the south where the water seemed to stretch on forever. "I think you're good."

"We should move on and cover as much ground as we can before nightfall," Steigauf said, climbing onto his steed. Arnald followed suit, awkwardly clambering onto his horse. "You all right?"

"Yep," the boy answered.

"Good," the soldier nodded. "And to answer your question, the shore doesn't turn to the east until we reach Shiverwind. With any luck, we'll see it tomorrow."

"We'll reach Shiverwind tomorrow?"

"No." Steigauf chuckled. "I said we may see it tomorrow. With luck, we'll ride into town the day after."

The wolf trotted ahead and waited for the riders a little farther along the road. The goat bleated a protest as the horses started trudging away.

———◆———

As the sun made its way across the sky, gradually falling towards the mountains far away to the west, the she-wolf kept her distance ahead of the riders. She sniffed the ground here and there, cocked her head and turned her ears to listen, and moved in and out of the tree line to explore.

Arnald noted her tracks in the snow on either side of the road. He looked about cautiously for a sign of other living things. A few birds sang happily in the trees and fluttered about, but there wasn't anything else to see.

"Not even a rabbit," the boy remarked.

"What's that?" asked the Pit Guard.

"I've been watching her," he jutted his chin to the wolf, "moving in and out of the forest. I thought she might have been hunting, but she keeps coming back with nothing."

"Probably taking a piss," the other replied.

"Maybe," Arnald said. "But then I noticed hers are the only tracks. There aren't any deer or rabbits. Rabbits are everywhere. We should have seen some tracks of something."

"It could've snowed here last night," the soldier suggested. "Their tracks could be covered."

"It's the afternoon," the boy reminded him. "Something would have come out and run across the ground at some time today."

"I know," Steigauf agreed. "It sounded silly coming out of my mouth as I said it. You're right. It's very odd."

Arnald looked at the forest, trying to see between the trees for a sight of deer or elk.

"I've heard that wolves can hunt some places dry," he said. "That's what Uncle Ibore called it. Hunting it dry."

"He's right," the soldier agreed. "Sometimes they get into a frenzy and kill for pleasure. It could be the wolves we encountered back at your village may have cleared this area of prey and moved north to claim fresh territory."

"Which means they could come back. This area is still theirs, as they see it," Arnald added.

"Precisely," the old man replied. "We should try to get as much space between us and them as we can before we need to stop to set up camp."

<hr />

They rode on, chatting about other trivial matters like the War of Six and battles Steigauf took part in, tanning skins to be sold at markets, and fishing. The latter was something they could both do.

"Net or line?" the old soldier questioned.

"Netting's easier if you need to catch fish," the boy replied. "A line is more sporting. I enjoy using a line."

"Do you have one?"

"No." Arnald shook his head. "Everything of mine was in the house and lost in the fire."

"Well," Steigauf said as he peered at the cove. "I suppose we won't be fishing anytime soon, then. We might see what the anglers in Shiverwind have available for purchase when we sell those arrowheads."

"And the goat," the boy said, glancing at the little beast walking behind the packhorse.

"And the goat."

Arnald's gaze moved to something among the trees to their left, near the water's edge.

"What's that?"

Steigauf pulled his horse to a stop. The packhorse followed suit, but the goat continued until the rope around her neck became taut and she couldn't go any further.

"It's a hut," the soldier replied. "And it's as good as any place to set up camp for the night."

"Could be someone in there," the boy suggested, peering at the little log cabin with no windows, as far as he could see. A little stone chimney poked from its roof on the front left corner and the door sat slightly ajar.

"All the better," the soldier said. "A little extra company might be a welcome change for both of us. But I doubt anybody is here."

"Why's that?"

"No smoke," Steigauf answered, edging the horses towards the shack.

The soldier dismounted his steed. Arnald started to do the same.

"No," Steigauf ordered him, handing him the reins to his horse. "Stay here and get ready to run if I call for you to do so. Understand?"

Arnald nodded as the soldier pulled his blade free of its sheath strapped to his saddle. The wolf stayed by the roadside, staring at the forest across the way.

The door creaked noisily as the Pit Guard pushed it open wider before stepping inside.

Arnald watched hesitantly as the man disappeared into the dark void beyond the door. He listened to the slow footfalls of the soldier cautiously moving about inside. A soft thud resounded, then another before Steigauf emerged through the door.

"Nothing," he said. "The furniture has been tossed. Maybe the attackers who raided your village visited here as well. There're some clothes in a cupboard. A man, by the looks. And stale food in another. Nothing of value and no sign of anyone being here for a while."

"Is it safe?"

"I think so," he answered. "We can light a fire in the stove and sleep inside. The place appears to be intact."

"Do we take all of this gear off the horses?" Arnald asked as he lowered himself to the ground.

"Yes," Steigauf replied. "They need a rest from carrying all this as much as we need a rest from riding. We'll unload it all and put it inside with us. I'll tether the horses and this little monster out here." He gave the goat a scratch on the head as he moved to the packhorse.

"What about her?" Arnald looked at the wolf, still staring into the forest.

"We'll let her decide," the Pit Guard told him. "She can stay inside with us or run about freely."

Arnald set to unloading his equipment as the soldier dug a length of rope from a duffle bag among the load on the packhorse. As the boy carried a load into the hut, Steigauf strung the rope between two trees near to the hut before looping the reins of his horse over the cord.

Arnald, in the meantime, plonked his equipment onto the floor by the door. He peered about the room, seeing the small stove in the corner to his left, a bench with cupboards underneath, stretching along the back wall. A single bed, with its covers dishevelled, rested against the wall to his right and an overturned square table and two chairs lay on their sides in the middle of the room.

He repositioned the chairs, turning them upright, before placing his attention on the table. As he lifted it, tilting it onto its legs, he noticed long and deep scratch marks on the floorboards beneath it. More marks, like those on the floor, stretched across the table's surface.

Upon carefully scrutinising the scratches, he believed he looked at the product of an animal that searched the cabin for food. He placed his fingers on the ones running over the table from one side to the other. Four marks side-by-side.

Maybe a bear, he thought.

Checking the back of the door for a latch or lock, he saw more scratch marks. They looked rough and wildly placed, almost as if the animal had trapped itself inside and swiped the door repeatedly until it broke the latch. The sight of the broken latch didn't bring the boy any comfort.

However, the alternative to finding the hut would have resulted in sleeping on the ground outside. He counted his blessings and silently thanked the gods for a roof over his head as he moved the chairs into position at the table.

"Still more gear outside," Steigauf said as he entered the cabin, his arms loaded with items from the packhorse.

"I think a bear got stuck in here," Arnald told him, moving to the door.

"What makes you say that?" the soldier asked, dropping his load on the floor next to the boy's.

"Scratch marks on the table and floor," he pointed out. "Some more on the back of the door. It looks as if it broke the latch."

Steigauf examined the table as the boy retreated outside. Like Arnald, he carefully ran his fingers over the markings, placing his fingers into each of the deep scratches. He peered at the marks on the floor before partially closing the door to look at the broken latch. Again, he ran his fingers over a set of markings crossing the surface.

The soldier scanned the room, stopping when his eyes landed on the tossed bed. He stepped over and lifted a blanket, holding it out wide before him to see tear marks through its middle. Something had ripped the mattress beneath the covers to shreds, exposing old stuffing of straw and feathers.

"So, what do you think?" Arnald questioned as he dropped another load on the floor. "Was it a bear?"

"Maybe," the soldier answered. He moved his gaze over the marks again before looking at the boy. "Which of your swords do you feel comfortable using?"

"My swords?"

"Yes," said Steigauf. "The smaller one, your mother's. Correct?"

"The others are too heavy for me," the boy admitted. "But I have used none."

"Sleep with your mother's sword tonight," the soldier instructed. "You'll take the bed. I'll take the floor beside you. The wolf sleeps inside with us tonight and we put everything we have against the door."

"In case the bear returns?" asked Arnald, his voice trembling slightly.

"I hope it's only a bear," the soldier answered.

"What else could it be?" the boy questioned, believing he already knew the answer.

Steigauf ran his fingers over the marks on the table again.
"A man-wolf."

Chapter Eight

"**WHAT ABOUT THE HORSES** and the goat?" Arnald queried as he pushed the table against the door.

"Sorry, Arnald. But, better them than us," the soldier answered as he dragged a heap of their equipment across the floor to push under the table and against the door. "Besides, we can always replace the horses. And we intend to sell the goat."

Arnald nodded as he took hold of his saddle and placed it against the pile of equipment under the table. Steigauf noticed the worried look on the boy's face as he placed his own saddle next to Arnald's.

"Look," the old soldier began. "There's a good chance this thing is miles away. Once a man gives in to the creature, he become the creature and instinct takes over. It could be far in the mountains hunting or sleeping. Perhaps, the man changed back again, realised what he was and stayed out there, naked as the day he was born to let the cold take him. It's what I would do. And take a look for yourself. He's been gone for some time. The food's stale. This," he gestured to the pile under the table, "is just a precaution."

"I know," Arnald replied. "It's just..."

The boy looked at the door.

"You've got a gentle heart, Arnald," Steigauf told him. "That's good. Unfortunately, we can't bring the animals inside with us. There's barely enough room for the three of us."

Arnald lifted his bedroll from the floor and carried it to the bed. The Pit Guard watched him place his bedding over the mattress. Having no words to ease the boy's concerns, Steigauf took his own bedroll and placed it on the floor beside the bed as Arnald laid his mother's sheathed sword on his bed.

"Have you seen a man-wolf before?" the boy asked.

"I've seen a few," the soldier replied. "Not since the war, though."

"What are they like?" Arnald sat on the bed, watching Steigauf place his own sword on the bedding.

"Big," he answered. "They stand much taller than any man I've seen. Much broader, too. They're very quick. Agile. You know what *agile* means?"

"They move quickly," the boy answered.

"And leap far," the soldier added. "And very strong. Everything about them is unnatural."

"What do they look like?" Arnald pressed. "I mean, beyond big and broad."

"A lot like her." Steigauf jutted his chin to the she-wolf lying by the warmth of the stove. "Only their bodies are shaped like that of a man."

"They run on their legs like men?"

"Sometimes," the Pit Guard replied, moving to a leather bag on the floor by the stove. "You hungry?"

"There's still some chicken in my saddlebag," the boy said, getting to his feet to retrieve the bird.

"Yeah, get it out," Steigauf said, digging through the bag. "We'll have some pork with it."

Arnald placed the wrapped chicken on the table as the soldier dropped a sizeable chunk of pig next to it with a thud. The wolf lifted her head and licked her lips in anticipation. Steigauf shot her a quick glare. "Be patient."

The soldier took out a knife from his saddlebag and carved several large slices from the meat and divided them between the boy and himself before tossing the rest to the wolf.

"Sometimes they run on two legs, like men," the Pit Guard continued. "Sometimes they run on four, like a wolf. One thing I noticed during battle; was they didn't pick things up like men. We fought many man-wolves at a place south of Shadowfort. The dead left plenty of swords, axes and pikes lying about, but not one man-wolf picked any of them up to fight with. They chose tooth and claw for their weapons. It's as if they forget what it is to be a man.

"Take that latch." Steigauf pointed to the door as he took a slice of pork and sat in a chair by the table. "He could've simply used his hand to open it. And, yes, the man-wolves have hands with thumbs and fingers, like us. Instead, he broke the door to get out. They must forget how to do things."

Arnald sat and chewed some chicken as he gave thought to what it must be like to change into a man-wolf.

"It must hurt," he muttered. "Changing like that. To become something so big."

"I presume so," the soldier said. "I've not seen it happen, myself."

"You said you fought south of Shadowfort," said Arnald, tearing more meat away from the chicken's breast.

"That's right," Steigauf replied, continuing to chew the portion of pork.

"Did you go north of there and see the mountain fall?"

"You know about that, do you?"

"My father and uncle were there," Arnald told him. "My father said he saw the neophyte witches fall when the mountain crumbled."

"He must have been close to them when it happened," the soldier opined.

"Did you see them fall?"

"No," Steigauf answered. "I fought on the southern side of the range. Where The Dragon's Teeth met The Barrier Ranges. The mountain fell, and now The Dragon's Teeth don't meet The Barrier anymore. What did your father say happened there?"

"He said they fought against lots of enemies, including man-wolves, and the ground opened up and swallowed the witches," Arnald replied. "He said it was the gods."

"Maybe." Steigauf tore a leg from the chicken. "If not the gods, someone with terrible power."

"Terrible?"

"I don't mean evil," the soldier explained. "I mean great. Enormous. To tear down a mountain like that would require powerful sorcery."

"My father said they hunted the Elvish King after that," Arnald said, reaching for a slice of pork.

"He joined us for that, did he?"

Arnald nodded, "My uncle too."

"Did they see him hang?"

The boy nodded again. "Did you?"

"I didn't see Elene and Lycia fall with the mountain," Steigauf replied, recalling the rope in his hands as he slid it over Amalith's head. "But I made sure not to miss seeing that bastard swing from the tree."

Arnald slept uneasily, waking often at every sound; a moan from Steigauf as he rolled onto his side, or the snort from the wolf as she repositioned herself near the warm stove was enough to make the boy jump out of his skin. The thought of a man-wolf set his nerves on end. The idea that the horses and goat tethered outside could become an appetiser for the creature had his mind racing.

The thud of heavy snow falling from tree branches, just outside the hut, created a picture of the monster's feet creeping about, lurking around the cabin to find a way in. The creature snarled silently, curling its lips, licking its yellow teeth as it smelled the prey resting inside, just as the she-wolf did when Steigauf carved the pork on the table.

Its hand-claws flexed and contracted slowly, as if reaching for Arnald's neck.

Somehow, it found its way inside, stepping quietly over the wolf and man on the floor, careful to let them sleep.

No, not sleep.

They were slain.

The man-wolf had slaughtered them silently before turning its attention to the boy.

It lunged, latching its jaws around the boy's shoulder.

"Arnald," it called.

He jumped awake, glaring straight into the eyes of the old soldier.

"Time to get up, laddie," the Pit Guard said. "The sun is on her way."

Arnald felt relieved.

"I need help to clear this stuff from the door," Steigauf told him as he dragged some equipment across the floor. "I need to piss. I think the wolf does, too."

The boy quickly aided the Pit Guard with the task. He, too, needed to empty his bladder.

Once outside, the boy checked on the animals. They had eaten all the straw laid out for them.

"Should I feed them?" he called to Steigauf.

"After," the old man shuffled away speedily towards the water. "You may want to stay upwind of me. And keep the wolf away if you can. I need to shit."

"Oh," Arnald replied, moving into a thicket of trees. He unlaced his trousers and looked to the ground around the base of his chosen privy. Small chunks of bark and wood shavings sat in an untidy clump at the tree's base. After relieving himself, he tied his cords and peered up the tree's trunk to see long scratch marks, like those on the table and door, just above his head.

"We need to push on," Steigauf told the boy as they started along the road. "If I think we can reach Shiverwind tonight, we'll risk travelling that little bit farther. Do you understand what I'm saying, Arnald?"

He understood.

The sight of fresh markings made during the night was enough to drive a pang of fear through the boy's heart. Clearly, the Pit Guard felt the same upon seeing the scratches.

"Why the creature didn't take one of the horses, I'll never know," the soldier said as they trotted away. The little goat bleated as the rope yanked its neck again and again.

"We need to stop," Arnald called.

127

"Why?" Steigauf turned, looking at the boy quizzically.

"She can't keep up," he replied, gesturing to the goat. "And she hasn't been milked."

"We don't have time for milk, laddie," the old man criticised.

"It's not about the milk," Arnald told him, slowing his horse down. "She's full and needs to be emptied. My father said milking animals, like cows and goats, need to be emptied each day if they don't have young to do so for them. He said it can hurt them if they're not emptied."

"I'll admit, I don't know much about milking animals," Steigauf said. "Do you need a bucket?"

"Do you want milk?" Arnald queried.

"No," the Pit Guard answered. "I just said we don't have time for milk."

"Then the ground will do," the boy said, dismounting his horse to approach the goat.

She bleated again as Arnald crouched and squeezed her teats. Milk spurted onto the road, forming a small puddle. Before long, the boy completed the task and returned to his horse.

"I'm sorry, laddie," the soldier said. "I was in such a rush to move on, I didn't give any thought to the needs of this one."

"It's all right," Arnald told him. "No harm done. She seems to be fine, and it's still early. As good a time to milk her as any, I suppose."

They moved off again. The wolf stopped to lap the puddle of milk before trotting quickly to re-join her travelling companions.

"Waste not, want not, I guess," Steigauf said, eyeing the wolf, milk dribbling from her chin. She stopped to sniff the ground, allowing the riders to pass her by.

Arnald turned in his saddle, peering back to her. She stared at the cluster of trees surrounding the hut. Deep shadows lingered there as the sun peeked her head above the water. A chill shiver ran along his spine as the thought of something watching from the darkness entered his mind.

The man-wolf hid there, watching them ride away.

He knew it.

—◆○◆—

Some time passed before either of them spoke.

"How would you feel about carrying that goat on your lap?" Steigauf asked.

"What?" Arnald's mind was elsewhere. His stare fixated on the ripples of the water as they sauntered along the road.

"I'd like to pick up the pace a bit," the soldier explained. "I don't think we could do that for very long with her in tow. Could you carry her?"

"I can try," he replied.

"All right then." Steigauf pulled his horse to a stop and dismounted. "I'll lift her, and you put your arms around her rump to cradle her."

Arnald shifted himself and prepared to take the animal.

The Pit Guard untied the rope from the goat's neck and lifted her into his arms. She bleated in his ear.

"For fuck's sake," he huffed. "I think I'm deaf now."

Arnald stifled his laughter as the soldier hoisted the goat into his lap. She tucked her legs beneath herself and nestled against him as he hugged her with one arm while gripping the reins in the other. All the while, the she-wolf watched on curiously, cocking her head as she took in the sight.

"All right," Steigauf said. "That was easier than I thought it would be."

"We haven't started moving yet," Arnald put in.

"If she becomes too much, just drop her," the soldier told him as he tucked the rope under some baggage on the packhorse. "We'll just tie her back on here and do what we have to do."

Soon, they were off to a canter and going at a reasonable speed. Arnald held the goat tightly with one arm, scratching her chest with his fingers as they rode. She pressed her face against his torso and closed her eyes. He wondered if she did so out of fear, not wishing to see the world pass by at a great pace, or because she enjoyed the sensation of being petted.

The she-wolf ran alongside him, peering up at the boy now and then as they moved. Occasionally she stopped, turned, and peered back along the road from where they had come. They travelled like this for what seemed a long way before the horses tired and slowed their pace to a walk again.

"We may need to stop for a bit," Steigauf announced, looking at the sun high in the sky. "I need to stretch my legs and the horses need a rest."

Soon, the soldier guided them to a patch of open ground on the side of the road. After dismounting, he dug some straw from the load on the packhorse and placed it on the ground before taking the goat from Arnald. The boy quickly jumped from his horse and led it to the small mound of straw before moving away to relieve himself.

Steigauf unpacked a small portion of pork and threw it to the wolf, who snapped it up speedily. He turned to face the boy as he fished out a portion of meat for himself.

"I'd suggest you pack some food for the rest of the day into your saddlebags," the soldier offered. "I don't plan on stopping again until we need to."

Arnald understood this to mean they wouldn't be stopping until they either reached Shiverwind or to set up camp for the night.

"I'll take a chicken," he replied, tying his cords, and returning to the horses.

"A whole chicken?"

"I'll break it up and eat a bit here and there," he answered. "It could last me all the way to Shiverwind."

"That's good thinking." The soldier smiled. "I told you already how wise you are, didn't I?"

"Yes," the boy said with a grin, searching the packhorse's bags for a wrapped bird.

"We'll let the horses eat and get moving again," the old man informed the other. "How's the goat? Are you both comfortable?"

"I don't know about her, but I'm fine," Arnald answered. "She fell asleep for part of the journey."

"Fell asleep?" Steigauf laughed. "How about that?"

Arnald looked to the wolf, chewing on a chunk of pig, then at the road they had just come along.

"She kept stopping to look back that way," the boy reported.

"I know," the Pit Guard said. His demeanour changed from jovial to solemn in a heartbeat. "I think she senses something following us."

"The man-wolf?"

Steigauf looked at the road and followed their tracks with his eyes off into the distance.

"Something," he muttered.

Chapter Nine

───────◆◇◆───────

T HEY SPENT THE REST of the day riding without stopping. The sun sank below their sight, vanishing behind the treetops of the forest which grew right up to the road's edge and casting deep shadows across their path. It was still light around them, however, with a bright blue sky stretching above and a pleasant view of the cove to their left.

As snow fell, the temperature dropped little by little as they travelled, growing colder as they passed through the shade of the trees. The road rose high above the water in places, allowing Arnald to view the shoreline twisting and turning into the distance. A few times, he thought they must be approaching the place where the coast turned towards the east, until he saw the point of land touching the water, or a bluff overlooking the lapping waves in the distance. The falling snow gave a foggy appearance to things far away.

"There it is." Steigauf pointed across the coastline to the south.

Arnald squinted, trying hard to see through the grey mess before him.

"There what is?"

"The southern edge of The Cove of Safe Keeping," the soldier answered.

"I can't see anything," the boy replied.

"It's there," said the Pit Guard. "Trust me. It's a little darker where the land meets the water."

Arnald thought the old man was losing his mind. Given that he and

Jörgen had seen the ship before the attack, where others had seen nothing, gave him the sense that there was nothing where the soldier pointed.

"I don't think we'll make it before we need to stop for the night," Steigauf told the boy. "We'll ride a little farther. When we're ready for the night, I want you to get your bow and quiver."

"Why?"

"I told you I'd teach you a thing or two," the soldier replied. "I haven't kept my promise. We should start, don't you think? I'll stay with you for a while in Shiverwind and teach you some more before I move on. But I don't intend to stay long."

Arnald nodded, solemnly.

"Don't fret," the old man told him. "There are others in Shiverwind who will guide you. People I know. There may even be a garrison from Dendadia there to teach you. Most of the larger settlements have a military post. Shiverwind has a barracks house near the wharves."

"Is that the plan?" Arnald questioned. "To recruit me into the military?"

"No." The Pit Guard turned to look at him. "You can do whatever you want to do. We'll speak with the magistrate and sheriff about what happened to your village first. After, we'll find accommodation at the barracks house. If the same man is in command there still, he'll take you under his wing and train you better than I. It's what he trained to do. Train others. Even if you don't intend to become a soldier, you must admit that any skill you learn from a man like him is worth learning."

"Did he train you?"

"Me?" the Pit Guard chuckled. "No. I'm old enough to be his grandfather. Maybe his great grandfather. No, he trained under a colonel in the Dendadian infantry, who was under my command during the War of Six. He was a lieutenant then, the colonel, that is. No, this man, in Shiverwind, is Captain Piers Kraayen. If he's still there and if they have not promoted him. It's been some time since I've been in Shiverwind. It might be populated by goblins for all I know."

"Or man-wolves," Arnald put in, gripping the goat tightly as he turned to look at their trail in the snow behind them.

"I don't think we need to worry too much about that thing, anymore," Steigauf said. "I've seen some tracks here and about as we've been riding.

There are certainly rabbits and squirrels about."

Arnald looked to the side of the road, peering to the base of the trees to see nothing but snow. He wondered if the old soldier was inventing the information to ease his fears, or if the falling snow covered the little tracks.

"Do you think that's why there were no animals back there, at the hut?"

"The man-wolf, you mean?" Steigauf asked.

"Yes," Arnald replied.

"I have no doubt about it," the soldier answered. "I think it must have hunted enough big game to scare the rest away. It may be why the wolves came to visit your hut. They may have been chased out of their territory and came to lay claim. That said, the wolves could have simply been attracted to the scent of pig hanging in your workshop. But yes. The man-wolf hunted or chased the other animals out of the area."

"Could it follow us to try and get our supplies?"

"Possibly." Steigauf nodded. "I hope not. I intend to take what pork and chickens we have left for the next leg of my journey. With your permission, of course."

"Take it, please," Arnald replied. "What would I need any of it for if I'm to stay in Shiverwind?"

"Thank you, laddie," the Pit Guard said. "If not the military, what do you think you will do with yourself?"

"I'm a good tanner," the boy answered.

"There's always a need for a good tanner," Steigauf said.

Jörgen suddenly entered Arnald's thoughts, standing before the attackers before they killed him and hearing his words. *I will be a Pit Guard one day.*

"I will be a Pit Guard one day," Arnald muttered.

"A Pit Guard?" Steigauf turned to look at the boy. "So, the military it is then."

The boy felt a sudden burst of fire in his chest. He couldn't shoot a bow and didn't know how to wield a sword.

A Pit Guard?

Why not?

The old man said the military in Shiverwind would provide him with training.

133

Why not?

Arnald nodded and lifted his head high. "I will be a Pit Guard one day."

———————◆◇◆———————

"Right then," Steigauf said, sitting on a fallen log with the wolf by his feet. She sat up attentively, watching the boy. Arnald held his bow in one hand, the quiver of arrows in the other. "Let's see your stance, laddie."

The boy slung the quiver across his shoulders and onto his back before lifting the bow. He turned towards the campsite where they tethered animals close to the fire.

"No," the soldier said, getting to his feet. He took the boy by the shoulders and turned him to face the cove. "See that tree?" Steigauf pointed to a thick oak near the water's edge. "That's your target. Not the horses."

"I haven't even loaded an arrow yet," Arnald protested.

"Good," the other replied, resuming his seat. "Now, show me your stance."

With his feet firmly in place, Arnald raised the bow and pulled the string back.

"What are you doing?" the soldier asked.

"Showing you my stance," the boy offered, furrowing his brow.

"You have your bow raised," Steigauf noted.

"Yes," Arnald replied.

"So, what do you intend to shoot? Air?" the Pit Guard smiled. "Load it, laddie. An empty bow feels different to a loaded one."

The boy reached over his shoulder, plucked a shaft from the quiver, and placed it on the string. Pulling to his shoulder, he heard the creak of the string tightening. He aimed the tip to the oak, his target.

"Hold it," the old man commanded.

A small twinge exploded in Arnald's bow hand.

"Hold it," Steigauf repeated.

The boy felt his arm shake.

"Loose!"

Arnald let the arrow fly. It zipped through the air, gradually descending,

descending, passing the tree on the left to vanish into the water.

The boy shook his head.

"Jörgen said I can't shoot for shit," he said. "He's right."

"You just need more practice," Steigauf said confidently. "Your stance is fine. Your aim and strength need some work. Did you see how the arrow arced downward?"

Arnald nodded.

"That's because of three things," the soldier told him. "First, you need to pull that string back farther, past your ear and even farther, if you can. Make it real tight. Bend that bow back. Second, build those muscles in your arms and back. You can do that by holding that loaded string in place for longer. I bet you felt the shakes just now, right?"

"In this arm," Arnald replied, holding the bow up.

"You need to train your arms for the bow," said the soldier. "Third, you need to train your eye to the arrow. That comes with practice. I suggest you move over there." Steigauf pointed to a patch of ground by the water's edge.

"Over there?" the boy pointed with the bow. "Why there?"

"You will be shooting sideways to the water and the camp from there," the soldier informed him. "That way, you won't hit the animals, or me, and you shouldn't lose any more arrows to the water. Your target is still that big tree that you somehow missed. Come on. The sun's already down and night is approaching."

Arnald hurried to the designated position, loaded the bow, and took aim.

"Good," said the Pit Guard. "Hold it. Count to ten slowly before you release."

"One...two...three...four...five..." A sharp stabbing pain ran along the base of the boy's thumb into his forearm. "Six...seven...eight..." His arm shook increasingly with each number. "Nine...ten."

He released the arrow.

It grazed the tree and planted into the ground.

"Very good," the soldier said, getting back to his feet. "Keep that up until you've emptied that quiver. When you're done, collect your arrows and come over to the fire. While you do that, I'm going to get something for us to eat."

The old man walked away as Arnald loaded the bow for another attempt. The wolf stayed, sitting up to watch the boy observantly.

Arnald pulled the string back tight to his ear. "One...two...three..."

He rubbed his shoulder as he chewed on a piece of hot pork. Steigauf warmed another portion over the fire on the end of a dagger. Keeping his hand on the wolf's head, Arnald closed his heavy eyes and drifted away as he listened to her deeply, softly breathing beside him.

"You'll get used to it eventually," the soldier told the boy. "Your body adapts to those things you do the most often. Keep practising and it will become second nature."

"I managed to hit the tree a lot, by the end," Arnald said proudly.

"I saw," the other said with a smile. "Next time, we'll try a smaller target."

"I could practise some more," the boy suggested.

"No." The soldier shook his head. "You've had enough practice for now. You need to rest. Besides, it's dark, and I'd rather you didn't lose any arrows. We stay by the fire for the rest of the night. It's safer here."

Arnald heeded Steigauf's words as he lay upon his bedroll across the fire from the soldier. He'd almost forgotten about the man-wolf.

"Would he follow us here?"

"I don't know," the Pit Guard replied, biting a piece of meat from the tip of his dagger. "You want any more?"

"No, thank you," Arnald answered. "I heard man-wolves only become man-wolves at night. But you said the man can give in to the creature. Can they be man-wolves in the day?"

"Yes," Steigauf returned. "I fought them in the daylight. Men who gave over to the instinct of the beast. They changed form and never returned."

"They chose to do this?"

"That, I don't know." The soldier swallowed the rest of his warm pork and lay down. "I've heard some have fought the urge so they could remain as men, but still change when the moon is full."

Arnald instantly looked at the silver orb in the sky just above the horizon.

It reflected in the water so perfectly it appeared as if two moons glared back at him.

"It's full now," the boy said.

"I'm aware," the Pit Guard replied.

"Do you think this man-wolf is one that changes with the full moon?"

"I don't think so," the old man answered. "That stale food looked pretty old to me. I think it might have been there for about a month."

Arnald pulled his covers over him to his ears. He felt soreness throughout his arms, tired from the long day and uneasy sense about the creature that preoccupied his mind. The wolf lifted herself from her place by Steigauf, walked around the fire and lowered herself delicately against the boy. She licked his face, as if sensing his concerns, attempting to bring comfort.

"I told you; she likes you." Steigauf smiled. "She may choose to stay with you instead of pressing on with me. I'll be a jealous man if that happens. Would you be fine with that?"

"You being jealous?" Arnald asked with a grin, reaching his hand out from the covers to rub the wolf's ear. She emitted a pleasant groan, closing her eyes. "I certainly would."

"Good," the Pit Guard chuckled, pulling his covers up and rolling on his side to face the fire.

Chapter Ten

———◆———

F AR TO THE EAST, across Kedielewen, sat a small hamlet nestled at the end of The Dragon's Teeth Ranges. Many of the residents extinguished candles and lamp lights, retiring for the night as the moon climbed higher over The Barrier, a range of high, rugged mountains stretching from the north to the south across the lands of Ananduil. Only a small gathering remained at the tavern, drinking and joking in the small establishment by the side of the Great Northern Barrier Road.

The snow fell steadily as a gentle breeze from the north rocked the sign hanging from a beam outside the establishment. It creaked softly as it swung back and forth in the wind. The words carved into the swinging timber panel read THE LAZY TRAVELLER. Another sign posted on the ground beside the road read, WELCOME TO MOUNTAINFALL.

"Last drinks," called the tavern keeper, a stocky old man with a thick beard and a white apron. The small band of seven men collected around the fireplace groaned. They ranged in ages from a young, brawny man with dark hair to his shoulders to an old man with a ring of snowy hair circling a shiny scalp.

"My round," the young man called. The men cheered.

"That's a boy, Nichol," the old one said, patting the younger man on the back.

"Then you go home to your loving wives," Nichol said as he made his way to the bar. The men groaned again.

"Seven more?" the tavern keeper asked.

The young man nodded. "Thank you, Humphrey."

"How about you go home to our loving wives, and we stay here?" another man called from by the fireplace. "They'd all like that."

"Thank you, Ivan," Nichol replied, looking at a young lady wearing an apron, standing near the end of the bar. "I think I might be a little busy."

"Oooh!" the men chorused.

She smiled, blushing as she looked at the floor, a lock of her dark hair falling over her face. She pulled it back behind her ear.

"I didn't see you come in," Nichol said as he placed seven coppers on the bar. "You're a sneaky one, aren't you?"

"Only when I need to be," she answered, leaning with her elbows on the bar. His gaze instinctively fell upon her cleavage.

"What a fine woman you are, Helena," he whispered, resting his arm on the bench.

"Your place, or mine?" she asked quietly, reaching over to touch his forearm.

"Your place is too far," he replied. "If I walk all the way out there, this fire in me will go out. Then what fun will I be?"

"Your place then," she said, standing upright to take some freshly filled mugs from Humphrey. She placed them on a tray to carry them to the men by the fire. "Stay here."

"Yes, my lady." He smiled as Humphrey handed him a mug of ale.

"You best treat her nicely, Nichol Kent," Humphrey told him when she had walked out of earshot.

"I intend to, Humphrey," he replied, watching the young woman gracefully weave between tables as she walked across the room. "And I don't just mean tonight."

"Good," the tavern keeper said, pouring himself a mug. "Because I think she really likes you. And after what she's been through! Well, you know about that, right?"

"I know her parents died during the war," Nichol answered after taking a swig. "I know she came from the other side of The Stone Curtain. And I know she wasn't received well when she first arrived here."

"Aye," said the tavern keeper as Helena turned to retrace her footsteps. The men by the fire ogled her as she moved. "No one from over there is ever received well. So, you best treat her nicely."

She smiled brightly as she approached, dimples forming on her cheeks.

"What are you two talking about, then?" she asked, circling around the bar.

"You," Nichol replied.

"Me?" she queried, placing the empty tray on the bench. "What's so intriguing about me?"

"Humphrey wants me to treat you nicely," the young man told her.

"Humphrey, you big bear." She giggled, leaning over to kiss him on the cheek.

"Oooh!" the men by the fire chorused again.

"Oh, shut it," the tavern keeper barked.

"Don't let Anne know about that," Ivan called. The others laughed.

"Drink your drinks," Humphrey instructed them. "And go home."

The men chuckled quietly as they returned to their conversation.

"You not drinking?" Nichol asked her. "Last drinks. I'm buying."

"I want to be clear-headed when you take me home," she smiled. He felt mesmerised by the deep green of her eyes. He couldn't recall seeing anyone with eyes like hers.

"Where did you come from?" he whispered. She gave him a curious glare. "I don't mean the place you were born or raised. It's just, there is no one else like you. No one. You're perfect."

She leaned over and touched his forearm again.

"And you're the most handsome man who has tried to lure me home," she returned. "For tonight, that is."

Nichol laughed quietly, unable to take his gaze away from hers.

"All right," Humphrey said, before draining his mug. "That's it. I'm done for the night. I need to get upstairs to my wife. Scull them dry, lads. I'm locking up."

Moments later, all emptied mugs sat together on the bar, and the gathering made their way to the tavern's door. Ivan, first to venture outside, called over his shoulder as a wall of chill air raced into the establishment, "Goodnight, Humphrey. Give my best to Anne."

"What's that supposed to mean?" the tavern keeper asked jokingly.

They laughed before the other men said their farewells, stepping through the door into the night.

"Remember what I said," the tavern keeper said to Nichol, who wrapped his cloak around Helena's shoulders, hugging her into his body tightly. "Treat her nicely."

"He will, Humphrey," she said before the young man could respond. "He always does."

"Goodnight, Humphrey," Nichol said, slapping a friendly hand on the other's shoulder. "Now, shut this door before you catch a chill."

With that, they followed the others outside.

They came to a sudden stop, hearing the door close and latch behind them, seeing all six other men standing dumbfounded in the snow.

"What is it?" Nichol asked, stepping over to Ivan, still holding Helena in his arms.

The old man pointed to the road with a shaky hand, his mouth opened to speak but made no sound. The gentle squeaks and creaks of the tavern's sign rocking in the breeze broke the silence intermittently.

Nichol and Helena followed his gesture, turning their heads to see what held the men's attention.

A tall pike stood in the middle of the road with its tip stabbed into the ground. On top sat a severed head of a man with his nose and upper jaw smashed in.

"By the gods," Nichol murmured as Helena buried her face into his chest.

PART THREE

The Lawless Are Not Welcome Here

Chapter One

———◆———

A S HE RODE, STEIGAUF squinted, peering through the bare oak and maple branches to the sun climbing high in the sky. His armour clinked softly as he repositioned himself. He then looked to the coastline of the cove, twisting ahead into the distance. Fog covered the view of the shoreline, turning to the east like a low cloud hovering over the water.

"We should arrive in Shiverwind before nightfall," he said, turning in his saddle to face the boy riding behind the packhorse. "With any luck, that is."

Arnald nursed the goat on his lap as he bit a mouthful of meat from a chunk of pork before tossing the remaining portion to the wolf.

"How long have you been feeding her like that?" the old soldier asked with a grin.

"Like what?"

"Tossing her your scraps," Steigauf clarified.

"They're not scraps," the boy replied. "They're pretty big pieces."

"How long?" he asked seriously.

"Since we left the village," Arnald answered.

"No wonder she likes you." The Pit Guard turned to face forward, looking at the distant fog on the water. "You'll get fat, girl."

The wolf paid no attention to the remark, looking to the boy for the next treat. Arnald understood the subtle rebuke.

"No more, my lady," he said to the wolf. "Sorry."

"My lady?" Steigauf laughed. "That bitch licks her bunghole clean, and you call her *my lady*?"

Arnald laughed softly.

After some time of travelling in silence and realising there were no more offerings to be had, the wolf returned to sniffing the ground and trotting ahead of the riders. "See that?" Steigauf pointed to her.

"Yes," Arnald replied, watching the wolf move on the trail ahead of them.

"That's what we need her to do," the soldier told him. "Scout ahead. She's good at it. If there's danger out there, she'll let us know. If you feed her while we're riding, she won't focus on the things that matter. And neither will you."

Steigauf turned to see a downcast expression on the boy's face.

"You want to be a Pit Guard, correct?"

"Yes."

"Then you need to be alert all the time and let go of compassion sometimes," the soldier explained. "Wanting to feed animals and be their friends is a natural thing for most people. But out here in the wild world, things aren't that simple. In the wild, she would have to fend for herself, or be part of a pack that works together to survive. To her, we are her pack. If you feed her all the time, she'll get used to that and rely on you for everything and forget she is a wolf. In this pack, she has a job to do, just as we do. Understand?"

"I think so," Arnald answered.

"Feed her when we eat," Steigauf added. "The pack eats its meals together. In the morning, at night, and if we stop along the way. Grazing from your saddlebags is for you alone. If she wishes to snack, she can be a wolf and hunt for a rabbit or something."

"She's not a dog," the boy said, watching the wolf trot off the road to the right, into some deep snow.

"Correct," Steigauf said, looking back to the fog.

Arnald peered in the same direction, noting the thick band of fluffy mist snaking across the water far away.

"Are you certain Shiverwind is there?" he asked. "It looks as if that cloud is eating everything in sight."

"It's there somewhere," the Pit Guard replied. "If you look carefully, you can see the hills and forest just at the top of the fog. When we get closer, you might see the mountains far in the distance. Right now, there's too much glare coming from the water. But it's there."

Squinting, the boy gazed at the top of the cloud and noticed the light, shady grey outline of land. From the back of his horse, he couldn't determine whether forests, barren hills or rocky mountains lay there.

"I see something," he told the soldier. "I can't tell what it is. Everything is covered with snow everywhere. It all looks the same from here. Especially with that cloud in the way."

"True," Steigauf agreed, digging into a saddlebag for a chunk of pork. "We might need to stop soon."

"Hungry?"

The soldier looked at the meat in his hand.

"Well, yes," he answered. "But that's not the reason. I really need to piss."

———◇———

The townsfolk of Mountainfall collected in The Lazy Traveller. Most sat at the establishment's tables with a couple at the bar or by the door as Humphrey stood behind the bar. The room remained practically empty with only a dozen or so people, the entire population of the tiny township, occupying the area.

"When's drinks?" Ivan called from a seat by the fireplace. Others seated around him chuckled.

"No drinks during the town meeting," the tavern keeper replied, receiving a chorus of complaints. He waved his hands, signalling for the gathered to quiet themselves. "We're here to discuss last night's discovery, then take a vote as to what action we take."

"We should elect a leader," called a woman with young features, standing by the door. She wore a long, hooded cloak that reached to the floor, green with thin gold decorative trimmings on the sleeves and hems. The trimmings bore the design of an ancient elvish rune knot pattern. Another stood beside her wearing a similar garment, only crimson. "Someone we can trust to make decisions on behalf of the community," she continued.

"Now, that's a good idea." Ivan pointed to the woman. "I think it should be you, Humphrey. You own this tavern, and it's the only place big enough to hold meetings like this. Makes sense. We could have drinks when we discuss important things and stuff."

Others joined in, nodding, and speaking their approval to one another.

"Hold on," Humphrey called out. "Just wait. Yaleni has a good point. We can call an election after we've dealt with the matter at hand. Some poor bastard's head was stuck on top of a stick right outside these doors. We need to send someone to Northwell to inform the magistrate there."

Several nodded, agreeing with soft murmurs.

"Why not send someone to Rockmill?" Helena asked, seated beside Nichol at a table in the middle of the room. "It's much closer than Northwell."

"Rockmill is on the other side of The Dragon's Teeth and lies in the lands of Asalethwen," Nichol explained. "The magistrates there do not deal with problems in these lands. We need a magistrate from Kedielewen. Northwell is the closest."

"That's stupid," said a woman by Humphrey's side. "Who makes these rules?"

"The Council of Four, my love," the tavern keeper said, touching her on the back.

"Anne has a point. We should elect a magistrate of our own," uttered a young man leaning against the wall near the bar. His small wiry frame, straight black hair and almond-shaped eyes set him apart from the others in the township.

"What say we do?" Humphrey responded. "We elect a new magistrate for Mountainfall, and we are still the same group of people dealing with this problem. Nothing changes. We are a small community who needs help. What can we do besides farm, peddle goods, and drink my tavern dry?"

"The Council of Four appoints magistrates," Ivan informed the others. "And they're all the way over in Dendadia. Besides, we're a new and small community and not a big enough town to warrant the appointment of a magistrate. So, we can't elect one and we can't get one."

The crimson cloaked woman stepped forward, pushing her hood off her head to reveal her blonde braided hair and two pointed ears.

"My sister and I will ride for Northwell immediately," she said, gesturing to the other cloaked woman. "With hard riding, we should reach there the day after tomorrow."

"And kill your horses along the way, Aralore," Nichol said. "That's a five-day journey at best, and that's pushing it. Besides, you and your sister are our best archers. We may need you here in case this murderer returns."

"Or murderers," Ivan said. "Travellers have told rumours of raiders attacking villages along the coast up to Coldwolf."

"We're a long way inland," the young man by the bar put in. "And we'll need more than two elvish archer ladies if they've come all the way to Mountainfall. That aside, two elvish ladies shouldn't go to Northwell, anyway."

The cloaked women appeared offended by his words.

"Why not?" asked Yaleni, lowering her hood to reveal her hair fashioned like her sister's, only silver.

"I hear they're not as open-minded about elves over there," he told her.

"We are citizens of Dendadia," Yaleni protested, pointing to the lad. "Just as you are. Just as all of you are. We registered our business here with the magistrate's office in Port Coldspring to show our loyalty and good standing. That's more than some others have done in this town. You lodged it for us, did you not?"

"Indeed, I did, and I will always support you both. But you are elves from Legilawen," Nichol said, turning in his seat to face her.

"So?" she queried, furrowing her brow. "What of it?"

"Legilawen is the land of the Elvish King, Amalith," he continued. "Some people still hold contention towards the people of Legilawen because of what he and his followers did. Some in these lands still say the only good elf is an elf from Wyrwen or a dead elf."

"It's not our fault we were born on the wrong side of the mountains," Aralore snapped, stepping forward. "Our parents never supported Amalith's ways. They were flayed for standing up to him. My sister and I fled and hid during the war. We were starving and homeless for years. We sought refuge here because we are still not accepted by our own people in our homelands. And we aren't accepted here either." Tears streamed over her cheeks as she spoke.

Nichol stood and wrapped his arms around her. "You are accepted here. You're a part of this community. One day, you'll ride into Northwell or Port Coldspring with your head held high and those pretty, pointed ears of yours on display for the whole world to see."

She laughed softly, wrapping her arms around his shoulders.

"Thank you," she whispered before letting him go.

"I'll go," he said, turning to Humphrey. Helena grabbed his sleeve and gave him an objecting glare. "I'll go," he repeated, looking at her.

"Not alone," the young man by the bar put in.

"Yeah?" Nichol asked him. The other nodded. "All right, Jaysh Shen-Jon and I will go to Northwell to inform the magistrate."

"Are you certain?" Humphrey queried.

"Why do you ask?" Nichol replied.

"I'm asking Jaysh," the tavern keeper clarified.

"Yes," the young man answered, peering around the room curiously.

"I'm asking because, like our elvish friends here, your people came from the Shattered Isles," Humphrey explained. "You might be looked upon with hostility as well."

"First..." Jaysh held up a finger. "My people call it Selemar Graekath."

"I apologise," Humphrey said sheepishly.

"Second, they're not my people," the young man continued, becoming excited. "I was born in Springhollow, as were my parents and their parents. There are plenty of exotic and beautiful people like me roaming your lands."

"I'm sorry," the tavern keeper frowned.

Outside, the wind picked up, whistling through the tiny gap under the door as Helena continued to give Nichol a displeased glare as the room offered their approvals.

"It's settled then," Humphrey said. "Nichol and Jaysh will go to Northwell..."

"And you'll be our temporary leader until we hold elections," Ivan broke in. "Now that's all settled, when's drinks?"

By late afternoon, Steigauf and Arnald reached the outskirts of Shiverwind. At first, they passed by houses and small cottages dotted throughout the landscape. Sightings of sheep and cattle huddled together in the cold, close to stables and houses and shielding themselves against the falling snow, became more frequent. Some people braving the weather, farmers mostly, offered a wave of the hand to which the soldier and the boy responded in kind. The appearance of the wolf often changed an onlooker's demeanour from friendly to surprised. Arnald smiled each time this happened.

When they held the town's edge in their sights, the boy looked on, awestruck. Great wharves and warehouses enveloped the water's edge to his left almost as far as he could see. Buildings with two levels lined paved streets that crisscrossed each other, filled with pedestrian traffic, horses, and carts. The bustling township behaved like a living, breathing creature.

"Bigger than I thought," he told Steigauf.

"You can get lost pretty easily here, laddie," the soldier replied. "Best stay close."

Arnald nodded as the wolf moved closer to his side, walking slowly next to his horse, as if guarding him.

Before they could enter the town, a band of armoured men on horseback lined the street before them, blocking their way.

"Evening." Steigauf nodded, smiling as he pulled his horse to a stop.

"Good evening, sir," said a young rider near the centre of the line. "We've been watching your approach and wonder what business you have in Shiverwind?"

"Business?" the old soldier replied. "What's your name, boy?"

"I'm Lieutenant Gerard of the Shiverwind Cavalry," the rider answered. "And who might you be?"

"They have cavalry now," the Pit Guard said to Arnald. "That's new."

"Sir," the rider called. "Your name and business?"

"Osman Steigauf," the old man reported. "One of The First. Guard of

151

the Temple of Four."

The officer appeared taken aback by the information.

"Do, do you have proof of this, sir?"

"Proof?" Steigauf thumped his breastplate. "How about this?" He then put his hand on the hilt of his sword. "How about this for proof?"

The riders instinctively placed their hands upon their weapons, ready to retaliate.

Arnald felt his stomach tighten into a knot.

The wolf bared her teeth, growling as she raised her hackles.

"Sir," Gerard ordered. "Control your animal."

"Control yours first," Steigauf returned. "Then, fetch Lieutenant Kraayen or Zain Demeara. They'll vouch for me."

The Lieutenant eased his posture and signalled his men to relax.

"You must mean Captain Kraayen," Gerard offered.

"Bastard got promoted," the old soldier whispered to Arnald.

"Magistrate Demeara holds council at this hour," the lieutenant informed the Pit Guard. "I'll send for him as soon as possible. If you could follow us, we will take you to the barracks."

"All right." Steigauf took his hand from his sword.

Gerard leaned over to the rider on his left and said something neither Arnald nor the old man could hear. The rider quickly responded by turning his horse to race through the streets, dodging traffic effortlessly at high speed.

"So, where's he off to?" Steigauf queried.

"To inform Captain Kraayen of your arrival," the other replied.

"Good," the Pit Guard said. "Lead on then."

A moment later, the riders made their way into Shiverwind. The people parted, making the way clear for the troop. Arnald felt every eye upon him, almost as if he walked naked through the street. He wanted to look around at the township, at all the unfamiliar things the place had that he had never seen in his life. Instead, he looked at his sleeve where Gertrude rested.

"I wish you were here with me," he told her. The goat bleated. Arnald smiled. "Not you, silly."

"Stay close," Steigauf said before turning to look at the boy and the wolf. "Both of you."

Chapter Two

THE EARLY MORNING BROUGHT a gentle drift of snow to Mountainfall. A small gathering collected by the stable house behind the tavern to see Nichol and Jaysh on their way. With two steeds packed lightly for a hasty ride with bedrolls, water skins, two bows and two quivers, each containing a small collection of arrows, the riders prepared to leave.

Helena held Nichol tightly, wrapping both in her bearskin cloak, her head on his chest. Her tears soaked into his cloak as she sobbed.

"You be careful," she whispered to him.

"I will," he replied, kissing her on the top of her head. "And, until I return, I want you to stay here, in town, in my house."

"I'm not that far away," she protested quietly, peering up at him.

He looked at the forest and shook his head.

"Yes, you are," he told her. "I can't see it from here, so it's too far. Stay in my house until I return, please."

She nodded reluctantly, tightening her hold around his waist.

"You hurry back to me," she commanded.

He nodded before planting his lips on hers.

"I wish someone would say farewell to me like that," Jaysh Shen-Jon muttered to himself.

"I'll kiss you if you like, boy." Ivan smiled.

"No thank you." The other appeared disgusted.

"Well, have this then," Ivan said, pulling a sword, sheathed in an old animal's skin, from beneath his cloak. He offered it to the young man with both hands. "She's old and might need sharpening. I haven't taken it out in years. She served me during the war but saw little action."

"I have my own," Jaysh replied, flicking his cloak behind his waist to expose a thin, curved sword strapped to his hip. "But thank you."

Ivan looked disappointed, lowering his arms to hold his sword against his stomach.

"I'll take it," Nichol interjected. "If you like?"

"You will?" Ivan looked at him with a grin. "She's not much, but she was good enough to cut down two Adaerwen warriors when we battled here, before the mountain fell."

"Thank you," Nichol said earnestly, letting go of Helena to take the prized possession from the old man.

"Only two?" Helena asked, wrapping her cloak around her tightly.

"Yeah," Ivan replied bashfully. "Some cunt hit me from behind and knocked me out. I spent the rest of the fight with my face in the mud, asleep. When I woke, the battle was over. The mountain had fallen, and I missed the whole thing."

"Unfortunate," she said.

"Not really," he told her. "I'm fucked at fighting. Much better in the sack, if you get my meaning."

"You have got a way with words, old man." Jaysh Shen-Jon shook his head.

"Fuck you and your tiny sword," the old man bit back.

"This sword was forged in the great furnaces of Umakoth." The young man pulled the blade free of its sheath. The blade reflected light like a mirror as he rapidly swung it around his body. It cut through the air swiftly, emitting an impressive whoosh with each move. Jaysh sheathed it as quickly as he had pulled it free without glancing to his waist to make sure he had done so correctly, as most men would. "It's been in my family for a century, passed down from father to son until now."

Helena stepped to Nichol's side as he strapped Ivan's sword to his horse. She watched Jaysh Shen-Jon intently as he placed his cloak back over his blade.

"You must practise using that thing a great deal," she said.

"Every day," he returned. "But never on an actual enemy. At least, not while it has been in my possession."

"But it has cut before?" Ivan asked, clearly interested after witnessing the lad's display.

"My father cut hundreds down with this blade during the War of Six." He patted his hip. "It left warriors of Adaerwen and Legilawen in pieces all over the battlefield. Or so I was told by the men who brought my father home."

"Brought your father home?" Helena asked.

"Not a good story," Nichol said, holding his hand up to Helena before turning to the young man. "You don't need to—"

"It's all right," Jaysh said before addressing all gathered. "I've only ever told Nichol my story. My mother died when I was an infant. My father raised me on his own. Before I could even talk, he went away to war, and he left me in the care of the women in Springhollow for three years. He returned with many other fallen men of Springhollow, and I watched him burn on a pyre when I was four years old. A magistrate handed me my father's sword when I turned five. As soon as I became of age, I left Springhollow to find the place they told me my father fell. I've been living here ever since."

"I'm so sorry, son," Ivan said, placing a hand on Jaysh's shoulder.

"It was a long time ago," he replied.

Helena looked at Nichol, placing a hand on his chest to gain his attention.

"I'm glad he's going with you," she told him.

"As am I," he returned. "He's a good friend."

"He's good with that sword," she said. "I feel better knowing he'll be there to keep you safe."

He kissed her forehead.

"I'll be back," he promised, pulling her into him.

"What's with the long faces?" Anne called, walking from the back door of the tavern to the stable house with Humphrey in tow. She carried two small steaming hessian sacks. "You're going to Northwell. Not the ends of the world."

"What's that?" Ivan piped up, pointing to the sacks.

"Hot bread for our travellers," she replied. "It should last the journey to Northwell."

The two riders thanked the woman, packing the sacks into their saddlebags before mounting their steeds.

"Good luck, lads," Humphrey said. "And don't be away too long."

"We'll return as soon as we are able," Nichol replied before turning his attention to Helena. "I love you," he mouthed silently.

"I love you," she repeated in the same manner before blowing a kiss.

With that, both riders turned their horses north to gallop along the Great Northern Barrier Road.

Helena remained by the roadside, even when the others had gone back inside to escape the cold, watching Nichol ride away out of view. She frowned and wiped a tear away before turning to cross the road where she entered the forest on the other side.

⁘

"How did you sleep?" Steigauf asked Arnald upon entering the mess hall of the barracks. The boy sat at the end of a long table on a bench with the wolf lying on the floor by his side. A group of soldiers sat at a nearby table, scoffing down their breakfast of porridge and toast.

"Well," he answered the old man as he picked up a slice of toast from his plate. He gestured with his thumb to the table of men. "They put me in a room with these men. Some of them snore loudly."

The soldiers closest to the boy chuckled.

"As long as you're comfortable," Steigauf said as he sat across from him. "You're not eating?"

"I ate at the inn," the old man answered before looking at the wolf. "Did you feed her?"

"She ate," the boy told him.

"Better than any of us," a soldier wearing a friendly smile piped in. "And she hasn't left the lad's side. Not once."

"I think she's claimed you as her own," said the Pit Guard to Arnald.

156

"Now we need to sort a few things. Captain Kraayen has decided to accommodate you and the wolf here for the first part of your training, which begins today."

"Today?" The boy sounded excited but bore a worried countenance.

"Today's as good as any day," Steigauf replied. "But listen. I spoke to one of the cooks here and I think we'll need to donate the food we gathered. He said he can use the chickens to make soup and the pork to make stew, with your permission."

"Of course," Arnald agreed. "But what will you take for your journey home?"

"Well..." The other cocked his head, raising his brow. "I'm going to stay awhile. Just to see how you get on with your training. See if it's what you really want to do. When I think you're settled in, I'll depart."

The boy nodded, happy to have a familiar, friendly face stay with him for a little while longer.

"I met with the magistrate and sheriff last night," the old man continued. "I told them of your situation. Magistrate Demeara ordered riders to take flight to Dendadia. It'll take them a while to get there. Perhaps a month, at least. It's a long journey from here. The sheriff wanted to send a troop to investigate the village. I talked her out of it."

"Why?" asked Arnald.

"By now, the snow would have covered everything if there was a trace to be found of the raiders," Steigauf explained. "The marks from the boats by the water's edge would be all but washed away. You burned all the bodies you could find. There's nothing left to investigate."

The boy looked at the toast on his plate as he pondered the old man's words.

"I also told them about the scratch marks we saw at the hut," the Pit Guard continued. "That, I told them to investigate. The last thing anyone needs is a man-wolf slaughtering the flocks we passed on the way into town. So, I suggested she send a troop of well-armed men back along the road to take a look."

He looked at the boy for a long moment, almost dotingly and absent-mindedly.

"Oh," Steigauf said suddenly, reaching to a pouch on his hip. "This might cheer you up. Here." He placed a gold coin on the table next to Arnald's plate.

"Blimey," said a soldier. "That's worth more than we get in a year."

"For the goat," the Pit Guard told the boy.

"A gold for a goat?" another guard queried. "Must be some goat."

Steigauf shrugged and looked at Arnald uncomfortably.

"I might have sold the whole *little boy, lone survivor of a raid* thing to get that," he said. "Whatever, the coin is yours."

Arnald picked up the coin and examined it. Almost the size of the palm of his hand, the coin bore engravings on both sides. Stencilled into the surface on one side were the words, *By The Authority of the Council of Four and its Treasury*. On the other side, the four women stood with their swords before them, like those on Steigauf's breastplate.

"I've never seen one so big before," Arnald said before placing the coin into a leather pouch on his belt. "Coppers and irons are all I've seen."

"Few people have ever seen a treasury goldie, laddie," a soldier sitting near him remarked. "You're very lucky to have one."

"Be sure he doesn't misplace it." Steigauf gave the men a cautious glare.

"Aye, sir," they choroused.

"The goat?" Arnald asked, lifting his toast to take another bite. "Did she go to a good home?"

"Good enough," the old soldier answered. "What's it matter? You have a goldie and she's just a goat."

"She's a good milker," the boy replied, thinking about how he had carried her along the road for countless miles. He recalled the many times she nuzzled against him under his cloak, keeping warm, and how he had scratched her behind her ears.

"You need to remember why you're here," Steigauf said sternly, bringing him back to the present. "You're not here to worry about goats or anything else that takes your mind anywhere other than where you need to focus. Understand?"

Arnald nodded.

"Good." The Pit Guard smiled. "Now, eat your toast and get ready to follow these men. You train with them today. Consignment drills if I heard correctly."

"For fuck's sake," one man, further along the table, whined.

"What's consignment drills?" Arnald asked, chewing on a mouthful of toast.

"Lots of hauling, loading and unloading wagons," one seated closer replied. "I swear that's all we ever do. With no wars to fight, we load someone else's shit on and off wagons or ships. We've become the town's labour force."

"It's good strength building and promotes teamwork," Steigauf told them all. "And, yes, the town needs their supplies moved about and you're providing a service to the people, so the drills serve dual purposes. You're all better men for it."

Chapter Three

⸻

Aʀɴᴀʟᴅ ᴄᴀʀʀɪᴇᴅ ᴡʜᴀᴛ sᴜᴘᴘʟɪᴇs he could on his own, mostly small boxes of carrots, turnips, radishes, and sacks of potatoes. By midday, his legs ached, and his shoulders throbbed. He paused momentarily, leaning against a warehouse doorframe, to watch the men of the troop partner up to lug larger crates containing farming implements, taking them from the docks to awaiting carts lined up by the wharves.

"Come on, laddie," a young soldier called as he returned from loading a box onto a wagon to collect a new load. "Get your back into it. No breaks until lunchtime."

"And when will that be?" the boy asked, rubbing his thighs.

"When they say so, I guess," the other replied, crouching by a larger, longish box. "Come on and help me with this one, will ya?"

Without hesitation, Arnald scooted over and lifted the crate from the other side.

"This one's heavy," he stated. "What's in it?"

"Dead bodies, for all I know," the soldier replied, shuffling his feet as they carried the load a few feet to the awaiting cart. "Put your side up first."

Arnald lifted his end onto the wagon before moving to the soldier's side to help push it onboard.

"That's it." The soldier smiled, glancing at the boy. "There're no bodies in there. It's farming supplies from Southfog and Vertdell. They'll all be delivered to different farms across the lands between here and the Long Spine."

The boy peered at all the wagons. He counted thirty lined up along the docks with loading underway, and a further twelve in a line that stretched behind a warehouse out of view, waiting for their turn.

"Must be a lot of farms," he said, walking beside the soldier to collect another crate.

"Not really," the other said, looking at the multitude of boxes, sacks and cases stacked along the waterfront. "It looks like a lot of stuff. But it isn't. Most of it's consumable."

"What's that mean?" Arnald questioned as he lifted his end.

"It means, it won't last forever," the soldier replied. "Like the potatoes. They'll turn bad. So, they need to be consumed."

"Eaten, you mean," the boy clarified as the two carried the crate to the wagon.

"Exactly," the other said. "Your end first, again."

Arnald repeated his actions from earlier, lifting the crate onto the carriage before helping the soldier push it all the way on board.

"Name's Johaan," the soldier said, reaching out to the boy.

"Arnald," said the lad, shaking the soldier's hand.

Before long, they loaded another crate onto the wagon. They had turned to gather another when a sharp whistle blew from a warehouse nearby.

Turning, they saw a tall, broad-shouldered, bearded man in an officer's dress uniform, deep blue with the insignia of an eagle carrying a battle axe. Beside him stood Steigauf and the wolf.

"Lunch," the officer called.

"That's Commander Erik Reigler," Johaan told the boy as they walked towards the warehouse. "He's navy, he is."

"He's in charge?" Arnald asked. "I thought Captain Kraayen was in charge."

"Reigler is commander of these vessels here." The soldier jutted a thumb over his shoulder to the ships moored along the docks. "It's his job to make sure we're well fed for the day. By the gods, I hope it's not porridge again."

⬦

As the day drew on, the two riders from Mountainfall, far to the east of Kedielewen, made considerable ground during their journey. They followed the well-worn road north, guiding their horses into higher lands, closing their distance to the feet of the mountains.

With the wind picking up around them, and the sun falling lower in the western sky, they stopped to set up camp in a rocky shelter built into a crevasse, a short and easy climb on a mountain's side. The sheltered area had natural high walls almost surrounding them on all sides save for one, the opening they entered from, giving them a clear view of the road below.

After tethering the horses to a tree within the shelter, Jaysh Shen-Jon set a fire while Nichol gathered snow into a pot.

"I've some terrible news," Nichol said, placing the pot onto the flames.

"What's that?" the other replied, returning to his horse to remove his bedroll from the saddle.

"I forgot to pack the tea," replied Nichol, retrieving his own bedroll.

"Bread and warm water for dinner, then," the younger man returned, rolling his bundle out by the fire. "For you, that is. I, on the other hand, packed the finest tea from Vertdell."

"You did?"

"Absolutely." Jaysh smiled. "Because I knew you would forget many things in your state of mind."

"State of mind?" Nichol queried, rolling his bedding on the ground on the opposite side of the fire. "What's that supposed to mean?"

"Helena." Jaysh held up a hand apologetically. "Don't get me wrong. She's sweet and pretty. But you have been absolutely preoccupied with her since you both made eyes for one another. You're lost all the time."

"I'm in love," Nichol admitted.

"That's never easy for a man to admit unless he means it," Jaysh Shen-Jon said, retrieving a tiny hessian sachet from a saddlebag. "And I know you mean it. But that's not what I mean. It's as if she..."

"Has a hold on me," the other finished.

"Yes." He nodded, sitting upon his bedding before plonking the sachet into the pot of water.

"What are you doing?" asked Nichol.

"Putting the tea into the water," the younger replied.

"Just like that?"

"Yeah, why?"

"We've got days ahead of us," Nichol explained. "You're going to use up all your tea on the first night."

"That's tonight's portion," Jaysh pointed to the pot. "I've prepared enough of those little bags for a week and then some."

Nichol looked at his friend, surprised.

"I apologise," he said.

"See, that's what I mean?" The younger man stabbed a finger towards Nichol. "You would have thought to do something like this if she wasn't in your head all the time. And now you're shocked to find that I did it instead. She's got you by your—"

"Balls," the other conceded.

"I was going to say, heart," Jaysh Shen-Jon returned. "But now that you mention it."

Nichol observed a thin layer of steam grip the water's surface inside the pot. Jaysh dipped a stick in to stir the liquid gently.

"So..." Nichol smiled wryly. "When are you going to find yourself a woman?"

"Don't you fucking start." Jaysh pointed the stick at his friend.

They both laughed, their chuckles carried away in the wind blowing wildly above them, sweeping over their sheltered spot.

"Seriously, though," Nichol said. "Is there anyone?"

Jaysh frowned and shook his head.

"I don't think there's any that would take a foreign-looking boy like me."

Nichol's heart sank upon hearing Jaysh's words.

"I wouldn't be so quick to dismiss them all, yet," he said.

"Why? What do you know that I don't?"

"There might be someone," Nichol teased. "Back home."

"Who?" Jaysh peered at Nichol, a look of uncertainty on his face, wondering if his friend played some kind of game.

"One of the elves," the other told him.

Jaysh sat up, attentive.

"No," he murmured. "You lie."

"So!" Nichol pointed his finger at Jaysh. "You do like her. I knew it."

"Does she like me?" he pressed. "Really? I mean, I thought about asking her to take a walk with me before the snow fell, but I..."

"She watches you all the time when you aren't looking." Nichol smiled. "I noticed it a while ago. So did Helena. I'm surprised you haven't after all this time."

"I should let her know," the younger man said. "Right? I should tell her how I feel."

"You should."

"As soon as we return, I'll let Aralore know how I feel about her."

"What?" Nichol snapped. "No, I meant Yaleni."

"Yaleni?" Jaysh Shen-Jon. "Oh my. This complicates things. So, Aralore doesn't like me, then?"

"I don't know," the other replied. "I've only noticed Yeleni has eyes for you."

Nichol watched his friend struggle with the thought.

"Oh my," the younger man uttered.

"You don't like Yeleni?"

"Of course, I do," Jaysh returned. "She's as beautiful as her sister. It's just..."

"You're drawn to Aralore," Nichol finished.

Jaysh nodded. Nichol pondered this for a moment.

"You could have them both," he suggested.

"No, I bloody well couldn't." Jaysh shook his head.

"Why not?" Nichol put forward. "They won't find husbands elsewhere in the Northerlands. And you're the only eligible bachelor left in Mountainfall."

"I don't know if I'm comfortable with that, Nichol," Jaysh replied.

Nichol nodded, moving his gaze to the plume of steam rising from the pot.

"You should think on it," he said eventually. "What have you got to lose?"

The patrons of The Lazy Traveller nursed bowls of steaming stew while soaking up the warmth the fire provided inside the establishment. Humphrey served drinks but wasn't doing as well with refills as Helena did with her hot casserole. Anne found it hard to keep up with each serve, buttering fresh bread to go with each bowl.

"Back for more?" Humphrey asked Ivan, who held his bowl out for another refill. "This is your third."

"It's bloody good stuff," the old man replied. "I'd like to know what you put in it."

"Nothing much," Helena admitted. "A fresh lamb from Kain Drovo's flock." She pointed with the ladle to a man seated at a table by the door. He noticed and waved back with his spoon before digging into his bowl of stew. She directed the scoop to another seated by the fireplace. "A few beets and radishes from Eowal Pendash's stores. Some herbs from Yaleni's collection." Helena scanned the room. "She's not here. And I picked some mushrooms from the forest."

"Mushrooms from the forest?" Anne asked. Helena nodded. "When did you collect them?" the tavern keeper's wife queried.

"Today," Helena replied. "After Nichol left, I went to my hut to collect a few things before going to his house. I needed a change of clothes and some other items."

"You went on your own?" Humphrey pressed.

"Yes," she answered. "It's all right. I wasn't gone long."

"Helena, you promised Nichol you wouldn't go back there until this problem is over," the tavern keeper reminded her. "You can't go back there on your own. Not again."

"I won't," she agreed, tears welling in her eyes.

Anne put the butter knife down on the bench and wrapped her arms around the girl.

"It's all right, lassie," she said. "We're just worried. We don't want anything to happen to you."

"I know," Helena sobbed.

Ivan placed his bowl on the bar.

"Tell you what," he started. "Next time you get the urge to go back to your hut for something, or to collect more mushrooms, you come and get me or one of the other lads here. We'll accompany you."

"Thank you," she said, wiping her eyes on her apron.

"Any time, deary," the old man assured her. "Now, how's about a little more of that stew of yours?"

Arnald felt sore from the top of his head to the soles of his feet. He fell onto his cot face down and closed his eyes. A numbness covered his skin so that he couldn't sense the wolf licking the palm of his hand hanging over the side of his bed.

"You did well today, Arnald," said a familiar voice.

"I hurt all over," the boy groaned.

"You skipped the evening meal," Steigauf said, sitting on the edge of the cot. "You should eat something."

"Too tired," Arnald mumbled.

The Pit Guard chuckled.

"Fair enough," he said, standing up. "Sleep well, then. You have sword drills tomorrow."

"Sword drills?" The boy turned his weary head to look at the old soldier. "I'll need my swords."

"No, you won't," Steigauf replied. "I'll keep them safe for you. You'll be using practice swords. Wooden."

Arnald nodded before dropping his head back to the bed, causing the Pit Guard to chuckle again.

"Good night, laddie," Steigauf said, walking away to the door. The boy gave no reply. He already fell asleep. The old soldier looked at the wolf, who lowered herself onto the floor beside Arnald. She glanced at the Pit Guard before resting her head onto her front legs. He nodded to himself as he exited the room, leaving the wolf and boy for the night.

Ivan staggered, making a zigzag pattern in the snow behind him as he walked alongside Helena.

"You didn't need to escort me home," she said to the old man.

"Nonsense," he told her, burping as he brushed building snow from his shoulders. "Sorry. A little too much to drink, I think. Besides, Nichol's house is right near mine. So, it only makes sense that I walk you home because I am the closest to you."

"Thank you," she said, pausing at a small gateway in a picket fence. "This is it."

"I'll wait for you to be inside, like a gentleman," he slurred. "You latch the door and I'll be off. All right?"

"All right," she agreed. "Goodnight."

"Goodnight," he returned as she made her way along a snow-covered path leading to the door of a quaint log cabin with shutters closed over the windows. She stepped onto the timber porch and gave Ivan a wave before stepping through the door.

He waved back as he watched her close the door and latch it shut behind her. Turning, he continued along the road a little further to a smaller hut. After entering, he staggered around a table and chair to the fireplace, stoked the embers with a poker to reignite the flames, and dropped onto his bed. Within an instant, he fell asleep, snoring noisily.

Javanakhan!

Suddenly, his eyes opened.

He peered at the fireplace. The embers glowed red. The flames burned out long ago. His sense of time was lost on him.

A rumble exploded within his stomach. Intense warmth swept over his body.

He stood and took off the outer layer of clothing, pants, and shirt.

Sweat trickled down his back, over his brow and under his arms.

The room seemed to swim around him.

Swirling.

Swirling.

Still too hot, he took off the rest of his garments and stood in the middle of his hut, naked.

The room warped and bent, twisted and turned around him.

The heat intensified.

He opened the door, exposing himself to the elements.

Snow drifted gently onto his skin as he stepped outside.

He scooped some from the ground and rubbed it against his naked flesh.

It didn't help. He felt unbearably hot all over.

Javanakhan!

His stomach rumbled again.

His gaze fell upon the forest.

He knew what he needed lay within.

Urging himself forward, he crossed the road and walked through the knee-deep snow on the other side. The wind howled about him. The world continued to swirl.

Javanakhan!

Placing a hand upon the trunk of a pine tree to steady himself, he gripped his stomach with the other as it bubbled and growled like a wild beast. Peering around to see the world swimming and swirling, he saw others to his left and right moving farther into the woods. He couldn't see them clearly, only that they were the forms of people.

He winced as pain from his belly intensified, as immense heat flowed over and through his flesh.

Javanakhan!

The pull to go on felt too great. He needed to move on. Forward, he pressed. Deeper into the woods.

Deeper.

Deeper.

Chapter Four

THE SUN HAD YET to peek above the horizon, but the troop set to training with wooden swords and shields. While some sparred, others fought against timber dummies lined along a wall at the edge of the barrack's training grounds, surrounded by tall stone walls.

Steigauf leaned against the wall, observing Arnald hack at his enemy. Crudely formed from thick posts planted into the ground with a cross beam tacked on to resemble arms, the enemy soldier simply stood there and took each blow without complaint. The wolf rested on the ground a few paces away from the boy, her head on her paws and eyes closed.

"Remember where the vital areas are," the Pit Guard said. "Put the blade to the neck and ribs. Picture it in your head. They used to paint these things to show you the best places to strike your enemy."

"They never painted them in the time I've been here," Johaan Heilig told him as he chopped at his wooden warrior's head.

"And just how long have you been here?" Steigauf questioned.

"Three months, sir." Heilig swung his sword into the target's middle.

"Three whole months!" The Pit Guard chuckled. "That explains a few things."

"Explains what?" The young soldier stopped to look at the older man. Arnald paused and quickly looked at each of them, sensing bitterness in Heilig's words.

"It explains why you're hitting your enemy incorrectly," the old man said.

"Incorrectly? How?"

"You hit your enemy in the head with the fuller," Steigauf replied.

"Fuller?" Heilig glanced at the boy curiously. "Do you know what he's talking about?"

Arnald shook his head.

Steigauf pointed at the boy.

"Don't stop," he said, approaching the young soldier. "Keep killing this piece of wood."

Arnald resumed his hacking as Steigauf took the wooden blade from the young soldier's hands. He then pointed to the flat side of the sword. "This is the fuller. Hitting some bastard in the head might knock him out. But, if they're wearing a helmet, you're fucked. Hack them with the blade. Every single strike you make needs to be with the blade if you want to kill. Understand?"

He handed the wooden sword back. Heilig took it and nodded.

"Why you don't have someone here to train you, I'll never know," Steigauf muttered, returning to his place by the wall as he looked up and down the line where others exhibited poor fighting skills. He looked at those sparring and shook his head. Their movements seemed rehearsed. As one brought a sword down, slowly, the other put his shield up to block it, slowly.

"It's a numbers thing," Heilig told him, hacking at the dummy with his sword's edge. A tiny chunk of timber splintered away from the wooden warrior's neck.

"That's better," Steigauf pointed at the wound. "And what do you mean, numbers thing?"

"We don't have an officer assigned to us as the troops in Dendadia do," the younger man answered. "We're given our orders daily and are expected to follow them to the letter. Every now and then, someone of rank comes by to check on us or tell us it's time to eat. But that's all."

Arnald stopped to watch the old soldier walk past him and a little onto the training grounds.

"You keep chopping." Steigauf pointed at the boy without turning to look at him. Arnald complied immediately. The old soldier walked over to a rack of wooden swords and took one before turning to the sparring men. "This is not a dance," he hollered.

The men stopped their training to turn and listen.

"The man you face is not your friend," Steigauf hollered as he approached the closest shield-bearer. "He's your enemy."

With that, the old soldier raised his wooden sword and swung it down towards the shield-bearer with immense force. Fear swept over the young man's face before he instinctively raised the shield to block the blow. Steigauf relentlessly attacked again and again. The strikes echoed loudly off the stone walls noisily as the Pit Guard roared mightily.

Arnald felt his stomach tighten into a tiny ball, believing the old man intended to kill the young soldier.

Chunks of timber broke away from the frail shield as Steigauf persisted with his attack. The sound of crumbling wood, the echoing hits, and the terrifying cry of the Pit Guard penetrated every man on the training ground, filling them with terror and confusion.

The shield-bearer fell on his back, continuing to hold his shield before him, emitting tiny cries of dread.

More and more timber shards broke from the shield before a large crack formed on its surface.

"I yield," the soldier called. "I yield."

But Steigauf didn't stop.

He hacked some more until he saw tears in the young man's eyes.

"Your enemy won't wait for you to lift your shield," the Pit Guard yelled, looking up at the stunned faces around him before tossing his wooden sword to the ground. "He won't be using little play swords and you won't be carrying flimsy shields. And he won't care if you yield. He will kill you, dead!"

Steigauf turned to look at the boy and wolf, who now stood, alert and ready for a fight. The boy watched on, wide-eyed and petrified.

"I'll train you," the old man called to all around him. "Your real training begins today."

Nichol and Jaysh rode side-by-side as the road descended to lower ground, gradually turning away from the mountains and towards the forest lands to their left. Keeping their steeds at a steady gallop, the men tried to gain as much ground as they could with the limited time they had.

They travelled many miles before both horses tired, slowing to a trot. Nichol reached down to pat his horse's neck.

"There, girl," he said before turning to the other rider. "I think we should walk them for a while. Give them time to catch their breath."

Both men dismounted and led the horses along the road. Jaysh Shen-Jon peered up to the mountains and saw a tall structure high on the ridge.

"What's that?" he asked, pointing to the stone object.

"I think it's one of the guard towers posted along the range," Nichol replied. "They're not manned anymore. Not since the war."

Jaysh squinted, hoping to make his eyes see it more clearly. It was too far to identify any specific features. To him, it just appeared like a distant stone pipe.

"Why build them here?" he queried. "Isn't the Frozen Waste on the other side of these mountains?"

"I guess the people on this side thought the Witch Queen or the Elvish King might send their troops across Haeraweth," said Nichol. "They didn't, obviously. Only the very brave or utterly stupid would try to cross those lands."

"How many towers are there up there?" Jaysh asked.

"I don't know. Most of the charts I've seen show six or seven. But I think they're just the larger outposts. For each of them, there would have to be another ten towers or more to protect such a distance. Don't forget, the range stretches all the way south to Blackborough on the coast."

"Not quite," Jaysh Shen-Jon put in.

"What's that?"

"The range doesn't quite reach all the way to Blackborough," he explained. "It stops far inland from the coast. I know because I've been to Blackborough."

"You never told me this before." Nichol looked at his friend. "How did you come to Blackborough?"

"I thought I did," the younger man replied. "I told you I've been to the

Mud Dragon?"

"Yes," the other said. "I know about your visit to the Mud Dragon Inn. I know about your exploits with the innkeeper's daughters."

"Five of them." Jaysh held up his fingers.

"The innkeeper's five daughters," Nichol corrected himself.

"Yeah," the younger man said. "Bastard ran me out of town. I won't be going back there anytime soon. You think he'd be happy. All his daughters were... I don't know."

"Plain looking?"

"I was thinking ugly as shit. But your way sounds better. Anyway," the younger man said, getting back to the story. "I left Springhollow by ship and travelled to Blackborough. I bought an ass there and rode it to the Mud Dragon. I stole a horse at the Mud Dragon to get away from an angry, murderous innkeeper and we've been together ever since." He rubbed his steed's muzzle. "Another reason I can't go back anytime soon. I wonder whatever happened to that ass?"

"Maybe they ate it out of spite." Nichol smiled.

"Or the innkeeper adopted her for his sixth daughter." Jaysh laughed.

They walked in silence for a short time before Nichol spoke.

"Why are you against taking both Aralore and Yaleni?" he asked. "If they'll have you, that is."

"What?"

"I'm just curious because you said you enjoyed the company of the innkeeper's daughters," Nichol said. "There were five of them and only the two sisters in Mountainfall."

"I didn't take all five at one time," Jaysh explained. "I mean, how does someone do that? I've got one... you know... and they are more than one. It's impossible."

"All right," Nichol conceded. "I understand."

"Haven't you wondered, though?" Jaysh pressed. "Do you line them up and..."

"Enough!" The other pressed his hands to his ears. "I don't want to hear this. I'm sorry I asked."

Jaysh chuckled as he peered back at the tower.

175

Helena kneaded a thick ball of dough on a bench in the tavern's kitchen. Anne, standing at another bench beside her, broke another clump of dough into smaller, fist-sized chunks before rolling them into balls to place on a baking tray.

"Will you make more of your stew for tonight?" the older woman queried. "You should. It was very nice."

"I was hoping there would be some left over," Helena replied. "A stew is often better on the second and third nights. But it was all eaten last night and I've no more mushrooms."

"Shame," Anne said, crossing the room to place the tray of rolls into the oven.

A knock at the door leading outside made them turn. The top half of the double-hung door sat open. Yaleni leaned on the lower door's shelf, dangling a woven straw basket in her hand.

"Good morning," she sang from beneath her snow speckled green hood. "Is Humphrey around?"

"I haven't seen him all morning," Anne replied, wiping her hands on her apron as she moved to open the lower half of the door to admit the visitor.

"Probably in the cellar conducting inventory," suggested Helena.

"Drinking the inventory, you mean." Anne smiled.

"Give him some allowance," the younger woman returned. "He never drinks when he's tending to customers."

"I'll go see where he is," Anne said to Yaleni, brushing by her to go outside. She didn't need to go far. The cellar doors were only a few paces from the kitchen door, lying almost flat to the ground. She bent to pull one panel open, but it being too heavy, she dropped it with a loud clunk.

"Let me," the elf offered, placing her basket on the bench before stepping to Anne's side. With one arm, she opened the door with ease.

"Thank you," the older woman said as she stepped into the dank space beneath the tavern. "Humphrey," she called. "Are you in here?"

No reply came.

She moved on into the cellar and called his name again.

"Strange," she said. "I thought he would be here."

"Eowal is missing, too," Yaleni told her. "I was just there and Tsami said he is probably out checking his traps for rabbits. You didn't notice Humphrey leave this morning?"

"No," Anne replied. Her voice shook. "I woke up, and he wasn't there. I didn't think much of it."

"Tsami said the same," the elf said as Anne climbed the steps back out of the cellar. "Eowal was gone when she woke."

"What do you think it means?" the older woman asked.

"I don't know."

"It could be nothing," Helena said from the tavern's back door. "It's no good getting worried about anything until we know more. Maybe he just went for a walk."

Anne gave her a questioning look.

"Do you know any time when Humphrey ever walked anywhere?" she returned, before looking at the elf-woman. "Why did you come this morning, Yaleni? Obviously not to put worry in my mind."

"I have some tea and spices I wanted to sell," she answered. "I was hoping for some of the bread you're baking in return. But it seems trivial now. I'll fetch my sister and we'll begin a search."

"Thank you." Anne gently touched the elf's arm.

Chapter Five

THE WOMEN OF MOUNTAINFALL met in the tavern gathering, sitting at the tables by the fireplace. Helena, Yaleni and Aralore set to serving tea as concerns were raised and tears fell.

"It makes no sense," a dark-haired woman muttered, dabbing her eyes with a white kerchief. "Durskka wouldn't just leave during the night. I always wake him. Otherwise, he'd sleep all day."

"I agree, Angela. It doesn't make sense." Anne reached over from her seat to touch her friend on the knee. "Humphrey hardly ventures outside of the tavern. Where would he go?" She looked around at the other faces and noticed how young they all were. All except for her.

"Somebody took him," Angela sobbed. "Took all of them. All the men are gone. Where?"

Helena carried a tray with a few cups of steaming tea. She placed them on the bar to reach over Angela's shoulders and hug her.

"Your man may be too late to seek help for us," Angela said. "It might be a waste of time."

"If he lives," another put in.

"Tsami." Aralore shot the other a scolding look.

"I heard the rumours about raiders attacking villages to the north," the other returned. "If they came here to take our men, they would have come by the road both Nichol and Jaysh travel along now, if they live."

Helena stood upright. Her hands trembled and her lip quivered. Tears erupted from her face as she quickly turned to dash back to the kitchen.

The elves were on her heels, Anne not far behind as the others offered Tsami reprimanding stares.

"She didn't mean it," Aralore said, placing her arms around Helena's shoulders. "I'm sure Nichol is fine."

"She's just upset and scared, deary," Anne added. "They all are." She looked at the elves and saw the concern on their faces. "We all are."

"I know," Helena muttered, wiping her face on her sleeve. "But what if she's right? What if Nichol lies in the road?" A surge of emotion overcame her, causing her to burst into tears. "We have seen no travellers for days. What if everyone is dead?"

"Don't be silly." Yaleni reached out to Helena, wrapping her arms around the sobbing girl and her sister both. "It's winter. Travellers stay home in winter."

"Besides..." Anne moved in to join the group embrace. "We had supplies delivered just a week ago. There are people still living outside of Mountainfall."

"From the south," Helena returned.

The other three women looked at each other questioningly.

"What's that, deary?" Anne asked.

"The supplies came from the south," she clarified. "Nichol rode north. The stories of raids come from the north."

A worried expression crept upon Yaleni's face. She noticed both her sister and the innkeeper's wife reading her expression.

"I'm certain Nichol is safe," she said, tightening her hold on the others, drawing Anne into the group with one arm. "I'm sure Humphrey and the others are fine, and all this trouble has a simple solution."

———◆———

"There should be guard posts by the road's side," Nichol announced, turning around in his saddle to see Jaysh peering at the mountain peaks. "If what Ivan told me is true, there are quite a few old huts used by the military during the time before the war. There should be one around here somewhere. Some more along the way to the turn for Northwell."

"For what purpose?" Jaysh asked.

"Ivan said they were a barracks of sorts," Nichol replied, turning to look forward again. "Soldiers slept there when they weren't on duty. Otherwise, they'd be up there on the mountain tops, guarding."

"Are they close to the road's side?" Jaysh Shen-Jon questioned, looking at his friend.

"I don't think so," answered Nichol. "I've travelled this road a few times and can't recall seeing anything of the sort. Mind you, I wasn't looking for them."

"Then they probably aren't by the road's side," Jaysh returned. "They're probably farther in the forest or a pile of rotting ruin. Or both."

Nichol nodded, scanning the trees to the right and left as they trotted along the road.

"Probably," he said.

"Still," Jaysh put in, looking back to the range. "We should keep an eye out for one. Those clouds don't look too friendly."

Nichol peered to the mountains. A long band of dark, ominous cloud smothered the tall peaks.

"No, they don't."

"Some shelter might be a pleasant treat," the younger man said.

"I agree," Nichol peered into the forest to his left. Dense snow-covered pines, twisted leafless limbs of oaks and maples stretched on for as far as he could see. "We may need to seek refuge in the forest and make a shelter if we don't find one of Ivan's guard posts."

"Sun's still high," Jaysh observed. "We could ride a little harder and make some more ground before those clouds reach us."

"I think we should take whatever opportunities first present themselves," said Nichol. "We'll pick up the pace, but if we see one of these guard posts, we'll take shelter for the night there. No matter how high in the sky the sun is."

"And if we don't find one of Ivan's guard posts?" Jaysh queried.

"We make do with what we're presented with." Nichol grinned. "Or get wet."

Steigauf glared at the soldier, lying on his back, the boy standing over him with a wooden sword in his hand.

"Get up," the Pit Guard growled. "Pick up your sword and attack."

"He's just a boy," Heilig returned.

"Who knocked you on your arse," the old man barked. "Now get up and don't go easy on him."

Arnald shot the old soldier a look of concern.

"You need to learn what it feels like to be hurt, laddie," Steigauf told him harshly. "Better to do that here where your wounds can be tended to instead of out there where you'll be left to die. Now, get ready."

The boy planted his feet firmly on the ground, tightened his grasp on the practice sword, and blocked out the clatter of others sparring around him as he prepared for Heilig's attack.

The young soldier raised his sword and stepped towards Arnald, bringing the timber edge down in a chopping motion with ferocity. The boy drew his sword upwards to block the blow. His arms trembled; a shattering sensation moved from his wrists into his shoulders.

Heilig attacked again, aiming each strike towards the boy's head. Every hit against his sword sent more tremors into Arnald's arms, weakening his grasp on his sword. He fell to his knees, continuing to hold the sword over his head, blocking every attack made by the young soldier.

A look of concern spread over Heilig's face. He turned away from Arnald to face Steigauf.

"This isn't right," he complained. "The boy could be seriously hurt."

As he spoke, the boy knocked his feet out from beneath him. Heilig planted face-first onto the ground, hitting with a hard and loud thud. The wind in his lungs burst violently from his mouth and nose with a noisy grunt and streams of mucus as Arnald jammed his wooden blade against the young soldier's neck.

"Good," Steigauf said, folding his arms and nodding proudly. "You've picked this up very quickly. We need to work on your strength to help you with counterattacks."

Heilig struggled back to his feet.

"Are you all right?" Arnald asked, crouching beside the other.

The young man plonked onto his rear and held up a hand to the boy.

"I just need to rest a bit," he wheezed.

"You," the Pit Guard said, addressing Heilig, "should never turn your back on the enemy. Never."

Heilig nodded as he struggled to his feet. He bent to pick up his sword, almost losing balance before peering at Arnald.

The boy stood ready for another spar.

The young soldier took a deep breath. His lungs burned as he exhaled.

"You ready?" Steigauf asked.

Heilig nodded.

"Don't go easy on him," the old soldier told him. "He won't return the favour, as you have just seen."

"I'm ready," the young man said, tightening his grasp on his wooden sword.

Arnald prepared to attack, stepping forward with his practice sword over his head.

"Clear the way," a guard called from a tower at the far end of the training ground. The gate's two enormous timber panels opened to allow a troop wagon pulled by a single horse into the compound.

"I need help," the driver, a grit covered soldier, called.

"Come on," Steigauf called to the men as he trotted across the training ground to the wagon as it pulled up by the base of a set of steps leading into the dining hall. As he drew near, he notices blood trickling down the horse's front left leg, emitting from a wound high on the shoulder. Shallow scratches there reminded him of the marks he and Arnald saw on the table, floor, and door of the hut they had stayed in their way to Shiverwind.

He looked to the driver of the wagon, who leaned back in his seat, wincing as he moved. Steigauf's attention fell upon the dark bloodstain smeared over the backrest behind the man.

"Are you all right?" he asked, regretting his question immediately. He realised the man was not all right.

"Bastard got me on the back," the other grunted.

"Help him down," the Pit Guard commanded two men standing nearby.

"In the wagon," the driver said, as he lowered his leg over the side of the carriage. "The lieutenant's in the back."

Steigauf peered into the wagon, at the floor space between the bench seats lining both sides, to what at first looked like a pile of freshly butchered meat. Copious amounts of blood covered the decking of the wagon with the barely recognisable form of a man lying in the middle of it all.

"By the gods," a soldier whispered as another turned to vomit on the ground.

The Pit Guard stood shocked by the vision before him. He turned to see Arnald standing by his sparring partner, staring at the bloody mess.

"Johaan," Steigauf called softly. The young man stood captivated by the wagon's load. "Heilig," the old man called again, a little louder.

The soldier snapped back to reality and looked at the older warrior.

"Sir?"

"Take Arnald inside," the Pit Guard instructed. "He's seen enough."

"Yes sir," Heilig replied, taking the boy by the shoulders to lead him away to the dining hall.

A bursting cough of blood from the body caused everyone standing about to jump.

"He's alive," a soldier blurted. "How the fuck is he alive?"

"Help me get him to the infirmary," Steigauf said, reaching into the wagon to lift the man as gently as he could. "Carefully, now."

Three others aided the old man, placing their hands under the severely wounded lieutenant, cradling him against their bodies as they moved together to another door beneath the tower.

Steigauf felt his stomach tighten as he surveyed the extent of the injuries. Deep gashes crisscrossed through the man's leather breastplate into his flesh. Tear marks stretched over his face from his forehead to chin. With his right cheek gone, the old man could see the lieutenant's teeth all the way to his jaw.

As they carried him into the infirmary, the wounded man's left arm and leg flopped unnaturally. Steigauf assumed they were broken, along with many other bones throughout the lieutenant's body.

"On the table," said the physicker, an old man in a black tunic, upon seeing the men enter the room. He stood over the wounded wagon driver, who sat on a stool at the side of the room, scrutinising the man's wounds as his assistant, a young woman in an apron with a wimple over her head, wiped the blood away with a damp cloth.

As the men lowered the lieutenant onto a bench in the centre of the infirmary, Steigauf peered around the room and noted the many shelves of potions and powders in a variety of differently shaped and coloured bottles and jars.

"By the gods," said the physicker when the men stood back from the table. He turned to a soldier standing at his side. "I need water. Fetch me a fresh bucket." The soldier stared, dumbfounded. "From the well," the old surgeon clarified grumpily.

"Easy on him," Steigauf said as the soldier hurried from the room. "This is the first time any of them have seen blood like this."

"Mine too," the physicker replied. "But if we don't act quickly, it might be too late for this man. It may be too late already. Who is he?"

"Lieutenant Gerard," the wagon driver reported, groaning as the young woman continued cleaning his wound.

Steigauf saw teeth marks on the man's right shoulder, reaching over both front and back, and four long scratches stretching across from his spine to his left side under his armpit.

"What happened?" said a voice from the doorway. Steigauf turned to see Captain Piers Kraayen entering the room. "Where are the rest of the men?"

"Dead, sir," the wounded driver replied.

"Dead?" the captain asked. "All of them?"

"All except myself and the lieutenant," the driver reported.

"What's your name, soldier?" Kraayen queried, moving past Steigauf to stand near the driver, looking at the wounds the young woman cleaned.

"Callum Immeril, sir," the other answered.

"Callum," Kraayen repeated. He looked at the young woman. "How are his wounds?"

"They are deep, my lord," she told him. "But they will heal."

Kraayen nodded thoughtfully.

"His wounds will heal," the physicker put in. "But this one is beyond my help."

The captain turned to the table in the middle of the room. His eyes fell immediately to the bloodied body.

"You have yet to remove his breastplate," Kraayen observed.

"I'm afraid to," the other replied. "It may be what holds him together. His wounds are extensive, and he has lost a great deal of blood. It's a miracle from the gods he's still alive."

Steigauf approached the Immeril. "What happened, son?"

"We went north yesterday," the other answered, wincing as the young woman wiped across the scratch marks over his back. "We went to investigate a report of a man-wolf sighting."

"I ordered them to go after what you told me about what you saw at the hut," Kraayen said to the Pit Guard.

"I gathered." Steigauf pointed to the scratches on the soldier's back. "Those are the same marks the boy and I saw."

The captain inhaled slowly.

"Tell me what happened," he instructed Immeril.

"We found the hut," he started. "The lieutenant went inside and found the marks exactly where you said they were, sir. The rest of us searched the surroundings and found more on trees. Janryc, one of the soldiers, found some tracks a little further north, leading across the road and into the forest. We followed them a short way before we were attacked. It took Janryc first. I tried to kill it, but it was too strong and too fast. It bit me and threw me against a tree. I saw the lieutenant leading others on horses to attack, but I must have passed out. When I woke, everyone was dead. Lieutenant Gerard was the only one still alive. I got him onto the troop wagon and drove through the night to get him back here."

"What of the beast that attacked you?" Steigauf asked. "Is it dead?"

"The only dead beasts I saw were most of the horses torn to pieces and crows picking at the bodies," Immeril answered. "I didn't want to stay to find out if that thing still lives or not."

The Pit Guard turned to the captain, looking him squarely in the eye.

"We have a serious problem," he said. "Can we talk outside?"

Kraayen nodded.

"Outside, lads," the captain ordered the other soldiers before turning to the physicker. "Do your best to ease his pain."

"The poor man isn't conscious at the moment," the other replied. "I think keeping him in that state until he passes is the best thing for him."

"Do what you must," Kraayen said as he followed Steigauf out of the room.

The Pit Guard crossed the training ground towards the troop.

"I want you to all go into the dining hall and wait for me," he ordered them.

"What's happening?" one of them asked. He pointed towards the infirmary. "What happened to them?"

"You'll be told what you need to know when I'm ready to tell you," Steigauf replied. "Now, go into the dining hall and wait for me there."

The men complied, moving up the steps into the room. Some did so hesitantly, looking to the door leading into the infirmary and back to the captain and the Pit Guard before entering the dining hall.

"The serious problem you wanted to speak of," Kraayen said after the last of the men disappeared from view. "What is it?"

"The man-wolf may still be alive," Steigauf replied. "And now he has a taste for the blood of men."

"We'll need to send another patrol," the captain said. "More archers than swordsmen. Then they can kill it from a distance."

"I don't think that would be wise," the other told him.

"What do you suggest?"

"Close the road," said Steigauf. "Divert all north-bound travellers to the Long Spine Road. Send riders to Driradia to inform the magistrate there of the situation, with instructions to close the coastal road from their end."

"What about the people who live along the coastal road?" Kraayen queried. "How do we keep them safe?"

"The boy's village is the closest to Shiverwind and the largest along the road," the Pit Guard said. "There aren't many others between there and Driradia, and they're not much more than small fishing communes much further to the north. This man-wolf seems to be keeping to the area near the hut. I think the other people along the coastal road will be safe for now."

"I can't believe Gerard and his men are..." the captain turned to look at the infirmary door.

"Which brings me to another serious problem," the old man frowned, following other's gaze. "You've got a man-wolf in there. Perhaps two."

Kraayen turned to Steigauf.

"What do you mean?"

Steigauf pursed his lips and sighed.

"The young man," he started. "Immeril. He's been bitten on his shoulder. He'll turn at the next full moon. And Gerard should be dead. I think he's been bitten as well. His wounds are many and I couldn't see any distinct bites, but I think he might have been. How else is it he still lives?"

"What do I do?" Kraayen asked. "I can't just murder them."

"They'll murder you and everyone in Shiverwind if you let them live," the Pit Guard told him.

Kraayen scratched his beard, sauntering towards the blood-soaked wagon as he considered Steigauf's words.

"I'll need to think about this some more," he said, looking at the infirmary door again. "In the meantime, I need to organise another party north to find this creature."

"I'll go," Steigauf said. "Give me some seasoned archers, and my boys, and I'll go."

"I sent ten cavalrymen and five infantrymen," Kraayen returned. "What makes you think you and these boys can defeat this creature?"

"Your cavalry and infantry went to investigate," Steigauf explained. "My boys and I will go to hunt and kill."

Chapter Six

———◆◇◆———

THE TROOP SET OFF early. It was still dark, and the stars twinkled in the sky and the moon sat low in the western sky. Arnald, rugged up in his cloak, looked to the cloth wrapped around his forearm, giving thought to Gertrude and how he now set out to possibly face his own death. His stomach tightened into a ball of nerves as the sound of excited horses snorted behind him as the troops gathered in two lines behind him and the Pit Guard.

"I know what you meant, laddie," Steigauf told him. "We'll see how we fare. I'd rather get there during daylight than set up camp in the dark."

Turning in his saddle, he counted twenty riders. All of them were unskilled, untrained, unknowing of how to fight, except for what Steigauf had shown them. None had seen battle.

After seeing the state of Lieutenant Gerard lying in the troop wagon, and hearing that all his men except for one other were dead, Arnald wondered if twenty men would be enough. He looked at the bloodstained cloth again before rolling his cloak back down to cover his arm.

"Perhaps I'll see you soon, Gertrude," he whispered.

"What's that?" the Pit Guard asked, turning to face the boy.

"Nothing." Arnald shook his head.

The old man mumbled something and looked at the wolf standing beside Arnald's horse.

"Are you ready, girl?"

The wolf licked her lips, keeping her eyes on the barred gates of the compound.

"Try to be safe out there, Osman," Kraayen called from the top of the steps leading to the dining hall. "Bring everyone back."

"Eight archers and twelve infantrymen on horseback. And not one of them has seen battle." The Pit Guard smiled. "I'll do my best, Piers."

"Open the gates," Kraayen called.

Two guards lifted the bar from the gate and swung the panels open.

Arnald's heart drummed in his ears. His breath came in quick gasps.

"Let's go," Steigauf called, urging his steed forward. The boy followed suit, turning to see Heilig behind him with his hood over his head. Quick puffs of vapour escaped the young soldier as they rode out of the compound. Glancing about, he saw fear in many faces of those riding in the two lines behind him.

He watched the gates slowly close behind the troop. A loud clunk signalled the bar dropping in place, locking them out of the compound, committing them to their mission.

Turning to look forward, Arnald felt a growing sense of discomfort, knowing the soldiers feared this expedition as much as he did.

The wolf offered a soft whine as she looked up at him, as if sensing his concern. He tried to bury his feelings as they rode through the empty streets of Shiverwind, but they only intensified as they neared the edge of the township.

"Come on," Steigauf called, nudging his heels into his horse's sides to increase speed to a trot. The troop urged their horses to follow their commander. Before long, they were out of Shiverwind's streets and heading north on the coastal road. "We should reach the hut by mid-afternoon, if we time this right."

"Will we rest the horses at any point?" a soldier behind Heilig asked.

"We just set out and you already want to stop," the Pit Guard growled playfully.

"I just meant..."

Jaysh Shen-Jon cowered beneath his canvas sheet, lying on his bedroll with the covers pulled over his head. Pelting rain battered so noisily against the canvas he could barely hear Nichol calling him.

"We need to move on," the brawny man hollered over the din, loading his equipment back onto his horse.

Jaysh flipped his covers to expose his head. The rain instantly soaked his face and hair. He pointed to the crumbling stones forming a partial corner and a stone pipe. A small part of the roof stretched over him, but it proved useless as the wind forced the deluge to fall at a sideways angle.

"Some great shelter these guard posts," he barked. "We should have stayed under a tree."

"It's not my fault," Nichol replied.

"I barely slept a wink thanks to this." He gestured around him with an open palm to the weather as he pulled his hood over his head with his other hand.

"At least the lightning and thunder has moved on," Nichol said.

"Thank the gods," Jaysh returned, carefully rolling his bedding beneath the canvas to keep the inner layers dry. "I almost shat myself, many times over. I swear it struck the ground right by my head."

"Well," said Nichol as he pulled a roll of bread from a saddlebag. "We survived, and now we need to move on."

"All right." Jaysh wrapped the canvas around the bedding, tying it together with a strap. "No need to push."

Nichol held his hands up, feigning surrender as Jaysh passed him to load his horse. The steed moved nervously, jumping, and turning away from him as he placed the bedroll on the animal's back.

"Stand still, you bitch," he growled.

"Are you going to be this grumpy all day?" Nichol asked, climbing into his saddle.

Jaysh settled the horse and strapped the bedroll in place before offering his companion an angry glare.

"Yes," he told Nichol. "All fucking day."

Nichol chuckled, trying to stifle his response by turning his face away.

"All right," he said. "Maybe things will brighten up. This weather can't remain. It'll pass."

"It's set in," Jaysh returned as he mounted his steed. "It poured all night. It's still pouring. This is our life now."

Nichol laughed again.

"You ready?" he asked before biting off a mouthful of bread.

"The sun can't even get through this mess," Jaysh complained, looking to the thick clouds above and the drab landscape around them. He urged his horse forward. "Let's go. Daylight is wasting away somewhere."

Before long, the two riders trotted along the roadside by side, the ground squelching beneath the hooves of their mounts. The pure, white snow turned to slush, caking the horses' lower limbs in mud.

I wonder why there aren't any other villages out here," Jaysh said suddenly, looking at the trees on their left. "I mean, this forest stretches all across Kedielewen from east to west and from The Dragon's Teeth to Northwell and Port Coldspring, right?"

"It's a lot of forest," Nichol admitted, noticing the other man's attitude change.

"Why have none settled there?" he asked. "Surely there are plenty of animals to hunt, plenty of timber for building, and lots of land to farm if you clear some away. It makes no sense."

"The Witch Queen," replied Nichol.

They rode a little farther in silence. Jaysh waited for more information until his patience grew thin.

"Well?" he said. "What about the Witch Queen?"

"Hmm?" Nichol turned. "Sorry. I thought you knew the stories."

"Obviously not," said Jaysh.

"So," Nichol began. "During the War of Six, the Witch Queen, Akasha Miroslava—"

"I know her name," Jaysh interjected. He pointed to the forest. "Just tell me why no one lives in this."

"All right. She sent part of her forces into these lands. The forest was swarming with man-wolves, men infested with skull-worms and other dark creatures from the lands of Legilawen and Adaerwen. There once were people living in the forest. Most of them were isolated farmers and a few small communities. The Witch Queen's forces wiped them out. If they weren't eaten, they put their heads on pikes along the roadside from

Shiverwind to Northwell."

"Just like that poor bastard outside The Lazy Traveller," Jaysh replied.

"Exactly like that," Nichol returned. "So, the reason nobody lives in the forest is that many still believe there are still some of the Witch Queen's forces hiding in there."

Jaysh considered this as they rode some more, peering into the woodlands. He looked at the spaces between the trees where dark, ominous shadows lurked.

"Do you think raiders killed that man, as the others believe?" Jaysh queried, keeping his gaze on the forest.

"I don't know what left that head outside The Lazy Traveller," Nichol answered. "But it wasn't raiders."

Yaleni placed a silver strainer over her cup before pouring the tea from the pot. Streaming steam billowed from the surface as she took the strainer away.

"What's in this mixture?" Aralore asked her sister as she passed through the door to her bedroom, into their living area. It was a little room with a small iron stove set in one corner, a bench against the wall, a table with two chairs and a couple of rocking chairs on a sheepskin rug, and a settee by a window.

"Just some mint," Yaleni replied, seeing the bow and quiver in Aralore's hands. "Nothing out of the ordinary. What's this?"

"I'm going into the forest to find the missing men," she replied. "I might do a little hunting. Some rabbit or deer might be a nice change."

"You're sick of my cooking?"

"No." Aralore shook her head. "You'll be cooking my rabbit or deer when I bring it back. I'm just a bit tired of lamb and beef. It's all we eat."

"It's all Kain Drovo has," Yaleni replied.

"Shelba Drovo," the other corrected. "If we can't find Kain, she'll have to tend to the livestock on her own. And they have chickens too."

"We could buy a chicken," the silver-haired elf offered.

"I'm tired of chicken," Aralore said. She looked at the steaming cup of tea. "Smells good."

"Would you like one?"

"No," the blonde elf answered. "I want to be back well before dusk. I'd best go now."

"The sun is barely in the sky!" Yaleni laughed. "And you're already concerned with dusk?"

"The time goes quickly when you're having fun," her sister said, hoisting her quiver onto her back and pulling her crimson hood over her head. She placed her hand on the doorknob and paused. "Best buy that chicken, just in case."

Yaleni smiled.

"I will," she replied. "Good luck and be careful."

Aralore closed the door behind her and started down the road towards The Lazy Traveller, a little farther along the way. The wind felt cold against her cheeks as snow drifted gently, almost lingering in the air, so she pulled her scarf over her mouth and nose.

"Aralore," a familiar voice called from behind her. She turned to see Helena trotting towards her. "Where are you off to?"

"I thought I'd take a look in the forest for the men," she told the other.

Helena looked at the bow and quiver.

"Are you expecting trouble?"

The elf shrugged. "Best to be safe."

They continued towards the tavern, walking side-by-side.

"Have you any idea where to start?" asked Helena.

Aralore pointed to the tree line at the top of the rise across the road from the tavern's front door.

"I thought I'd start there and go to your hut," she replied. "From there, I might head in the direction of the mountains before circling around to follow the stream back to the bridge down the road there."

The elf gestured to a wooden crossing to the south of their position. Helena kept her gaze on the forest as they walked.

"Aren't you afraid of what might be in there?" she questioned.

"You went in there on your own," said Aralore.

"That was before everyone vanished," Helena replied. "I'm afraid."

"I'm armed," Aralore pointed out.

They paused outside The Lazy Traveller.

"Just be extra cautious," the young woman implored.

"Don't fret," Aralore told her. "I'm an elf. Whatever lives in there must be blessed with exceeding trickery to best an elf."

"I hope so," Helena said, moving towards The Lazy Traveller's door.

Aralore waved and crossed the road, leaving Helena at the tavern.

As she entered the woods, she switched to the mindset of a hunter, loading an arrow on the string of her bow as she scanned the area before her. She made each step deliberately, mindfully, without making a sound. Searching for tracks, marks or signs of any kind that might show the way to her missing friends, she moved stealthily into the woodland.

Deeper and deeper, she went, following a path of sorts that Helena had made over time traversing from her hut to the township and back. Snow covered the track now, leaving only a long indentation on the otherwise smooth surface for most of the way, otherwise forcing Aralore to retrace the path from memory.

Eventually, she came to a series of knolls. The path wound its way between them, snaking between the mounds to a small hollow where Helena's tiny hovel stood.

The elf admired the little hut, stopping to take in the scene. Constructed from logs, the cabin had two tiny square windows covered by timber shutters and a small wooden panel door. Jutting from the snow-covered steep apex roof, a stone chimney emitted light smoke into the cold air.

Smoke?

Aralore tensed.

She moved warily to the hut, focusing her attention on the door.

"Who's in there?" she called, pulling back on the bowstring. "Show yourself."

Not waiting for an answer, she stepped closer to the cabin. Closer. Closer.

"Show yourself," she called again, now within arm's reach of the door.

Not hearing a reply, and with her inquisitiveness increasing with each breath she made, she relaxed the bowstring and reached for the door latch.

Slowly, she opened the door with a long creak, revealing a dark room lit only by the low flames in the fireplace to the side of the room. Besides the usual trappings, the room appeared empty. It held a table and chairs, an empty bed and not much else.

Aralore pushed the door open wide to step inside.

"Elf," a raspy, mucous saturated voice breathed into her ear.

She turned abruptly to stare into the face of a grotesque figure; twisted, furrowed, and vile. Her heart seemed to stop and burst from her chest at the same time as she locked her gaze on the other's black, hollow eyes.

The figure lifted a closed hand and extended her gnarled fingers to expose a small mass of brown powder. With a puff from the creature's mouth, the powder blasted into Aralore's face, entering her nostrils.

A sense of suffocation overwhelmed the elf.

She gasped desperately for air as she crumpled to the ground.

Letting go of the bow, she turned onto her stomach and clawed at the ground, trying to scream as the world around her spun and swirled.

The figure suddenly gripped the elf's scalp, squeezing tighter and tighter before pulling the crimson hood away from the elf's head.

Aralore tried to scramble away on all fours, only to be flipped onto her back before the creature dropped onto her waist, pinning her to the ground.

Slowly, the figure leaned closer to the elf's face, moving its twisted hands to touch Aralore's cheeks gently before running its tongue over the elf's lips.

She tried to protest, wanting to turn her head or strike back, but she couldn't move.

The creature lowered its face to Aralore's ear.

"Javanakhan," it murmured.

Chapter Seven

———◦◦◦———

THE WEATHER EASED DURING the day. Instead of rain, the weather now offered a soft drift of snow as the two riders approached the intersection, which split in three directions; south, north and west. A tall, thick post stood to the eastern side of the crossing, topped with a crossbeam with an empty gibbet cage swinging on chains from each end.

"What's that?" Jaysh queried.

"They used to stick criminals in those and leave them to rot," Nichol answered. "They thought it might deter others from a life of delinquency."

"Did it?" the younger man asked.

"No," said Nichol, looking at the post.

Jaysh stared at the cages, listening to the soft squeaking of the chains as the breeze pushed the gibbets, causing them to sway gently.

"Why are they still here?" he inquired. "Surely they don't use them anymore."

"The cages, no," Nichol replied, gesturing to the thick shaft. "But the post points us towards our destination."

It was only then that Jaysh noticed the three timber markers jutting from the upright beam. Weather and time had been unkind to the signage, making it difficult to read the words engraved on the panels. One pointed south with the word *ASALETHWEN* carved into its surface. Directed to the north, another bore the word *COLDWOLF*. The last signalled to the west with the engraving of *NORTHWELL*.

"Asalethwen," Jaysh muttered. "Not Mountainfall."

"The sign is older than Mountainfall, my friend," Nichol explained.

"Then it should be corrected."

"I agree," the other said, turning his horse left to follow the road to Northwell. "Shadowfort is the next closest point of destination after Mountainfall. It should be stencilled up there instead of naming the whole of the Southerlands."

The younger rider looked at the strange road sign as he followed his friend.

"Perhaps the makers of that thing didn't know the names of places beyond The Dragon's Teeth," he suggested. "Perhaps they simply enjoyed hanging bodies out to rot."

"Everyone who ever existed knew of Shadowfort," said Nichol. "Even before the War of Six, it was a mighty stronghold. No, I think the men of these lands once bore some animosity towards outsiders. As far as they were concerned, anything beyond The Dragon's Teeth, The Great Northern Barrier and the Long Spine Mountains weren't worth knowing about. That's what I think, anyway."

Considering the other's words, Jaysh turned in his saddle to take another look at the gibbet post. The empty cages rocked back and forward slowly as the chains continued to squeak softly.

"It must have been a horrible way to go," he said. "Starving away to nothing."

"I couldn't think of many other ways more saddening," Nichol said, keeping his eyes forward. "Left to nothing but your own thoughts on what you did to be put in the cage, the people you hurt, the ones you loved. Then, the long hours without food, water, privacy. The gut pains of hunger, the thirst, and how long do you wait before you relieve yourself publicly? And when you do, you've taken your first step from being a man to something else, a creature. I suppose that's when madness sets in, and you can only wish for death to come. If it were me in one of those contraptions, I'd beg every passer-by to set me free or kill me quickly."

Jaysh frowned reflectively and nodded.

"So," he uttered, a smirk growing on his face. "You've given this some thought, then?"

"Fuck off," Nichol retorted with a smile. He looked at the sun sinking towards the horizon ahead of them. "We should set up camp soon."

———◄○►———

Her eyelids felt heavy, almost as if they were stuck in place and needed prying open. The muscles in her arms and back ached tremendously. As she regained consciousness, she realised she hung from the rafters in Helena's hut, her hands bound with rope over one of the timber beams. Her toes swung inches from the floor.

"Elf," it whispered to her.

She turned her head to see the form of a disrobed young woman silhouetted by the light emitting from the fireplace. Her vision remained blurry; the world continued to swirl inside her head.

"Who are you?" Aralore said, her voice barely a whisper.

"We are," the other replied, slinking slowly across the floor to the elf's feet. She touched Aralore's bare ankles gently with her fingers before sliding her hands up to her prisoner's exposed thighs. It was then, the elf realised that the creature had removed her clothes before hoisting her up.

The figure slowly stood, running her tongue in a line over Aralore's stomach, between her breasts, stopping at her neck. "We are, we are, we are," she whispered, her warm breath brushing the elf's face.

Aralore trembled with fear as she tried to see the woman, to determine any discernible features. The deep shadows hid her from the elf's failing sight. The colour of her hair, the tone of her skin, remained imperceptible.

"Where is the other one?" she questioned.

"Other one," the figure wheezed, slipping behind Aralore, touching her fingertips to the elf's spine. Aralore felt an uncomfortable tingle shiver to her neck.

"The old woman?" Aralore pressed, her voice trembling slightly. "Where is she?"

"We are here," the woman answered, wrapping her arms around her prisoner's waist. She pressed her cheek to Aralore's back. "We are always here."

The elf let out a soft cry of despair.

"This is my friend's house," she said, trying to sound confident, knowing she didn't. "You shouldn't be here."

"Friend's house," the other hissed, slinking around the elf, moving across the floor to the table by the fireplace.

Aralore saw her cloak draped over one chair, her tunic and trousers over another, and her boots on the floor between them by the fireplace.

This makes no sense, she considered. Setting her clothes like so would be something she would do to dry them if they were damp.

"What do you intend to do with me?" the elf inquired, tears streaming down her face, believing she already knew the answer to her question.

The figure stood with her back to the elf, lifted a long knife from the table and carved into something in front of her that Aralore could not see.

The woman lifted something, dangling a long, wet strip between her thumb and fingers as she tilted her head back and opened her mouth. The elf could tell it was meat of some sort. Slowly, the woman lowered the moist strip of flesh past her lips before turning to face Aralore again. Gripping the knife tightly, she moved aside, taking something else from the table in her other hand.

At that moment, Aralore wished her sight hadn't returned.

She saw a severed leg, cut neatly high on the thigh, sitting in the middle of the table. Its knee sat bent slightly and the toes cast shadows across the table's surface as the flames in the fireplace danced.

"By the gods," the elf gasped. Her gaze quickly turned to the approaching figure.

The woman held an upturned fist to Aralore's face.

"What are you going to do to me?" the elf said, crying.

The woman opened her fingers and blew across her palm, sending a cloud of powder into the elf's face.

The room swam and swirled as the woman cackled.

Shadows churned and spiralled, growing around Aralore as the other pressed her lips to the elf's ear.

"Javanakhan," she whispered.

Aralore's eyes grew heavy as her head swirled and darkness swept upon her again.

The troop reached the little hut by the side of the road as the sun dropped below the horizon. With enough light left in the sky, the men set tents and equipment in place as near to the cabin as they could.

"Make the fires high and keep them burning all night," the Pit Guard commanded as he approached the cabin with his bedroll in his arms. "I want two teams of seven and one team of six. Three archers and four infantrymen in each team."

"Sir?" one archer queried as he raised his hand.

"What is it?" Steigauf asked, turning to face the man.

"We archers only number eight altogether," the man explained. "We can't divide into three teams the way you ordered."

"Correct," the old warrior agreed, addressing the entire troop, not just the inquisitive archer. "One team will have two archers instead of three, by my calculations. So, as I said, two teams of seven and one of six. Report to me when you've organised yourselves."

Steigauf entered the structure with the boy and the wolf. Arnald rested on his knees to lay his bedroll on the floor as the old man placed his bedding on the timber bed by the wall. The boy stopped and looked at the Pit Guard.

"You didn't place me in a team for the watch," he said. "I should be in one of the teams. I'm training with them, so I should be on watch with them. Shouldn't I?"

"You are," the other replied, sitting on the bed. "You and I will join the shift before sunrise."

"So, there's to be no hunting for the man-wolf tonight?"

"Absolutely not," he answered. "We just travelled all day. We all need some rest. My hope is that the fires will deter the man-wolf from approaching and allow us some well-earned sleep. We'll start our search tomorrow."

Arnald finished straightening out his bedroll in time for the wolf to drop onto it.

"And where do I sleep?" he asked the animal. She responded by licking him across the face before lowering her head onto her paws.

"She'll move for you when you want to get beneath the covers," Steigauf told him. "Besides, she'll be back on her feet when we get something from our supplies to eat."

With a nod, Arnald rubbed the wolf's neck, curling his fingers through her soft fur.

"I'm pretty hungry now," the boy said.

"Me too," the old man admitted, rising to his feet. "You get yourself something to eat. I'm going to collect some wood for the stove and light her up."

The boy stood up and started for the door. As Steigauf predicted, the wolf jumped up and followed Arnald outside. The Pit Guard was on her heels, moving outdoors to gather kindling for the stove, to be met with all twenty men standing in three groups beside the hut.

"All organised, sir," Heilig reported. He gestured to the gathered soldiers. "Two groups of seven and one of six."

"Good," Steigauf replied, pointing to a group of seven. "First group takes first watch for three hours." He gestured to the next group of seven. "Second group takes watch for the next three hours and the third group watches for the final three hours. I'll join you on the third watch," he said to Heilig.

"Yessir," the young soldier replied.

"First watch begins as soon as you've finished eating," the Pit Guard said. "And eating begins now."

With that, the men dispersed to light fires and prepare meals from the supplies in their saddlebags.

It wasn't long before the veil of night covered the sky and the watchers moved to the edge of the encampment, spreading around the perimeter. The rest of the troop retired to their tents as Arnald, Steigauf and the wolf shut the door of the cabin to recline on their bedding.

Arnald turned on his side to face the stove, watching the flames dance in the little furnace as the wolf pressed herself against his back. His thoughts returned to his village as he touched the cloth wrapped around his forearm.

"Osman, are you awake?" he asked after some time.

"Yes," the Pit Guard replied. His voice sounded weary.

"What does *Müqin sì* mean?"

Steigauf let out a soft sigh.

"I don't think it's wise to dwell on such things, laddie," he said.

"That man said those words to my brother," Arnald said. "Then, Jörgen died. It was the last words my brother heard. I'd like to know."

"Mother dead," the Pit Guard replied. "That's the closest I can translate into the common tongue."

Arnald felt a tear roll down his cheek.

"Thank you," he replied, the tremor in his voice exposing his emotion.

Steigauf frowned, rolling on his side to look at the boy. The wolf obscured Arnald from his sight.

"But it wasn't the last words your brother heard," the Pit Guard said. "Remember. You told me he said one more thing before he died. He heard his own words. What were they?"

"Fuck you all." Arnald sobbed softly.

"I didn't quite hear," Steigauf pressed.

"Fuck you all!" the boy said louder.

"They're the words," the old soldier said. "They're the only words that matter when you face an enemy."

Arnald wiped his eyes and peered at the flames.

"Close your eyes, boy," the Pit Guard commanded. "Try to get some sleep."

Doing as instructed, he shut his eyes and tried to empty his thoughts. Focusing on the wolf's breathing and the crackling of fire in the stove, Arnald felt himself drifting away.

For a moment, the boy felt at ease, peaceful and calm.

He felt as if he floated on air between the states of reality and a dream.

Part of him watched his brother fight bravely against the raiders while another part sat with Gertrude on the pier.

The pier.

He held Gertrude's hand, interlacing his fingers with hers, stealing kisses when he thought no one watched them.

He so wanted to stay here, with her on the pier.

A sudden shake of the shoulders brought him back to the cabin.

"Time to get up, laddie," Steigauf said, standing over him.

"I just fell asleep," he answered, wiping the sleep from his eyes.

"Afraid not. You've been asleep for some time; as have I," the old soldier replied, dressing in his armour. "You'll need your sword, quiver, and bow."

"I can't shoot a bow," the boy replied, standing to dress. The wolf stood, crossed the floor and plonked herself in front of the stove.

"You shoot better than half of those men out there," Steigauf replied.

"That's not saying much for them." Arnald sat on a chair to put his boots on.

"That's true," the Pit Guard said. "But you're right. You need a little more practice."

"A lot more practice," the boy corrected, standing to strap his mother's sword to his waist.

Steigauf moved his arms, checking he'd fixed everything in place, that he could move unobstructed, before reaching for his sword leaning against the wall beside the bed. When he had it buckled on his waist, he looked to Arnald. The boy had his quiver and bow slung over his cloak.

"You ready?" the old man asked.

"Some more sleep would be nice," he answered.

"Agreed," the old man said. "But duty calls. Come on."

With that, he opened the door and stepped outside. Arnald followed, with the wolf in tow. They crossed the ground, circling the tents and campfires to a cluster of men gathered nearer to the road.

"Any place you'd like us, sir?" asked Heilig as the Pit Guard drew near.

"One archer to the north by the road." Steigauf pointed. "The other to the south. The boy and I will stay here. The rest of you send the second watch to bed and take their positions."

With that, the men disbanded to fulfil their roles.

Arnald folded his arms across his chest as he peered at the stars as he wished to be back in his bedroll.

"Now comes the boring part," the old man whispered. "Waiting for the sun to rise."

"How long for that to happen?" Arnald questioned.

Steigauf turned to look across the cove. The dark sky glared back at him, showing no sign of approaching light.

"Not any time soon," the soldier answered. He pulled his cloak around his armour. "Always colder at night without clouds in the sky. Have you ever noticed that?"

"No," the boy replied. "I'm usually tucked up in my bedding."

Steigauf smiled as the wolf positioned herself on the road in front of Arnald. She turned to look at the forest across the way, a little to the north.

"Have you had to do this before?" the boy asked.

"Night watch?" the soldier queried.

Arnald nodded.

"Not since the war," Steigauf answered. "Everyone had to do their share of watch duty back then. Especially on the field camps near Shadowfort. I'd say your father and uncle would have seen their fair share of night duty during their time out there."

"I don't know," the boy replied. "My father and uncle talked little about it. Except when Baba told us stories."

"Stories?" the Pit Guard asked. "Stories of battle?"

"Not really," Arnald said. "More about the people in the battles. I think he left the bad parts out, so Jörgen and I didn't get frightened before bed."

"He told you about the man-wolves and the skull-worms, but not what they truly did to those on the battlefield?"

"No," the boy answered.

"He told you about Lycia and Elene and how they fell into the mountain, though?"

Arnald nodded, watching the wolf stare off into the distance, slowly cocking her head.

"Neophytes, he called them."

"That's a big word," Steigauf said, looking southward to where an archer stood watch. "That's probably enough, then. I'll say this much, Arnald. The real thing is always far worse than any story, no matter how gruesome the details."

"He told me of the chase after the elf king and that he and my uncle watched the hanging," the boy added.

"And I told you I was there as well," the Pit Guard replied with a shake of his head. "I must have set eyes on your father and uncle at some time.

There were a lot of us there on that day. But, if he watched Amalith swing from that rope, we must have been within eyeshot of each other."

The wolf emitted a soft growl.

Both man and boy looked at her curiously.

"What is it, girl?" Steigauf asked, leaning over to rub her neck.

She set her hackles on edge and bared her teeth, intensifying her snarl.

A sudden, bloodcurdling cry burst from the forest, sending a chill along Arnald's spine. The cry turned into a long howl, much deeper and more monstrous than any wolf the boy had heard before.

Arnald hand reached for the hilt of his sword. He didn't need to ask the Pit Guard what made the terrifying sound. The howl echoed on and on as a tight ball formed in Arnald's gut.

Steigauf pulled his sword free and glared to the woods across the way, just to their north.

A towering, dark shadow emerged from the tree line.

It flexed its claws on its forelimbs, leering towards the camp with vivid, yellow eyes.

Arnald felt his legs quiver and his arms shake as he stared transfixed at the most terrifying creature he ever laid his eyes upon.

The man-wolf.

Chapter Eight

———◆◇◆———

"I SUPPOSE WE WON'T need to go hunting today, after all," Steigauf uttered, glancing at the boy beside him.

Arnald gripped the hilt of his sheathed sword nervously, fixing his stare on the monster near the edge of the woods. It lowered itself onto all four limbs, appearing much like a wolf as it slunk along the tree line.

"Get your bow ready, Arnald," the old man said. "You really don't want that thing getting close enough for you to engage it with your sword." He turned briefly to face the camp. "Watchers, wake the company. We need all hands. Archers, shoot that bastard down."

The archer to the north, being the closest to the man-wolf, didn't hesitate. He fired his first two arrows in haste, sending them into the forest behind the creature. The third struck the beast on the leg.

The man-wolf appeared undeterred, picking up its pace a little to glide closer to the roadside. It glared at the archer with its yellow eyes, baring its teeth in a wide snarl.

The second archer bolted past Steigauf and Arnald, loading an arrow onto the string as he ran.

"I need all archers now," the Pit Guard hollered.

"Coming, sir," called a half-dressed man, wearing only his trousers and boots as he sprinted over the snow with his bow in his hand and quiver on his back. Like the second archer, he loaded his weapon on the run.

"Coming, sir," another shouted, fully clothed and following the shirtless man.

The four bowmen sent a small barrage of bolts to the man-wolf. Shafts stuck into the creature's shoulders and back. The man-wolf yelped when a few arrows hit deep into its flesh.

The she-wolf stepped forward, edging towards the monster. Her lips curled over her teeth.

"Not yet, girl." Steigauf held out a hand to her.

She licked her lips, looking at the old man before returning her gaze to the man-wolf. The Pit Guard could see her eagerness to attack in her stance and the urgency to kill the intruder in her stare.

"Where are the rest of my archers?" he called.

"Sir," one of them shouted as the remaining four bowmen burst from their tent to hurry across the campground to their comrades.

The man-wolf lifted its arm to block arrows from striking its head, only to have several bolts smack into the forelimb.

It glanced back to the forest, turning away from the archers.

"I think it's about to run," Steigauf called before looking at Arnald. "Load your bow, laddie."

Arnald, still fixated on the beast, hearing his own heartbeat rapidly thundering in his ears, suddenly snapped back to reality.

"Load my bow," he muttered, reaching over his shoulder for an arrow to load onto the bowstring.

"Take aim," the Pit Guard instructed. "Take your time."

The boy pulled the string back as far and hard as he could.

"Take your time," the old warrior repeated. "Steady your breathing."

Arnald closed his eyes and tried to silence his heart, still thudding loudly in his head.

Calm yourself, he told himself.

Opening his eyes, he saw the man-wolf turn and charge towards the archers. It lunged over the road, tackling the shirtless bowmen to the ground.

A fine spray of blood exploded from the man as the creature bit into his neck and tore his back wide open.

Arnald felt a tight knot form in his stomach as he let his arrow fly.

It zipped through the air at great speed only to fly a little wide of its intended target, sticking into the ground a short distance behind the monster.

Twelve infantrymen charged in, swords raised, to defend the archers against the creature.

The man-wolf flung the shirtless man onto the road before tearing into another bowman with its long claws.

A swordsman stuck the creature deep in the side, to which the beast responded with an ear-piercing yowl as it gripped the soldier's sword hand with its claw. It gave a tug, tearing the infantryman's arm away from his shoulder.

The soldier screamed, falling to the ground. Arnald looked on, stunned at the sight of the swordsman's arm flailing about in the man-wolf's grasp.

Another's blade pierced the creature in the back. It turned, hitting the attacker with a backhand strike. The swordsman lifted from the ground to smack hard into a tree, knocking the wind out of him.

Surrounded by infantrymen on all sides, the man-wolf roared angrily as it searched frantically for a way out. It swung its forelimb claws wildly at the men.

"Cut it down," Steigauf shouted. "Cut it down."

The men hacked and chopped at the creature. Several blows hit the beast but didn't slash deep enough to cause substantial damage. It yelped, growled, and roared in response as it lashed out, snapped its jaws and lunged at the soldiers.

Finally, Heilig buried his sword deep into the monster's back. It gave a terrifying howl as it reached over its shoulder, attempting to pull the blade from its back, but the sword stuck in place just out of reach.

The man-wolf lifted Heilig by the neck and threw him across the road, thus opening the surrounding circle of men to offer a way of escape.

"No," Arnald cried upon seeing his friend skid across the ground to land in a heap.

The beast leaped away from the other soldiers towards the woods.

"Girl," Steigauf uttered, signalling the wolf to dash towards the creature. She closed the ground quickly as the archers took to firing bolts at the man-wolf again.

"Hold your fire," the Pit Guard yelled, as the wolf vaulted onto the monster, sinking her teeth into its neck. She shook her head violently, tearing fur, skin, and tissue open.

The beast fell hard to the ground, allowing the wolf to reposition herself on his back, out of the man-wolf's reach.

Shaking her head again, she widened the wound, spilling a thick stream of blood over her muzzle and onto the ground.

"Get in there," Steigauf called to the soldiers, running after the wolf with his sword in his hands. "Kill this thing."

Arnald sprinted to Heilig's side, dropping to his knees to examine the young soldier.

"Johaan," the boy called, reaching to touch the other's shoulder.

"I'm fine," Heilig wheezed. "Just got the wind knocked out of me."

The soldier rolled onto his side to watch the other warriors gather around the creature. Swords plunged and ploughed into the beast's flesh over and over.

It yelped and howled, each cry growing fainter and fainter until it cried no more.

"All right," the Pit Guard called, stepping back from the man-wolf. The rest of the troop followed his lead, holding their bloodied swords in their hands to regard the monster.

The wolf climbed from the creature's back to trot over to the boy. She licked the blood on her snout as she pressed her body against him.

Arnald, like the other men, watched the man-wolf carefully.

As blood spilled from the many wounds over the creature's flesh, the fur covering its body receded slowly, exposing pink skin. The beast's arms, legs, and muzzle shrank.

The boy stood up, not quite believing his eyes, as he watched the monster's form change to that of a man half its size.

"There it is," Steigauf said, peering down at the body of a naked individual with a torso covered with piercing wounds and flesh torn away from his neck. "The man-wolf in all its glory."

Javanakhan!

Aralore opened her eyes.

She saw brightness surrounding her and felt an icy breeze on her face. Her vision remained blurry, but she no longer hung from the rafters in Helena's house. With the bindings on her wrists now removed, she padded and ran her palms over her body, feeling her clothing instead of bare flesh.

Sweeping her hand to her side, she felt her bow and quiver in the snow beside her. Furrowing her brow, confused at the situation she found herself in, she wondered why the woman dressed her again and where she'd left her.

"Hello," Aralore cried, tears streaming over her cheeks, feeling a sudden surge of relief to be alive. "Is anyone there? Please help me."

She called again before sobbing uncontrollably.

"Hello," she screamed as loudly as she could. "Please, somebody."

The sound of a door opening drew her attention. It wasn't far away.

"Hello," she called again.

"By the gods," she heard a familiar voice say. "Aralore?"

"I can't see you, Anne," the elf replied, trying to sit up. Her legs didn't respond and her back remained flat on the ground, paralysed. "I can't move," she whimpered. "I can't move."

"Wait here," she heard the older woman say. "I'll get your sister. Don't go anywhere."

Aralore laughed a little as she continued to weep.

"I won't," she replied.

Anne's footsteps crunched in the snow, growing fainter as she moved away. The elf looked in the sound's direction and could see a large, blurry, grey blob. The Lazy Traveller, she assumed. The woman in the woods returned her to where she started her journey.

Why?

The brightness of the daylight stung her eyes, so she closed them again. Listening to the surroundings, hearing birds twitter in the forest and the wind rustle through the trees, she waited for her sister and silently thanked the gods for her life.

It wasn't long before she heard hurried footfalls in the snow.

"Aralore," her sister called, sounding frightened. "Who did this?"

"We should get her inside," Anne interjected before the elf could reply. "The tavern or home?"

"Home," Aralore said quickly. "Take me home, please."

Feeling two people lift her from each side, placing her arms over their necks to carry her, she recognised Yaleni's form and knew the other wasn't Anne.

"Who is this?" Aralore inquired.

"It's me," Helena answered.

The elf nodded, turning her head towards her sister.

"My bow," she said.

"I have it," Anne returned. "And your arrows."

Soon after, they placed Aralore on her bed.

"Who did this?" Yaleni asked again.

Aralore shook her head, "I don't know. Two women, perhaps more. I saw one old and one young."

"Would you recognise them if you saw them again?" the silver elf asked.

"No," the other replied. "They both used some strange powder to render me unconscious. When I woke, I couldn't see anything but shapes. I saw things a little more clearly after a while when they held me prisoner in Helena's house."

"My house?"

Aralore nodded.

"I only saw the young one there," the blonde elf told them. "She had me bound and hanging. And she draped my clothes over your chairs by the fireplace."

"You were stripped bare?" Anne asked.

"So was she," said Aralore. "It was so strange and frightening."

Yaleni touched her sister's face, offering comfort.

"What else did you see?"

Aralore felt her stomach turn as she remembered the grotesque sight of what rested on the table.

"Someone's leg," she answered. "A man's. The woman sliced a portion off and ate it."

"By the gods," Anne muttered.

The blonde elf gripped her sister's arm tightly.

"You must promise me you will not go out there," she implored.

"If I do, I'll go with others," Yaleni assured her sister.

"No," Aralore snapped.

"Someone's in my home," Helena added. "I'd like them to leave."

"No," the elf said again, looking toward Helena, still not able to see clearly, tears streaming from her eyes. "That leg. It must belong to one of the men from here."

"Humphrey," Anne blurted suddenly, sobbing quietly at the thought of her husband becoming food for some fiend in the woods.

"If they couldn't escape these women," Aralore continued, "you won't either. Promise me, you will all stay in Mountainfall until we hear from Jaysh and Nichol. Please."

Yaleni stroked her sister's arm.

"I promise," she replied. "I'll stay here with you until we hear from Jaysh and Nichol."

"Oh, Humphrey," Anne cried, moving away from the bedroom.

"Helena?" the elf asked.

"I won't," she answered. "I should see to Anne."

Aralore listened to the footsteps moving into the living quarters.

"Who do you think these women are?" Yaleni asked, holding Aralore's hand.

"I think they're witches from Adaerwen," the blonde elf said quietly. "They both spoke a word native to the Land of the Dead. *Javanakhan*."

"A mind spell," the other said. "This is dire news."

Aralore frowned as she shook her head slowly.

"What is it?" asked Yaleni.

"I can't work out why I still live," she said, setting off more tears. "Why spare me and return me home but butcher and eat our men?"

Chapter Nine

F OR SOME STRANGE REASON to Jaysh Shen-Jon, the world seemed new, refreshed. The scent of the pine trees filled his nostrils, the sun felt warm as it embraced his back and shoulders, and the clear sky ahead of them appeared far more welcoming than the looming clouds he and Nichol had travelled beneath for the past couple of days.

A broad grin stretched over his face as he rode, peering around at the landscape. The road ahead turned slowly to the right, vanishing into the surrounding forest of tall, pointed trees planted in neat rows. Many thin columns of smoke rose in the distance, their source beyond his view. He closed his eyes and inhaled.

"I swear I can smell bacon, eggs and finely buttered toast," Jaysh said.

"After we speak to the magistrate, we'll find a tavern and indulge," Nichol said with a laugh. "What do you say?"

"Oh, yes," the younger man agreed. "Give me a decent, hot meal at a table any day."

The road eventually straightened out to reveal a large township spread out before them. Two gibbet cages, one on either side of the road, swung from tall beams marking the entrance to the settlement. A large timber sign sat beneath the cage to the left with letters engraved in the common tongue. Another sign on the right, was written in elvish.

Welcome To

NORTHWELL
-The Lawless Are Not Welcome Here-

"I guess the message is clear enough," Jaysh said, raising his brow at the sight.

"You've nothing to worry about here," Nichol replied. "You're one of the most law-abiding people I know."

While the aroma of freshly baked bread, brewed tea and warm food drew the riders past the posted greeting, the unpleasant stares from people moving about burned into every exposed part of the younger man as his horse plodded slowly behind Nichol's.

"Friendly bunch," he said to his companion.

"Wary," Nichol told him. "My guess is they don't see many travellers from the east."

"We always see travellers coming from Northwell," Jaysh returned. "You would think they'd be used to it."

"From Northwell," the other said. "Not going to Northwell. This might be a rare thing for some of them."

Jaysh saw three children standing by a woman he assumed to be their mother, under a sheltered shopfront. He smiled and offered a friendly wave as he rode by. One youngling, a little girl, smiled and waved back. The mother quickly gave a disapproving look to the girl before gathering the children together with her hands to guide them away from the newcomers.

Soon, the riders neared the centre of Northwell, looking around for signage for the magistrate's office. It proved pointless as a small group of leather armoured men brandishing swords gathered in the middle of the road ahead. Nichol and Jaysh pulled their steeds to a halt as one man slowly stepped towards them.

His dark beard draped over his barrel chest and his shoulder-length hair fell untidily over one eye.

"My name is Clay Wallace," he growled. "I'm the Sheriff of Northwell. These men are the welcoming party. We request you to relinquish your weapons during your stay. Elsewise, keep riding through, turn around or step down from your horses so we can welcome you in a less than traditional manner."

"We'll relinquish our weapons," Nichol said quickly. "We came to speak to the magistrate."

"The magistrate has business in Port Coldspring," Wallace replied. He pointed behind him to a hitching post by the side of the road, outside a small stone hovel. "Tie your horses there and follow me inside. You'll speak with me in his absence."

After hitching their steeds, the two men followed the sheriff into the little hut. Inside, there wasn't much more than a stove set into the wall opposite the door, a table and an assortment of chairs placed around the interior. A set of iron bars stretched from ceiling to floor along one side of the room, creating a cage of sorts. One of the other men with the sheriff followed the others into the room, moved to the cage's door and unlocked it with a key chained around his neck. It opened with a loud squeak.

"Your weapons, gentlemen," he said, holding out his hands.

"This is Jeren Telsh," said Wallace, pausing by the warm stove. "My deputy."

"My sword is on my horse," Nichol replied.

Jaysh unbuckled his sheath and handed his weapon to the man by the cage.

"I'll get that back, right?" the young man queried.

"Of course you will," Wallace said, plonking onto a seat by the table before gesturing around the room. "Pull a chair over."

Both men complied as Telsh placed Jaysh's sword onto a rack by the wall inside the cage. He closed and locked the cage door before leaving the room.

"I'll check their horses," he said, before closing the door behind him.

Jaysh and Nichol looked at Wallace questioningly.

"Check our horses?" Nichol asked.

"For weapons you might have hidden," the other replied.

"He did hear me when I said my sword is on my horse?"

"He heard," the sheriff nodded. "Don't worry. You're here. You seem like honest lads who want to avoid trouble. If he finds anything, he'll lock it in there, and that'll be the end of it. You'll get it all back when you leave. So." Wallace leaned his elbows onto the table and gazed at the two men across from him. "When will you leave?"

"We just got here," Jaysh replied.

"And why are you here?"

"To see the magistrate," Nichol put in. "But, given you said he's not here, I suppose we're here to see you."

"That you are." Wallace raised his brow. "But, why?"

"Ah." Nichol looked dumbly at the table, suddenly lost for words. "Where do we begin?"

Jaysh shook his head and leaned forward.

"We found a severed head stuck on a post outside the tavern in Mountainfall," the younger man told the sheriff. "We don't know how it got there, who he was or where he came from. Our people sent us to get help from the magistrate. None of us are fighters. We're a very small village of farmers, craftsmen, and not much more. Travellers have spoken of raiders attacking places along the shores of Kedielewen and we're afraid. That's why we came."

Wallace leaned back in his chair and ran his fingers through his beard thoughtfully.

"You don't believe a traveller could be responsible?" he asked.

"The last traveller through was some time before this occurred," Nichol replied.

"And you don't believe one of your own villagers could have done this?" Wallace pressed.

Nichol shook his head. "No way."

At that moment, the door opened, allowing a burst of cold air into the room. Telsh entered with Nichol's sword in his hands. The sheriff watched his deputy open the cage door and place the weapon on the rack beside Jaysh's blade.

"It's worth investigating." Wallace leaned forward again. "Jeren."

"Sheriff," the other answered, shutting the cage and locking it behind him.

"Find Kurst and Aamon," Wallace commanded. "Bring them to me. Also, get Torm to prepare two Eluvian horses."

Telsh left the room in haste.

"Eluvian horses?" Jaysh gasped.

"Horses bred by the elves, lad," the sheriff said matter-of-factly.

"I know," Jaysh replied. "I just never thought there would be any this far north."

"They come in very handy," Wallace told him. "They're exceedingly fast and can run at full gallop for miles and miles before they need a rest. And even then, they only need to slow to a canter to rebuild their strength. Amazing animals."

Nichol watched the sheriff scratch his beard for a while in silence.

"So, what about us?" he asked, eventually. "Are we to just go home now?"

Wallace shook his head. "You'll stay here, in Northwell, until I hear from my riders. Aamon will ride to Port Coldspring and inform the magistrate of the situation. We will request support to accompany us to your village so we can investigate this murder. Kurst will go to Mountainfall and speak to the people there before returning to confirm your story. I must inform you that support may take some time. The closest garrison equipped for dealing with raiders, if that is what has done this, is based in Shiverwind."

"Shiverwind?" Nichol whispered, not believing his ears.

"This could take some time. Perhaps a week," the sheriff finished.

"A week?" Jaysh shook his head. "We need to go back to our friends."

"I can't allow that." Wallace crossed the room to the stove and held his hands out to the warmth. "If danger resides in Mountainfall, sending you back puts you in danger. That goes against the Dendadian Charter. My position is to protect you, and that means keeping you here in Northwell until we're ready to go. I'm sorry, lads."

Nichol dropped his head into his hands.

"What is it?" Wallace inquired.

"He left his woman to come here," Jaysh answered, placing a comforting hand on his friend's back.

Wallace stepped to Nichol's side and squeezed his shoulder.

"I am sorry," he said. "This is of little comfort, but I'll set you up in The One Eyed Hag. It's the best inn in all Northwell. Halstein and Elke are two of the best people I know. Hot food. Warm baths. You'll be well taken care of."

Captain Piers Kraayen stared, perplexed, at the body lying on the physicker's table. He shook his head in disbelief as he took in the sight before him.

"How could someone like this cause so much damage?" he asked.

Steigauf shifted his feet and shrugged.

"He didn't look like this when he attacked," the old soldier replied. "He was at least twice the height, double the width and a great deal fiercer in appearance."

A small smile crept upon the captain's face.

"Always the smart arse," he said, before turning his attention to the corpse's face, a younger man staring blankly at the ceiling. "I don't recognise him. How long do you think he's been out there?"

"Hard to say," the Pit Guard answered. "Man-wolves don't age like the rest of us. Could be that he was bitten recently, at least a month ago, which means another man-wolf still lurks out there, somewhere. Could be that he's a relic from the war who moved into that hut. Who can say?"

Kraayen nodded.

"We should burn the body," Steigauf added.

"The magistrate and sheriff will want to see it first," the other replied, turning for the door. "But, yes, we will burn the body. How did you defeat it without so many casualties? The men who accompanied you weren't as seasoned as those who went with Gerard."

"I suspect Gerard was caught off guard," the old man said, following the captain outside. He looked over at Arnald, petting the wolf by the gate to the compound. "We had her to warn us. Otherwise, I think I wouldn't be here now."

Kraayen turned for the dining hall.

"Did you see any of the others?" he asked, stopping at the base of the steps leading inside. "The dead, I mean."

"No," Steigauf answered. "It's possible the man-wolf had a lair and took the bodies there. It's also possible the snow covered them, only for them to be discovered when the warmer season arrives."

Both men entered the dining hall where the men of Steigauf's company solemnly sat and ate their meals. Kraayen paused to look at them.

"You lost one to that thing," he said quietly to the Pit Guard. "It seems to have hit the others hard."

"They're young," the old soldier told him. "They haven't seen battle, let alone trained for it. What happened to their friend was monstrous. Still, they did their duty. They're good men."

"They need a good leader," Kraayen uttered. "Will you stay and train them?"

"I'll stay for the boy," Steigauf said. "At least until I think he's ready to go on without me. He wants to be a Pit Guard."

"He'll need to go to Dendadia to complete the training." The captain turned to face the old man. "Does he have what is takes?"

"Not yet," Steigauf answered.

"Stay then," Kraayen urged. "Train them. Take them on and command them."

"I'm old and plan to return to my homeland," objected the Pit Guard.

"You still can," the captain said, looking at the men. "Just see what's left of the winter out here."

"It's always winter here."

Kraayen smiled.

"I'll officially assign the boy to this lot," the captain added. "You can train him and them at the same time. When you think he's ready to move on, I'll write up the references and accompany him to Dendadia myself."

Steigauf breathed long and deep, scanning the men silently seated at the long benches.

"There's no need for you to do that," the old man said. "I can give him my armour and sword to carry to the temple. He just needs to tell the priests my name and they will take him in."

Kraayen looked at Steigauf questioningly.

"You won't stay?"

"I'll stay," the soldier nodded. "I'll train these men until I'm ready to move on."

Chapter Ten

TWO RIDERS SPRINTED OUT of Northwell, one to the east and the other to the west. Their horses galloped swiftly, kicking up a fine spray of snow and sludge behind them as they raced along the roads.

Nichol observed the steed taking flight along the eastern road to Mountainfall. It ran so swiftly, its hooves appeared to barely graze the ground. Kurst, the rider, practically lay prostate on the horse's back. The horseman was much smaller than Nichol, and his outstretched arms gripped the distinctively shortened reins at the sides of the charger's neck. The shortened stirrup leathers enabled the rider to tuck his knees higher.

The rider and horse vanished from sight, bolting around the long bend that wound into the forest. The snow and sludge settled back to the ground and the sound of galloping hooves grew fainter until Nichol could not hear them any longer.

"How can he ride like that?" Nichol asked, turning to Wallace who leaned against the sign by a gibbet cage post.

"Kurst just needs to hold tight," the sheriff answered. "Naril will do the work. That horse knows what to do without having to be told."

"So..." Nichol stared at the empty road. "He doesn't need to steer or urge the horse at all?"

"Nope." Wallace smiled, turning to walk back into town. "Come on. I think we need a hot meal. It's bloody cold out here."

Nichol turned to follow, glancing over his shoulder to the road.

Wallace noticed, responding with a pat to the other's arm.

"Don't worry," the sheriff assured. "Kurst will be in Mountainfall by tomorrow evening. Naril may slow when she gets tired, but she won't stop until she reaches her destination. Both Eluvian horses once ran to Shiverwind and back in just a little over three days." He paused to allow that bit of information to sink into Nichol's head. "Shiverwind! Your Mountainfall isn't that much farther away from here than Shiverwind. It's just in the other direction. Kurst will be able to pass on that you are safe and well and your beloved, what's her name?"

"Helena," Nichol replied.

"Yes, that's it. Your beloved Helena will be content. He'll come back from there and give you news of her, and you'll be content. By then, we should have news from Port Coldspring and be on our way to investigate this incident. Nothing to worry about."

Nichol saw the severed head on the pike flash through his mind.

Nothing to worry about.

Before long, the two men stepped upon the long, timber porch of The One Eyed Hag. The double-storey building stood taller than any other structure in town, except for the watchtowers along the edges of the settlement. It reminded Nichol a little of The Lazy Traveller, with its little sign swinging from a post near the door, its glass windows with wooden shutters and unmistakable odour of ale wafting through the air.

Wallace held the door open for Nichol and they saw Jaysh sitting at a table, his back towards the bar, digging into a steaming plate of ham, eggs, and finely buttered toast. Nichol furrowed his brow, standing by the door to look at his friend, befuddled.

"I thought you were going to see the other rider off," he said.

"I was," Jaysh replied after swallowing a mouthful. He scooped up a lump of eggs with his fork. "But, then I didn't."

"Two more please, Elke," Wallace said to an attractive young lady behind the bar.

Elke smiled politely, and turned to a large, rectangular portal window behind her that opened into the kitchen, where a man of similar age sliced a loaf of bread on a countertop.

"Halstein," she blared, causing all three men to jump. "Two more."

"I'm right here," the man in the kitchen replied. "You don't need to yell."

She turned, holding her smile for the three patrons. "Won't be long."

Wallace nodded dumbly as both he and Nichol sat by Jaysh.

"By the gods," he whispered when she returned to her task of wiping the countertop.

"Been like that since I got here," Jaysh quietly reported, stuffing his mouth with toast. "I'm guessing a bit of a lover's quarrel."

"Could be," Wallace growled. "They're siblings, you know."

Jaysh and Nichol stared silently at the sheriff.

"Siblings?" Nichol asked. Jaysh blinked and swallowed hard.

"Oh, yeah." The sheriff nodded slowly. "Fucking crazy, I know. But each to their own. No law against it. Probably should be."

Jaysh nodded, agreeing.

The three men sat in silence for a short while until Wallace let out a long breath.

"Yep!" he said, raising his brow.

"So." Nichol turned his attention to his friend. "Why didn't you go to see the rider off to Port Coldspring?"

"Too cold," his friend answered, shovelling another morsel into his face. "Too hungry. Besides, Jeren, the deputy and some other man went."

"Torm," Wallace put in. "The horse tamer. He's got a soft spot for Naran, the horse. Naril's brother."

"So," Jaysh continued. "I came here and ordered some food instead."

Nichol couldn't argue with the logic.

"You missed a spectacle," Wallace told him.

"I've seen horses before," the younger man said. "I own a horse. I can look at it whenever I want."

"Seeing an Eluvian horse run is something you can never get used to," the sheriff replied.

"He's right," Nichol put in. "I couldn't even begin to describe it."

"That's because you're bad with words," Jaysh opined.

Nichol shook his head. In the corner of his eye, he noticed Elke approaching the table.

"Can I get you, gentlemen, something to drink while you wait?" she asked.

"A pot of tea to share with my guests, thank you," Wallace replied.

"A pot of tea, it is," Elke said. "And we can hear you over there. Halstein and I are not siblings. We're cousins."

Jaysh started coughing, something sticking in his throat from gasping and swallowing simultaneously. Elke smacked him hard on the back with an open palm, ejecting a chunk of ham from his mouth and back onto the plate.

"Thank you," he croaked.

"Quite all right." She peered at each man seated around the table. "So, if you don't mind, we would appreciate any discussion about laws around non-traditional relationships kept to a minimum on our premises."

Wallace and Nichol nodded respectfully.

"Absolutely," Jaysh said, holding his hands up in surrender. "I admit, the idea of brothers and sisters doing that kind of thing is weird to me, but after just being saved from choking to death, I'm all good with cousin fuckers."

———⊷◇⊶———

Thin purple clouds drifted past the towering peaks of The Great Northern Barrier and into the deepening red sky over Mountainfall. Snow fell as a cold breeze swept through the tiny township, causing the hem of Helena's dress to waft around her ankles and brush against her boots with a soft hiss as she stood by the roadside on the corner near The Lazy Traveller.

Yaleni watched thoughtfully from the patio of the tavern, hugging her cloak about her tightly as she nursed a steaming cup of tea, leaning against a support beam. Her observations led her to believe the girl longed for her man. Helena's gaze had remained fixed on the road to the north since the sun first crept below the horizon, and she'd been wringing her hands fretfully for hours.

"Helena," the elf called calmly so as not to alarm the girl.

A moment passed before Helena responded, almost as if she didn't hear Yaleni's voice. The girl turned her head to peer back, a glint in her eyes from crying.

"Come inside. The night is here. You'll catch your death out here."

"I miss him," Helena said, turning to look at the road again.

"I know," Yaleni replied, stepping off the patio, moving to the girl's side. "Come inside and get warm. You're no good to him if the cold takes you from him."

Helena seemed to consider the elf's words.

"What if he's hurt?" the girl asked.

"You can't think like that," Yaleni answered. "By now, he'll be in Northwell. He's probably spoken to the magistrate already and preparing to return. Staying out here to watch for him won't hasten his journey. Come inside, please."

Keeping her gaze on the road, Helena nodded reluctantly.

Together, the two women entered The Lazy Traveller, where a blazing fire filled the room with welcoming warmth. The women of Mountainfall moved about the room, busying themselves with setting cutlery and mugs on tables, while Anne and Aralore prepared lamb stew and freshly baked loaves of bread in the kitchen.

"Are you all right, kitten?" a young woman asked, placing mugs onto a table by the door before reaching out to touch Helena's shoulder.

"I'm all right," the girl answered, smiling gingerly.

"Let's get you by the fire," Yaleni said, placing a hand on Helena's back before glancing at the other woman. "Could you fetch a cup of tea, Tsami?"

"Of course," Tsami replied. With that, she briskly moved to the bar.

Yaleni guided Helena through the room towards a seat by the fireplace.

"How's Aralore?" the girl asked. The question seemed to come from nowhere and struck Yaleni with surprise.

"She's fine," the elf said as Helena lowered herself into a chair. "She's right there, in the kitchen."

Helena nodded upon seeing the other elf.

"I was worried about her after..." Her words drifted away. She seemed to compose herself, peering into the flames. "I'm glad she's up and on her feet again."

"As am I," Yaleni said, dragging a chair from a nearby table to sit next to Helena. She placed her cup of tea on the table to take Helena's hands in hers. They felt like ice to the touch. "Are you sure you're all right?"

Helena nodded. "I miss Nichol. That's all."

"You're cold," the elf said. "We need to get you warm inside and out. Let me fetch you a bowl of Anne's stew."

Yaleni stood, turning to move away. She felt Helena squeeze her hands tightly, causing her to look back to the girl questioningly.

"Does it have mushrooms?"

Yaleni furrowed her brow.

"The stew?" she said. "No. There are no mushrooms. Just lamb, potatoes, turnips and parsnips with a few herbs and spices from my collection. Why?"

Helena looked into the flames and shook her head.

"I don't feel like mushrooms, is all," she replied.

Yaleni glanced at Helena before turning away. She passed by Tsami who smiled at the elf as she carried a fresh cup of steaming tea for Helena. Yaleni replied with a polite smile and nod.

"Well done, lassie," Anne said quietly as the elf entered the kitchen. "I was really worried about her being out there on her own."

"I still am," Yaleni whispered, stepping to the older woman's side. "I need a bowl for her. She's cold right through."

Anne complied, ladling out some stew into a bowl.

"You'll have no need to worry after she eats that." Anne grinned.

"It's not the cold I'm worried about," the elf replied. "She's... I don't know. Not herself."

"She has been standing outside for a long time," Aralore put in. "Perhaps her mind needs warming from the cold."

Yaleni tilted her head, raising her brow in contemplation.

"I'll get this to her," the elf said.

Anne glanced through the kitchen door to the others setting tables in the tavern. A broad smile stretched across her face.

"I'm so glad they all came," she said. "We should make this a daily event. Coming together for the night meal, I mean."

Aralore nodded. "I think that's a terrific idea. What do you think, sister?"

Yaleni observed the women setting tables, holding little discussions themselves, smiling, laughing, supporting each other. Her gaze moved to the girl by the fire, sipping tea as she peered into the flames.

"I agree," the elf said. "We all need this right now."

<hr />

As night set in Naril, the Eluvian horse slowed her pace to turn southward at the intersection onto the Great Northern Barrier Road. Kurst, her rider, gripped tightly to the reins as she increased pace again.

"With any luck," he said to the steed, "we'll be in Mountainfall sometime tomorrow."

Naril snorted before offering a small whinny.

"By morning, you say?" Kurst queried, not really understanding the horse at all. For all he knew, the horse snorted to clear a bug from its nostrils. Speaking to the horse helped to pass the time. "Well," he continued. "You'll need to run really fast to get there by sunrise. It's a long, long way from here."

The horse raced onwards into the night, seemingly oblivious to the rider's words.

<hr />

Far to the west, Naran slowed to a trot as he carried Aamon into Port Coldspring. Aamon straightened his posture, placing his hands on the back of his hips before stretching his back.

The streets appeared empty, save for a few men milling around an inn a short distance inside the edge of town. They watched the rider and horse cautiously as Aamon steered Naran towards them.

"Pardon my intrusion," he called. "I have a message for the magistrate. Do you know where I can find him at this hour?"

"Where are you from, stranger?" one man called, his voice slurry from drinking.

"Northwell," Aamon answered. "Our magistrate is here, and I need to speak with him urgently. Any help you could offer would be greatly appreciated."

The man pointed towards the bulk of the township.

"Good chance the magistrate is at the town hall near the town square," he replied. "Follow that road and you won't miss it."

"Thank you," Aamon said before directing Naran away.

It wasn't long before rider and horse reached a large open area hemmed by shops and neat garden beds covered with snow. Bare trees lined the sides of cobbled pathways, winding and crossing over one another through the locale, branching from a primary artery that led to the base of the stairs into the town hall.

Aamon noticed flickering light emitting from the open doors of the hall. He directed Naran towards the building, a gigantic stone structure with a steep, gabled roof.

"Stay here," he said to the horse as he dismounted. He dashed up the stairs and inside.

Two guards standing on either side of the doorway stepped into his path.

"State your business at this hour," one man said, placing a hand on the hilt of his sword. Aamon stopped in his tracks and measured the men before him. Both stood a good head and shoulders over him, clad in dark leather breastplates, vambraces and greaves.

"My name is Aamon," he replied. "I come from Northwell, and I need to speak to the magistrate urgently."

"Which one?" the other guard asked.

"Sorry?" Aamon offered the man a perplexed stare.

"Which magistrate?" the guard clarified. "Yours or ours?"

"Both," the rider answered.

"They're together in the magistrate's chamber," the first guard told him. "Follow me."

Aamon followed the guard through the main auditorium, past many bench seats positioned in neat rows, to a tall timber door to the side of the room. He signalled for Aamon to stop before knocking.

"Who is it?" a raspy voice called from within.

"A rider from Northwell, sir," the guard called back.

A moment of silence followed, allowing time for Aamon and the guard to exchange awkward glances as they waited for a response. The guard feigned drinking from a cup, signalling to Aamon that the magistrates' meeting involved a little more than just talk.

"Show him in," commanded the raspy voice.

The guard opened the door to reveal a large room with lavish furniture and two men seated in plush chairs by a small fireplace. Aamon recognised one man immediately. He was a young burly man with a fiery red beard resting upon his stout belly.

"Magistrate Shylton," the rider said, stepping into the room.

"Aamon," the other replied. "What brings you here?"

Aamon looked at the other man cautiously as the guard closed the door behind him.

He stared at the rider with deep eyes. The lines on his clean face showed years of experience. His wiry frame told the rider he lived his life a little less lavish than his counterpart.

"Sorry, sir." Aamon bowed to the older man.

"Quite all right, young fellow," he said, rising to his feet, extending a hand. "Magistrate Bowyar."

"Aamon," the rider replied, taking the magistrate's hand.

"Best state your business so we can get back to drinking, laddie." The old man returned to his seat.

"I have a report from Mountainfall, sir," Aamon replied.

"Mountainfall?" Shylton queried. "Does that place even fall under my jurisdiction?"

"You're the closest magistrate to them in all Kedielewen," the rider answered.

Bowyar chuckled as he reached to a small table by his chair for a mug.

"Guess that places them in your jurisdiction, Kane," he said, before taking a sip.

Shylton grimaced and gestured to Aamon.

"Go on."

"Someone posted a severed head outside the tavern," the rider reported. "They express concerns regarding stories of raiders to the north. They fear the raiders have moved inland and threaten their township."

"There's nothing out there," the young magistrate retorted. "What could raiders want with nothing?"

"It's not raiders," Bowyar added. "Too far inland. The raiders are sticking to coastal settlements. Nothing to worry about."

Aamon gave both the men a contemptuous glare.

"I just rode all the way from Northwell with a message," the rider said. "Sheriff Wallace believes this is worth investigating and sent me to relay his request for a troop to escort him to Mountainfall."

Bowyar shook his head.

"Unfortunately, lad, all our men are out patrolling the shoreline to the north searching for these raiders. We barely have enough men here to form a squad. The only men who may be available are in Shiverwind."

Aamon turned and put his hand on the door handle.

"Where are you going?" Shylton asked, getting to his feet. "You just arrived."

"I'm going to Shiverwind to find men who will aid us," Aamon answered, his face set like flint.

"There's no guarantee of any men there," Bowyar said, standing to move to his counterpart's side. "They could be out patrolling their shores like ours. And, if there are men there, you have no guarantee they will come."

"There's no guarantee they won't, either," Aamon told him before exiting the room to dash through the auditorium and back outside to where Naran waited.

PART FOUR

Javanakhan

Chapter One

———⟡———

S TEIGAUF STOOD ATOP THE stairs leading into the dining hall, folding his arms as he watched the boy attack a dummy with a steel practice sword. A small smile crept upon the old man's face as he witnessed newly learned skills developing into habits. Arnald spun on his toes and heels as he manoeuvred around the dummy, ducking beneath imaginary blows, slicing his blade under its timber armpits and across its wooden neck.

"Good," he called to the boy. He flashed his gaze along the line of other men, practising their sword skills on other dummies. "Very good."

Johaan Heilig chopped into his allotted dummy with the edge of his sword. The blade offered a dull clang, barely leaving a mark on the wooden post.

"These new practice swords are useless," he complained, dropping his sword arm to his side. "They don't cut and they're twice as heavy as my actual sword."

"They're not twice as heavy," Steigauf retorted, stepping down from the steps to move across the ground towards the man. "They are heavier, though. They make them heavier so you can build your strength. This way, you're able to fight more swiftly, respond more quickly when you engage in battle. Their blades don't cut because they are a training tool, not a weapon." The Pit Guard positioned himself behind the soldier. "And, before you bitch about it anymore, the boy seems content to use the same

235

tool as you without complaining. His sword is just as blunt and just as heavy as yours. What's the problem?"

"My shoulder aches," Heilig said, turning to face the old man. "I think it's still repairing after the man-wolf tossed me."

Steigauf looked at the soldier's arm. A thick woollen tunic and leather breastplate covered the soldier's shoulders, obscuring any signs of injury.

"Was there blood?" the old man asked.

"During the fight?" Heilig queried. "Yes. But it wasn't mine."

"You're certain?" The Pit Guard gripped the soldier's upper arm with one hand as he pressed firmly against the shoulder with the other. Heilig winced, emitting a small grunt.

"I went to the physicker as soon as I could after we returned," Heilig said. "He told me there were no piercings or abrasions. The pain I'm feeling must be muscular."

Arnald stopped to listen to the conversation.

"Keep going," Steigauf barked, pointing at the dummy standing before the boy. Arnald immediately returned to fighting his wooden enemy.

"There was blood on my shirt," Heilig said, lowering his voice. "But it wasn't mine. Perhaps it came from the man-wolf?"

"Perhaps." Steigauf frowned, as he continued to inspect the soldier's arm.

Heilig stared at the old man for what seemed a very long time.

"You aren't sure," the young man eventually said.

The old man shook his head.

"I have no marks," Heilig assured. "No claw or tooth reached me."

Steigauf moved in closer to speak quietly into Heilig's ear.

"The man-wolf can heal quickly," he told the young soldier. "Very quickly. Not only when it takes the form of a monster, but also when it is in the form of a man. I cannot be certain, but I will be watching. When the hunger comes, and it will, you will change."

"I don't want to," Heilig whispered, tears welling in his eyes.

"It's beyond your control, laddie," Steigauf replied.

"The full moon is a way ahead of us," Arnald said, standing beside the Pit Guard. The old man furrowed his brow as he looked at the boy.

"How did you get here so quietly?" Steigauf asked. "And why aren't you attacking that dummy?" He peered around to see all the other soldiers of his unit watching on quietly. "I don't recall giving the order to stop."

"Sorry, sir," one soldier said. "We just can't ignore what's going on here. Is Johaan a man-wolf?"

Steigauf pursed his lips, looked to the ground, and folded his arms.

Heilig cried, lowering himself to sit on the ground.

"I don't know," the Pit Guard eventually replied.

"Well," the other soldier said as he pointed his practice sword to Arnald. "The boy has a point. The moon won't be full for some time. Surely, there's something we can do."

Steigauf shook his head and sighed.

"The problem we have is that we like to believe the stories we've been told as children," he said. "A man-wolf can change into the beast at any time. I've seen them in daylight, not just at the time of a full moon. When the creature gets hungry, it comes out to hunt. That said, we have no proof Heilig is a man-wolf."

"So, what do we do?" asked another concerned soldier. "Wait for him to change?"

The Pit Guard nodded slowly.

"That's exactly what we do," he answered. "We wait."

———◆———

Arnald watched Heilig from across the table in the dining hall, observing the man stirring his porridge slowly as it slowly turned cold. The soldier stared blankly at the bowl with a sad scowl stamped upon his face.

The boy peered around quickly to see the others of their troop sitting at other tables, offering sideways glances at the alleged cursed man. When he returned his gaze to Heilig, he found the man staring at him.

"You can go to them if you prefer," the young man offered. "I wouldn't want you near if I suddenly changed."

"I'm not afraid," Arnald told him. "You're my friend."

Heilig's chin quivered.

"Thank you, Arnald," he replied. "I think you might be my only and best friend here. But I don't know what I might do to you if I change into this thing they believe me to be."

"We can face that when or if that happens, Johaan," the boy returned. "Now, eat your porridge. You need your strength."

"I can't," he said, pushing the bowl to the middle of the table.

"Well, I can," said a gruff voice from behind him. A young soldier sitting on the bench beside Heilig reached over the table to the bowl and scooped the slop into his mouth, spilling a little onto his beard. "I'm Viktor."

"We know who you are, Viktor Benten," Arnald said, eyeing the man warily. "Why aren't you with your friends over there?"

"Friends?" the other queried, looking around the room to the other members of the troop. "Them? They're nothing but associates. Comrades in arms. Let's see how friendly they are if we ever see real battle, huh?"

"We've seen battle," the boy said.

"You refer to the man-wolf?" Benten smiled. "No, that wasn't battle. That was just a hunting trip. I mean real battle, proper battle, facing an actual enemy. Some of those bastards will run away like frightened children. You wait and see."

Arnald felt a lump form in his throat as he remembered cowering away when his village, his family, were murdered.

"You know what I might be?" Heilig said. "What they all think I am?"

"Yeah, so?" Benten replied, scooping more porridge into his mouth. "You're no monster yet. Besides, I heard if you pat a man-wolf's tummy, they become loyal as dogs. I'll be the first to try that if you turn."

Benten gazed at the others as both Arnald and Heilig exchanged curious glances. Suddenly, Benten smiled.

"I just made that up," he chuckled, pushing the empty bowl to the middle of the table. He gestured to the other men in the dining hall. "Look, fuck those ones. Maybe they will fight by your side. Maybe they will stab you in the back. But I will fight with both of you. I've been watching you train. You both have the qualities of skilled warriors. Especially you." Benten pointed at Arnald. "Your sword skills are outstanding. Your bowman skills are shit, though. But I'd rather fight by your sides than any of them."

"Better chance of survival?" Heilig asked.

"Exactly." Benten smiled.

Chapter Two

"TAKE YOUR TIME," STEIGAUF whispered.

Arnald pulled the string back to his shoulder. The tension in his forearm holding the bow increased, slowly building to a dull pain. He glanced at the piece of cloth protruding from beneath his sleeve; Gertrude, making herself known, wrapped around his arm. The boy lowered his brow, staring straight down the arrow's shaft at the woven rope target posted against the stone wall.

"Steady your breathing," the Pit Guard added, standing a short distance behind his young apprentice, bare of his armour and weapons. "Release."

His fingers let the string free, allowing the arrow to catapult towards the target. For a moment, the bolt seemed to fly directly towards the centre of the target.

For a moment.

TWACK!

The arrowhead stuck into the left side of the target, a good six inches from the little red bullseye painted in the middle of the rope coil.

"I hit it." Arnald smiled.

"That you did," the old man agreed.

The wolf lifted herself from the ground by Steigauf's feet and approached the boy. She licked his fingers where the indent from the bowstring slowly dissipated.

"Does that hurt?" the old soldier asked.

"Not really," the boy replied, looking at his fingertips. "A little."

Steigauf strode to the target and retrieved the arrow.

"Perhaps we should get you a glove," he said as he retraced his footsteps to Arnald. "Just while you're perfecting your archery skills."

"No," Arnald replied. "I need to build strength in my arms and fingers."

"Some of the best archers wear gloves, boy," Steigauf told him, handing the arrow over. "You'll get callouses on your fingers without them."

"Like the ones you have?"

"Precisely." The old man held his hands out for Arnald to see. "Look at those ugly things."

Arnald saw nothing revolting about the soldier's hands. In fact, they reminded him of his father's hands. Hardworking hands.

"No gloves," said Arnald as he loaded the arrow onto the string.

"All right," replied Steigauf as he and the wolf took their places behind the boy. "No gloves. Now, take your time."

"Steady my breathing," the boy added as he pulled the string back across his chest to his shoulder.

"General," a voice called from across the yard, near the dining hall's door.

The sudden interruption caused Arnald to let the arrow fly. It whistled through the air and scraped the side of the target before bouncing off the stone wall behind it.

"Shit," the boy spat before turning to see the intruder. A very young elf-woman stood tall at the base of the stairs leading to the dining hall. Her long golden hair rested over her shoulder in a braid tied off with thin leather strips. Clad in dark hunting attire, sword slung on her back and dagger strapped to her right hip, she appeared both beautiful and dangerous to Arnald.

"Sheriff," Steigauf replied. "How may I assist?"

As she approached the old man, Arnald noted how she almost appeared to float, taking long strides with silent footfalls. She craned her long neck, keeping her steely, curious blue eyes on the boy as she drew nearer.

Beautiful and dangerous, Arnald considered.

"Captain Kraayen summoned the magistrate and me," she told him.

"And we need your assistance."

"Assistance?" the old man asked.

"I don't believe this is something we should discuss so openly," she replied, nodding to Arnald. "Especially in front of ears so young."

"You're not that much older than he is," Steigauf said. "Besides, he's probably seen much worse than you have. This is Arnald Oberlin, the boy I told you about."

Her countenance suddenly changed. Her gaze softened and her shoulders appeared to relax.

"I am sorry, Arnald," the sheriff said.

He understood her sympathy related to his loss of family, not for the guarded attitude she displayed moments earlier.

"It's all right," he replied, running his fingers through the wolf's fur as she moved to his side.

The sheriff observed the interaction between boy and wolf studiously, holding her gaze for some time before speaking.

"I'm Kysha Naberyn," she told him, introducing herself formally. "Sheriff of Shiverwind."

Arnald nodded warily. He looked at the Pit Guard.

"She can be trusted," the old man told him.

"We must speak," she said to Steigauf. "A rider from Northwell has arrived. The magistrate would like you to hear what he has to say."

"Northwell?" Steigauf furrowed his brow. "That's a long way from here. Surely, you should have received a dispatch from Coldspring to relay a message from Northwell. Isn't that the way they do things anymore?"

"It is," Kysha answered. "This is very unusual. It's why the magistrate sent me to fetch you. You need to hear this yourself."

Arnald tentatively followed Steigauf into the office of the barracks commander. The room was dark, barely large enough for the large timber table positioned in its middle. A map of Kedielewen stretched across the table, almost covering its surface. Instantly, Arnald absorbed key landmarks from the image. The Cove of Safe Keeping was near the centre, Driradia to the top-left, the Long Spine Mountains bordering the left edge of the map, then the Great Northern Barrier Mountains and the road sharing its name to the right. A large chunk of Haeraweth to the other side of the eastern mountain range showed nothing but blank canvas. There lay the frozen waste where barely a man had set foot.

Sighting Coldspring on the map, resting on the eastern shore of the cove, Arnald guessed his little village sat across the water directly to the west of it. He followed the road from Port Coldspring with his eyes to Northwell, from Northwell to Shadowfort. The Dragon's Teeth Ranges and The Barrier Ranges met there.

"This is an old map," he blurted.

"Indeed, it is," a voice said from a chair across the table from him. Arnald glanced up to see Magistrate Zain Demeara, a man he'd met a few times in the company of Steigauf. "You've got an astute eye, young soldier."

The boy looked away, embarrassed for speaking out loud without invitation.

Captain Kraayen, seated at the table's end closest to a small blazing fireplace, noticed the boy's awkward look.

"What makes you say that Arnald?" he asked.

"The mountains join there," the boy pointed to the map. "That's where the mountain fell."

"You're correct," Kraayen said. "Although, it wouldn't be noticeable on a map of this size. I've heard the newer maps in Dendadia have exaggerated the break in the ranges. There is a small settlement there now. Mountainfall. That's the reason this rider has come." The captain gestured to a man seated at the far end of the table.

The man rose to his feet and bowed slightly.

"Aamon Martano," he announced. "At your service."

"Arnald Oberlin," the boy replied politely.

"Osman Steigauf," the old man grunted impatiently before pointing his finger to others gathered about. "Zain Demeara. Piers Kraayen. Kysha Naberyn. Now that we know each other, let's talk." The Pit Guard pulled two seats out from the table. "Park yourself, laddie."

Arnald complied, sitting next to the old soldier as Kysha moved gracefully around the table to sit nearer to the magistrate.

"Tell the commander what you told us, Aamon," Demeara said, waving his hands towards the Pit Guard.

"General," Kysha corrected the magistrate.

"I hold no rank," Steigauf told her. "I'm a Pit Guard."

"What do I call you then, sir?" Martano asked.

"Osman," the old man answered. "Steigauf. Sir. Commander or General, if it takes your fancy. I don't really care. Just don't call me grandfather."

"The Pit Guards hold the right to command armies according to Dendadian legislation," Martano said. "General seems fitting."

"Fine." The Pit Guard twirled his hand slowly. "Why are you here?"

"I rode from Northwell to make a request for men to accompany me back."

"Back to Northwell?" Steigauf asked.

"Yes, sir," the rider said.

The old man regarded the map, nodded slowly, and rose to his feet.

"Well," he said, offering a wry smile to Captain Kraayen. "That was indeed a very interesting piece of information. Now, if you don't mind, I'd like to return to the archery grounds to continue training Arnald."

"There's more," the captain returned. "Please, sit down."

Steigauf sighed and lowered himself into the chair. He looked at Martano and waited.

"Two men from Mountainfall came to us with news of an attack," the rider explained. "They found the head of a man sitting on a pike outside the tavern there. They wanted to speak to Magistrate Shylton to organise an investigating party. The men believe raiders might be nearby."

"Near to Mountainfall?" Steigauf queried. He reached past Arnald and pointed to the place where the two mountain ranges met on the map. "All the way inland, there?"

"With all the news of raids along our coastline, it's not unreasonable for people to think the worst," Demeara put in.

"Perhaps." The Pit Guard rested his back in the chair. "What did your Magistrate Shylton have to say?"

"Magistrate Shylton is currently meeting with Magistrate Bowyar in Port

Coldspring," Martano replied. "I spoke briefly with them the night before last. They both seemed certain they could spare no men, considering the threat of raids along the shore. Most of the men are thinly spread to deal with those reports."

"Fast horse," Steigauf said softly, winking at Arnald.

"What?" Kraayen asked.

"I said, fast horse," the old man answered. "For Mister Aamon Martano to ride all the way from Port Coldspring to here, in what? Two days? Must be one really fast horse."

"A day and a half, to be exact," Martano told him defensively. "The horse's name is Naran, and he's Eluvian. So, yes, he's a really fast horse."

Steigauf stared at the rider for a long time. The thick silence lingered in the room.

"I want you to go," Kraayen said eventually.

Steigauf turned to look the captain square in the face.

"What?"

"I can't spare all the men you took with you before," the other told him. "I want you to select six men to accompany you to Mountainfall."

"Six?"

"The boy can stay here to continue his training, of course," continued Kraayen.

Arnald shot a concerned glance at Steigauf.

"The boy comes with me," the old man said.

Magistrate Demeara waved his hands in protest.

"Let's not be hasty," he interjected. "It's dangerous out there. Reports of raiders and let's not forget the man-wolf you encountered. He has a bed here, a roof over his head and hot food."

"The boy comes with me," Steigauf repeated. "He's learning the ways of the Pit Guards, not the ways of an average soldier. He'll learn best from a Pit Guard. He comes with me."

Arnald peered at the faces around the table. They all looked at him as if he were an object, not a person. All except Steigauf and Kysha.

"You're being unreasonable," Kraayen put in. "We agreed he would train here, and I would take him to Dendadia myself. The road to Mountainfall is no place for a boy."

"He comes with me, or I don't go," Steigauf argued. "I'll take him directly to Dendadia instead."

"Don't be silly," Demeara added. "You're the only one here we can spare to investigate this issue."

"Spare?"

"I merely mean you're skilled and have had experience," the magistrate clarified. "There are no others here that fit that description. The boy's not ready. Let him stay."

"No," Steigauf barked.

Kysha stood to her feet sharply.

"Stop," she snapped. "Look at him."

The men turned to see Arnald cowering in his seat, frightened.

"Arnald," the elf called softly. "Are you all right?"

The boy nodded.

"What would you like to do?" Kysha asked.

"You'd let him decide?" Demeara queried.

"It's his fate," the elf sheriff answered. "Not yours. Or yours." She glanced at the old man sitting beside Arnald.

Steigauf nodded thoughtfully before turning to face the boy.

"It's up to you, laddie," the old man whispered. "What do you say?"

Arnald slowly moved his gaze across the map, tracing the line marking the road from Shiverwind, through Port Coldspring and Northwell to Shadowfort. He moved his fingers to the cloth sticking ever so slightly from his sleeve.

Coward.

"I'll go with you," he said.

"Good lad," the Pit Guard said, smiling, patting his hand on the boy's knee.

"As will I," Kysha said, lowering herself back into her seat.

Magistrate Demeara looked at her disapprovingly.

"You cannot. You're the sheriff. You're needed here."

"I hereby resign from my duties as Sheriff of Shiverwind," she told him.

"But why?" the magistrate asked, continuing to shake his head in disbelief.

She looked across the table at Arnald and smiled.

"I'm young and have yet to see the world," the elf replied. "Seems there is no better time than the present."

Chapter Three

"THEY'RE TAKING A LONG time with the food," Viktor Benten growled softly. He sat directly across from Arnald and Heilig, the only other two occupants of his long table near the main door of the dining hall. The other men of the troop positioned themselves at other benches around the room. "We've usually been fed by now. Why do you think they're taking so long?"

"I'm guessing you're a little hungry." Arnald smiled, looking over his shoulder at the wolf resting on the floor behind him. Keeping her chin on her paws, she glanced at him quickly before moving her gaze to the open door leading outside. The boy followed her line of sight, expecting the Pit Guard to enter at any moment.

The late afternoon light turned to deep purple dusk before deepening to a pitch black. Benten justifiably voiced his irritability. The troop was growing impatient as their hunger increased and the night was dragging on.

They'd never waited this late for their meal.

"Look at them," Heilig muttered, tightening his fists on the table's edge. "They all fear me."

Benten turned to see several men giving side glances to the trio seated on their own, far across the room.

"So what?" he offered. "Let them fear you. You don't need them. You have us."

Arnald offered Heilig a grin, smacking his hand against his friend's arm. Heilig released his hands, placing them flat onto the table's surface, nodding slowly to himself.

"You're right." He looked over at Benten. "I don't need them. You're the best friends I've ever known." He moved his gaze to Arnald. "Which is why I need you both to make me a promise."

The boy nodded.

"What promise?" Benten queried.

"If I turn," Heilig started, "into a man-wolf, I mean."

"I got what you meant." Benton sighed. "What about if you turn?"

"If I turn, or if I start to turn, I want one of you to kill me," said the young soldier. He jutted his chin to the others seated across the room. "Not one of them. They'll massacre me so that nothing remains. And not Steigauf, either." Heilig glared intently at Arnald. The boy noticed, for the first time, flecks of yellow and green in his friend's eyes, reminding him of those belonging to the wolf resting on the floor behind him. "I respect the man, but I don't know how he'll react if I change. Will he make it swift or kill me slowly? I'd rather die quickly and painlessly. Promise me. Both of you."

"I promise," Benten replied, sounding solemn.

Heilig offered the man a thankful nod before turning back to the boy. "Arnald?"

"Of course," he replied, tears welling in his eyes.

Benten peered towards a door at the side of the dining hall, one that led to the galley. The aroma of meat cooking in the kitchen continued to grow thickly throughout the room. His stomach rumbled loudly as he shifted uncomfortably in his seat.

"Might be sooner than you desire," he offered. "Especially if that beast inside you is getting as hungry as I am."

At that moment, the wolf rose to her feet, keeping her gaze on the open door leading outside. Arnald followed suit, gazing to the door just in time to see Steigauf, dressed in his armour, enter the room. Captain Piers Kraayen passed through the door next, with Sheriff Kysha Naberyn close on his heels. One man offered a high whistle as she appeared.

"Stow that shit," Steigauf roared.

Kysha stared coldly at the offending man.

Beautiful and dangerous, Arnald thought.

Kraayen stepped towards the middle of the room to address the men.

"I apologise for the delay in the night's meal," he began. "We've been in conference, and it was crucial for us to get this right. Unfortunately, several of you are about to be removed from this company and regrouped into a separate party. We don't take these kinds of decisions lightly, hence the setback tonight.

"When I call your name," he continued, pulling a piece of folded parchment from his coat pocket, "you are to immediately and silently move to the troop wagon waiting in the yard outside this door. Your equipment has already been moved, so there is no need to return to your barracks." Kraayen read from the paper, "Fridmund Agdestein."

A wiry man with a long, dark beard, seated near to the kitchen door, stood, took a deep breath, and moved across the floor towards the door.

"He's the best archer," one man muttered.

"Not bad with a sword, either," whispered another.

"Silence," Steigauf bellowed.

"Ulfar Wynneiros," the captain called.

A tall, broad-shouldered man with straw-like hair rose from the table and followed Agdestein to the door.

"Kolfinn Sigemaer."

Sigemaer grinned from ear to ear. He stood a little shorter than the other men. He offered a little wave goodbye to the men at his table before moving away swiftly.

"Ospak Runolffson," called Kraayen.

A powerful, impressive man stood slowly. Strands of his golden hair draped over his expressionless face as he sauntered through the room towards the door.

"Viktor Benten."

Benten looked at both Arnald and Heilig. The colour drained from his face as his usual cheery demeanour turned sour. Silently, he offered them both an apologetic expression as he lifted himself from the table to move to the door.

"Now what?" Heilig whispered softly to Arnald.

"Don't worry," Arnald replied knowingly, almost inaudibly.

The young soldier furrowed his brow as he peered curiously at the boy.

"Johaan Heilig," Kraayen called.

Heilig's furrows grew deeper as he cocked his head, still looking at Arnald, rising to his feet.

"And Arnald Oberlin," the captain finished. "Make your way to the wagon."

Arnald followed his friend to the door, the wolf moving to his side. He glanced over to Steigauf, who offered a wink and a nod.

<hr />

The ride in the troop cart was slow going. Arnald, seated beside Heilig on one of the long benches lining the sides of the carriage, peered over the back of the vehicle to see the wolf following closely. Steigauf, dressed in his recently polished armour, rode through the barracks gates behind them on his dark steed with the elven sheriff, Kysha Naberyn, trailing upon a brown and white spotted stallion.

"Where are our horses, general?" Kolfinn Sigemaer called, seated across from the boy. His face still bore the cheeky grin he wore in the dining hall. Arnald wondered if the feature stuck permanently on his face after the wind changed one day, something his uncle used to warn him of when he poked his tongue out in spite.

"Ahead," the Pit Guard replied. "You'll be united with them soon enough."

The carriage turned onto a cobblestone street as the barracks gates closed with a gentle thud. The horses' hooves clopped loudly against the surface, echoing, and reverberating off the facades of the houses and shops tightly lining the sides of the road. Arnald heard the raucous laughter and boisterous voices resonating from the tavern by the waterfront where the dock workers congregated after a hard day's labouring, a stark contrast to the silence of the usually busy street they moved through. Now, with the night well and truly set in, orange lights flickered from upper windows, behind closed curtains, as inhabitants settled in for the night.

"You can talk, lads," said the driver, a cloaked man with his hood pulled over his head. "We've got a way to go."

Arnald peered around the group. Four of the men, seated on the bench across from him, set their eyes on Heilig. The silent glares made him feel uncomfortable, a knot forming in his stomach.

"What are you looking at?" Viktor Benten, seated on Heilig's other side, growled at them.

"His eyes," Ulfar Wynneiros eventually answered.

"What about them?" Benten persisted with growing anger in his voice.

"They glow," the other replied.

This caught Heilig's attention. Until then, he'd peered at the floor of the troop carriage.

"What do you mean, glow?" he asked.

"Just that," Wynneiros told him, his straw-like hair blowing over his face. He pointed to the wolf following them. "They glow like hers."

Arnald turned to his friend to see the strong yellow surrounding the pupils had increased and the light from the streetlamps reflecting from within the dark holes, like the eyes of an animal.

"Arnald?" Heilig queried.

The boy nodded.

A deep frown struck the man's face as a lone tear streamed over his cheek.

"I'm turning," he whimpered.

"If you do," Wynneiros started, tightening his hand on the hilt of his knife attached to his belt.

"I'll kill him," Benten interjected. "Or the boy will. Not you. Take your hand from your knife."

Arnald felt the tension grow colder than the surrounding air.

"He could turn at any moment," Wynneiros protested. "I'd be doing him a favour."

"I'd be doing us all a favour if I slit your throat now," Benten returned, sliding his own knife from its sheath.

A long silence ensued as the men held one another's gaze.

"Put your knife away," Ospak Runolffson said emotionlessly, staring at the road before them. "No one is getting his throat slit. No one is killing the man-wolf. We are chosen. We fight together. We live together. If we fight one another, we are weak. Put your knife away."

Benten complied, keeping his eyes on Wynneiros.

"And you..." Runolffson turned his face to the straw-haired man. "Put your hatred away. This man is your brother."

"Brother?" Wynneiros blurted. "This monster?"

"We are all brothers now," Runolffson told him. "We might even be all monsters when we complete the mission they have for us."

A deep silence fell upon them all.

The horses' hooves clopped loudly on the cobblestone street, reverberating off the facades of the houses and shops lining the streets.

None spoke a word, except the Pit Guard and the elf, who remained a fair distance behind the troop wagon. Arnald couldn't hear their words and their faces became drawn into the shadows as they passed from the cobbled streets, lined with lamps onto a muddy road leading out of the township.

Tightly packed houses opened out, spread apart. The glow of flickering fires and candlelight now emitted from the windows of dwellings surrounded by fenced yards, followed eventually by farmhouses separated by expanding space.

Grunts and snorts of disapproval from the steeds pulling the wagon occasionally resounded as their hooves moved through the wet slosh of the road beneath them.

"Come on, girls," the driver said soothingly. "Not too far now."

"That's good," Benten offered. "I'm famished. Can any of you smell that? Someone's cooking a roast."

The other passengers turned their faces towards the road ahead. Sure enough, the faint, sweet aroma of food floated in the air towards them.

"Smells like pork," Wynneirros whispered. "By the gods, it smells so good."

"I wonder if they're having taters with it," muttered Sigemaer. "I could go a pile of taters with some pork... And crackle. Can't forget the crackle."

"And gravy," Agdestein put in. "Lots of gravy all over it."

Runolffson shook his head, pulled his cloak around himself tightly and moved his stare to the wagon's floor.

"Not interested in food, my friend?" asked Benten, noticing the large man's reaction.

"You're all wasting your time," he answered. "It's a dream. We're infantrymen. We eat porridge and slop. Whoever it is that meal is prepared for is no member of this troop."

The others responded by relaxing their postures, returning their own gazes to their boots.

Wynneiros pursed his lips and glared at Runolffson. "Nice way to end the party," he growled. "We had a moment here."

"Sorry," the other replied, his face remaining expressionless.

"Mmph," Wynneiros grunted, shuffling in his spot as he pulled his own cloak tightly around him.

"He's right, lads," the driver offered. "No good dreaming about what isn't when all you have is what is. But fortune sometimes favours the stupid. Tonight, you feast. See up ahead. That's where we stay tonight."

The passengers peered past the driver to see orange light flickering from a large building with many windows resting on the side of the road.

"Is that a tavern?" Arnald queried.

"No, laddie," Benten answered. "That's The Maidservant Inn. Only the best establishment of its kind in all Kedielewen."

"The best?" the boy inquired, unable to take his eyes off the building as they drew nearer. He noticed soft light emitting from upper rooms and wide-covered verandas surrounding both the lower and upper levels.

"Is this some kind of joke?" Heilig asked the driver. "They won't let someone like me or the lad in a place like that. Surely, you intend to take us to a stable house, or something of the likes."

The driver shook his head.

"My orders are to drive you here," he answered. "Then we stay the night before returning to the barracks."

Wynneiros sniffed the air.

"By the gods, that smells so good," he said. The aroma of roasting pork grew thicker and sweeter as they closed upon the inn.

"Maybe I'll get some of that crackle, after all." Sigemaer chuckled.

"Crackle?" Agdestein laughed. "We're arriving at The Maidservant Inn and you're speaking of crackle?"

"Why is it the best?" Arnald asked, peering around at the excited faces of all the others, except for Runolffson, who held no expression whatsoever. Arnald wondered if the man could even show emotion.

"The whores," Benten answered with a wide grin.

Arnald furrowed his brow.

"You know? Ladies who offer services to weary travellers for exchange of currency."

"I know what whores are," the boy said. "We had them in my village, too. I just don't understand how whores could make a place the best."

Heilig sighed and leaned in close to Arnald.

"When a man has either come from a long journey on a merchant ship, or by horse along the road from Port Coldspring or the Long Spine Mountains, a woman's honey-pot can be quite enticing," he said. "That's why it's the best. It's also the only establishment of its kind in Shiverwind."

"No." Sigemaer shook his head, smiling from ear to ear. "It's more than that, laddie. These girls are magical in their ways. They do things that no other woman would even think of doing."

"Like what?" Arnald asked.

"Well..." The other tilted his head back and looked at the sky. "Where do I begin?"

"You don't," Steigauf growled. His voice suddenly alarmed the passengers. They hadn't noticed him close the distance or for how long he'd been there, listening. "The boy is a boy and doesn't need to know your filth."

"Sorry, sir." Sigemaer bowed his head.

"Tonight, you get a hot feast, a warm bed and a woman, if you so desire," the Pit Guard announced to the men. "Each of you will have a room for yourselves. Except you, Arnald. You will share."

The boy nodded.

"Will the wolf stay inside with us?" he asked.

"She will." Steigauf nodded. "She will be with you. Not me."

Arnald offered the old man a quizzical look.

"I don't understand."

"Your friend, Mister Heilig, is correct," the Pit Guard replied. "Long journeys get lonely."

Arnald grasped what the old man was saying.

"Who then?" The boy looked around at the others.

"Me," Kysha said from the back of her horse.

Benten raised his brow and whispered, "Lucky bastard."

The boy certainly didn't feel lucky. He looked to the sheriff, who glared back, boring into him with her piercing blue eyes.

Beautiful and dangerous.

"Will you look at that?" Agdestein uttered. All heads turned to The Maidservant Inn's open door. A voluptuous figure, silhouetted by the light issuing from within, stood in the passageway. The woman's form, her curves, the outline of her breasts, and her long legs were clearly visible through the sheer gown she wore.

"Must be cold," Kysha observed.

"Might be she longs for my warm embrace and came running to the door when she heard us coming." Benten smiled.

"Might be that you're an idiot," the sheriff retorted.

"Good evening, gentlemen," the woman said as the carriage pulled to a stop. She looked to the elf and added, "my lady. Your meal for the night is roast pork, potatoes, carrots, and freshly baked bread."

"Taters." Sigemaer grinned.

"What about gravy?" asked Agdestein.

"Of course." The woman laughed. "Plenty to drown your food with."

The archer turned to Arnald, a wide grin on his face.

"Can't wait," he said.

The woman stepped back into the well-lit room and invited the travellers to enter with a wave of her hand.

"Your rooms are prepared," she informed the men as they filed off the back of the carriage. "Your equipment is located against the wall at the base of the stairs and your horses have been fed and taken care of in our stables behind our fine establishment. They'll be ready for your departure in the morning."

The Pit Guard and the elf continued past the troop carrier, steering their horses slowly along the side of the building. The wolf stared after Steigauf, offering a faint whimper.

"Where are you going?" Arnald called after them.

"Putting the horses in the stable," the old man replied. He pointed to the wolf. "Take her inside with you. Get something warm into you both. This might be the last decent meal in a very long time."

With that, Steigauf and Kysha disappeared around the back of the inn.

The men of the troop followed the woman through the door while Arnald and the wolf kept their attention fixed on the edge of the building where the Pit Guard had gone. Eventually, he felt a hand pat his shoulder.

"Come on," Heilig urged him. "The commander gave you an order."

Arnald nodded and followed the others inside with the wolf on his heels.

Chapter Four

THE THICK SMELL OF roast pork filled the room. To Arnald, the aroma invited him, enticed him to take another step. Lantern lights adorned the walls, along with a large iron chandelier hanging from the ceiling in the centre of the room, ensuring the place was well-lit.

Several round wooden tables placed around the space, each with four timber chairs, ensured adequate seating places for the troop. A large bearskin rug rested on the polished timber floor by an open fireplace blazing away at the side.

Bags, knapsacks, weapons, and other items belonging to the travellers rested against the wall on both sides of the hearth. A wide stairwell climbed to an upper platform, where it turned to the left to continue upwards, vanishing through a passage in the ceiling.

A long timber bench sat directly beneath this section of the stairwell. Jugs of ale and mugs set upon table trays, ready to be served, waited patiently along its top. Behind the bar, a reflective surface covered the wall; not clear enough to serve as a looking glass, but sufficient to throw back more light into the room. Shelves placed on its surface housed many bottles and jugs of varied colours, shapes, and sizes.

Several young women, dressed in similar attire to the woman by the door, stood on the stairwell observing the new arrivals, whispering to one another. Some gasped quietly as the wolf stepped to Arnald's side.

"I am Hilda," announced the woman in the sheer gown. The bright light emitting from the surrounding lanterns provided Arnald with the opportunity to see everything beneath the thin material. A quick glance around and the boy noticed that the other men of the troop were as taken as he by her appearance. "These are my ladies."

The men and the women on the stairs exchanged smiles and cheeky waves. Arnald counted eighteen maidservants.

"Are there others arriving tonight?" he asked.

"Others?" Hilda looked at Arnald curiously. "Why do you ask?"

All eyes fell on the boy, waiting for an answer.

"You have nineteen maidservants," Arnald replied, choosing his words carefully. "We don't number—"

"Arnald," Kolfinn Sigemaer snapped. "Some of us might be quite all right with two or three maidservants serving us." He turned his attention to Hilda. "That is, if you aren't expecting others, my lady."

"We aren't," she said with a grin. "The Maidservant Inn has been procured for this night for you. And..." she turned to Arnald. "We have twenty-six maidservants here tonight. Some are upstairs putting the finishing touches to your rooms. So, more than enough to meet all your needs, young soldier."

Arnald felt a strange knot form in his stomach. His hand shot straight to the cloth wrapped around his other arm. Gertrude.

"Choose a table," Hilda continued. "Sit wherever you like. Together or spread out. Your choice. The place is yours tonight, gentlemen. Food will be served shortly."

A hand fell on Arnald's shoulder. He turned to see Heilig by his side.

"Come on," the young soldier said. His eyes glowed, flickering a yellow reflection from the surrounding light. "Let's sit close to the fire."

Arnald sat in the chair, placing the fire to his right and the main door of the inn to his back. Heilig sat across the table from him, putting the stairwell behind him. The wolf plonked herself onto the rug in front of the fire, stretching out to soak in the heat.

Benten joined them at the table, removing his cloak and draping it over the back of his chair, facing the fireplace. Arnald and Heilig watched him with curiosity.

"We're inside," he told them matter-of-factly, as if they should understand. "We're next to a fire and we're about to partake in a hot meal. You two can sweat your holes off... if you wish."

Heilig nodded, offering a small grin.

"He's right," the young soldier said to the boy as he removed his own covering. "We don't need our cloaks. Not tonight."

Arnald followed suit and draped his cloak over the back of his chair as a young lady wearing an apron, headscarf, and an outfit much less revealing than the others, emerged from a door behind the bar. She glanced around the room before locking eyes with Arnald. Quickly, she skirted the side of the bar, hastily making her way to the boy's table.

"Jana," Hilda called from the centre of the room. Her expression appeared stern.

"Sorry, my lady." Jana bowed her head respectfully, stopping in place. "The commander instructed me to serve the boy and wolf immediately."

"Commander?" Hilda glanced at the door behind the bar.

"He's tending to his horse," the young woman explained. She gestured to the ladies on the stairs. "He said he wants the boy and elf girl fed and in bed before..."

"I understand." The other smiled. She looked at the boy and then at her maidservants waiting in place. "Modesty please, ladies. And someone, fetch my robe."

"Aw, come on," Sigemaer complained from his seat across the room.

Hilda offered an apologetic smile as the maidservants filed up the stairs and out of view.

"Just a temporary holdup, gentlemen," she announced. "We'll feast and make sure the youngsters are tucked away in bed before resuming regular business."

"Regular business will bear limitations," Steigauf announced as he entered the room from the door behind the bar. "We have an early start in the morning. I do not want any complaints, meaning I don't want any hungover soldiers. Understood?"

"Yes sir," the men chorused.

Jana made her way to Arnald's side, crouching slightly to his level.

"We're serving pork, potatoes, carrots, cabbage and parsnip," she told him in a low voice. "I can add extra of what you like or take away anything you don't."

"Is there crackle?" he asked.

"Yes," she said. "You'll get some crackle. Would you like butter or gravy on the vegetables?"

"Butter on the vegetables and gravy on everything," Arnald replied, hoping this was an option.

"Good man," Jana approved, looking across the table and straight into Heilig's burning eyes.

"Same for me," he told her.

She nodded nervously.

"And me," Benten put in. "And a loaf of buttered bread, if it's there."

"Absolutely," she replied, lifting herself to full height. "I'll bring a loaf for the table."

"I'll have the same," announced Kysha, brushing behind Jana to sit in the empty seat between Arnald and Heilig. Jana moved away to the bar as all three occupants of the table glanced at each other questioningly before moving their gazes to the elf.

"What's the problem?" she asked, looking at each of them. "Do you dislike girls? Do you have a problem with people in authority? Or do you just hate elves?"

"I don't hate elves," Arnald quickly said.

"We just didn't expect anyone to sit with us," Heilig replied.

"Would you prefer I sit elsewhere?" She locked eyes with him.

"I didn't say that..." the soldier answered. "I welcome you, Sheriff."

"As do I." Arnald nodded.

Benten remained silent, looking past the elf to the flames in the hearth behind her.

"And you?" she pressed.

"I hate elves." He looked down at the table.

Arnald felt the tension in the air tighten all around him. He noticed Benten's lips pursing tightly, quivering as the muscles in his jaw twitched.

"Do tell," Kysha said, her voice calm, unemotional.

"Elves killed my father and mother," he whispered, just loud enough for the others at the table to hear. "Not before making me and my father watch as they took turns raping my mother. Then, with their sharp Eluvian blades, they stabbed into the stomachs of my parents slowly. It took a long time for them to die. I remember their screams that turned to sobs that turned to silence, and I felt grateful when they died. I was happy they weren't suffering anymore." A tear streaked over his cheek. "And then it was my turn. They beat me. They beat me to hear me cry and scream. When that wasn't enough, they raped me. This went on for three days, and all the while my parents' corpses watched on. When they had their fill, they beat me to within an inch of my life and left me to die." He lifted his gaze to meet hers. "I was three years old."

Heilig reached out and placed his hand on Benten's shoulder.

"I'm so sorry this happened to you," he said earnestly. "So many abominable things happened during that war."

"The war was over," Benten growled. "It was a band of elves who fought for Amalith. They escaped the purge that followed. As they moved across from one side of Asalethwen to the other, they raided isolated farmhouses and tortured the occupants along the way. A garrison from Dendadia, who was hunting the band of elves, found me trying to bury my parents at our little farm near Springhollow. By then, the band of merry elves would have crossed the border into Wyrwen. The garrison men were kind, staying with me until they found suitable people to take me in, and all the while their prey were getting further and further away."

Benten returned his gaze to the table and fell silent.

Arnald waited for him to finish the story. Instead, Benten sobbed.

"Did they catch them?" the boy asked, instantly feeling shame for his naivety.

The man slowly shook his head.

"Highwaymen killed my parents," Kysha stated. "I don't remember any of it, except flashes. I remember seeing lots of blood, everywhere. I was not even a year old, but according to my grandparents, I was smart enough to stay silent and hidden. They took nothing from the wagon. We had nothing worth taking. Nothing of value. My grandparents raised me until I turned ten, when my grandmother, after being a widow for two years, passed away. Zain Demeara, the magistrate, and Captain Kraayen took care of me afterwards. I still live in my grandparents' house. My house, now. But

Magistrate Demeara helped to keep me fed while Captain Kraayen trained me for peacekeeping duties."

"Why peacekeeping?" Heilig asked.

"I never want what happened to my parents to happen to anyone else," she answered.

Arnald noticed a strange glint in her eyes as she briefly furrowed her brow. He believed she only told part of her story, keeping something more painful than the brutal deaths of her mother and father to herself.

Kysha moved her gaze back to Benten. "I am very sorry for what happened to your parents. I really am."

With his belly full, and the taste of pork and gravy fresh on his tongue, Arnald ascended the stairs to the upper level with the she-wolf on his heels. He glanced quickly to Steigauf, sitting in a chair by the fireplace with Hilda on his lap. The Pit Guard lifted his mug of ale, offering a nod and wink at the boy before placing his attention on the young maidservant.

Arnald noticed every man watching as he climbed, only they weren't observing him. Rather, they regarded the elf as she ascended the stairwell before the lad.

"Lucky bastard," Sigemaer called, raising his mug to Arnald. Slightly offended, the boy stopped to protest the other's assumption. Kysha took him by the forearm, gripping his sleeve under which the stained cloth rested.

"Ignore it," the elf said softly, pulling him after her.

The men reacted with a cheer.

"You made it worse," Arnald whispered.

"Let them think what they will," she returned, leading him onward.

At the top of the stairs, the floor levelled out, branching to the left and right in a long corridor with doors on one side and windows on the other.

"Your room is the last in that direction," said a maidservant, gesturing to the right. She appeared a little apprehensive as the wolf reached the top of the stairs. "It's my room. I won't be joining you, obviously. That's usually what happens. We usually use our rooms when... But I'll be in another room tonight. So, you will take care of it, won't you?"

"Of course," Kysha replied, furrowing her brow. "What do you believe our intentions to be?"

"Oh, not you," the maidservant said apologetically. She gestured to the wolf.

"She'll be well behaved," Arnald assured her. "You have nothing to fear from her."

"I'm more concerned with what you need to do if she needs to..." the maidservant pointed to the closest window. "You know, find a tree or something."

"She and I just went," the boy replied. "We won't need to go again until morning."

The maidservant nodded.

"I should return to the men," she said, starting for the stairs.

"Miss," Arnald called after her. She stopped on the top step and turned. "Could I ask a favour?"

Kysha eyed the boy cautiously.

"Of course," the maidservant answered, taking a tentative step towards him.

"My friend, Johaan Heilig," he said. "I have a feeling the other men might have whispered in the ears of the ladies here already, telling them about him."

"The man-wolf," she interjected, authenticating Arnald's suspicions.

"He hasn't transformed yet," the elf put in. "He still may not, ever."

"I saw his eyes," the maidservant replied.

Arnald sighed, running his hand through his hair.

"Please, consider keeping company with him," he said. "I'm not asking you to bed him. Just sit and talk. Have a mug of ale or two with him."

"You're a strange boy, Master Arnald," she offered with a small grin. "A boy your age speaking of such things."

"How many boys my age do you know?"

She contemplated his words, nodded, and resumed descending the stairs.

Arnald watched her until she vanished from his view.

"Come on," the elf said, taking him by the arm again.

Once they were in the room, Kysha let go of Arnald's sleeve and crossed the floor to the enormous bed sitting in the middle of the room with its headboard against the windowsill on the far wall. Floral curtains draped across the glass panels; tulips and daffodils, carnations and periwinkles provided a certain level of privacy from people passing by on the road outside. Two candles flickered from the top of two bedside tables, one on each side of the bed.

"Latch the door," she said, unbuckling her belt. Arnald did so, nervously fumbling with the device before successfully fastening it in place. "Now, take off your clothes."

Arnald felt a knot form in his gut as all his joints froze in place.

"What?"

"Take off your clothes," she repeated, sitting on the edge of the bed to remove her boots. "Keep your undergarments on. I won't have you sharing a bed with me if you intend to wear that filthy outfit. Especially after you promised to take care of that young lady's room for her."

Arnald moved to his side of the bed and undressed, focusing his attention on the wall closest to him, trying to not think about the beautiful Eluvian woman behind him. Once he stripped to his undergarments, he slipped beneath the covers of the bed, rolling onto his side to face away from her. The sheets were cool to the touch. A shallow shiver ran along his spine as he tightened his body into a ball.

The bed shook slightly as she followed his lead.

"Blow out your candle," she instructed before extinguishing the light on her side. He craned his neck and shot out a blast of air from his lips.

Darkness.

"We will warm quicker if we move closer together," she suggested.

He touched the cloth on his arm, thinking of Gertrude. He imagined her glaring at him disapprovingly.

Before he could respond to Kysha's suggestion, the she-wolf leaped onto the bed and settled between the two occupants. A wide smile spread across Arnald's face.

"It seems she has other ideas," he said.

"She's very protective of you," Kysha replied, sounding disappointed.

Arnald felt troubled by the tone in her voice.

"I'm twelve," he said, reminding her of his age. "I'll be thirteen next autumn. I was promised to a girl, and we would have been wed the following spring if everything didn't die when it did."

A momentary silence followed, enough time for tears to spill from the boy's eyes.

"I'm sorry, Arnald," she whispered back. "Please forgive me."

"It's not your fault," he told her, a smile creeping on his face. "I'm irresistible. Besides, the mood downstairs might be spreading."

"Might be." She chuckled. It was the first time he heard her laugh at all. "I'm not much older than you, you know. People assume elves age slower than men, but we don't. We're stronger and faster, but we are so much alike in every other way."

"How old are you?" he asked.

"Fourteen," she replied. "I'll be fifteen next winter."

Fourteen!

"Is that why Magistrate Demeara didn't want you to join us on this journey?"

"Yes," she answered. "He's been like a father to me for the past year."

"Then why did he just let you go?"

"I'm not his daughter," she said. "I can choose to go wherever I like."

Arnald turned onto his back, causing the she-wolf to grumble in protest.

"I don't understand," he said. "You don't know me or owe me anything. You don't know any of the men accompanying us. Why join us?"

She hesitated in answering. He stared at the blackness surrounding him as he waited for her response.

"I'm young and have yet to see the world," she said, repeating her words from the meeting in the magistrate's office.

Deep down, he knew she lied.

"We should try to get some sleep," he said, not wanting to press the issue.

"Good night," she whispered, rolling away.

"Night," he returned, touching the cloth on his arm with his fingers.

Goodnight, Gertrude.

Chapter Five

WHEN ARNALD WOKE, IT wasn't because he felt the natural urge to do so. Instead, the hot breath and unwelcome sensation of the wolf's wet tongue raking across his forehead pulled him from his slumber.

"All right," he whispered, hoping the actions of the she-wolf hadn't stirred Kysha from sleeping. The wolf stealthily climbed over the boy and landed silently on the floor. Arnald reached above his head to pull the curtain back from the window. Darkness and stars.

As gently and quietly as he could, he lifted himself out of bed and dressed, looking at the elf, hoping she slept deeply. The wolf stood by the door, emitting a soft whine.

"Shhh," the boy hissed as he laced and buckled his boots.

A groan from the far side of the bed made him freeze in place.

"Where are you going?" Kysha grumbled, lifting her head to look in his direction.

"Sorry for waking you," Arnald whispered. "She needs to go for a walk. Truthfully, so do I. Go back to sleep."

"Mmph," she grunted, flopping her head back onto the pillow.

Arnald draped his cloak over his shoulders before unlatching the door to let both him and the wolf out. Once they were in the corridor, he turned to close the door behind him as quietly as he could.

"Come on," he said to the wolf, walking towards the stairwell. The wall lamps flickered, illuminating the passageway with a dull orange glow.

As he descended to the lower level, he saw empty mugs, some overturned chairs, and smelled the thick aroma of stale ale. It almost appeared to him as if a battle took place during the previous night.

Both wolf and boy stepped cautiously through the room towards the door. Low flames lapped at the charred remains of logs in the fireplace. Arnald felt tempted to stoke them back to life, but the powerful urge to go outside compelled him to press on.

Unlatching the door, he let the she-wolf out first as a blast of cold air swam inside, causing him to shiver. She crossed the timber decking and dropped to the snow by the roadside, waiting for him to close the door behind him.

"You don't need to wait for me," he whispered to her. He followed her to the ground and pointed to some trees on the far side of the road. "I'm going there. You go wherever you like."

She stayed by his side until they reached some shrubbery by the edge of the woodland where he unlaced his trousers. She crept into the shadows beneath the trees, vanishing from his sight. This gave him some relief, as he didn't like her watching him during such moments.

More relief ensued as his body relaxed and released the previous night's reservoir. As liquid splashed against the side of the trunk of a tall pine tree, Arnald peered towards the waterfront. Lights in the distance reflected on the waterfront. Shiverwind didn't look all that far away, at least not as far as the previous night's journey seemed to show.

He peered up at the sky as the flow relaxed and slowed. The stars burned bright in the clear sky, exhibiting twisting bands where countless pinpricks in the black curtain of night drew close together and seemingly swept across the expanse. Some seemed so large and bright, he thought anyone could be forgiven if they reached out to try to take them out of the air. Others appeared dull and tiny, looking as if they were far, far away.

He laced his trousers, turning in place as he kept his gaze on the sky above, seeing a faint purple glow close to the horizon far to the east.

A low warning growl from the she-wolf behind him brought him back to earth. Kysha stood a few feet before him, at the side of the road, her hood pulled tight over her head.

The sight startled him.

"There's a perfectly good privy behind the inn," she told him, pointing back to the building.

He stood frozen in place, staring at her questioningly.

"You were watching me?"

"No," she replied defensively. "I just got here."

"I didn't hear you approach," he told her as the she-wolf moved to his side, keeping her eyes on the elf. "You should have announced yourself."

"I'm sorry." Kysha looked away shamefacedly. "I didn't mean to upset you. I just got here. I saw nothing. I just thought you might need company out here on your own."

"I'm not on my own," he reminded her, reaching out to rub the wolf's ear.

"I'm sorry," she repeated.

He let out a long breath, calming his nerves.

"I think we should go back inside," he said, walking by her. "The fire needs stoking and we should prepare for the journey ahead."

"Arnald," she interjected.

"Forget it," he told her, gripping his sleeve covering the cloth. "You saw nothing. No harm done."

She followed him back to The Maidservant Inn in silence.

Arnald held the door open for Kysha and the wolf before latching it shut behind him. He moved to the fireplace, picking up a poker leaning against the stonework to encourage the flames to live again.

"I'll see if there's more wood in the kitchen," the elf said quietly, passing through the door behind the bar as the she-wolf planted herself on the rug before the hearth. Arnald nodded, stoking the charred embers as best he could.

"Trouble in paradise?" a low voice said from the stairs. The boy turned to see Steigauf descending slowly, tightening the straps of his vambrace.

"What?"

"She doesn't appear happy," the Pit Guard replied, strolling to the fireplace to stand by the lad. "Did you two... you know?"

"No," Arnald answered, glancing at the door behind the bar. "We just slept."

Steigauf nodded.

"Don't let the boys know," he said. "They put money on it. All except your two friends. Those two believed you would be too much of a gentleman. Seems they're right."

"What about you?" Arnald asked, leaning the poker against the stonework.

"I bet you wouldn't," he admitted. "Not because you're a gentleman. But, because the two of you are still children and probably too scared to go through with such things at your age."

The boy watched the flames dance around for a short time.

"I think she fancies me," he said, confiding in the old man.

"Of course she does," the Pit Guard replied. "Elves are a funny stock. The moment she saw you, she was drawn to you. She'll be loyal to you through thick and thin, laddie. You could find another to love, and so could she, but a connection was made the other night when she first laid eyes on you in the magistrate's office. Perhaps before that— when she came to the barracks. You'd be wise to make sure your relationship with her stays positive. One of the worst things to have is an elf as an enemy."

Beautiful and dangerous.

"Would she kill me?" the boy asked.

"Probably not. I don't think it's in her nature to murder someone she considers an ally," Steigauf returned, stretching out to scratch the wolf behind an ear. "Then again, she is a woman."

Kysha stepped through the door, lugging a large canvas firewood carrier, loaded with chocks of timber.

"Hilda gave me this," she announced. "They're cooking breakfast."

"I hope it's not porridge," Arnald grumbled, taking a seat at the table he occupied the night before.

"Bacon, eggs and toasted bread made from last night's leftover loaves," the elf replied, crouching to load a few timber chocks into the fireplace. She peered up at the Pit Guard and offered a smile. "Good morning, General."

"Morning, Sheriff," he returned.

"Just Kysha, now," she reminded him. "I gave up being a sheriff, remember?"

"I do," said Steigauf.

Kysha looked at Arnald, wanting to say something, but opted to turn her attention back to the fire.

The Pit Guard gave the boy an intense glare, signalling with a tilt of his head to say something to her.

Arnald pursed his lips and nodded.

"I'm sorry," he said. She turned to face him. "I shouldn't have spoken to you the way I did."

"It's all right," she replied, standing to place the canvas carrier on the floor by the poker. "I shouldn't have approached you without signalling you first. I would have felt violated if you had done the same to me."

He momentarily locked onto her piercing blue eyes before his gaze drew to her golden braid draping over her shoulder, coming to rest upon her breast.

Beautiful and dangerous.

A strange sensation ran over the skin of his forearm where he kept the cloth.

He glanced away to the flames, dancing higher and brighter as they bit into the fresh chocks of wood.

"Truce, then?" he suggested.

She smiled. "Truce."

———◄O►———

The troop gradually took their places at the tables spread around the room. Heilig and Benten joined the elf and boy at their table by the fireplace where they all eyed each other silently, suspiciously. Eventually, they all broke into a laughing fit.

"So?" Benten asked, playing with his knife and fork as he moved his gaze from Kysha to Arnald.

"So," the elf repeated.

The other waited for more. When nothing followed, he pressed. "So, did you two... you know?"

"I really don't see how that is any of your business," she answered, cocking her brow.

Arnald glanced around the room and saw others looking their way.

"Did you?" he blurted, hoping to change the focal point of the conversation.

"Aye." Benten leaned back in his chair and smiled. "I had two of those lovely maidservants to myself. Oh, the things they can do. Let me tell you." He leaned forward, placing his elbows on the table to get in nice and close.

"Please don't," Kysha interjected.

"Why not?" He seemed offended. "If you two shared your adventure from last night with us, I'd be more than happy to hear all about it."

"I'm not you," the elf said, rising to her feet. "And I'd rather not know." She turned and strode to the fireplace, lowering herself beside the wolf.

"It's clear you're not me," Benten replied, shrugging his shoulders. "And I'm sorry if I upset you."

She ignored him, reaching out gingerly to rub the wolf's ears. To Arnald's surprise, the wolf allowed it.

"You asked," Benten whispered to him. "You got me in trouble just now."

"I didn't mean to," he replied. "I just don't want to talk about..." He shot a quick look in Kysha's direction. Benten nodded, seeming to understand.

"This one's looking better," the man said, nodding towards Heilig. "Don't you think?"

Arnald examined the young soldier sitting across from him.

"I don't know what he's talking about," Heilig told him. "He said the same thing when we met at the top of the stairs."

"Your eyes have changed," the boy explained. "They're not glowing like they were last night. Not like hers, anyway." He nodded to the wolf. "They're just green, now."

"A full belly and that young maidservant might have tamed the beast inside," Benten added.

"For how long?" Heilig asked.

Chatter from the other tables built as maidservants appeared from the door behind the bar, carrying plates of steaming bacon, eggs, and slices of buttered toast. Arnald could faintly hear the utterances of praises about *this one* and *that one* as the young ladies entered the room.

The maidservant whose room Arnald and Kysha stayed in overnight, approached the table, carrying one plate. She placed it before Heilig and smiled.

"Thank you, Johaan," she said, placing a hand on his shoulder.

"No." He shook his head, touching her hand with his own. "Thank you, Isabel."

Two others approached, one carrying two plates, the other only carrying one.

"Here you are, naughty boy," said the maidservant with one plate. She placed it in front of Benten.

"Thank you, my lady," he returned, slapping her on the rump. The other young lady put one plate in front of Arnald and the other in the empty place once occupied by Kysha.

"Will the young miss be joining you here?" the maidservant asked.

"I'll take it to her," Arnald said, lifting himself to his feet. He skilfully grabbed a knife, fork, and plate of food in each hand and carried them to the rug, where the elf and wolf waited. Lowering himself carefully into a cross-legged position, he held one plate out to Kysha. "Here."

The elf looked at him and smiled.

"She's letting me touch her," she said.

"I think you're growing on her," Arnald replied, still holding the plate of steaming food out for the elf. "Please, take this. My arm is beginning to hurt."

She did so, placing it on her lap.

The wolf lifted her head and licked her lips, eyeballing the bacon.

"Miss?" Arnald called to the maidservant, who was just making her way back to the bar. She stopped and turned to face the boy. "Could we get a plate of bacon for my friend here?"

"We've got one prepared," she replied. "Only, it has bacon and some leftover pork from last night, still on the bone. Will that be all right? We'll just throw it out otherwise."

"That will be fine," he answered before turning his attention to the wolf, who continued staring hungrily at the bacon on Kysha's plate. "Yours is coming. Be patient."

The wolf plonked her head down onto the rug and let out a soft whine.

———◆O◆———

After a hearty breakfast, the troop carried their equipment from the inn to the stable house behind the establishment where they loaded the horses. Arnald tightened the straps of his saddle on his white steed before feeding it a carrot.

"Where did you get that?" Kysha asked quietly as she fit a bridle over her stallion's head, peering about to see if others were listening.

"I took it from the kitchen," Arnald explained. "I have more here." He reached into a canvas bag hanging across his body on a sling stretching from his right shoulder to his left hip and retrieved another carrot.

"Put that away," she snapped in a low whisper. "You can't just take things like that."

"I didn't steal it," he assured her. "Hilda gave them to me."

"Hilda gave them to you?" the elf queried suspiciously.

Arnald put the carrot back into the bag and nodded.

"While you were sitting on the floor earning the wolf's trust, scratching her ears while really listening to the men boast about their night deeds," he said with a smile, "I helped with the dishes in the kitchen. They rewarded me with these carrots, a block of cheese, some boiled lollies, and a kiss from Jana."

Kysha appeared shocked.

"Jana kissed you?" she whispered.

Arnald nodded, scratching his horse's muzzle.

"Where did she kiss you?"

"In the kitchen." He grinned.

"Not there," she said, sounding frustrated. "Where *on you* did she kiss you?"

"My forehead," Arnald replied, peering into the elf's eyes, and seeing elements of insecurity, covetousness, and envy. "She kissed me on my forehead."

"Mount up," Steigauf hollered from atop his black steed. His armour glistened in the morning light streaming through the trees. "We have a long way to go."

Arnald lifted himself onto his horse, only to come face-to-face with Kysha already waiting in her saddle.

"Forehead?" she asked suspiciously.

He nodded as he turned his charger towards the doors of the stable house.

The men formed two lines as they filed upon horseback through the doors and past The Maidservant Inn. The young ladies gathered on the porch to wave and blow kisses to the men as they rode by.

"Good luck out there, lads," called the driver, sitting in the seat of the troop carrier, waiting at the side of the road for the soldiers to pass.

"We didn't see you at breakfast this morning, driver," Steigauf called.

"You never heard of breakfast-in-bed?" the other replied.

"Fair call!" The Pit Guard laughed.

Kysha, riding at the rear of the line with Arnald, searched the gathering on the porch with her eyes until she found Jana. The maidservant waved and blew Arnald a kiss, who, in turn, blew one back.

"Forehead, my arse," the elf growled.

Chapter Six

THE TEN RIDERS TROTTED along the road at a steady pace, moving beneath over-arching trees that resembled tunnels in places. The bare limbs of maples and oak twisted and stretched above them like malformed fingers. Occasionally, the way ahead opened with pine forest keeping mostly on their right.

Arnald's interest remained on his left, the crystal-clear water of the Cove of Safe Keeping. Its expanse spread so far to the horizon; it could easily be mistaken for a sea. Riding at the back of the troop behind two pack horses being led by Heilig and Benten, observing the glassy surface of the cove, he remembered home. In particular, he remembered sitting on the pier with Gertrude the day he and Jörgen first spied the dark ship. A strange twinge tickled his forearm where he kept the cloth.

Coward, she hissed deep inside his head.

A frown crept over his face as he moved his hand to his forearm.

"What's the matter?" Kysha asked.

He shook his head. She saw his hand gripping the sleeve of his right arm. Pursing her lips, she followed his gaze to the water. She tried to remain silent but couldn't.

"I know what you hide," she said eventually.

He continued to stare out to the cove, not making a sound.

"Why do you let her condemn you?" the elf pressed.

Arnald shot her a fiery, tear-filled glare.

"I'm sorry," she told him instantly, her expression bearing a hint of pain.

He wiped his eyes and shook his head again. "It's all right." Arnald glanced ahead to the other riders before peering down to the wolf trotting by his side. "Why didn't that rider from Northwell come with us, do you think?"

"You're changing the subject," she noted. "I guess he wanted to get back to his commander with the news about us coming. I'm uncertain."

"He could have ridden with us," the boy replied. "The more, the merrier."

"You don't seem too merry," said Kysha.

"I'll be fine." He wiped his eyes again.

The elf watched him for a small time before moving her gaze to the water again.

"He left last night, so he's most likely in Port Coldspring, by now," she told the boy. "Those Eluvian horses move quickly. If he doesn't stop, he'll be in Northwell before the morning comes."

"And us?" Arnald asked, looking at her with interest. "How long before we reach Port Coldspring?"

"At this pace?" She looked up to the arms of more maples and oaks reaching over the road. "We should arrive tomorrow night. Northwell, another two days after that and Mountainfall perhaps another three or four days."

"A week," he whispered.

"A week," she repeated. "I hope they hold out long enough for us to get there."

"It might be nothing," he put in. "Osman thinks it's too far inland for raiders to attack."

"A severed head on a pike isn't nothing, Arnald," the elf said. "Something, someone did that."

He considered her words and nodded.

"What if it's just someone from the village?" he asked. "Someone who saw an opportunity to rob a traveller, or to kill for fun?"

"It's not often we come across someone who kills for fun," she answered. "But those kinds of people do exist. This is why we need to investigate."

"Will you play the part of the sheriff again?"

"I suppose I'm still enforcing the law by being a member of this party," Kysha said. "But I don't believe I'll ever be sheriff again. Time will tell."

Arnald watched her as they rode on in silence. She kept looking about at the branches of the trees, watching small swallows weaving between the twisted limbs.

Beautiful.

The gentle twinge returned to his arm.

His hand instinctively returned to the sleeve.

Watching the elf, he realised his reaction was because of something of his own making. Gertrude was gone.

She wouldn't let him go because he wouldn't let her go.

"I don't know why," he said suddenly.

Kysha placed her attention on him.

"What's that?"

"I don't know why I let her condemn me," he explained, wiping tears away on his sleeves. "She was never that way in life. She was the sweetest person I ever knew, and I loved her."

She reached over and touched his thigh.

"It's not your fault, Arnald," she assured him. "You can't go on blaming yourself. You hear her voice, but they're your words."

"I know," he acknowledged, feeling as if a hard punch had struck him in the stomach. He buckled over in his saddle and quietly cried.

Heilig, riding just ahead of them, craned his neck and made eye contact with the elf. He gave her a knowing nod before returning his attention to the road ahead.

───◆───

With only a quick stop to allow the horses to drink from a small, chattering brook, the troop rode steadily for the rest of the day. Eventually, as the sun drew low in the western sky, Steigauf called for the horsemen to pull to a halt near the edge of a stone bridge. A flowing rapid passed beneath the crossing and a small clearing by the road's side on their right made for a suitable camping spot.

"This'll do," the Pit Guard called, pointing to a patch of flat, open ground. "Put the tents up there and a fire there."

Arnald dismounted his steed and gave the wolf a rub under her chin. She responded by licking his hands.

"Come and help me," Kysha said to him, dropping from her spotted stallion before leading it to the packhorses, where she retrieved a long rope. "We'll tie this between the trees over there to hitch the horses for the night."

Before long, the troop had tethered the twelve horses in place and assembled four tents in place. The fire, however, proved to be more stubborn.

"The wood's too wet," Wynneiros pointed out. "We need to let it dry."

"A tad bit difficult without a fire," Sigemaer retorted. "Have we got anything worth burning? Just to get this thing started."

"No," Steigauf grunted as he passed by to place some items in his tent. "You'll need to find a way, boys."

"Sir," Kysha called from Arnald's side, observing Wynneiros's feeble attempts to light the fire with flint rocks. Sparks burst from the stones, again and again, only to extinguish on the damp kindling.

"What is it, Kysha?" the Pit Guard returned, placing his attention on her.

"Sleeping arrangements?"

The old man nodded.

"My tent." He pointed to the small structure next to him. "Just me, and the wolf, if she desires. That tent." He gestured to one sitting to the left of his. "You, Arnald, Johaan, and Viktor. No wolf," he said to Arnald. "It'll be crammed in there with four of you." He turned to Heilig and Benten, who were gathering wood from the edge of the forest near to the tethered horses. "I'm trusting you to look after them."

"Aye, sir," the men chorused.

"I can take care of myself," Kysha argued.

"I know," the old man agreed before turning to enter his tent.

Wynneiros swore as more sparks landed harmlessly on the timber.

"Well, I'm at a loss," he said, looking around for support.

"What about you?" Sigemaer asked, looking at the elf.

"What about me?"

"You're an elf," he said.

"Excellent observation skills, soldier," Benten remarked.

"I mean, elves have magic powers," he retorted. "Maybe she could magic us a fire."

"Maybe I can magic this sword right up your bunghole," she replied, pulling her long blade free of its sheath.

"Wait." He held his hands up to her. "I meant no offence."

"Elves aren't any more magic than you or me," Heilig said, carrying his bedroll to the tent. He looked at Arnald as he lifted the tent flap. "Viktor and I will sleep by the walls, you two between us. All right?"

The boy nodded as Kysha slid her sword away.

"All right," she agreed. "But you're on my side. I don't trust Viktor's hands."

"What?" Benten gasped, appearing offended. He then shrugged his shoulders, "Yeah, all right then."

Sigemaer stepped forward, clearly not finished with the discussion.

"Elves are magic," he argued. "They don't age like men."

"You're incorrect," Kysha returned. "We do age like you. We're just stronger and better looking while you grow weaker and wrinkle. We're faster, quieter and better fighters than you."

Beautiful and dangerous, Arnald thought.

"Traits of their kind," Steigauf said, emerging from his tent. "Something I think she might be more than delighted to educate you about, soldier." The Pit Guard allowed the warning to sink in. "Now, light this fire or it will have to be carrots and a block of cheese for supper."

Arnald shot Steigauf a quick look. The Pit Guard replied with a simple cock of his head.

"What is for supper?" Runolffson asked, unbuckling his bedroll from his saddle. "Leftover pork from last night? Perhaps some of that bacon?"

"Oh, something better." Steigauf smiled, moving to one packhorse to retrieve a small hessian sack. "Oats to make porridge which contains all the nutritional goodness every soldier needs."

The troop let out a long groan of disappointment.

Wynneiros paused, lowering the flint stones to the ground.

"I'd rather die of starvation," he grumbled.

"That's a possibility," the Pit Guard told him. "Especially if you don't get that fire started soon."

Arnald briskly made his way to the packhorse and started rummaging through the equipment still strapped to its back. After moving to its other side and rummaging some more, he found what he sought. A small hatchet.

"What are you doing?" Benten called after him as the boy quickly made his way through knee-deep snow towards the nearest pine trees. "We already have enough wood. All of it is useless, so why would you want to get more?"

"I don't think any of you grew up here, in Kedielewen," the boy replied. "So, none of you would know how to find dry wood."

He pushed his way into the thick growth of a tree, through the snow-laced needles to its trunk. There, he started chopping into a low limb. Within moments, he dragged the branch onto open ground and hacked the timber into a few portions about the length of his forearm. Discarding the portions with pine needles, or removing them entirely, he carried the pieces of wood to the fire.

"They'll smoke a bit," he told Wynneiros, who stared at him wide-eyed, still holding the flint stones in his hands. "But, with the help of a bit of the dry stuff, on the ground way under that tree, you'll get this fire started."

The other men stood befuddled, gawking at the boy.

"Well, you heard him," Steigauf hollered at them. "Get in there and get some of that dry stuff."

Sigemaer dashed through the gap the boy made under the tree, returning in a flash with his arms filled with dry twigs and brown pine needles. Agdestein was quickly on his heels, doing the same.

As soon as the fresh kindling rested in place with a couple of pieces of wood Arnald supplied, Wynneiros attacked with the flint stones again.

Smoke and tiny orange flecks of light ignited. A loud cheer echoed around the campsite as flames took hold, biting into the fresh logs.

"Well done, laddie," Steigauf said, resting a hand on Arnald's shoulder.

Late into the night, Arnald stirred awake. The sound of the tent flap rustling dragged him from his sleep. The first thing he saw was Kysha's golden braided hair, illuminated by the firelight seeping in through the opening. She nestled herself against him; her face pressing gently against his neck.

Then, his gaze moved to a pair of yellow eyes, almost glowing, reflecting the dull light coming from outside. They appeared to be locked onto him. Arnald felt momentarily tense with fear.

"Johaan. Viktor!" Runolffson's impressive form crouched at the tent's entrance. "It's your watch," he whispered.

Kysha moved slightly, grumbling as if irritated.

"Sorry," the large man uttered before lifting himself to full height and closing the tent flap.

Arnald, however, kept his gaze on Heilig.

"Are you all right?" the boy whispered.

"No," the other growled. "I can feel the change, Arnald. I'm scared."

Benten let out a quick snort, still fast asleep. Heilig shot a quick look to the other man before glancing at the orange glow dancing on the closed flaps of the tent.

"Why is it happening now?" Arnald asked. "You seemed fine earlier."

"I think it has to do with meat." The soldier's voice remained low, guttural, almost animalistic. "The porridge filled the man, but the beast inside needs something else."

"You can't have us," the boy returned, placing an arm over the elf.

"I wouldn't do that," Heilig told him.

"You were watching me," said Arnald. "I saw you."

Heilig sat up, causing Kysha to stir again.

"I wasn't watching you like that," he explained. "I felt the urge to get up and was trying not to wake you two. I promise. I am still very much myself."

"You don't sound yourself," Arnald countered, referring to the soldier's voice.

"I know." Heilig reached for his boots resting by the tent's entrance. He gestured to Benten, sleeping beside Arnald. "Give him a nudge, will you?"

With a quick jab with his elbow, Arnald woke the other man.

"What?" Benten grumbled, lifting his head to gawk grumpily at the boy.

"It's your watch."

Benten flopped his head back down. "I was back at The Maidservant Inn with two of their best, if you know what I mean."

"I'll speak to the commander," Heilig assured Arnald as he slipped his boots on.

Benten sat upright.

"Speak?" he blurted. "What? About my dream of being at The Maidservant Inn? I'd prefer you didn't."

"Stupid," Arnald hissed. "Not that. Keep quiet. You'll wake her."

"She's awake," Kysha grumbled, squirming beneath the covers.

"Sorry," Benten offered.

Heilig picked his sword up from the floor and strapped it to his waist.

"Get dressed," he said to the other soldier. "We're on duty."

With that, he lifted his cloak and withdrew outside.

Benten shuffled about, making a small racket as he quickly dressed and prepared for the watch.

"I am terribly sorry," he whispered, directing his apology to the elf before leaving.

She emitted a soft grunt and pressed herself against Arnald.

Arnald wanted to go back to sleep, but the vision of two yellow eyes staring at him stuck in his mind.

The elf's breathing eased, signalling she had dozed off again. He let his arm stay over her back, too afraid to move in case he woke her.

So, instead of sleeping, he simply lay there under the warm covers, waiting for the sun to rise.

Chapter Seven

K YSHA RODE AT THE front of the line with the Pit Guard, the
wolf trotting by their side. Arnald could see they were in deep
conversation but riding at the back of the troop placed him too far away to
hear any of it. Ospak Runolffson became his riding partner, following the
two packhorses led once again by Heilig and Benten.

"Where do you come from, Arnald?" asked Runolffson, using his fingers
to guide strands of his golden hair away from his face and behind his ear.

Arnald furrowed his brow.

"You know where I'm from," he returned.

"I know your village was attacked," the other stated. "I know everyone
was murdered. I know you wear a dirty rag on your arm to remind you of
one you loved dearly."

Arnald felt his stomach tighten, unsure whether to be offended by the
insensitive reference to the cloth bearing Gertrude's bloodstain.

"I want to know about the people," Runolffson continued. "I want to
know about life in your little part of the world. What did you do there?
Not just you. Everybody. What did everybody do?"

The boy stared out at the water in the cove.

"I don't know," he replied. "They were just people doing whatever they
did."

"Were they farmers?" the man pressed. "Fishers? Goat fuckers? What?"

"Goat fuckers?" Arnald smiled.

"There are some strange people out there," Runolffson answered, his countenance remained unchanging. *Like stone*, Arnald thought. "Some believe their gods will only answer their prayers if they do some very strange things."

"Like..." the boy started.

"Goat fucking," the man said.

Arnald shook his head, continuing to smile as he returned his gaze to the water.

"We had quite a few fishing boats and a long pier to tie them to," he eventually said.

"So, your village was made of fishers?"

"And hunters. And farmers. Mostly livestock like pigs, sheep, chickens, cows, and..." he faced Runolffson, "...goats."

A small glint crept into the big man's eyes. Arnald could have sworn he saw a very faint hint of a smile.

"What about your father?" Runolffson asked. "I heard he fought in battle and saw the mountain fall."

"He told me that one night before the raiders came," the boy said. "He told me he and my uncle saw two witches fall with the mountain. He told me he saw the Elf King Amalith hang. I never saw him fight. Not really. The night when the raiders came, I hid."

Runolffson looked at Arnald for what seemed a long time.

"You did the right thing," the man told him.

"I was a coward," the boy returned, tears welling in his eyes.

"You were wise," Runolffson said. "If you had tried to fight, you would be dead."

"Maybe I should be," Arnald wept.

"You are meant to be here," the big man explained. "You are meant to be with us. For the moment, we are your brothers. We are your family. We are your village. We need you here."

Runolffson's words filled Arnald with a sense of status. He wiped the tears away before returning his gaze to the man riding beside him.

"Now," Runolffson continued, "tell me more about this village of yours. What did your father do there?"

Arnald's mind raced back to the workshop with the little sign swinging from a post.

"He was the tanner."

The day wore on as Runolffson and Arnald continued to talk, and all the while the Pit Guard and the elf continued with their conversation. Just as the discussion between the boy and the man changed topic now and then, Arnald was sure both Kysha and Steigauf didn't stick to one issue either.

"You fancy her," Runolffson uttered quietly so that others couldn't hear.

"What?" The boy shot him a puzzled look.

"The elf." The golden-haired soldier gestured to the front of the line with a nod. "You like her. Can't say I blame you. She's a handsome girl."

"I don't..." Arnald paused, feeling uncomfortable. His hand touched his sleeve, fingers picking at the hem.

"You don't know me well," Runolffson said. "And I am sorry if I say something that upsets you. But your Gertrude is gone, Arnald."

"I know," the boy snapped, momentarily wishing he never shared his story with anyone. But that's what each of them in the troop did. Over time, as they trained, ate, and talked before sleeping in the bunk house, they shared their stories. At least, the parts they wished to share. Arnald had opened up to most of the men, telling them about his family, his feelings for Gertrude and how he hid during the attack on his village, when the raiders murdered everyone he loved. He lowered his gaze to his horse's mane and frowned. "I'm sorry. It's just that I was promised to her."

"And you feel guilty for what happened," the other put in.

Arnald nodded.

"I already told you, and I'm sure others have also told you, it wasn't your fault," Runolffson let him know. "It was the raiders. Not you."

"I know." The boy peered at the water's edge to watch small waves lapping the shore. "I want to find them and kill them all."

"Perhaps one day," Runolffson returned, "I and your new brothers here will help you do that. Huh?"

"Perhaps," Arnald replied, looking back at Kysha at the front of the line. "What do you think they're talking about?"

"The commander and the sheriff?" the man clarified. "The weather. Fishing tips. How the snow falls. You. Who knows? What do people ever talk about when they ride together?"

"Lots of things," he replied with a grin, thinking about the many things he and Runolffson had been discussing.

"Did I mention how I came to be in the service of the infantry?" the man asked.

"No."

"Well..." Runolffson brushed his hair away from his face with his finger. "Remember, I mentioned about how, when I was a child, the physicker told my parents my face couldn't show a great deal of expression because of muscle deformities."

"Yes," the boy said.

"Those deformities almost cost me my life," said the man. "I probably shouldn't tell you this story. But, considering you spent a night in a brothel, it might be all right.

"So, just a little under a year ago, I finished a hard day's work on our little farm and still had some energy to spend. I rode my horse into Jomaandia..."

"Near the Bay of Hope," Arnald said.

"That's right," Runolffson agreed. "Great fishing in the bay. But that's nothing to do with this story. I visited a brothel, paid for a service, and got what I paid for. I fell asleep, as most men do afterwards. But the young lady didn't. She left the bed, dressed, and went downstairs to find another client. I don't know.

"In that time, someone cut her throat open and left her to bleed on the stairs," said the man before exhaling a long sigh. "She didn't deserve that."

Runolffson peered up at the trees.

"The owner of the brothel woke me up," he continued. "He told me to dress and get out of there. He knew I didn't do it, but Jomaandia isn't a large town, and people visiting brothels aren't looked upon favourably, just as brothels aren't looked upon favourably. So, according to the owner, the townsfolk already made their judgement and were gathering in the town square to get me."

"But you didn't kill her," Arnald reiterated. "The owner said so. Surely, the sheriff would hear your argument."

"Jomaandia has no sheriff or magistrate," Runolffson replied. "A little like your own village, I suspect."

"What did you do?"

"I fled," the man answered. "The good people of Jomaandia didn't care about a dead whore. But the opportunity to kill a monster as big as me, who cannot smile or cry, who lives way out of town with his parents. Now, that's something.

"I found a fishing boat captain who took me on board where I offered my services in return for passage to Aliedia," he continued. "From there, a travelling merchant let me ride in his wagon to Driradia. After that, I got some work on the docks, then a trade ship to Shiverwind."

"Then you joined the infantry," Arnald said.

"Then I joined the infantry," Runolffson agreed. "It's good, honest work. I get to help people. And I'm free."

"You have to follow orders and do what you're told," the boy put in.

"All right." The man quickly glanced at Arnald. "Maybe, I'm not free. But I'm alive."

They rode in silence for a while, with Arnald peering at Kysha.

"Have you heard anything of your parents since?"

Runolffson shook his head.

"I have no doubt the community shunned them," he replied. "They were already isolated because of me, long before the brothel. What kind of baby doesn't smile when you tickle it? Or not cry when it is hungry?"

Arnald watched the man as they rode. His expressionless face glanced about, looking at the scenery passing them by. The boy then noticed something residing deep in the man's eyes.

Sadness.

"The people in Jomaandia are wrong about you, Ospak," Arnald told him. "You're not a monster."

"What am I then?" he entreated.

"My brother."

⊷◆⊶

"We should set up camp," Sigemaer called to Steigauf from his saddle. The sun quickly fell towards the horizon, causing the trees to cast deep around the riders. "Don't you think, sir?"

The Pit Guard, still riding beside the elf, turned and gave the soldier an irritated glare.

"We ride on," the old man said, loudly enough for all to hear. "It'll be dark when we reach Port Coldspring."

"Will we be lodging in another fine establishment?" Wynneiros asked with hope.

"No," the Pit Guard replied abruptly, turning to face the road ahead. "You will set up camp on the far side of the town. Kysha and I will make a quick stop at the barracks before joining you."

"Should we be concerned, sir?" Sigemaer asked.

"Yes," Steigauf replied. "You should be concerned with whether you let Ulfar keep the stones for lighting fires. Arnald would be a better choice. I would hope you would have a pot of porridge hot and ready for my arrival."

Arnald felt a sense of pride wash over him.

"Aye," Runolffson called. "Let Arnald have the stones. He can be our fire keeper."

"So, I couldn't light the fire," Wynneiros sang out. "Let's all complain about my poor fire lighting skills."

"All right," Benten replied. "Your fire lighting skills need improvement."

"Your ability to produce flames is wanting," Heilig added.

Both men chuckled.

"Very funny," Wynneiros remarked.

"Ooh, I got one." Agdestein the archer chuckled. "Your flair for fabricating flames is fucked."

Everyone but Wynneiros and Runolffson laughed.

"You can all lick my arse!" Wynneiros shouted.

"With tongues of fire," Arnald called out.

The riders burst into a fit of hysterics, even Wynneiros. Runolffson nodded, offering Arnald an approving wink.

Port Coldspring's streets appeared empty. For Arnald, the dim street lanterns and flickering glow from windows provided the only evidence of life in this township. That, and the two guards, both older men, standing at a post by the edge of the settlement.

"What business have you?" one of them called as the troop slowed their approach.

"We're on assignment from Shiverwind to Mountainfall," Steigauf replied. "A rider must have passed through on his way to Northwell."

"Aye," the guard acceded, eyeing the approaching riders suspiciously. "What's his name?"

Steigauf looked at Kysha, riding by his side.

"Aamon Martano," she called. "He rides an Eluvian horse named Naran."

"Aye," the guard said again. "And you're a little girl."

"She's an elf," Steigauf informed the guard. "She's Kysha Naberyn, Sheriff of Shiverwind."

The news appeared to spark interest in both sentries.

"And you?" asked the second guard.

"Osman Steigauf," he returned as they drew nearer. The guards studied the old man's armour, spying the four engravings of women and swords across the chest piece.

"You're a Pit Guard?" the second inquired.

"I am."

"He's one of The First," Kysha offered.

"One of The First?" The guard gasped before dropping to a knee. "It's an honour, my lord."

Steigauf scrunched his face and shook his head.

"Get up, ya silly fart," said the Pit Guard. "I'm nobody's lord."

"Apologies," the other replied, lifting himself to full height.

"Stupid," the second sentry uttered, offering the first a deriding sneer.

"I need to see the commander of the barracks here, the magistrate and the butcher," Steigauf told the guards. "Where can I find them?"

"Bones for your dog?" the second guard asked, gesturing to the she-wolf.

"What?"

"Bones for your dog," he repeated. "Is that why you want to see the butcher?"

"That'd be my business," the Pit Guard replied. "And she's a wolf, not a dog."

The wolf glared at the guard.

"Oh," the sentry said, tearing his gaze from the she-wolf, and looking back to the Pit Guard. "The commander should be at the barracks. Raiders to the north have kept us pretty busy around these parts. He tends to spend his days and nights holding conferences in his chambers. Most of the infantrymen are elsewhere, hunting these bastards."

Arnald's ears tuned into the discussion. News of such things reached the barracks in Shiverwind but, now he had confirmation. The raiders attacked other places along the shores of the cove. Not just his little village.

"Must be why they have a couple of old men, like yourselves, standing watch," Kysha put in.

"The young men are spread thin," the second sentry said.

"Not the kind of news you should share with strangers on the road," the elf returned.

"Now wait," the second started, his voice emitting a hint of anger. "You said you're on assignment from Shiverwind."

"We could be anyone," she returned. "Lucky for you, we are who we say we are. The magistrate?"

"What?" The sentry furrowed his brow.

"Where is the magistrate?" she elaborated.

"Probably in a tavern," the first guard replied. "Probably drunk under a table or in a whore's chamber. You'd be wasting your time trying to speak with him. You'd have better results with the commander."

"Or the butcher," the second added.

The first pointed to the road behind him.

"Follow this road and turn left at the first intersection," he instructed. "That road leads to the docks and market square. The butcher's dwellings are behind his shop. He'll be there. The barracks are at the far end of the dockyards. You can't miss it."

"My men will set up camp on the other side of the township," Steigauf informed the sentries.

"Not staying at the barracks, then?" the second guard inquired.

"Come on," Sigemaer whispered, barely audible. "Please."

"No," the Pit Guard replied to the guard. He turned in his saddle to face Sigemaer. "We won't afford ourselves any more luxuries until our mission is complete. Understood?"

"Yes sir," the men chorused.

The first sentry pointed to the road behind him once again.

"If they follow this road around to the other side of town, they'll come upon another sentry post with another two old farts, like us," he said. "There is a field where you can set up camp there. Tell them Terence and Rupert say hello."

"Their names?" Arnald called from the back of the line.

"You have a boy with you?" the first guard queried, standing on his toes to peer along the row of riders.

"Yes," Steigauf answered. "We have a little elf girl and a young boy in our company."

"Perhaps," the first guard suggested, offering a concerned look to the Pit Guard. "Perhaps they'd be better staying with us here in Port Coldspring? The road isn't the safest place for children."

"And Port Coldspring is?" the old soldier returned. "What, with all the raiders in the area, only old men for protection and a drunkard magistrate? I think not."

"Their names?" Kysha asked, repeating Arnald's question.

"Willem and Ivor," the guard replied.

Steigauf turned in his saddle and peered along the line.

"Ospak," he called.

"Yes, sir," Runolffson replied, straightening his posture.

"You are in charge during my absence," the Pit Guard said. "Take the men, set up camp and have a pot of oats bubbling before I join you."

"Yes, sir," the other repeated, urging his steed forward, leading the others past the sentry post to traverse the road around the township.

"Now," Steigauf said, returning his attention to the guards. "If you don't mind, gentlemen. I have business and limited time to conduct it. Good evening."

Chapter Eight

———◆◆◆———

THE TROOP RODE MOST of the way around the outskirts of the township of Port Coldspring before Arnald realised the wolf followed a short distance behind him. She appeared to slink in the shadows on the farthest side of the road to the settlement, weaving in and out of the trees, lingering in the light just long enough for the boy to notice.

"Come on, then," he called to her, patting his thigh.

She lowered her head to sniff the ground and trotted into the scrub, out of view.

Before long, the riders found the sentry post where two more guards stood by a fire on the edge of the road.

"Willem and Ivor?" Runolffson called.

"Aye," replied one of the elderly men. "Who might you be?"

"Ospak Runolffson," the rider answered. "We are infantrymen from Shiverwind."

"Come to relieve us?" the guard asked.

"Afraid not," Runolffson told him, pulling his horse to a stop. "We're on assignment and were told by the guards on the other side of town to set up camp hereabouts."

"Terence and Rupert," Arnald called from the back. The two elderly guards looked at the boy and nodded. "They say hello."

"Well, hello to them," the other guard, wearing a long white beard, offered. "I hope they're freezing their nut sacks off over there."

Sigemaer snickered.

"You've a wolf on your tail," the first guard said, lifting his sword from the sheath on his hip.

"She's with us," Runolffson informed the men.

"With you?"

"She's the travelling companion of the boy and our commander," the soldier said.

The guard slid his sword back into place and pointed to an area of open ground a few yards from their position.

"You should set up your camp there," he said as he turned his hand towards an enormous pile of timber chocks behind him. "We've got plenty of wood for a fire. You're welcome to it."

"Thank you," Runolffson said before turning to Wynneiros. "Give the firekeeper the stones and then help Johaan and Viktor carry some of that wood."

Wynneiros bore a disappointed look.

"All right," he muttered, reaching under his cloak to retrieve the flint stones in his coat pocket.

"The rest of us will set up camp," Runolffson ordered, urging his horse forward. "Arnald, you'll need to get that porridge sorted before the commander returns."

———◆◇◆———

It wasn't long before Arnald made a fire and set to preparing a pot of porridge for the troop. Heilig, Benten and Wynneiros joined the boy by the fire after piling extra chocks of wood close by, enough to get them through the night. Runolffson assembled the tents with Sigemaer and Agdestein. The task took a little longer to fulfil than expected. Eventually, all seven men, one boy and the she-wolf, were resting by the fire by the time Steigauf and Kysha returned, their horses laden with extra cargo.

"How's that porridge coming?" the Pit Guard asked as he directed his horse past the men towards the other steeds tethered nearby.

"It's ready," Arnald answered. "We were waiting for you."

"Good," the old man said. "Johaan and Viktor. Come and help us with this."

Heilig and Benten jumped to their feet and followed the two riders away. Arnald watched the exchange between the Pit Guard, elf and two men as Steigauf tethered his horse to the hitching rope with the other steeds. He couldn't hear what they said to one another at such a distance. Not that it mattered. The talk around the fire picked up, drowning out all surrounding ambiences.

"Where are you from, Kolfinn?" Runolffson asked Sigemaer, seated across the fire from him.

"A small village near Blackborough," the smaller man answered. "It has no name. It stands on top of a tall cliff overlooking the gulf. Some of the best scenery I've ever seen in my life."

"What are you doing here?" Agdestein, the archer asked, combing his long beard with his fingers.

"Work," the other replied, offering his usual cheeky grin.

Arnald watched on as Kysha took a large satchel from her horse's back before passing it to Heilig. He draped it over his shoulder as she spoke to him, touching him briefly on the arm. The boy's stomach tightened at the sight.

"Please elaborate," the archer said to Sigemaer, turning his hand like a wheel.

"I come from a poor family," Sigemaer explained. "The local landowners didn't have enough places for farmhands, or hunters or anything. It came down to either I work there, and my father misses out, or he works, and I miss out. So, I did the only thing I could think of doing."

"You enlisted in the infantry," Wynneiros interjected.

Continuing to look on, Steigauf signalled to Benten and Heilig to take a large bundle from his horse. The men complied and started back towards the camp.

"Not yet," Sigemaer said. "I joined the merchant marines first. It didn't last too long, though. I couldn't get used to the motion of the sea."

"Kept losing your breakfast?" Runolffson asked.

"Lunch and supper, too. I made it all the way from Blackborough to

Shiverwind, stopping at every port in between. At first, the other sailors kept telling me it takes time for your sea legs to form. By the time we reached Driradia, they told me I should look for other work because I was probably going to die out there on the seas."

"So, you enlisted then?" Wynneiros said.

"As soon as we reached Shiverwind," Sigemaer replied.

The boy watched Benten unravel the bundle near the allotted tent for himself, Kysha, and the two men he observed. Meanwhile, Heilig placed the satchel given to him by the elf into their tent, before returning to Benten to assist with the bundle. Both men stretched the bundle out flat. It appeared to be a thick canvas sheet. Benten and Heilig lifted two short poles resting in the middle of the sheet, previously wrapped within the package.

"Arnald," Steigauf called, approaching the two men. "Come over here, laddie."

Jumping to his feet, Arnald made his way over with the wolf on his heels.

Kysha tethered her steed, offering him a quick smile before untying her bedroll from her saddle.

"Fetch your bedroll and equipment," the Pit Guard instructed.

"It's a tent," Arnald said as he watched Benten slip one end of the pole into a tiny canvas lip before hoisting it up to plant the other end onto the ground.

"It's a small tent," Steigauf told him. "Meant for one man. But you and Kysha will occupy this one. You're both smaller than any of the rest of us. So, it should suffice."

Arnald touched his sleeve and gave the Pit Guard a puzzled look.

"It's not a request, laddie," the old man told him. "I'm ordering you and Kysha to use this tent."

"May I ask why?" Arnald moved his gaze to Kysha as she approached, carrying her bedroll in her arms. "We're fine with Johaan and Viktor, aren't we?"

"Arnald, please," Heilig interjected with a gentle growl, lifting his end of the smaller tent into place, peering at the boy with yellow eyes. "This isn't about you or Kysha."

Benten tied a guideline onto the pole at his end of the tent, offering the boy a stern look.

Don't argue, it said.

"All right." Arnald nodded, understanding. He looked at Heilig. "But I don't think you could ever hurt us. I don't think you could let yourself do that."

"I need to be sure," Heilig returned. "Because I'm just not as certain about that as you are."

Arnald stood in place for what seemed a long time. He wanted to say something but could think of nothing.

"Get your things," Steigauf commanded.

With a nod, Arnald did what he was told.

After the troop filled themselves with porridge, Arnald retrieved a rag from a satchel usually packed with cooking utensils, bowls, and cutlery. He dipped the rag in a small tin pot of steaming water sitting at the edge of the fire, soaking it through. Sitting back from the flames, leaning against a fallen log the men dragged into place earlier for something to sit upon, Arnald cleaned the larger pot in which he'd cooked the porridge. The interior appeared all but bare already as Wynneiros had scraped the remains out with his fingers earlier.

"We've nothing for breakfast, now," Benten muttered, aiming his comment at the broad-shouldered man.

"There was nothing left," Wynneiros told him. "At least, not enough for breakfast. Not even for one of us to have breakfast."

"I can make more in the morning," Arnald put in. "It's no bother."

"There," Steigauf added. "The firekeeper will make more porridge in the morning."

Arnald put the large pot to his side and stared into the flames, watching them twist through the chocks of timber positioned neatly in the hearth.

"We should get some sleep," Kysha said from across the campfire. Arnald knew she intended the comment for him.

"I'm not ready for bed yet," Sigemaer returned.

"Silly oaf," Agdestein whispered, just loud enough for all to hear.

"She's talking to Arnald," Steigauf said before turning his attention to the boy. "And she's right. It's been a long day and, if you are going to make breakfast for us, you will need to be up early. Off to bed. Both of you."

Arnald immediately rose to his feet.

"A very dutiful soldier," Heilig growled, observing the boy's obedience. "You'll make a great Pit Guard."

A lump formed in Arnald's throat.

"That he will," Steigauf agreed.

He stood in place, as if stuck, wanting to say something in return but not finding the words. A hand gently grabbed his elbow and tugged him toward the small tent.

"Come on," Kysha whispered. "If you need to get up early, so do I."

The wolf lifted herself from the ground beside Steigauf and followed the elf and the boy.

"Not tonight, girl," the Pit Guard told her before she had wandered too far. The wolf lowered her ears and tucked her tail between her legs. Steigauf reached out and rubbed her neck. "There's no room in there for you."

"Barely room for the two of them," Agdestein observed as the Kysha and Arnald crawled into their new tent.

"They'll be fine," the Pit Guard assured the wolf. Arnald watched her as she lowered herself beside the old man again, looking back at him as the boy closed the tent flap.

"You will make a great Pit Guard," Kysha said, kneeling on her bedroll as she unbuckled her sheath and scabbards. Arnald's eyes slowly adjusted to the dark interior, using the faint glow of the fire against the tent walls to help find his way around. The cramped space placed him uncomfortably close to the elf as she undressed.

"Thank you," he replied, taking off his cloak carefully, trying to keep to his side of the tiny interior.

She shifted gracefully into a seated position to slip her boots off before placing them near the entrance of the tent. Arnald clumsily fell on his side as he attempted to remove his own boots. Kysha giggled as she slid under the covers. She then draped her cloak over the top of her bedding and settled on her side, facing him.

Watching him.

Eventually, he followed her lead, leaving his equipment by the tent flap before climbing under his blankets. Lying on his back, he looked at the flickering glow touching the apex of the tent.

"We should consider combining our bedding into one instead of two," she whispered into his ear.

A feeling of unease swept over him as he realised how close together they were, on their own, in the dark.

"Do you mean having only one bed for the both of us?" He touched the cloth on his arm.

"It's practical," she replied. "It's winter. It's cold. The heat from our bodies will keep us both warm."

He continued to stare at the glow above him for some time.

"Arnald?" Kysha breathed. "Are you asleep already?"

"No," he answered, returning his thoughts back to when she and Steigauf arrived at the camp earlier in the evening. "What's in the bag you gave to Johaan?"

"Dried meat," she answered.

"Dried meat?"

"The commander and I believe Johaan's new hunger might be subdued if he eats meat," Kysha told him.

"You're basing this on how he was after eating meat at The Maidservant Inn?"

"Yes," she said. "Both the commander and I spoke with him about it early this morning, before we started on the road. The commander and I talked about what we could do to help Johaan. I suggested we purchase dried meat from the butcher here in Port Coldspring."

"And what did you say to Johaan when you gave him the bag," Arnald asked, "and touched him on his arm?"

Jealousy drove his questioning but didn't understand why. *Do I like her? Do I want her?*

Confusion swirled around in his mind as he shifted between thoughts of Kysha and Gertrude, who still stayed with him in his heart.

The elf inhaled slowly.

"I just told him not to tell anyone what's in the bag," she explained. "If the others knew we had meat, they might react angrily."

Arnald moved his hand away from his sleeve.

You fancy her, he heard Runolffson say in his head.

"You can move closer if you wish," he told her. "But I'd rather keep to my own bedding."

"Thank you," she said, shuffling closer, nestling against him. "Good night."

You fancy her.

Arnald closed his eyes as he pulled his blankets over his head.

"Good night."

Chapter Nine

—◦◦◦—

ARNALD FELT HIMSELF ROCKING from side to side violently. He woke to the sound of Kysha's whispering voice urging him to get up as she shook him.

"All right," he grumbled. "I'm awake."

"You need to get breakfast made," she told him, moving away towards the tent's entrance.

Arnald peered about, trying to make his eyes adjust.

"It's still dark," he complained.

"The sun is on her way," the elf replied, slipping her boots on.

"How can you tell?" the boy asked, wiping his eyes as he sat up. "Is it an elf thing?"

"Yes," she answered with a hint of sarcasm. "It's an elf thing."

By the time he finished stretching and reached for his own boots, Kysha had buckled her scabbards in place, draped her cloak about her and lifted her sheathed sword from the floor.

"Come on," she pressed. "You prepare breakfast. I'll pack our equipment."

"I bet Osman's sleeping at the moment," Arnald grumbled.

"The commander is entitled to do so," Kysha said as she rolled her bedding.

"And Viktor and Johaan," he continued as he laced his boots. "I bet they're sleeping soundly, too. Do you know why?"

"Why?"

"Because it's still night time," Arnald told her, waving a hand around, gesturing to the darkness.

She snickered.

"Go and make breakfast," she said, continuing to pack her gear.

"All right." He put his cloak on and lifted his sword.

"Leave it," she instructed. "I'll strap it to your horse. Don't worry. I'll pack everything the way you like it."

He looked at her thoughtfully, hoping to glimpse her face. She continued to busy herself with packing, and it was too dark to make out her features.

"Thank you," he said, opening the tent flap to leave. "Ooh, and it's cold, too."

She giggled as he clambered outside, closing the flap behind him.

Sigemaer and Agdestein sat by the fire.

"Keeping watch?" Arnald asked derisively as he approached. The scent of baking bread filled his nose. He peered at the township of Port Coldspring, not too far away, and surmised the aroma came from there.

"Don't really need to with those lads over there," the archer explained, pointing to the sentries by the road.

"What's for breakfast, Firekeeper?" Sigemaer inquired.

Arnald lifted the large pot from the ground.

"Porridge," he replied.

"Ooh, how exciting!" the soldier said with a cheeky smile.

"I don't know about you," Agdestein started. "But I don't really feel like porridge for breakfast today. What about you, Kolfinn?"

"No," Sigemaer put in. "I don't believe I do, either."

Arnald felt his stomach tighten.

"It's all we have," the boy told them as he started away with the pot in his hands.

"Not if you put that pot away and fetch the skillet," the archer told him.

Stopping in his tracks, Arnald turned to face the men. Both were wearing broad grins.

"What if we told you we got two loaves of freshly baked bread, some bacon rashers and fresh eggs?" the archer continued.

Arnald's ears perked up. The information came from Agdestein, which meant there might be some genuineness to it. If Sigemaer had told him, he would've doubted the information.

"Do you have some bacon rashers and fresh eggs?" the boy asked.

Both men giggled gleefully, like little children as they gestured like travelling mummers to a large woven handbasket sitting on the ground with a red and white checked towel covering the contents.

"Where?" Arnald pressed.

"The guards over there brought them at their shift change," Sigemaer replied.

"We checked it," Agdestein told him. "There's enough for two days, at least. If we stick to one egg and two rashers each for breakfast today, we'll be able to do the same tomorrow. Twenty eggs and forty rashers. That's enough for all of us, counting the wolf. With two loaves, we can divide one among us now and keep the other for tomorrow."

"What do you say, Firekeeper?" Sigemaer asked, as if seeking Arnald's approval.

"That's very nice of those men," the boy said, peering at the sentry post. "Isn't it?"

"They brought it from the barracks," the archer explained. "I think the men on watch when we arrived might have put in an order for us when they were relieved from duty. Those lads dropped this off when they arrived."

With a nod, Arnald turned and made his way towards the horses with the large pot in his hands. The two men watched him curiously.

"Where are you going?" asked Sigemaer.

"To put this away and fetch the skillet," the boy answered before hearing both men giggle again.

Benten peered over his shoulder to Arnald from his saddle.

"Best breakfast ever, Firekeeper," he said. "I can still taste that bacon on my tongue."

307

Arnald smiled, quite pleased with himself. His ability to fry rashers of bacon and eggs in a skillet wouldn't win wars, but it made everyone happy before setting out for the day.

With Port Coldspring far behind them and the Cove of Safekeeping becoming a memory, they followed the road east, away from the coast. Gradually, the forest closed around them, bringing the aromatic scent of pine and the melodious songs of robins flittering through the growth. The sun felt warm and barely a cloud rested in the blue expanse above.

"It's a good omen," Kysha told him, looking about at their surroundings.

"What is?" he asked. He reached down to rub his steed's white mane. The horse nickered gently as it continued trotting behind the packhorses.

"Everything," the elf replied. "The blue sky. The happy birds. It's not raining or snowing. The sun is warm. Today is a good day. Don't you think?"

He watched her intently, soaking in everything he saw. Feeling an uncomfortable sensation on his arm where he kept the wrapped cloth, he forced himself to remain unresponsive to the urge to touch it.

You fancy her.

Part of him admitted to it. Another part wrestled with guilt and condemnation. Gertrude remained in his heart.

You fancy her.

He did.

She turned to face him, waiting for an answer. He found himself immediately lost in her blue eyes.

"Arnald?" She smiled.

"It is," he replied. "It's a very good day."

The road passed close to a wide river, flowing away in the direction from which they had ridden. Arnald observed Steigauf glancing about here and there before turning to peer at the sun high in the sky, creeping slowly towards the west.

Idle conversation with Kysha caused the boy to lose track of time. They hadn't spoken of anything of value that he recalled. They simply talked.

"We'll find a place to camp just up here," the Pit Guard announced to the troop.

Runolffson glanced at the sun and back to the commander.

"Begging your pardon, sir," he called. "It's not far past noon. Are you certain you want to set up camp now?"

"We set up camp rather late last night," Steigauf replied. "I think we deserve a longer rest before an early start tomorrow. Besides, I'd like to take Fridmund and Arnald on a hunt."

"Sir?" Agdestein queried.

Arnald listened intently upon hearing his name. Hunting seemed a peculiar task, considering the troop had made him their firekeeper. Surely, he served a better purpose in preparing food rather than chasing it, given his poor hunting skills.

But Steigauf answered the archer and Arnald understood.

"The lad needs to practise shooting arrows," the Pit Guard said. "Who better to show him than the best archer in this company?"

"I'm the only archer in this company," Agdestein put in.

"Correct," the old man agreed with a nod.

The troop crossed a shallow, chattering tributary and pulled to the side of the road. Quickly, they unpacked the horses and set up camp. Arnald took the hatchet from the equipment and started for the closest pine tree.

"I'll do that," Benten said, intercepting him and taking the axe. "I think the commander means to go hunting right now." He nodded towards Steigauf, who had removed his armour, placing it neatly by the opening of his tent.

"Oh," Arnald said, preferring to cut wood rather than fire his bow.

"Best give me the flints," Benten said. "Unlike Ulfar, I've lit a few fires in my time. I'll have it bright and burning for you before you know it."

"All right." The boy reached into his pocket to retrieve the stones.

Arnald left Benten to perform his duties, starting back to his camp where he left his bow and quiver.

Jörgen's bow and quiver.

"You'll be fine," Kysha said softly as he entered the tent. She was setting both hers and his bedding in place. "Just listen to his instructions and do your best."

"I've been doing just that since I met him," he replied. "I can't shoot a bow."

"You can," she corrected him. "You just need to practise your aim."

"And chasing live game will help me with that?"

"Your enemies won't sit still for you, waiting for you to perfect your aim," the elf told him.

He grabbed the bow and quiver and gave her a worried look.

"You'll be fine," she told him again.

He crawled back out of the tent and crossed the camp to where Steigauf, Agdestein and the she-wolf waited.

"Ready, laddie?" the Pit Guard asked as he tightened the buckle of his scabbard, holding a dagger.

"I suppose so," Arnald answered sheepishly, peering at the weapon on the old man's hip. "You're not taking a bow?"

"You have your bow," Steigauf answered. "Fridmund has his. More than enough."

"What if we get into trouble?"

"You have your bow," the Pit Guard repeated. "Fridmund has his. I have a dagger and this bitch has very sharp teeth." He reached over and scratched the wolf behind the ear.

"Don't worry, Arnald," Agdestein said. "We won't get into any trouble. I can shoot the beak off a finch in full flight. If trouble comes, it stands no chance against my arrows."

Arnald smiled, not believing the archer's ability to hit a target so small and quick.

"Come on," Steigauf said, moving towards the forest, snow crunching beneath his boots. Arnald quickly stepped in line, following the old soldier with Agdestein and the she-wolf by his sides.

Soon, they were weaving through thick growth, working their way deeper into the woodlands.

Chapter Ten

A RNALD FOLLOWED STEIGAUF CLOSELY, stepping as close to the old man's footprints in the snow as possible, holding his bow in both hands against his chest. If the old soldier ducked beneath a low branch instead of going wide to avoid it, the boy did the same.

He noticed the wolf to his side with her head low, eyes darting to scan the undergrowth. A few tiny birds flitted about, chasing each other as if playing.

"Arnald," Agdestein murmured so softly the boy almost thought it a trick of the brain. He turned his head to face the man following him, noticing the archer rested an arrow on the string as he walked. "Load your bow. You must be ready."

He hadn't considered that. His father, uncle or brother usually did the hunting while he carried the knife for skinning and carving.

Carefully, quietly, he reached over his shoulder and retrieved a shaft. As he followed the Pit Guard, he placed the nock onto the string.

They started down a long slope, where the forest opened to a wide clearing.

Steigauf signalled for them to stop. The she-wolf complied first, stiffening her body as she peered in the direction the old man faced.

Without turning, the soldier pointed to Arnald and beckoned him with the same finger. Trying as hard as he could to avoid making sounds in the snow, the boy edged forward.

Moving his finger to point forwards, Steigauf directed the boy to the intended target.

It took a little time for Arnald to spy the large black rabbit huddled against the trunk of a pine tree, deep in the shadows under the branches. *The old man has extraordinary eyesight,* Arnald thought.

"Take your time," whispered Steigauf.

Arnald raised his bow and took aim, pulling back on the string just as the old man showed him. The sound of his heart thudded in his head.

"Steady your breathing," the Pit Guard told him.

The boy lined up the fletching, shaft, and tip of the arrow with the rabbit's head.

"When you're ready," the old man said softly.

Arnald released the shaft.

It whistled through the air, racing towards the target.

Racing.

Racing.

TWACK!

The big black rabbit bolted away into the woodlands, leaving the arrow sticking from the tree trunk far behind.

Arnald lowered his arms, disappointed.

"Don't feel bad, Arnald," the archer said, stepping forward to pat the boy on the back. "That shot was difficult, and you didn't miss by much."

"Shhh," Steigauf hissed, suddenly holding his hand up to signal the others to be quiet. He pointed to a large patch of shrubbery not too far from where Arnald's arrow had stuck. Steigauf pointed to Arnald again. "Load again, laddie."

Without hesitation, Arnald loaded his bow, seeing the head of a doe sticking up from behind the shrubbery, startled by the sound of the arrow striking the tree.

"Take your time," the old man repeated as if it were a prayer.

The boy pulled back on the string, hearing it creak as it became increasingly tense. He lined up the fletching, shaft, and arrow with the deer's head.

"Steady your breathing."

Arnald inhaled deeply and let out all his air slowly. When his lungs emptied, he let the arrow free.

It zipped with a high whistle for an eternity. Arnald felt a knot form in his stomach as the doe spun her head towards him, responding to the sound of the approaching shaft.

TWACK!

It planted deep into her snout. A spout of bright red blood splashed across her face.

She called out, a sudden and frightening scream. It caused a shudder to run through Arnald's body.

The deer shook her head as she turned to flee, sending a spray of blood over the snow around her hooves.

Another arrow plunged into her eye, causing her to fall, dead.

The boy turned to see Agdestein in a firing stance, holding his bow out before him after taking the shot.

"Good shot, laddie," Steigauf grunted as the wolf raced forward to inspect the kill.

"Fridmund made the kill," Arnald replied.

"Yes," the Pit Guard acknowledged. "You're right. But that was the best shot I have seen you make so far."

Arnald followed the old man down the slope, shaking his head.

"You're too hard on yourself, Arnald," Agdestein said, slinging his bow over his shoulder. "It was a great shot. You're getting better. And you're better than you give yourself credit for."

"But I didn't make the kill," the boy replied. "All I did was wound it."

"Your arrow would have killed it eventually," the archer said as they drew near to the shrubbery.

"From blood loss and pain," said Arnald.

Steigauf crouched by the doe and made a deep cut in her groin with his knife before slitting her stomach open.

"Think back to when you were content in your little village with your family and your beloved Gertrude," the old soldier said. "Could you even hit a target?"

"No," the boy answered as Steigauf reached into the deer to scoop its innards out.

"No," the Pit Guard repeated. "When I first brought you to the barracks in Shiverwind, could you hit the target then?"

"No," Arnald said.

"But you hit that tree," the old soldier said as he pointed with his bloodied knife, "just an inch from the rabbit. You hit this doe when it moved its head. An unskilled archer would have far less success than you. You're improving, laddie. Take our word for it."

Arnald felt a sense of confidence building inside. Agdestein gave the boy another pat on the shoulder with an assuring nod.

The wolf licked her lips hungrily as Steigauf scooped the deer's entrails onto the ground. She whined softly, bobbing her head up and down as she glanced from Steigauf to the organs and back impatiently.

"Yes," he told her. "All right. Go for it."

With that, the wolf buried her muzzle into the mess.

"How are we going to get this back?" the archer asked. "I only expected to nab some rabbit. Not something this big."

"Aye," Steigauf agreed, standing to full height to assess the situation.

"We could cut it up here," Arnald suggested. "Just the legs. That's where most of the meat is. Leave the rest for the forest."

The old man nodded, twirling the blade with his fingers. He crouched again and sliced into the flesh around the doe's hindquarters.

Before long, the four hunters made their way back to camp, Arnald and Steigauf carrying a hind leg each over their shoulders while Agdestein managed the two forelimbs. The she-wolf bore a wide bloodstained grin on her face after devouring the insides of the carcase. The scent of faint smoke wafted through the forest, showing they were getting closer to the campsite.

"Do you think you can carve this into portions, laddie?" Steigauf asked as they trudged through the forest.

"I think we should roast one of the hind legs tonight," he suggested. "I can carve the rest, cook it up on the skillet and store it for another time."

"Good idea," the old soldier agreed. "We should reach Northwell sometime tomorrow. Perhaps we should purchase some beets and potatoes to make a stew."

"We don't have anything to carry a stew in," the boy replied, moving the leg from one shoulder to the other.

"Well," Steigauf said. "Just make enough each evening to satisfy our needs. You can make more the next night, then the next night."

"Is that the role of the firekeeper?" the archer queried. "To be our cook also?"

"No," Steigauf answered. "It's his role to learn all the skills necessary to survive out here on his own and when commanding other men. That is, if he still wishes to be a Pit Guard."

"I do," Arnald immediately replied without hesitating.

The old man frowned and nodded.

"Why?" Arnald asked.

"Well," the Pit Guard said, "I just thought you and Kysha look to be getting along well together. Maybe, you might consider... I don't know."

The boy gave the old man a curious look.

"What? Settling down to have children together?"

"Why not?" Steigauf asked. "She's beautiful, don't you think?"

Beautiful and dangerous.

"Watch it, Arnald," the archer warned. "You might be a victim of entrapment here."

"Not at all," the old man protested. "I'm just saying, the two of you are sharing a tent now. Surely, you've given thought to such things. Perhaps, given in to such things?"

"We have not," Arnald answered.

"Sir?" Agdestein interjected. "They're still children."

"The boy was promised to another," he replied before turning to peer at the boy. "Sorry Arnald."

Arnald shrugged his shoulders or tried to as best he could with a deer's leg resting on them.

"Next spring, if I recall," the old man continued, speaking to the archer. "They were to be wedded then. I don't believe the intention, in Arnald's village, is for the newly married couples to wait for what we might consider adulthood before consummating. Do you? Would you? I wouldn't."

"Seems wrong," Agdestein put in. "It is wrong."

"Things are tougher up here in Kedielewen," Steigauf told him. "Young families are of benefit to communities like Arnald's little village."

"But Arnald's parents weren't so young when they had him," the archer said before turning to the boy for confirmation. "Were they Arnald?"

"No," Arnald replied. "My father and uncle fought in the War of Six before moving to our village. That's where Baba and Mama met each other. But Osman is correct. It is... was the tradition of my village to marry young. Gertrude and I were to marry either this coming spring or the next and have children as soon as we could. Our parents were still negotiating when the wedding should take place before the raiders attacked. But..." he returned his attention to the Pit Guard. "I have done nothing like that with Kysha. We share a tent. That's all."

"But you like her," the old man said, weaving around a tree.

"I don't know," said Arnald. "Perhaps. I think so."

"Let it run its course naturally," the archer proposed. "Friendship first. Build the relationship. If the other things are meant to happen, they'll do so in their own time."

"That's how you live your life, is it?" Steigauf smiled. "You were pretty quick to take what you wanted at The Maidservant Inn. So much for letting the course run naturally."

"That's different, sir," Agdestein answered, grinning from ear to ear.

Arnald surmised a fond memory of the night returned to the archer's thoughts.

"Yes, it is," the old man agreed.

They walked on in silence for a short distance before the old soldier glanced at Arnald.

"I know she likes you, laddie," he said.

Arnald felt a new knot form in his guts. He knew this to be true as well. Kysha had all but said so herself. But the memory of Gertrude weighed heavily upon him, and the urge to touch his arm where the cloth rested continued to return every time he gave his mind to her or the elf.

They trudged onward as Arnald continued to wrestle with his feelings. The scent of smoke increased with each step.

"Sir," Agdestein called suddenly. The she-wolf trotted back to the archer, who stood by a tall pine tree.

"What is it?" Steigauf asked, turning around.

"You need to see," the archer answered, staring at the trunk.

The Pit Guard and the boy moved to the man's side and followed his gaze.

Two lower limb stumps jutted from the stem, sap spilling from the fresh wounds. Below them, several long, deep marks crisscrossing each other.

"Bear," Agdestein told them.

"Aye," the old man agreed. "Big fucker, too."

Arnald felt the knot in his stomach grow tighter.

Chapter Eleven

—◆◇◆—

AFTER HANGING THE DEER'S hind leg from a low tree branch for half of the day, Arnald skinned the pelt and carefully removed the bones from the flesh with his dagger. He placed the meat into the large pot usually used for making porridge and positioned it in the fire, moving the embers around it with a stick before loading more chocks of wood against its sides.

He then took the skillet and sat it on the fire near the pot. Lifting the other hind leg, Arnald skilfully removed the skin. While the rest of the troop rested in their tents, Heilig, Benten and the wolf sat by the fire watching the boy as he sliced portions of meat from the leg with expert ability before dropping them into the pan.

The loud sizzle and the alluring aroma of venison frying brought an instant reaction to the men and the wolf. Benten let out a long groan of pleasure. The wolf licked her lips.

"By the gods, that smells good," Heilig growled.

"You can't have it," Arnald told them, pointing with his knife at the skillet. "This is for later." He directed the blade to the pot. "This is for supper. It will take some time to cook. You'll both be better off if you do something to occupy the time until it's ready."

"Like what?" Benten asked. "We've set up camp, and the sun is still high."

Kysha approached, carrying a satchel over her shoulders.

"You could fill all the water skins if you can't sleep," the elf said.

Reluctantly, the two soldiers stood and moved away. Arnald smiled as he sliced another thin portion of meat from the leg before placing it into the skillet next to the others.

"Can't sleep?" he asked Kysha.

"No," she answered, crouching next to him as she reached into the satchel. She drew out a small leather pouch with a drawstring and gestured to the pot. "Rosemary for the meat, with your permission."

Arnald nodded.

She tipped a small mound of green herbs into her hand and sprinkled it into the pot. The powerful scent wafted into the boy's nostrils.

"A drizzle of honey would be nice," he said. "You don't have any of that in your bag there, do you?"

"Sorry," she said. "We can't have everything."

Using the tip of his blade, Arnald flipped the small portions of venison over in the pan. They sizzled and spat noisily as he returned to carving another slice from the leg. Kysha reached around him to retrieve a bundled cloth resting in a pile of others on the ground beside him. She spread it out wide, anticipating his next move.

Arnald placed the new strip of meat into the skillet before lifting the first piece out. He then placed it in the centre of the cloth and retrieved the second slice, positioning it on top of the other.

And so, it went. He carved more slices from the leg, fried in the skillet, and piled onto the cloth. All the while, the wolf watched as piece after piece sizzled.

Eventually, the leg bore no more flesh. At least not enough for Arnald to carve. He tossed the bone to the she-wolf, who snatched it before it hit the ground, carrying it away towards the boy's and elf's little tent.

As she gnawed noisily on the bone, Arnald lifted a forelimb and repeated the process. Kysha wrapped the cloth around the cooked meat portions, tying a knot on the top before dropping the bundle into her satchel. She then reached for another cloth and stretched it out on the ground, ready for the next lot.

Later that night, the troop picked the pot clean, devouring the meat from the hind leg within minutes. The only member of the company who didn't benefit from the feast was the she-wolf, whose belly remained swollen from the innards she ate on the hunt and the bones she's crunched near Arnald's and Kysha's tent.

"By the gods, that was good." Wynneiros patted his belly, sitting on the ground by the fire with his back against a log. "You cook well, Firekeeper. If this Pit Guard thing doesn't work for you, you could always open a tavern with the sheriff there. You'll have customers from miles around, you will."

"Thank you." Arnald eyed the man suspiciously, uncertain if he complimented or insulted the elf and the boy.

"I think the rosemary brought out extra flavour," Heilig put in. "Don't you think, Viktor?"

Benten glanced at the elf girl sitting beside Arnald, before returning his gaze to the flames.

"Sure," he said reluctantly. "It was a good addition."

Kysha tensed, taking in a deep breath as she looked at the fire. Arnald, sensing her trouble, reached around and placed his hand on the small of her back. It seemed to have the desired effect, as she relaxed slightly, leaning towards him, into him. He put his arm around her.

Steigauf, seated on top of the log, noticed the embrace. They all did.

"It's about time you put your differences aside," he told Benten. "She is not one of the elves that wronged you."

"I know, sir," Benten replied. "I'm trying. I like the girl. I really do. But I see those eyes of hers and those pointy ears and I know those were the same kind of eyes and ears my family saw before they were slaughtered."

Pressing herself harder against Arnald, Kysha sobbed quietly.

"This goes for all of you," the Pit Guard said. "Get over your prejudices and disagreements. Not just with each other, but with everyone and everything. You're a part of the Dendadian Infantry. That means you serve everyone and everything in the three lands of the west. Men, sorceresses, trolls, orcs, and elves. All fall under our protection. During the War of Six, I found the strangest allies in the strangest places. If I harboured any hatred towards any of them previously, it is well gone now. Had I continued to harbour any hatred, I would most probably be dead. You need each other. You're a company. A small company at that. So, learn to get over your past and work with each other."

"We are brothers," Runolffson immediately added. It seemed to Arnald that this was the Jomaandian's *go to* statement, constantly returning to arguments of *brotherhood* and *solidarity*. "We are brothers and one sister. Where are your families now? Dead, or they abandoned you."

"Thank you for that inspirational speech, Brother Ospak," said Sigemaer. "Our families are dead, or they abandoned us. Words to live by my brothers and one sister. Words to live by."

Arnald stifled his laughter, causing his body to shudder. Kysha looked at him curiously, wiping tears from her eyes.

"Sorry," he whispered. "That was funny."

She shook her head slowly, returning her gaze to the fire.

Agdestein snickered, setting off others around the fire. Soon, all the members of the troop chuckled together, except Benten and Kysha. When the sniggers faded away, Benten peered over to the elf with glazed eyes.

"I'm sorry," he said. "I'll try harder. I will."

She nodded, accepting his apology.

"As will I."

It was then Arnald noticed the wolf rising to her feet, hackles on edge and teeth bared. She stared across the fire, past the company of men to the far side of the clearing. Following her gaze, the boy saw a set of eyes reflecting the firelight brightly. His body stiffened.

"What is it?" Kysha asked.

He said nothing, watching the eyes of the intruder.

The she-wolf snarled and raced forward at tremendous speed, around the troop and directly towards the thing across the way.

Steigauf shot to his feet and bolted for his tent to fetch his sword, with Agdestein the archer quick to follow. Something triggered Arnald at that moment to stand up and run for the tent, leaving Kysha by the fire.

"Arnald," she called. "Where are you going?"

"Get your weapons," he called to everyone. "Bear."

The unmistakable roar of the creature signalled the others into action, making them run in all directions to retrieve their swords. Heilig fell to the ground, his hands gripping both sides of his head, squeezing his eyes shut.

"Johaan," Benten shouted, crouching by his friend. "What is it, Johaan?"

Heilig opened his eyes.

Yellow eyes.

"Run," he growled. His voice was guttural and animalistic.

"Shit!" Benten raced towards his tent as Heilig writhed and rolled around by the fire.

Arnald watched his friend from a distance. With nothing he could do to help, he draped his quiver over his shoulder and placed an arrow on the bowstring. Agdestein fired three arrows at the bear, causing it to bellow ferociously with each strike.

"Don't hit the wolf," Steigauf commanded, hearing her snarls and growls as she attacked the beast.

"I won't hit the—" the archer began, interrupted by a sudden yelp. "That wasn't me," he said. "I didn't fire."

"The bear got her," said the Pit Guard, brandishing his sword. He glanced at Heilig, who had moved to his hands and knees, screaming in pain as his shoulders appeared to pop and contort. "By the gods."

A loud crunch emitted from Heilig's face as his nose and mouth protruded, forming a snout. Strands of coarse grey and black hair appeared on his neck and face as his ears extended and fingernails grew.

Heilig's scream became a deep roar, far more monstrous than the bear's, before he stood to full height.

Arnald froze in place as Heilig, the man-wolf, turned his head to glare hungrily at the boy. The creature stood taller, its form broader, and far more impressive than Runolffson's.

Heilig took a step towards Arnald, cocking his head as if measuring the lad. The boy noticed the man-wolf's clothes bore little rips and tears here and there, but his shredded boots opened to reveal his enlarged claw-like toes.

"Johaan," Arnald called, as if trying to wake his friend. He didn't know where the courage to do so came from, but it had an effect.

The man-wolf stopped in place, as if stunned.

"There is no Johaan," Benten called, racing from his tent with his sword in his hand.

The bear roared again, lumbering across the open ground towards the camp.

Heilig snapped his head around, locking onto the beast racing towards them.

Arnald seized the opportunity to take aim and fire a shot at the attacking animal. The shaft suck in its shoulder, next to one of Agdestein's arrows. The bear continued forward; the arrow having no obvious result.

Like a flash, Heilig leaped into action and bolted towards the intruder.

The bear huffed and growled with each stride, approaching rapidly.

The man-wolf ran on all fours, closing the gap until it leaped, tackling the beast onto the ground. Heilig wrapped his legs and arms around the bear before sinking his teeth into the creature's face. Blood sprayed around the corners of the man-wolf's mouth as he swivelled his head back and forth, sawing into the bear's flesh.

The bear roared, swiping with its claws to knock Heilig away, causing the man-wolf to skid across the surface. Confused, it peered across to the man-wolf, lying motionless on the ground, before focusing on the men darting about near the fire.

Agdestein fired another shaft, striking the bear in the snout. It bellowed a loud, pain-filled roar.

Arnald followed suit and shot another into the side of the creature's head, near its ear.

Focusing its attention on the boy, the bear started forward again.

In desperation, Arnald reached over his shoulder for another arrow and fired without taking careful aim. He reached again for another before the first arrow struck the bear n the shoulder, the next on top of its head, and the next flew wide.

More arrows flung through the air as Agdestein and Kysha joined the attack, firing arrows rapidly at the attacker. Unlike Arnald's attempts, every arrow the archer and elf fired hit their intended target.

Suddenly, the man-wolf rammed the bear from the side. The two giant beasts tumbled across the ground before coming to a stop by the edge of the road. The bear, resting on its back, roared in protest as Heilig grabbed the top and bottom jaws of the beast with his hands.

Agdestein prepared to shoot another arrow.

"No," Arnald shouted. "You might hit Johaan."

A sickening crunch followed as the man-wolf ripped the lower jaws away, flinging them towards the tree line. The bear responded by gurgling a roar. Heilig buried his snout into the freshly opened wound, snapping, and chewing into the beast's throat. The bear swiped and rocked, trying to wrestle the monster off. Slowly, its limbs fell slack, and it gave up the fight.

Heilig, the man-wolf, let out a long howl, the sound resounding in the night air.

Agdestein took aim again as the man-wolf feasted.

"No," Arnald protested.

The archer offered the boy a confused look.

"He's a man-wolf, laddie," Steigauf told the boy. "He's tasted blood. Fridmund would be doing him a favour."

"He didn't attack me when I called his name," Arnald argued. "He's still in there. He's still Johaan."

"You don't know that," Wynneiros put in.

"Johaan," Arnald called, knowing some already made their minds up. The man-wolf lifted his head from the kill and peered at the boy. "If you're in there and you understand, you need to run right now."

The man-wolf glanced at the others, eventually locking its gaze on Agdestein, who was taking aim.

Like a flash, the man-wolf darted away into the forest, vanishing into the shadows.

"Now look what you did," snapped Wynneiros. "We'll need to go after him."

"Not tonight," Steigauf interjected, staring at the boy quizzically.

"Sir?" the soldier inquired.

"It's dark in that forest and I don't feel like hunting a man-wolf in there tonight. We'll look for him at first light," the Pit Guard replied, starting towards the tree line far across the clearing. "Come, laddie."

Arnald followed the old man across the open ground.

"Then, where are you taking the boy?" Wynneiros asked, puzzled by the commander's actions.

"To fetch the wolf," Steigauf answered.

Chapter Twelve

———◦◦◦———

A NNE FORD OPENED HER eyes slowly. Thick darkness gradually unveiled from her head like a cloud drifting just enough to allow the sun through.

Only, she could not see the sun. Only more darkness.

Her head struck something, causing a small, sharp pain to explode at the base of her skull. Anne then realised someone had her by the ankles, dragging her across the ground.

Looking about, twisting her head up to peer in the direction she had come from, she saw The Lazy Traveller in the distance. Orange light streamed through its open door, spilling onto the road.

Letting the heat out, she thought, her head swimming, spinning in a daze.

The pale moonlight revealed a track she left in the shallow frost behind her. Her eyes fell upon the house of the elvish sisters. Movement in a window, a fluttering curtain, drew her attention. No light emitted from the interior. No faint glow of a fire. But Anne knew, somehow, the sisters hid inside.

Hid.

The elderly woman felt a sudden surge of fear burst from her chest and spread over her body.

The sound of the ground scraping against her back increased, sounding like a far-off echo at first. As her senses became clearer, the noise increased.

Her senses grew more acute, feeling the damp cold soaking through her clothing and touching her skin. Shivering, she craned her head towards the sound of crunching snow. Footsteps methodically striding towards the forest with her in tow.

A band of cords wrapped around her wrists kept her hands together. Another length of rope encased her body from just beneath her shoulders, twisting around her to her ankles. There, the rope extended from a knot into a gnarled, ghostly hand.

From the hand, Anne followed the splotchy skin along the arm of a twisted figure, naked and old. The distinct shape of its ribs and jutting hips looked as if they might protrude through the flesh with each step taken. Stringy lengths of unkept, white hair hung over its back, revealing a jutting spine snaking down the length of its body. Its stick-like legs and wiry physique appeared barely able to carry itself, let alone drag Anne's hefty form. Yet, it did so without difficulty.

Unnatural, Anne thought.

Crunching step by step, they drew closer and closer to the dark forest. Anne's senses became clearer and clearer, and the urgency of her situation became apparent. Fear burst from her chest and stabbed into her stomach.

"Where are you taking me?" she squeaked. Her voice was barely audible, as if clogged by the fear she felt.

The rhythmic crunch of snow ceased.

The figure stopped at the edge of the forest and turned to the woman, revealing a pasty face with hollowed eyes and a wide, crooked smile filled with yellow teeth and blackened gums.

A deep, phlegm filled cackle spewed from its cracked and deformed lips as it lowered itself onto all four limbs. Slowly, it crawled like a spider over Anne, its hands and feet crunching in the snow on either side of the bound woman. The sound was more deafening, threatening, and frightening than anything she had heard before.

Pressing her head into the ground beneath her, Anne silently prayed to Areang, the earth god, to swallow her.

The figure lowered its face to within inches of Anne's, making her believe the creature might sink its yellow teeth into her flesh.

A string of saliva spilled from the figure's mouth and stretched down slowly to touch the woman's lips. Anne felt a knot twist in her stomach. The disgust and terror of her predicament overwhelming her, causing tears to well in her eyes.

The figure cackled softly again, seemingly amused by the woman's reaction.

What are you going to do with me? Anne wanted to ask, but a blubbering sound mixed with an unintelligible wheeze escaped her instead.

The creature lowered its mouth to Anne's ear and opened its mouth wide.

"Javanakhan," it said.

The world whirled and warped, plunging the bound woman back into darkness.

Rhythmic footfalls crunching through the snow resumed, drifting away, fading, fading.

Fading.

PART FIVE

The Stone Curtain

Chapter One

———◆———

S EARCHING IN THE DARKNESS, peering under the low branches of pine trees in hiding places among the undergrowth, Arnald eventually found her. The she-wolf lay awkwardly on her side, whining softly as she licked her hind foot.

"Over here," he called to Steigauf, searching beneath another tree.

"Is she alive?" the old man asked, jogging to the boy.

"She's alive," he answered. "But I think she's hurt."

Arnald crept forward, reaching out to the wolf.

"Careful," the old man said, grabbing the boy by the shoulder to stop his advancement. "She's a wolf. Not a dog. She might attack if she feels threatened."

Steigauf squinted, trying to see what the wolf gave her attention to.

"Too dark to see anything," he breathed. "We need to draw her out on her own."

"I could get one of the bones," suggested Arnald.

"No," the old soldier replied. "She already had a full stomach. Getting tossed like that would make her feel like shit. The last thing she would want right now is more food."

Arnald moved away a short distance and crouched. He patted his thighs and called her.

"Come on," he said. "Come here, girl." He repeated it over and over.

She cocked her head and whined. Pushing her good back leg, pulling with her forelimbs, she crawled slowly towards him.

"That's it, laddie," Steigauf approved, stepping back to the boy's side, joining him. "Come on, girl."

The she-wolf emerged slowly from beneath the tree, yelping suddenly as she tried to stand to full height. She lifted her left paw off the ground, hobbling towards the Pit Guard and the boy.

"Come on," Arnald continued to call as the wolf drew closer. She sidled up to him, whining as she pressed her head against his side. He slid his hand over her muzzle and across her head. "It's all right, girl."

"We need to get her back to the fire where we can take a look at whatever is wrong with that foot," Steigauf said.

The trio moved slowly back to camp, stopping a few times so the wolf could rest before continuing.

A long howl rang out in the distance, echoing in the night sky. The she-wolf looked back at the forest and let out a soft call.

"Johaan," Arnald whispered, peering at the woodlands beyond the clearing.

"Sounds like he's travelled a fair way," the Pit Guard observed.

They continued towards the fire where the troop waited, standing at the ready with their weapons after hearing the man-wolf's cry.

"Do you think he'll come back?" the boy asked.

"Not tonight, I hope," the old soldier answered.

Within moments, Arnald sat by the fire with the wolf resting her head in his lap. She continued to whimper as Steigauf examined the hind leg. A quick yelp informed the old man that he found the problem.

"She got a big splinter stuck between her toes," he explained. "It's in pretty deep."

"That's all?" Sigemaer inquired.

"You'd be crying like a baby if this thing was stuck in you," Steigauf growled. "Ospak, help Arnald hold her down. This is going to hurt."

"Yes sir," replied Runolffson, crouching beside the boy. He placed one big hand on the wolf's shoulder and the other on her hip. She growled quietly.

"It's all right, girl," Arnald assured the wolf. She returned to whimpering again.

"Hold her," the Pit Guard commanded as he dug with his fingers, trying to grip the end of the splinter with his forefinger and thumb.

Kysha raced from the tethered horses to the fire with a bundle of cloth in her hand.

"Hold her," Steigauf repeated as he pulled the splinter out slowly.

The she-wolf growled, baring her teeth, glaring angrily at Arnald.

She yelped as the Pit Guard lifted his hand away.

"Got it," he announced, holding a blood-soaked slither of wood the length of Arnald's pinkie finger. He tossed it into the fire as Kysha held a cloth out to him.

"Here," she said. The old man took it and immediately mopped the wound on the wolf's paw.

The she-wolf returned to whimpering softly as Arnald stroked the fur on her cheek.

"I need to wrap this," Steigauf said to the elf. "She won't like it, but it won't heal if dirt gets in there. Have we got anything big enough to cover her foot?"

"I'm not sure," Kysha replied.

"Pouches," Arnald suggested.

Agdestein peered curiously at the boy.

"What's that?"

"Pouches," he repeated. "We got some leather pouches with drawstrings with the supplies. Kysha uses one for the rosemary we seasoned the meat with tonight. There are others, different sized ones, with other things in them. Things we could store elsewhere."

"The cloths," Kysha put in, looking at the bundle in her hand.

"What about them?" Steigauf asked.

"I got them from one of the pouches," she answered. "We could pack the others in a saddlebag. The pouch might be a little large for her foot, but it might work. I'll get it."

The elf turned to leave, but Steigauf interjected.

"Wait," he said, holding his hand out to her. "Give me those first. I need to wrap this wound."

"Oh," she said, handing the bundle to the Pit Guard. "Of course." With that, she raced back to the horses.

The wolf licked Arnald's hand as Runolffson returned to his place by the fire, resting his back against the log. He glanced over to Benten who stood nearby, staring at the tree line at the far side of the clearing, wearing a concerned expression.

"Are you all right, brother?" the large man asked.

"No," Benten answered.

"We'll find him," Arnald said, sensing the other's worries.

"I'll take watch, tonight," said Benten.

"All right. The first watch is yours," Steigauf confirmed.

"I'll take all the watches, sir," the soldier corrected himself.

The Pit Guard shot him a sideways glance as he wrapped a cloth around the wolf's paw.

"All right," the commander replied. "But regular change will occur. I'll take the first watch with you. Ospak and Ulfar take the second watch. Kolfinn and Fridmund, third watch."

"Not necessary, sir," Benten protested, keeping his eyes fixed on the tree line.

"Orders," Steigauf told him.

Kysha returned with the leather pouch in her hand.

"Here," she said, holding it out for the old man just as he completed wrapping the cloth. He took the pouch and slipped it over the paw, tightening the drawstring just enough to secure it in place.

"She's not going to like it," he said, reaching over to scratch the wolf behind her ear. "But it's going to have to do."

———◆———

"Sneaky," said Arnald, sliding beneath the blankets. Kysha had laid the two sets of bedding in such a manner to make one bed for two.

"I get cold," she said, removing her boots.

"You live in the Northerlands," he reminded, resting on his back, his arms folded behind his head. "How can you cope? It's always cold here."

"My people didn't originate here," she replied, slipping into bed beside him. "Perhaps the blood of warmer lands flows through my veins."

"Perhaps," he agreed, looking up to the apex of the tent where the flickering light and shadows created by the fire outside danced on the canvas surface. "What's it like there?"

"Where?" she asked, nestling against him.

"In your homelands."

"I don't know," she answered. "My family moved a lot before I came along. They settled in a little village west of Shiverwind for a time. I don't remember it all that much."

Arnald took in a deep breath as he remembered his little village. He recalled the fishing vessels moored along the pier, the tiny stalls in the marketplace by the field. Little, simple huts, and farmhouses with simple folk to occupy them.

Much simpler, he thought.

A noise from outside brought him back to the present. He craned his neck to look at the tent flap.

"It's not him," Kysha told him, sliding her arm across his chest, nothing more than a gentle embrace, perhaps for her own comfort. But it also served as a restraint, keeping him in place, possibly also for her own contentment. "It's just embers cracking in the fire."

"I'm worried about him," Arnald said, relaxing back in place.

"I know." Her voice sounded drowsy. "But you won't be of any use to him if you don't get some sleep."

"What if he's injured?"

"He'll heal," the elf replied. "He's a man-wolf."

"We might never find him out there," Arnald fretted. "He might be lost for good."

"The general and I will find him," she said, yawning.

"You'll find him?"

"I'm an elf who was a sheriff," she reminded him. "I used to hunt wanted men and bring them to justice. How hard could it be to find Johaan who wants to be found?"

He considered her words as he watched the light and shadows dance above.

"Go to sleep, Arnald," she whispered.

He listened to her soft breathing and focused on it. Gradually, he closed his eyes and drifted away.

Chapter Two

E ARLY THE NEXT MORNING, Arnald and Kysha packed their tent and
horses well before the others. Agdestein knew the boy would choose
his friend over making a pot of porridge, so the archer prepared breakfast
for the troop. By the time the boy and the elf approached the fire, weapons
strapped in place and ready to go, two steaming bowls of sludge waited for
them.

"It's not as good as yours," Benten mumbled to Arnald between
spoonsful, eating quickly, eager and ready to begin the search for Heilig.

"Thank you," the archer said, forcing a smile.

"Hurry and eat." The other man pointed at the two bowls with his
spoon.

Moments later, the trio set off across the clearing on foot.

"What do I tell the commander when he wakes to see you've gone
already?" Sigemaer asked.

"Whatever you like," Arnald replied.

"The truth," Kysha put in.

Entering the woodlands, the three searchers followed a set of clear
imprints in the snow left by Heilig, the man-wolf. They trailed wide of
most trees, only vanishing temporarily where dense shrubbery clustered
across the path. There, broken tree limbs and torn undergrowth confirmed
their quarry's path.

After a long time of walking, Arnald broke the silence.

"Did you get any rest?"

Benten glanced away from the trail to make eye contact with the boy. "No," he answered. "Not a wink."

Arnald didn't know how to respond. Instead, he just nodded as Kysha overtook the two, continuing to follow the marks in the snow.

"He's moving very fast here," she informed them, peering to a rise ahead of them. "He might have been hunting."

"Hunting what?" the boy asked.

"I don't know," she answered, pointing to the top of the hill. "But he went up there quickly."

They ascended the slope, clambering on all fours on the steeper sections before reaching the top. From there, they saw the ridgeline weaved through the forest in both directions.

Beneath them, on the other side, a thin brook snaked through a tiny vale. Rocky outcrops jutted from the edges of the stream. A dismembered carcase of a stag rested on a flat section of stone across the waterway from the trio.

"There," the elf said, pointing a short distance further upstream from the remains.

Arnald and Benten followed her gesture and saw Heilig, the man, asleep and curled into a ball among a few large boulders.

"Johaan," Benten called, racing down the embankment towards his friend.

"Be careful," Kysha called after him.

The warning came too late, and the man slipped in the snow and slid on his backside down the steep hill.

"Viktor!" Arnald called after him, starting down the slope, carefully placing his feet with each step.

Benten seemed oblivious to his plight, continuing to call to Heilig during his rapid descent. Eventually, he came to a complete, sudden stop when his boots reached the water's edge.

Unharmed by the experience, he gracefully shot to his feet and crossed the shallow stream, running to the sleeping man's side.

"Johaan," he called again, dropping to his knees beside Heilig. "Wake up."

With a grumble and groan, Heilig slowly opened his eyes.

"What is it?" said Heilig, wiping his eyes with the back of his hand. Suddenly, he sat up and gawked about, aware of his surroundings. "Oh, my!"

"Are you all right?" Benten asked, peering at the blood on his friend's clothing.

"I think so," the other reported, looking down at his outfit, noticing the state of his boots.

Kysha and Arnald moved to Heilig's side, reaching out to help the man to his feet.

"Do you remember any of it?" Arnald asked.

Heilig spotted the stag on the rock and nodded.

"I remember everything," he answered. "I remember killing that thing and eating some of it. I remember it felt incredible. I remember wanting to kill and eat you until you called my name."

Arnald felt a stabbing pain in his gut.

"You chose not to?" Kysha put in.

"No," Heilig replied. He looked about and gestured up the slope. "We go this way, right?"

"Yes," Benten replied. They started back the way they came.

"I wasn't in control," Heilig explained, continuing to answer the elf. "*He* was. I was just watching and feeling it, like a dream. Just as he is watching now. I can feel him back there, behind my eyes."

"Sounds like a nightmare," Benten put in. "Not a dream."

Heilig nodded.

"It was," he agreed. "But it felt good at the same time."

<hr />

Arnald noticed Heilig shifting in his saddle, occasionally lifting his torn boots from the stirrups to stretch his legs out, turn his ankles and shake his feet. First his left, then his right, before putting them back in the stirrups. He'd ride for a while before repeating the process again.

"What's he doing?" Arnald whispered, hoping he spoke loudly enough for Kysha to hear.

"The bandage cloth he wrapped around his feet might give him trouble," she answered.

Arnald nodded, thinking of the strips of cloth Heilig encased his feet in to cover his exposed toes.

"Do you know if there is a cobbler in Northwell who could mend Johaan's boots before we need to leave?" the boy asked.

"Those boots need tossing," she said. "We need to find him some new boots, and he needs to learn to take them off before he changes again."

"I don't think that's how it works," Arnald told her.

"Maybe he needs to be trained," she smiled. "Like a dog."

Arnald's thoughts turned to the wolf.

Peering back along the road, Arnald observed the she-wolf hobbling a short distance behind the troop. They rode at a slow plod to cater for her injury, but not nearly slow enough. His heart sank as she drifted farther and farther away until she attempted to run, stepping awkwardly so her bandaged and pouched back foot didn't touch the ground.

"Maybe I should walk with her," the boy called to the old man.

"We're already moving too slowly," Steigauf answered, leading the company along the road.

"Maybe I could carry her on my horse," he persisted. "Like I did with the goat."

The men looked at each other questioningly before Wynneiros turned in his saddle to face Arnald.

"What goat?"

Arnald shook his head, dismissing the question.

"She's a lot bigger and heavier than that goat, laddie," Steigauf replied. "Unfortunately, she's going to have to keep up or choose to fend for herself in the wild. It's the way things are for wolves. Stay strong for the pack or lose your place."

Arnald felt his cheeks grow red hot.

"So, we abandon her?"

"We won't abandon her," the Pit Guard snapped. He took a deep breath and pulled his horse to a complete stop. The rest of the troop followed suit as Steigauf turned his steed about. He waited for the wolf to limp to the boy's side. "It's a long way to Northwell. At this pace, we might get there by nightfall, if we're lucky. But..." he continued, keeping his eyes on the wolf. "We'll go as slow as we can. When we get to Northwell, we'll find a physicker, or alchem, or witch who might help her better than we could."

With that, he turned his horse and moved on.

Arnald dropped his gaze and peered down at the wolf. He wanted so much to just pick her up, but Steigauf's assessment was correct. She stood almost half the size of his steed, far too big to carry.

"She's strong," Kysha said from his other side. "She'll make it."

"What goat?" Wynneiros repeated, glancing about to the others for an answer.

Nightfall came.

Kysha and Arnald lost sight of the troop as they fell far behind to stay with the she-wolf. The animal stopped at intervals, licking at the wounded paw now and then, showing it gave her painful displeasure. Still, she persisted, staying on her feet to limp after the two young riders.

It took a long time before they saw the faint lights of Northwell in the distance. More time passed before they reached the edge of the township. Runolffson waited for them there, accompanied by two older men holding lanterns. One of them stepped forward, lifting his light high.

"Who goes there?"

"Stupid man. It's them," Runolffson growled. "Arnald."

"Ospak," the boy replied. "Did you find someone who can take care of the wolf?"

"The commander found a healer who uses herbs and potions," the other replied as the riders drew closer. He peered at the wolf limping slowly behind them. "I don't know how much help she can be. The wolf needs rest and a lot of it. We need to leave in the morning."

"She'll be fine," Kysha said, dismounting to lead her horse on foot. "Which way?"

"I'll take you," Runolffson answered, turning towards the town.

The buildings sat tightly nestled together, almost appearing as one. Only small passageways between some buildings broke them up, along with tiny lanes and streets to divide the dwellings. The township appeared much smaller than Arnald thought it to be, expecting another Port Coldspring or Shiverwind, but finding something about half the size. Still, it was much, much larger than his little village.

"Old men guarding the town here, too," Kysha said.

"Not many," Runolffson told her. "All the men but a few, have gone north. They've been spread out to aid the men from Port Coldspring along the coastal region all the way up to Coldwolf. I think they're wasting their time."

Arnald cocked his head, frowning as he considered the big man's words.

"What about the report from Mountainfall?" he asked. "You don't think raiders are responsible?"

"No," Runolffson answered, leading the trio around a corner to the left. "I don't think raiders attacked that man. I don't think the threat came from the coast at all."

"So," Kysha said. "Who do you think killed the man in Mountainfall?"

Runolffson shrugged as he strode towards a larger building with a pointed roof, surrounded by a timber fence as tall as he stood.

"Perhaps someone in Mountainfall," he replied, passing two elderly guards standing post.

"Where are we?" Arnald asked as they passed the sentries, entering a wide yard.

"This is the infantry barracks and stable house," the big man told him, continuing towards the open doors of the stables. "We are staying here tonight. Food awaits us. The healer is inside, and the beds are not on the ground."

As they entered the stable house, the scent of straw and horse dung wafted deep into Arnald's nose. He welcomed it, along with the warmth that came from being inside the building. Several pens lined the walls along both sides of the structure. He recognised most of the steeds as those accompanying his troop.

"You can leave your horses here," Runolffson said, pointing to equipment neatly piled against the wall at the far end of the interior. "Your saddles and saddle bags should go there with the rest of our gear. Bring your weapons into the barracks. They stay with you."

As soon as they finished unloading the horses, the big man led them through another small, man-sized door and back into the cold. Arnald wanted to turn and go back in with the horses as a deep shiver ran through his core.

A few steps covered the distance to the barracks. Within moments, they stood inside a long room with a roaring fire at one end, resembling the dining hall of Shiverwind, except that ten small beds, just big enough for one man, lined the far wall and one long bench and table sat against the wall beside them. The men of the troop sat here, spooning some steaming brown concoction from wooden bowls. Sitting with them was a young woman with a hood drawn over her head and three men, one of which Arnald recognised from the office of the magistrate in Shiverwind. The rider from Northwell.

Steigauf stood to his feet when he noticed the newcomers. He beamed a smile when he saw the wolf hobbling behind the boy.

"You made it," he said, putting a hand each upon Kysha's and Arnald's shoulders. He turned to look at the woman sitting with the men. "L'Erieniul, this is your patient."

The woman stood and practically glided across the room to the trio. She crouched a short distance from the she-wolf and pulled her hood from her head to reveal fiery red hair, pointed ears, and ruby eyes.

Beautiful and dangerous, Arnald thought, once believing the words only applied to Kysha.

"Come," she said, her voice soft and soothing but commanding at the same time.

The wolf lowered her head and stepped forward slowly, careful to keep her wounded foot from touching the floor. A soft whine and whimper emitted from the beast as she crept closer.

L'Erieniul reached out to the she-wolf, stretching her fingers. The creature sniffed the woman's hand before licking her fingertips.

"She has a good heart," L'Erieniul said. "And a strong will. I will need to take her closer to the warmth of the fireplace. There, I will conduct my spell."

"Spell?" Arnald queried.

"Not what you think, boy?" she queried, eyeing him. "Not the healer you thought me to be?" She stood to full height, towering almost as tall as Runolffson. "I served in the War of Six, casting magicks against the harridan of Adaerwen and the hordes of Legilawen. But mostly, I healed our fallen men so they could fight another day."

Arnald followed her to the fireplace.

"Give me some time. Your wolf will be healed by morning," she assured him.

"She's not my wolf," he said as L'Erieniul kneeled upon a bearskin rug spread out on the floor.

"I know." The woman smiled. "But she is. Even if you do not see it. And she will be for some time." She peered at the wolf. "Come."

The she-wolf crossed the floor and lowered herself before L'Erieniul, who quickly removed the pouch and wrappings around the animal's foot. After a quick examination, the woman rubbed the she-wolf's leg and took in a deep breath.

"It will take some time," she said. "Best leave us to our business."

Steigauf placed his hand on Arnald's shoulder.

"Come on," he said. "You need to eat something."

Arnald sat at the table alongside Kysha, all the while watching L'Erieniul stroke the wolf's paw softly with her fingertips. An elderly man entered the room through a door beside the fireplace, carrying two steaming bowls. The wolf reacted, craning her neck to observe the new arrival.

"Shh," L'Erieniul breathed, moving her hand to the she-wolf's ear. The animal responded by lowering her head onto the woman's lap. As the man placed the bowls in front of the boy and the elf, the woman reached beneath her cloak to retrieve a vial of clear liquid about the size of her small finger.

"What's that?" Arnald asked.

"Quiet, laddie," Steigauf told him. "Let the lady work."

Only then did Arnald notice the entire troop watching, as if transfixed.

L'Erieniul removed the little cork from the mouth of the vial and poured the entire contents onto the wolf's foot upon and around the wound. It spilled slowly; obviously some kind of oil. After placing the cork back onto the vial, she returned the tiny container beneath her cloak before leisurely rubbing the liquid into the foot, running her fingers between the wolf's toes and over the wound.

"You should eat," Kysha said, bringing Arnald out of a trance. The elf girl dribbled a little of the steaming slop over her lips as she spoke. "It's very good."

Arnald felt a smile forming.

"You've got a little there," he said, pointing to her chin.

"Ooh," she said, wiping it away with the back of her sleeve.

Taking her advice, he tucked in. The brownish, greyish stew didn't look at all appealing, but it tasted marvellous.

By the time Arnald scraped the bowl clean with his spoon, the wolf had fallen asleep.

"We leave her to rest here," L'Erieniul said, rising to her feet before approaching the table. "In the morning, it will be as if the injury never happened."

Arnald watched her intently as she approached the main door.

"You're leaving?" he asked.

"Yes." she turned to look at him, penetrating him with her ruby eyes. "I've done my part. She's doing hers. Now, I must return home."

"Thank you, L'Erieniul," Steigauf said, standing.

"Thank you for the business, Temple Guard." She bowed slightly before turning for the door again.

Arnald watched as she lifted her hood back over her head before opening the door to step outside.

"Are all elves like this?" the boy asked.

"Like what?" Steigauf queried.

"Beautiful and dangerous?"

"Yes," Kysha put in before the old soldier had a chance to respond. A wide grin spread across her face as she spooned the last of the casserole from her bowl.

Chapter Three

THE WOLF SLEPT SOUNDLY, even with the rackety sound of someone clanging pots, plates, and cutlery in the kitchen behind the wall housing the fireplace. The men seated about the room chatted loudly, joking, and laughing together. Arnald feared the she-wolf would wake from the clamour, but she didn't. Her breathing remained slow and steady, as if she slept deeply.

He stroked her ears, seated upon the rug beside her, peering into the flames. A million thoughts raced through his head. He considered the wolf and her injury; particularly, whether she would be fit enough for the journey ahead. He thought of their mission and what might wait for them on the road. Memories of his home wafted in and out, with the faces of his family drifting before him in the flames. One lingered longer than the others. His hand touched his sleeve, hiding the stained cloth as he stared into the eyes of Gertrude.

She no longer called him a coward, or at least he didn't hear her do so. His own questioning voice boomed in his head, inquiring about the condition of his heart, his feelings for Kysha. Admittedly, he felt an attraction towards her but remained uncertain if his affections deserved encouragement. A frown formed on his face as he pursed his lips, wondering if his departed promised one silently scorned him for his internal struggle.

Seeing the elf approaching from the corner of his eye, he moved his hand back to the she-wolf. Kysha lowered herself beside him, holding two mugs of steaming liquid.

"Tea," she said, offering one to him.

He took it and sipped it slowly. His mouth stung from the heat, but his tongue savoured the sweet flavour. The reaction on his face must have spoken volumes.

"I put a little honey in," Kysha told him.

"A little?"

The elf smiled, raising her mug to her lips.

"She'll sleep deeply," she said, peering at the wolf. "Something in the ointment L'Erieniul used helps with the healing when the afflicted sleep."

"You know this, how?" Arnald asked.

"I'm an elf," she answered with a grin, as if that explanation was enough.

Arnald shook his head and smiled before raising the mug for another sip.

At that moment, Steigauf crossed the room and crouched beside them, reaching over to stroke the she-wolf's flanks.

"You two will stay in the commander's quarters," he said.

Arnald shot him a concerned look.

"What about her?" he asked, referring to the sleeping animal.

"I'll look after her," the Pit Guard answered. "You'll be taking my place in there. I'll stay in here with the men so I can keep an eye on her. We're expecting the sheriff soon. I presume it will be a late night of talking. I'd prefer you two to get some rest. We still have a long way to go, and we need to start early tomorrow."

Kysha appeared offended, cocking her head, and lowering her brow.

"I should be here when the sheriff arrives," she told the old man. "I'm not a child you can instruct. I was Sheriff of Shiverwind, remember?"

"True," Steigauf nodded. "But you are a child, like it or not. My instruction, however, is for Arnald to follow, and I know he will follow it. I would prefer two well-rested young people tomorrow rather than one grumpy elf riding everyone's arse because she didn't get enough sleep."

"All right," she sighed, moving her gaze to the fireplace.

"Thank you," the Pit Guard said earnestly, rising to his feet. He looked down at Arnald and pointed to the steaming mug. "Finish that and off with you. The kitchen hands will show you the way."

Arnald took his time to drink his tea, hoping to see the Sheriff of Northwell before retiring for the night. He wanted to be in the room to hear the conversation between the adults just as much as Kysha. He wanted to know everything firsthand rather than hear only pieces later as they journeyed. The steam rising from his mug eventually disappeared as the tea turned cold, causing his hopes to evaporate with it.

"Come on," the elf whispered, perceiving his thoughts. "We should go before the commander catches on to what you're doing. Drink up."

Arnald nodded, quickly swallowed the mug's contents, and turned for the kitchen door by the fireplace. As he placed his hand on the latch, a large barrel-chested man burst in through the entrance at the other end of the barracks accompanied by three men following closely.

"Good evening, gentlemen," he bellowed cheerily, closing the door behind them. "Bloody cold out there."

"You're late." Steigauf stood, crossed the floor, and shook the man's hand. The man peered at the boy and elf by the kitchen door.

"Early, I would say," he replied. "I don't think what we need to talk about is for the ears of younglings."

Steigauf shot Arnald a stern look before placing his attention back upon the newcomer.

"The boy has seen his fair share of blood, if that's your concern," the Pit Guard assured. "But I did try to send him off before you arrived."

"And the elf?" The tone in his voice bore slight disdain towards her.

"I'm the Sheriff of Shiverwind, if you must know," Kysha remarked defensively. "I dare say I've dealt with more scum in our dockyards in my time than you have in yours."

"Aye," the other smiled. "I bet you have. Shiverwind is much larger than our little, quaint, wholesome village. We haven't had to deal with any scum in some time."

"Probably put off by the sight of the gibbet cages you have hanging on the roadside," the elf quipped.

"And the signage. The lawless are not welcome here," he quoted as he crossed the room, reaching his hand out to her. "Clay Wallace. Sheriff of Northwell."

"Kysha Naberyn," she replied. "Sheriff of Shiverwind. Or I was."

"Was?" he inquired. "Not anymore?"

"Not anymore," she answered.

He placed a hand in his pocket and stroked his dark beard with the other as he measured her with his eyes.

"A little young to be a sheriff," he muttered.

"Don't be fooled," Steigauf told him, moving to his side. "She can handle herself."

"The boy?" Wallace asked, turning his attention to Arnald.

"I'm teaching him," the Pit Guard answered. "He's a quick learner."

"Then, perhaps they should stay." The sheriff reached out to the boy. "Clay Wallace."

"Arnald Oberlin," he replied, taking the man's hand.

Wallace's vice-like grip tightened on Arnald's knuckles, causing him to wince. The big man noticed and allowed a small wry smile before letting the boy free.

"He's a big one," the sheriff said, peering down at the sleeping wolf.

"She," Steigauf corrected him.

"What happened?"

"She was injured during a bear attack," the Pit Guard told him. "The healer saw to her and now she sleeps."

"L'Erieniul?" asked Wallace.

Steigauf nodded.

"She's a good elf." He smiled, turning back to the table, slapping the Pit Guard on the shoulder. "And I don't just mean with magicks. Come. Let's talk." He gestured to the men with him, both young and clearly out of place. Neither appeared to be trained infantrymen; nor did they seem like law enforcers either. One of them, with his dark hair and almond eyes, reminded Arnald of the men who attacked his village.

"These are Nichol Kent and Jaysh Shen-Jon from Mountainfall. They brought the news of raiders to our attention, particularly the discovery of a man's severed head outside the tavern there. They have been staying with us here in Northwell since. I refused to let them return home until your arrival. I think it's best if they accompany you back, for their safety."

The men took positions around the table.

Steigauf gestured for Kysha and Arnald to take a seat alongside him.

"Did Aamon tell you about the rider we sent to Mountainfall?" Wallace asked, peering across the table at the rider.

"No," the Pit Guard replied, looking around the table at his men to see if they had anything otherwise to say. All of them either shook their heads or gawked back dumbly.

"I thought it best to wait until you arrived," Martano put in. He locked eyes with the old man and leaned forward. "The day I set out from here, we sent another rider to Mountainfall. Kurst didn't return. Neither did Naril, his steed. We trained the Eluvian horses to return home if something happens to their riders. Protocol demands we then send other riders to search for the missing man."

"He could be held up in Mountainfall," Wynneiros suggested. "Might be some pretty woman he's shacked up with."

"It's a possibility," Wallace agreed. "But I believe he would return and fulfil his duty. I fear something terrible has occurred in Mountainfall."

Arnald noticed the two men with the sheriff shift in their seats uncomfortably. One of them, Jaysh Shen-Jon, pursed his lips as his chin quivered.

"Are you certain you want to return with us?" Steigauf asked them.

"It's our home," Nichol answered. "We have loved ones there." He wiped his eyes. "We need to know."

The old man contemplated the response, scratching the whiskers on his cheek. He then peered around the table at his men, who wore sympathetic expressions as they watched the two men from Mountainfall.

"Tell me," Steigauf began. "Did anyone see the attacker, the person who left the severed head outside this tavern of yours?"

"No," Jaysh Shen-Jon answered. "We didn't recognise the head." He furrowed his brow, clearly uncomfortable with his answer. "We didn't recognise the person."

"Victim," Kysha corrected. Her voice was almost soothing.

The young man from Mountainfall nodded.

"Victim," Jaysh said, repeating the word.

Runolffson shifted in his seat.

"And you found nothing else of him?" he asked.

The men from Mountainfall shook their heads.

"I don't need to know anything more," the Jomaandian announced. "This is a hunting trip. We need to find the ones responsible and bring them to justice."

"Aye," said Agdestein. "Putting a head outside a tavern..."

"On a pole," Nichol put in.

"What's that?" the archer inquired.

"The head was sitting on a pole."

"That's a statement, that is," Sigemaer said. "A warning or a threat."

"Like your gibbet cages," Benten added, looking across the table to the Sheriff of Northwell.

Wallace nodded slowly.

"I'm coming along with you," he said, turning to the Pit Guard.

"We leave at first light. We ride hard to make as much ground as we can," said Steigauf before peering over to the sleeping she-wolf. "I just hope she's ready for it."

"If L'Erieniul saw to her," Wallace put in, "she'll be ready."

Chapter Four

———◆———

ARNALD WOKE EARLY.

The she-elf's arm draped over his waist and her body pressed against his back. The combination of the soft bed and her warmth made for a convincing argument to stay where he lay instead of complying with the demands of his bladder.

Carefully, as gently as he could, he moved Kysha's arm and slowly got out of bed. Even with the red embers glowing and tiny orange flames spiralling in the fireplace built into the corner of the commander's quarters, a chill in the air bit into Arnald's skin as he fished on the floor for his coat.

After putting his boots on, he softly strode across the room to the door. Each footfall caused the floorboards to creak. Arnald winced as he heard the elf groan. He froze in place as she rolled over onto her other side and settled.

Continuing, he quietly unlatched the locking mechanism and opened the door. It squeaked noisily as cold air spilled into the room. Kysha groaned again.

Arnald slid out the door, closing it behind him. He peered at the sky as he moved around a corner of the structure, seeing the light of the moon trying to pierce thick clouds covering the sky.

Probably rain coming, he mused as he untied the cords of his trousers.

The sensation of relief swept over him. A sigh emitted a white vapour from his lips. When he finished, he laced his trousers.

"She's not who you think she is, you know," a voice whispered from the darkness.

"Shit!" Arnald gasped, turning to face the intruder.

L'Erieniul, the healer, stood with her back against the barracks wall. Her ruby eyes fell to Arnald's cords, still partially undone. She offered a small grin before returning her glare to his face.

"How long have you...?"

"Not long," she replied. "Not enough to see anything, if you're so concerned."

He continued lacing up his trousers, tying them with a quick loop knot.

"Why are you here?" he asked.

"Looking in on my patient," she answered. At that moment, the she-wolf trotted from the shadows and up to the boy. From Arnald's perspective, she didn't appear to be limping at all. She licked his fingers, offering a soft whine. He responded by rubbing her ears, something she seemed to like.

"The commander?" Arnald peered at L'Erieniul.

"They still slumber," she answered, striding gracefully to the wolf's side to stroke the thick fur on the beast's neck.

Arnald furrowed his brow and looked suspiciously at the healer.

"What did you mean when you said she's not who I think she is?"

"Your sheriff," the other replied. "She hides a secret from you. There is more to her than you know."

Arnald peered to the commander's cottage and pondered L'Erieniul's words.

"Does anyone else know this secret?" he asked.

"What a strange thing to wonder," she replied. "I would have thought you would want to know what her secret is."

"It's her secret," he said, returning his gaze to her. "She'll tell me if she thinks I need to know."

L'Erieniul nodded, offering a wise smile.

"The Pit Guard may know," she told him. "I know. Other elves scattered about may also know."

Arnald took a deep breath. "Is she dangerous?"

"Beautiful," L'Erieniul whispered. "And dangerous."

Her ruby gaze penetrated deep into Arnald, causing a sense of discomfort to build in his belly and a lump to form in his throat.

"To me?" the boy questioned. He nodded to the barracks. "To the men in there?"

L'Erieniul shook her head slowly.

"I don't need to read the signs to know she loves you," the healer explained.

"Loves me?" Arnald looked to the ground. "But she keeps a secret from me?"

The healer touched the boy on the shoulder.

"She's ashamed of it." L'Erieniul moved her hand to Arnald's forearm, to Gertrude. "And you are not ready."

The boy nodded, silently agreeing with the healer's projection.

"One day," she continued. "One day, you will be ready. You will need her, and she will need you. I see a day when you will guard the gods, and when the gods will serve you. On that day, the dragons will return to Ananduil."

"Dragons?"

L'Erieniul stepped back, gesturing to the wolf as she drifted into the darkness.

"I leave her in your hands," she said as she turned for the gate. "Take care, Arnald Oberlin, Firekeeper."

With that, she strode away, leaving the perplexed boy with the wolf standing in the cold.

<hr />

The men gorged on fresh bacon, eggs, and buttered toast for breakfast, remarking on how quickly the she-wolf recuperated. An elderly kitchen hand moved along the table, dishing out more bacon to the troop.

"We're going to run out of pig soon," he remarked. What with the way you lot are swallowing it down... Do any of you even chew your food?"

A couple of the men chuckled politely as they shovelled more meat into their mouths.

"It's unbelievable," Kysha muttered from Arnald's side.

"The men are hungry," Steigauf mumbled from across the table before biting down on some toast.

"Not that," she snapped. "The wolf. I've seen nothing heal so quickly, no matter what herbs or concoction were used."

"L'Erieniul is no simple healer," Wallace put in, wiping a piece of toast over his plate to collect the dregs.

"That's for certain," Arnald whispered, resulting in a stern glare from the elf.

"Do you think she's pretty?" Kysha asked.

Several men close by shot Arnald sideways glances.

Don't answer that.

Heilig subtly shook his head while Benten pretended not to hear, attacking some bacon with his knife and fork.

"I only meant that there's more to her than just a healer," Arnald replied.

"Like?"

He glanced around the table for help but found none. The men had all returned to their plates.

Letting out a long sigh, he turned in his chair to face her.

"She knows things," he answered.

Kysha looked at him quizzically. "What things?"

"Things about you," Arnald told her. "Things about me. She knows my full name, and I never told her."

"She may have picked that up from someone here," the Kysha put in. She returned her attention to her plate, piercing a rasher with her fork before pausing. "What does she know about me?"

"What?" the boy said.

"You said she knows things about me," the elf clarified.

"She didn't tell me," he replied. "She just said you have secrets."

Steigauf shifted uncomfortably in his seat.

"That's enough," he told them. "Eat your food and get ready to leave. We have a long way to go and not enough time to do so."

"Nothing?" Benten asked Heilig. The two riders led the pack horses, followed by Arnald and Kysha at the rear of the troop.

"Nothing," Heilig returned, peering about at the gibbet cage and sign on the town's edge.

NORTHWELL - The Lawless Are Not Welcome Here.

Arnald followed his gaze and saw L'Erieniul standing farther along the road behind them, watching them ride away. Her red hair drifted on a gentle breeze, reminding the boy of flames dancing in a fire. She offered a wave of her hand, to which he replied, returning the gesture.

She's not who you think she is.

"Not even an itch?" Benten queried, drawing the boy's attention back to the conversation.

"Itch?" Heilig smiled.

"You know," the other pressed. "Whatever it is you feel when, you know?"

"No." Heilig laughed. "No itchiness."

Arnald considered the discussion.

"Perhaps he's cured?" the boy put forward.

"Cured?" Benten turned in his saddle. "How does one cure themselves of being a man-wolf?"

"Bacon," the she-elf suggested.

Heilig burst out with laughter.

Arnald pointed to the wolf, trotting beside Steigauf at the head of the company.

"Maybe L'Erieniul did something while we slept," he offered. "The wolf is completely healed. Look at her. Maybe she did something to Johaan, too."

Heilig shook his head.

"I wish that were so," he said. "But no. I can still feel the monster inside me."

Benten looked at the man curiously.

"So, why do you think it hasn't tried to come forth?"

Heilig let out a long sigh as he looked around at the surrounding forest closing about them.

"I don't know," he eventually answered. "The sheriff might be right."

"What?" Benten looked around at Kysha and Arnald. "Bacon?"

"Food," Heilig shrugged. "Meat. Satisfaction. A full belly. I really don't know."

Arnald watched the two riders for a moment before he turned to look back at Northwell. They had moved some distance from the edge of the township, but he could still see people moving about. L'Erieniul, however, was nowhere in sight.

"It doesn't matter," Kysha said. "Maybe you have control of the beast, and it lies dormant."

"I don't think that's it," Heilig told her. "I believe we'll see the monster again."

"Not anytime soon, I hope," Benten said.

With Northwell far behind, the focus of the riders became the road ahead. For a time, it snaked alongside a wide river, giving the troop opportunity to fill canteens and let the horses drink. The sun climbed high into the sky and some of the men's guts grumbled.

Steigauf retrieved a small loaf of bread from his saddlebag, broke off a morsel with his hand and ate it, signalling the men to eat something. He then approached Sheriff Wallace, standing by the roadside with the two men from Mountainfall, where they fell into a discussion.

"I should be a part of that," Kysha muttered, crouching by the riverside, tightening a leather strip around one of her braids.

"What?" Arnald asked, oblivious to what the others were up to. His concentration focused on the bubbles popping at the mouth of his canteen as he dipped it into the stream to fill it up.

"That," she answered, nodding her head to the men by the road. "What are they talking about, do you think?"

The boy took a quick look. He saw the Pit Guard talking with the other three men briefly before the she-wolf blocked his view. She licked his face with her thick, wet tongue and huffed warm breath over his skin. Arnald snickered, reaching up to rub the thick fur under her chin.

"I was Sheriff of Shiverwind," Kysha continued. "I should be included if they're talking about dangers ahead or strategy."

"Osman will tell you everything you need to know," Arnald said, pushing in the cork to seal the canteen. "Who knows? They might only be discussing the weather. Sometimes, we don't need to know everything."

She stopped fixing her hair to look at him.

"L'Erieniul," she said eventually, knowing his thoughts.

"What?"

"You want to know my secret," the she-elf surmised, returning her attention to her hair. "The one that L'Erieniul claims I keep from you."

"I told you everything about me," he replied, sitting on the ground. The wolf lowered herself beside him, lying down to place her head on his lap. She closed her eyes as he rubbed her ear. "Not that there is much to tell."

Kysha looked at the boy pleadingly. "I would tell you, Arnald," she whispered so that others wouldn't hear. "But I can't tell you. If the others knew…"

"What are you two up to, then?" a voice asked, disturbing the moment.

Arnald looked around to see Fridmund Agdestein standing a short distance away, holding Arnald's bow and quiver in his hands, his own slung over his shoulders. The elf returned to fixing her hair, offering a quick smile to the archer before turning her face towards the stream.

"Just talking," the boy returned.

"Come on," Agdestein said, holding the bow out to its owner. "We should take this time to get some practice in."

Arnald glanced over to Kysha, who gave him the same quick smile she gave Agdestein.

"Go on, then," she said.

He could tell she didn't really want him to go. Rising to his feet, at the grumbling disapproval of the she-wolf, he placed a hand on her shoulder.

"Why don't you come with us?" he asked.

"I'll be fine," she answered, penetrating him with her blue eyes and smile. "Besides, my archery skills aren't lacking like yours."

He took his bow and quiver from Agdestein.

"We won't be long, my lady," the archer told her. "And you are more than welcome to join us."

She hesitated, glancing at Steigauf, talking with the men by the roadside.

"Come on," Arnald pressed.

The wolf licked her lips and whined as if earnestly imploring the elf to join them.

"All right." Kysha nodded. "Let me fetch my bow."

"Excellent." Agdestein smiled. "We should make a competition of it. Let's see how many more targets I can hit compared to you."

The boy and elf laughed.

"Pretty sure of yourself, aren't you?" Kysha returned as they approached her horse.

"Absolutely!" The archer grinned.

Steigauf called after the boy, at which Arnald turned to face the old man. The Pit Guard pointed to the bow in Arnald's hand.

"Take your time," he called.

"Steady my breathing," the boy returned.

Steigauf nodded and grinned before returning his attention to the discussion with the men by the roadside.

Chapter Five

———◆◆◆———

RIDING TALL, ARNALD SMILED uncontrollably as he trotted behind the packhorses. Two rabbits, strung by their necks from his saddle's horn, bounced against the steed's shoulder. He glanced over to the six coneys, dangling from the elf's seat and back to his two.

His smile broadened.

Both of his took shafts to the head. One of them hit directly in the eye.

All of hers received arrows through different sections of their bodies. One even had to be put out of its misery with a twist of its neck.

Wynneiros clearly won the competition, stringing nine rabbits on his charger.

Still, comparing numbers wouldn't stifle Arnald's pride.

Headshots! He smiled. *Both of them.*

"Happy with yourself," Kysha said, noticing the boy's demeanour. "Aren't you?"

"Yes," he said, lifting his chin high.

"As am I," she admitted. "It wasn't long ago you wouldn't have been able to shoot the ground. Now, look at you."

"I shot them right in the head," he told her.

"We know," Benten remarked contemptuously. "You did what the commander told you. You took your time. You steadied your breathing. You aimed. You shot. You killed rabbits. Now, shut the fuck up and ride quietly with that fat smile of yours."

"Leave the boy be." Heilig chuckled.

Arnald giggled, offering the elf a cheeky expression. Understanding his intentions, she smiled and shook her head.

"Don't," she whispered.

"Right in the head," he announced loudly. "Both of them."

Heilig's shoulders rose and fell rhythmically as he stifled his laughter.

"You little bastard!" Benten turned in his saddle to face him. The beam on the man's face informed the boy that he wasn't really upset.

"I did what the commander told me," Arnald continued, almost laughing. He aimed an imaginary bow at Benten. "I took my time and steadied my breathing. Then, *shoop*!" He fired the invisible arrow. "Right in the head."

"You're turning into a little shit, Arnald," the other replied, turning to face the road ahead.

"Turning?" Heilig queried.

Kysha reached over and slapped the boy on the thigh.

"That's enough," she whispered sternly.

He nodded, receiving her caution.

Peering about at the surrounding woodlands, Arnald continued to smile as he thought about the minor victory he experienced. Kysha was right. His skills had improved a great deal since he left his little village.

Looking down at the two rabbits near his knee, he studied the wounds he made on his trophies. He wondered if Jörgen shot so true with his bow; the one that Arnald now claimed as his own.

He couldn't remember.

By nightfall, the troop set up camp by the roadside, feasted on roasted rabbit and gathered by the fire to talk. While a few men ran whetstones over the edges of their blades, Agdestein did the same to each of his broadhead arrowheads. Arnald, seated cross-legged beside Kysha on the ground, watched with curiosity as the archer slid a shaft from his quiver, and stroked the small stone along the triangular tips.

"Does that even do anything?" Sigemaer asked, sliding his sword into its sheath.

"I'm not sure," Agdestein answered with a smile. "I think so."

Arnald watched him place the arrow of his focus on the ground beside him, neatly lining it up next to six others he's already attended to.

"What does it do?" Sigemaer continued. "Sharpening them like that, in your opinion?"

The archer let out a long sigh and frowned, considering his answer. He shrugged and cocked his head.

"I like to think it makes them fly faster," said Agdestein. He raised his hand and motioned like something zipping through the air. "Like a falcon diving for her prey."

Sigemaer chuckled, "The way you pull back on that bowstring does that, my friend."

"Perhaps," the archer said, taking another arrow from his quiver. "But I think it helps, and that's all that matters."

The other man nodded. "Can't argue with that," he said, taking his dagger from his waist to run his whetstone over its edges.

Arnald peered across the fire to the two men from Mountainfall. They watched the flames quietly, listening to the conversation between the soldiers. Both men bore heavy expressions, which the boy surmised showed a longing for their home.

The perplexing situation of not knowing the state of the people you care about must be a heavy burden, Arnald thought. No news had come to them about Mountainfall from travellers on the road as there had been no travellers. The unknown must be torture.

"My father went to Mountainfall," the boy said, locking eyes with the one called Jaysh Shen-Jon.

Steigauf, seated beside the men, looked over to him. Arnald couldn't read the old man's face, but he felt Kysha's hand on his knee tighten.

Take caution, her gesture informed him.

"Your father?" Jaysh returned.

Arnald nodded. "Long ago. During the war."

"He saw the mountain fall?" Nichol asked.

Arnald nodded again.

"That must have been a thing to see," Runolffson grumbled.

"Just rubble and rock now," Nichol said. "Overgrown with grass, field flowers and weeds in summer. Covered in snow for the rest of the year."

Arnald noticed a glint in the man's eyes.

"What's it like?" the boy asked.

Nichol and Jaysh glanced over at him.

"Mountainfall? Is it a big town like Northwell?"

"No," Jaysh replied. "It's very small. Very few people live there. Not even large enough to be called a village, really. A bunch of strangers who came together and became a family."

Nichol smiled. "The biggest thing in Mountainfall is The Lazy Traveller," he said. "It's where we all come together at the end of every day."

"The Lazy Traveller?" asked Arnald.

"The inn," the man answered. "It's bigger than the biggest barn there. Built for the many travellers who would pass through the gap made by the fallen mountain. Humphrey and Anne Forde, the owners of The Lazy Traveller, thought it would be a good investment. Where else could merchants and travellers stop as they pass between Kedielewen and Asalethwen?"

Benten nodded. "Smart."

Nichol smiled, letting out a soft snort.

"Not really," he replied. "Do you know how many travellers pass through Mountainfall in a year?"

Benten shook his head.

"Not many more than we have sitting around this fire," Jaysh Shen-Jon put in. "Not very profitable."

"Why?" Kysha asked, taking her hand from Arnald's knee to lean forward.

Steigauf shifted, as if uncomfortable. He stretched one of his legs out in front of him as he answered her question.

"There are many who believe the place is cursed." He rubbed his thigh. "Many died in battle there, including soldiers of the west, creatures of the east and two apprentices of the Witch Queen Miroslava. Not just that, but an entire mountain fell into the earth. Things like that are not easily forgotten."

"It's why Shiverwind is such a lucrative town by comparison to all other settlements in Kedielewen," Sheriff Wallace added. "So many travellers from the south and east choose to venture who knows how many miles and enter our lands through the gap near Deep Rock rather than take the shorter, more convenient path by Shadowfort and through Mountainfall."

Arnald looked at the flames and wondered if people would venture along the coastal road of the Cove of Safe Keeping, through his tiny, abandoned village, after news of what happened there spread over the lands. Perhaps people already regarded his homeland as cursed.

"That's silly," Kysha huffed, responding to the words of the old men.

"Superstition *is* silly," Wallace agreed. "Many beliefs of men, elves, orcs, and trolls are silly. But they continue to believe in them."

"Not me," she grumbled quietly, moving her gaze to the fire.

"So!" The Sheriff of Northwell looked at her quizzically. "What do you believe in then, little elf?"

"Nothing," Kysha returned. She paused a moment. "Me. I believe in myself."

"Nothing and yourself?" Wallace pressed. "You don't believe in the gods?"

"The gods?" She smirked. "Superstition is silly. You said that just now."

"Aye," he agreed, a small smile spreading on his face. "But they made a mountain fall right in front of a thousand witnesses. You can't deny that."

"Did they see the gods?" She lifted her head to lock eyes with the old man.

"What?"

"Did any of those thousand witnesses see the gods?" she persisted. "Did they see Grolle kill the people on the mountainside? Did they see Areang toss the ground about and drag the mountain into the earth?"

"They saw the mountain fall," he replied.

"But did they see the gods do it?" she asked, growing animated. "The cycle of nature makes grass grow, clouds fly, fire burn. Surely, it can make a mountain fall. So, did they see the gods?"

This time, Arnald placed his hand on her knee. To him, her temper sparked, and he wanted her to quench it before it flared. She put her hand on his, letting him know she was in control.

"No," Wallace replied. "No one has seen the gods. Only the actions they take or the evidence of what they have done. It requires faith to make the connection."

"Faith. Belief," she muttered, relaxing her tension, and returning her gaze to the flames. "Those are things I reserve for myself, Sheriff Wallace. In Shiverwind, drunken ship hands made advances, sometimes violently, on a lone she-elf child and none too often rushed to assist her when she cried for help. So, at the ripe age of ten, while one of them lay on top of her, she took his knife from his belt and buried its blade deep in his neck.

"He didn't die, but quite a few people called her a murderer, typically elf-like, and rallied for her to hang," she continued. "But an infantry captain saw something in her and persuaded the magistrate to allow her to be trained instead. Now, she carries blades and a bow, and she savours the fear in the eyes of men who cross her path.

"My faith is in my weapons. My belief is in myself. Not your gods." Her hand tightened around Arnald's.

Wallace nodded slowly, understanding.

"I'm sorry that happened to you," he told her.

"I'm not," she replied. "Those experiences made me who I am today."

"Surely, you must have some trust..." the Sheriff of Northwell prompted. "Some belief in these men around you?"

"I believe they fight with honour," she answered. "I believe the best trained them. I believe one of the best men I've known in my lifetime commands them. I also believe they don't stand a chance if they try anything towards me."

"We wouldn't dare try," Runolffson put in, flicking his golden hair over his shoulder with a toss of his head.

Several others concurred with nods and grunts.

"I took more conies than you," Wynneiros reminded, a small grin on his face.

Kysha smiled. "Yes, you did," she replied before looking across the flames to Benten. "But Arnald shot his two prizes right in the head."

"No!" Benten sat up straight and pointed a finger at the boy. "Don't you..."

Arnald took his cue. "I shot them right in the head," he said with pride.

Heilig burst out in an uncontrollable chortle.

"Fucking bastard." Benten snorted, breaking into a giggle.

A contagious din of hysterics spread around the campfire. Only Runolffson, Wallace, and Steigauf maintained their composure. The Pit Guard shook his head slowly and let out a long sigh as he stroked the ears of the she-wolf.

Chapter Six

———◆◇◆———

T HE EASTERN MOUNTAINS GREW taller and clearer as the troop journeyed along the road. They moved at a steady trot, hoping to gain ground and reach their destination without tiring the horses.

"This is my first time seeing The Great Northern Barrier," Arnald said.

"Some call it The Stone Curtain," Steigauf returned from the front of the pack.

Arnald studied the rocky range before them. It looked rough, steep, and unwelcoming. There appeared to be nothing resembling a curtain.

"Why?"

"Well," the Pit Guard said, moving his gaze from the road to the mountains. "It separates everything on this side from everything on the other side. On this side is everything we know, love, and hold dear. On the other is a world of strange customs, peoples, and oddities."

"Oddities?" the boy asked.

"Creatures unlike anything we have here, laddie," the old soldier replied.

Examining the range, Arnald considered the Pit Guard's explanation.

"I still don't understand," he admitted. "They should have called it a wall. Not a curtain."

"Aye," Wallace interjected, riding beside Steigauf. "It is stone, after all. But you can find a way through a curtain more easily. And, sometimes, one of those oddities makes its way over that monstrosity. Take those raiders who attacked your village." He peered at the Pit Guard momentarily. "What was the word, again? The one you said the boy overheard?"

"Müqin, sì," said Steigauf.

Jaysh Shen-Jon shot a quick look at the old man before turning to glance at Arnald. Their eyes met briefly before Jaysh returned his face to the east, almost as if embarrassed.

"Müqin, sì," Wallace repeated. "That tells me your raiders came from The Shattered Isles on the other side of The Stone Curtain."

The boy furrowed his brow.

"They came by boat," he put in. "They didn't climb over the mountains."

"It's just a saying," Steigauf replied, turning in his saddle to face the boy. "It's just places over there that are hidden from view, the way a curtain hides things."

Arnald nodded, not completely understanding, but getting the idea.

"It's still a silly name," he grumbled under his breath.

They rode on, idly chatting with one another to pass the time. Wispy clouds moved in from the north, carrying a chill breeze with them as the day carried on. The sun crept over their heads and slowly fell to the horizon behind them.

"What's that?" Kysha inquired, staring ahead.

Arnald followed her gaze and saw nothing.

"What's what?" Wynneiros asked, moving in his saddle to see past the hulking form of Runolffson.

"Something at the crossing," she clarified, before leaning towards Arnald, where she whispered, "It's my first time this far east, too."

"By the gods," Wallace huffed. "You've got a splendid set of eyes if you can see that far ahead."

"She's an elf," Steigauf reminded him.

Wallace frowned and nodded before turning in his saddle to face her.

"It's probably the cage you can see," he answered.

"Another gibbet cage?" She shook her head.

The Sheriff of Northwell returned his gaze to the road.

"They're a deterrent, more than anything else," he explained. "It's been a long time since any of them have been used."

"They're cruel," the elf spat. "Leaving someone to die of starvation and thirst."

"What's the alternative for a criminal?" Wallace asked cynically.

"Depends upon the crime," she returned.

"All right, Sheriff of Shiverwind," he said, a hint of annoyance in his voice. "Tell me how you punish the guilty."

"Thieves go to the cells at night, and we put them to work on the docks in the day," the elf told him.

"We don't have docks in Northwell," he argued.

"Find some other laborious duties, then," she returned.

He nodded. "Fair. What else? What if the crime was something heinous? A murder, for example?"

"Put them to the sword," she answered callously.

He swivelled to look at her, a surprised expression on his face.

"You've done this?"

"Many times," she replied.

He maintained his focus upon her, astonished. "You're so young and outraged by our cages," said Wallace. "But you have no difficulty executing a person without prejudice?"

"I wouldn't say without prejudice," she answered. "If they have committed the crime of murder, and there is no doubt, a beheading is swift and possibly the briefest of pains anyone could feel."

"Beheading?" the Sheriff of Northwell gasped.

"If using the sword to bring justice isn't something you can do, you could always try hanging instead," Kysha offered. "Or perhaps you're getting too soft in your old age and need to relinquish your position?"

"Kysha," Arnald whispered, warning she might have crossed a line with such a comment.

Surprisingly, Wallace didn't retaliate. He rode in silence for a short while, possibly considering his response.

"You may be right, little elf," he said eventually. "Fortunately for me, I've not had to deal with violent crimes in a very long time. These raids along the coast are the first in nearly ten years. And I have no captives to try and convict. Honestly, I wouldn't know what to do if I caught one. But the cages will stay in place for as long as I'm the sheriff.

"You might think it circumstantial," Wallace continued, "that no outsiders except the locals and occasional merchant use the roads around here. But we've not had any dealings with highwaymen or elf beatings in all the time I've been in my position.

"There are no other sheriffs in this entire area," he explained. "From Northwell to The Stone Curtain, to Mountainfall, all the way up to Coldwolf. Just me. And, because I'm Sheriff of Northwell, the eastern reaches of Kedielewen goes unwatched.

"The cages are a deterrent, as far as I can tell," said Wallace. "They stay in place but go unused. I hope you can understand that."

Kysha nodded. "I do," she replied softly. "And I apologise for my conduct."

"As do I," Wallace answered. "Sheriff Naberyn."

The troop rode the rest of the way to the intersection in silence, pulling to a stop near the cages. Arnald imagined some emaciated figure inside, curled in a foetal position, starving, and dying. The road stretched away to the north, south and west without a sign of another living soul in sight. The terrifying mountains, reminding him of giant, jagged teeth, sent a chill breeze from their icy peaks down to the road, biting through the layers he wore to his skin. He couldn't imagine how one would feel being abandoned in such an isolated, hostile environment. Even when he was alone in his village, after the raiders had taken everyone he loved, he still had the means to survive. Not so for the ones placed in these tiny prisons.

"They are cruel," he whispered to himself, reaching his hand out to Kysha by his side. She took it in hers.

"Aye," Heilig returned, keeping his voice low. "Not a good way to go."

"We should set up camp for the night," Steigauf called to the troop.

Kysha shook her head, looking at him in perplexity. "Not here," she said. "Please."

The old man furrowed his brow before glancing at the gibbet cages.

"They're empty, Kysha," he told her. "They haven't been used in years. Look, they're rusted through. Nothing but ornaments."

A quick breeze scooted along the road, causing the cages to rock gently. A high squeak emitted from the chains as a low creak resounded from the beams upon which the cages hung upon. A chill ran along Arnald's spine, sending a sense of unease over his body. He shuddered as he offered the Pit Guard a pleading look of his own.

"There are old structures farther along the road," Nichol Kent said. "If you're willing to forgo another hour of rest."

"Structures?" Steigauf asked.

"Old ruins," the other answered. "I think they're barracks houses, or something like that, for the men who once stood guard in the towers along the ridge."

The Pit Guard nodded, as if recalling an old memory.

"They're not that old," Steigauf said. "They were built not long before the War of Six began. The threats of war reached our borders. Small raids and skirmishes all the way along this range. Amalith testing the grounds before the tempest. Dendadia commanded the towers to be constructed, along with quarters for the sentries who guarded them."

"You've seen these structures, then?" Wallace asked the old man.

"Not these, no," he answered. "Those built in the south, yes. I was posted at one near to The Mud Dragon Inn during the early days of the war."

"Mud dragon?" Arnald asked, suddenly intrigued by where the name came from.

Steigauf understood the boy's question.

"There are no mud dragons," he assured the lad. "In fact, I've seen no dragons in all my days. I have my doubts they ever existed."

Arnald wondered if he should tell the Pit Guard of what L'Erieniul told him; *I see a day when you will guard the gods, and when the gods will serve you. On that day, the dragons will return to Ananduil.*

"All right," Steigauf called, turning his horse southward. "We press on. There's still enough light to spare an hour. Perhaps these ruins can offer a little shelter against the winds."

———◆———

Kysha huddled tightly against Arnald, tucked deep beneath the covers of their bedding. The she-wolf curled at their feet by the closed tent flaps, fast asleep. The wind beat against the tent relentlessly, a turbulent din forbidding the two from slumber.

"How does she do it?" Arnald whispered, feeling the wolf's form against his feet.

"What?" the elf asked.

"Sleep," the boy clarified. An incredibly immense blast struck the tent, as if something heavy fell against its side. "This bloody wind."

"So much for the ruins offering any shelter." Kysha chuckled softly.

Arnald felt a chill brush over his face, the only part of his body exposed outside of the bedcovers. Kysha must have felt it also as her arms tightened around him.

"Three days," he muttered.

"What's that?" she said.

"Osman said it will take three days to reach Mountainfall," he replied. "We'll be able to sleep in a bed there, he told me."

"You don't enjoy sharing a tent with me?" the elf queried.

Arnald felt trapped by the question. Whether he did or didn't required an explanation. In truth, he did like sharing the tent with her. He had grown fond of Kysha during the time he spent with her, feeling closer to her than he ever did with Gertrude.

And this feeling presented a profound sense of guilt which manifested through a dull ache beneath the bloodstained cloth wrapped tightly around his arm.

"I just feel constricted in this tent," he answered. "Especially with her down there. A bed in a room with a warm fire just feels overdue. Don't you think?"

Kysha nuzzled against him tighter.

"A bed does sound good," she admitted.

In silence, they lay together, listening to the howling wind and the thrumming of the tent walls. Arnald closed his eyes, hoping to drift away.

"What will you do afterwards?" the she-elf asked.

"Afterwards?" he asked. "I guess we'll investigate the death of the stranger in Mountainfall."

"No." She shook her head softly. "I mean after that."

"You already know," he told her, creasing his brow. "I'll travel with Osman to Dendadia to train as a Pit Guard."

"Will you go south or back through Shiverwind?" Kysha pressed.

"South, I suppose," Arnald answered. "I think Osman wishes to visit his homeland again. He was heading there before he found me."

"His homeland," she murmured before yawning. "I wonder where the general comes from."

"Wyvernmont," the boy said. "It will be a long ride from there to Dendadia. We'll almost have to come by Shiverwind again to pass through Deep Rock."

She laughed silently. He felt her quick breaths against the skin of his neck.

"How do you remember such things?" she asked. "I don't even know where Wyvernmont is. I would need a map to recall details like that."

"I've always been able to remember little details," he said. "The map I saw in Magistrate Demeara's chambers is in my memory."

"You're a walking map," she said with a giggle.

He wrapped his arm tightly around her waist, fighting the pain of guilt throbbing under the bloodstained cloth.

"Will you come with us?" he asked. "Or will you return to Shiverwind to resume your duties as sheriff?"

She remained silent for what seemed an eternity. Arnald feared she didn't wish to respond.

"I'll follow you, Arnald Oberlin," she said eventually, turning her face to his. "For as long as you want me."

"I do," he replied instinctively, surprised by the words escaping his mouth. Filled with sincerity, Arnald believed it. His heart froze mid-beat as his thoughts took their time to catch up to the moment.

But, before he could contemplate the situation, assess whether he had made a mistake and possibly offended Kysha, she pressed her lips against his.

His body tensed, and his eyes widened with astonishment. She held him there until he relaxed.

Slowly, she pulled away, allowing him some breathing room.

"Well," he whispered. "I'm beginning to enjoy sharing this tent with you now."

"Shut up," she breathed, pressing her lips to his again.

Chapter Seven

ARNALD EXITED THE TENT, carrying his mother's and father's swords bundled in his arms. The wolf followed at his heels. He turned and took a long look at Kysha, sleeping soundly, before closing the tent flap.

"Morning, Arnald," Agdestein said quietly. He sat on a log close to the campfire, running a small whetstone over the tip of an arrow. "Sleep well?"

"The wind kept me awake most of the night," the boy replied, sitting next to the archer. He pulled his mother's sword free of its sheath before retrieving a small whetstone of his own from his pocket.

"And Kysha?" the other asked. "Did she have trouble sleeping, also?"

Arnald cocked his head and peered at the man quizzically.

Agdestein returned the expression after a moment's silence.

"We only kissed," the boy admitted.

The archer's brows lifted upon hearing the news. A wide smile crept across his face.

"Only kissed?" Agdestein remarked. "Nothing more?"

"No," Arnald said.

The man chuckled softly, peering over to the wolf at the edge of the campsite as he lifted another arrow from his quiver.

"Must have been romantic with her in the room watching you." The archer nodded to the beast.

Arnald followed Agdestein's gaze to see the wolf squatting to empty her bowels. He turned his attention to sharpening the blade in his hands.

"I think I love her," the boy told the man.

Agdestein looked around to see if anyone else had heard. The sound of snoring emitting from the tents informed him that all others in the troop slept soundly.

"Obviously, she feels the same for you," he said, turning back to Arnald.

"She kissed me first," said the boy.

"How do you feel about it?" the archer asked.

Arnald nodded slowly.

"You may have a tough decision ahead," Agdestein said softly. "You told us you want to train to be a Pit Guard. But what if she wants to return to Shiverwind, or go someplace else to settle down?"

"She told me she would follow me for as long as I want her," the boy replied.

"The girl is smitten," the other said, placing a freshly sharpened arrow at his feet, where several others rested. He reached into his quiver for another. "That was clear the first time I saw the way she looks at you."

"I really like her," Arnald confessed.

"Enough to forgo your training?"

The boy ran the whetstone along the blade slowly, nodding.

"Yes."

"Then you must be in love," the archer told him. He used the arrow in his hand to point at Arnald's sleeve. "But how does *she* feel about it?"

Arnald paused, holding the whetstone mid-blade as he moved his gaze to his arm. He had forgotten about Gertrude. From the moment Kysha placed her lips on his, the memory of his promised one faded. Until now.

He put the sword and stone on the ground and pushed his sleeve up to his elbow, exposing the bloodstained cloth. His thoughts filled with the moments he stole kisses with Gertrude on the docks by the village when they thought none saw them, holding hands as they walked along the shore into the woods to steal more kisses.

Slowly, he carefully unwrapped and peeled the cloth from his arm. He stood to his feet and took a step closer to the fire, holding the cloth delicately in his hands.

380

"Are you certain?" Agdestein asked.

A tear streaked down the boy's cheek as he stared at the cloth.

A gentle breeze caused the fabric to wave like a tiny flag in his fingers. Slowly, he shook his head and placed the cloth into his pocket.

"It's all right, Arnald," Agdestein said. "These things take time."

<hr />

"Remember," Steigauf said, "the blade is a close contact weapon." He leaned against the trunk of a bare tree as he observed Arnald lunging, turning, pivoting in place as he thrust and swung his mother's sword at invisible enemies. "You'll be able to smell your opponent's breath on your face, see their sweat on their brow and taste their fear as they try to cut you down."

Arnald raised the blade above his head as if he intended to chop it through the middle of his enemy's head.

"Never open yourself to an attack," the Pit Guard snapped.

Arnald stopped to glance over at the old man.

"I was about to deliver my killing blow," the boy protested, puffing and panting.

"You're about to be sliced in two by the guy with the battle axe approaching from the side." Steigauf nodded to something beside the lad. Turning his head, Arnald saw the she-wolf sitting nearby, watching intently.

Steigauf retrieved the empty sheath by his feet and tossed it to the boy.

"That's enough for today," he said.

Arnald caught the case with one hand and slid the blade inside.

"You've grown accustomed to using that sword. You should try training with your father's. It's heavier and will help to put some meat on those stringy arms of yours."

The boy nodded, peering back to the camp, a short distance away, where the men busied themselves packing the tents, except Kysha and Heilig, who crouched by the hearth, cooking bacon and toast. As he watched, Heilig pushed a raw rasher into his mouth.

"How are things?" Steigauf asked, moving close to Arnald.

He gave the Pit Guard a quizzical look.

"Between you and Kysha?" the old man clarified.

"Fine," he answered, looking for Agdestein. He wondered if the archer betrayed their confidence, sharing the news of the kiss with the old man. "Why?"

"I just wondered," the soldier said, placing a hand on the boy's shoulder as they started back to camp. "I placed you two together rather hastily, never really giving thought to how you may have felt about it. I just thought two younglings together would be all right. But Ospak pointed out that you two are not as young as I'd like to believe you to be."

Arnald felt a knot form in his stomach. He scanned the camp and found Runolffson rolling a tent into a tight bundle.

How many people had Fridmund spoken to?

"So, I'm wondering if you two..." the old man continued, stumbling over his words as he spoke. "Whether you might have... She's a very pretty girl, so have you...?"

"No," the boy shook his head. "We haven't. She kissed me, though."

Steigauf stopped in his tracks and stared at the lad. He sucked in a deep breath and let it out slowly.

Arnald felt grateful for the Pit Guard's reaction. Agdestein kept his secret, after all.

"Did you kiss back?" he asked after a brief spell.

"Yes," Arnald admitted.

"Did you like it?"

"It wasn't my first kiss," he said, referring to the many moments he had with Gertrude.

"Of course." The old soldier smiled. He looked at the boy's arm. "How does *she* feel about it?"

Arnald recalled Agdestein asking the same question earlier as he slid his sleeve up his arm to reveal bare skin.

The Pit Guard offered a quizzical look.

"What did you do with it... her?"

"I put her here." Arnald tapped his coat pocket.

Steigauf responded by patting the boy on the back softly.

"Let's get some of that bacon before the wolf inside Johaan eats it all," the soldier said, watching Heilig stuff another rasher past his lips as they started back towards the camp again.

The troop set out southward, on The Great Northern Barrier Road, towards Mountainfall well before the morning sun breached the lofty peaks to the east. The sky appeared a clear blue and the way ahead looked pleasant. Pockets of green vegetation poked their heads through the snow here and there, and the powerful scent of pine filled the air.

"Should be a grand day," Agdestein proclaimed.

"Don't be too hasty to announce such things," Jaysh Shen-Jon said. "The weather can turn sour quite unexpectedly around here."

Arnald, riding at the rear of the party, gestured for Kysha to slow down. She complied, both allowing some distance between themselves, and the pack horses led by Heilig and Benten.

"What is it?" Kysha asked, keeping her voice low.

"Fridmund and Osman know," he told her.

She furrowed her brow. "Know what?"

"That," he said, giving her a puzzled look. "That we kissed."

She shrugged.

"So?" she muttered. "Let them all know. I don't mind."

He glanced quickly at the troop, making sure they didn't drift too far behind for any to notice.

"You don't care if they know we...?"

"I've never cared for what people think of me, Arnald," she replied. "Neither should you. If all you concern yourself with is what others think of you, you can never truly be you. Can you?"

Beautiful, dangerous and wise.

She nudged her heels into her spotted stallion's sides and closed the widening gap between her and the pack horses.

Arnald contemplated her words and found himself agreeing with them. He urged his steed forward, bringing himself alongside her. She captured him with her smiling blue eyes, and he believed, there and then, he had fallen in love with her.

Chapter Eight

A PAUSE BY A stream presented an opportunity for the horses to rest and for Arnald to practise his archery. Steigauf, Agdestein and the she-wolf escorted the boy past the tree line and into the woods, just out of view of the road and the troop. Reaching over his shoulder to his quiver, Arnald fumbled with his fingers as he attempted to lift an arrow.

"Try moving the quiver to your hip," Agdestein told him, gesturing to his own, which he wore similarly to a swordsman's sheath. "You can always strap your sword to your back. You need to get to your arrows quickly. You don't have time to fuss about."

"That's an advanced technique," Steigauf said before placing his attention on Arnald. "Take your time. Steady your breathing."

"He should be trying to get off as many shots as he can," the archer argued.

"He's still learning," the old man replied. "He needs to practise his aiming."

"He knows how to hit a target," Agdestein persisted. "I've seen him kill two rabbits, shot right through the head. What he doesn't know is how to shoot under pressure, when the enemy is advancing from all sides, when your heart is pounding in your ears and your hands shake from fear. He needs to learn how to point, shoot and hit his targets with speed and accuracy."

Steigauf shook his head. "He's not ready for that. When he is, I'll let you know, and you can teach him. And that's final."

Agdestein let out a long sigh and nodded. "Yes, sir."

"Now, laddie," Steigauf said to Arnald. "Move that quiver to your hip, as he said. Take an arrow and aim for that tree trunk."

Following the Pit Guard's instructions, Arnald loaded the bow and took aim at the thin trunk of a small pine tree. In truth, he'd rather try Agdestein's approach to training, or hunt for more rabbits.

"Pull back on that string," the old man continued. "Take your time. Steady your breathing."

Arnald let the arrow fly.

It whistled softly as it streaked through the air, emitting a loud *thwack* as it planted deep into the tree trunk.

The she-wolf, resting on the ground nearby, let out an unimpressed snort.

"Bloody good shot!" Steigauf laughed.

Before they had time to celebrate, the Pit Guard ordered Arnald to load another arrow and try again.

Arnald repeated the process again and again until his quiver emptied. As he retrieved his arrows, plucking them from the tree trunk, the men continued to debate over the boy's training.

"Enough," Kysha called, her voice reverberating through the trees.

The men fell silent, turning to see the elf approaching through the forest with a wooden pole in each hand. Arnald recognised them, the support poles for the tent he shared with her. She strode past the men, continuing towards the boy. Kysha tossed one of the tent poles past Arnald, landing it on the ground a few paces behind him before pointing to it.

"Time for close combat training," she said with a cheeky grin.

"We're in the middle of archery practice," Steigauf told her.

"Archery practice is over for the day," she answered.

"Archery practice is over?" the old man snapped. "Just who is in charge here?"

"You are, General," she said. "Now, run along. This boy and I have some serious sparring to do."

"Run along?" The old man shook his head and looked to Agdestein for help.

The archer shrugged and chuckled silently.

"She's a sheriff," he quipped. "I'm just a mere infantryman. Who am I to argue?"

"Right then," Steigauf said, turning back to face Kysha. "We'll leave the children to play."

Arnald watched the two men walk away as he carefully leaned his bow and quiver against a tree.

"Why are you really here?" he asked.

"Close combat training," she replied, twirling the pole around her playfully with one hand. With a nod, she gestured to the pole resting on the ground behind Arnald. "Pick up your weapon."

He glanced back towards the road. Steigauf and the archer were nowhere in sight.

"All right, then," he said, turning to reach for the pole. Clutching it, he turned to face her.

She was gone.

His heart skipped a beat as an icy shiver ran down his spine.

Creeping forward to where she once stood, he glanced about to the right and left, trying to see any movement among the thick growth, looking for tracks left in the shallow snow and finding none.

The wolf stood up, growling softly.

"It's all right," Arnald whispered, gesturing for the animal to relax.

At that moment, the elf struck, smacking him on the rump with her staff.

He buckled at the knees and fell as the sting expanded across his buttocks.

"You should always be on guard." Kysha giggled.

Arnald turned to confront her, jumping to his feet with the pole grasped firmly in both hands, ready to fight.

Gone.

He looked to the ground, finding no sign of footprints.

"How do you do that?" he called.

"I'm an elf," she said from close behind him.

He spun around to see her only inches away. Her staff plunged towards him with ferocity. Instinctively, he swung his pole, blocking her attack.

A moment too late would've resulted in injury.

"Hey," he snapped. "You could've hurt me."

"We're training, Arnald," she replied, whizzing the pole about her skilfully. "The enemy will not take your feelings into consideration."

Suddenly, she attacked with ferocity. Arnald blocked every blow but lost ground to her, stepping back with each strike.

With speed and precision, she pressed with her ceaseless assault. Arnald continued to deflect each strike but couldn't find an opportunity to turn the tables.

Farther and farther, she pushed him towards a tree. He knew once his back pressed against its trunk; she had him.

Desperately looking for an escape, Arnald ran a dozen scenarios through his mind. In every one of them, if he tried to attack, he would open himself to copping a hit in the face or body.

The broad smile she bore let him know she knew she had won.

She had won.

Strike after strike echoed through the forest as Kysha continued to force Arnald towards the tree.

Not knowing what else to do, not wanting to end up pressed against the tree, the boy dropped and rolled across the ground towards the elf.

She overreached with a blow and stumbled before he knocked her off her feet. As she fell on her face, a loud gasp spilled from her lips.

Arnald quickly shot to his feet, pole in hands at the ready.

Seeing her on the ground made him feel pity towards her. He softened his stance and stepped towards her.

"Are you all right?"

Kysha leaped to her feet and lunged for him.

She tackled him, knocking him to the ground hard. His pole bounced across the ground, leaving him defenceless.

The elf pinned him in place, pushing her weight against his body. She held his arms down with her own as she lowered her face close to his.

Pressing her lips to his, she giggled before pulling away.

"I win," she gloated, lifting herself from the ground.

He remained there, watching her as she bent over to retrieve her pole.

"You win," he conceded.

At that moment, the she-wolf appeared in his view and licked his face. The slobber and hot breath felt disgusting against his skin.

"Not you too," he protested.

Kysha burst into a laughing fit as Arnald tried to stand up, fighting the wolf's persistent attempts to lick him.

"Come on," Steigauf's voice echoed through the woods. The wolf instantly bolted away from the fallen boy towards the caller. "Time to move on."

Arnald lifted himself to his feet and retrieved the pole from the ground before fetching his quiver and bow, slinging them over his shoulder. In silence, he started back through the forest with the elf girl by his side.

As they followed the wolf's trail left in the snow, Kysha slowly reached over to him, taking his hand in hers, interlacing their fingers. Arnald grinned sheepishly, glancing over to her to see the same giddy look on her face he knew he wore.

<hr>

For the rest of the day, the boy and the elf rode side-by-side, talking about nothing and everything. They observed Heilig riding ahead of them, frequently digging into his saddlebags for dried meat as they journeyed. After some time, Benten shared his concern with his friend.

"Are you all right?" he asked, gesturing to another sliver of smoked pork held firmly in Heilig's hand.

"Hmm?" the other grunted, turning his face towards the other. His eyes bore a tint of yellow.

Benten's complexion changed, turning so white Arnald thought he almost blended in with the snow resting on the trees along the roadside.

"You're changing," he said before turning in his saddle to inform Arnald and Kysha. "He's changing."

"I'm all right," Heilig returned. "Just a little hungry, that's all."

Wynneiros couldn't contain himself, shouting out to Steigauf at the front of the party.

"Heilig's changing, sir."

"What?" the Pit Guard called back, pulling his steed to a halt.

Sigemaer howled before falling into a giggling fit.

"That's not funny," Steigauf hollered as he turned his horse to ride back along the line. The troop pulled to a complete stop as the commander approached Heilig. "Are you all right, son?"

"Just hungry, sir," the soldier replied before stuffing more dried meat into his mouth.

The old man looked at Benten. "How much has he eaten?"

"I don't know," Benton answered. "He's been at it for a while."

Steigauf placed his attention on Arnald.

"For about the last mile or so," the boy added.

Heilig shook his head and chuckled, "I'm fine."

The sound of hooves plodding announced the arrival of a concerned Sheriff Clay Wallace.

"Is everything all right?" he asked, glancing at Heilig.

"I'm fine," the soldier repeated sternly. "I can ride and eat. I have enough supplies."

Steigauf slowly measured Heilig, peering into the man's eyes intently.

"All right," he said after a long pause. He looked across to Arnald. "If he shows any sign of changing, you call out."

The boy nodded.

With that, Steigauf turned his steed and started towards the front of the line.

Wallace lingered, scrutinising the yellow-eyed soldier for a moment before turning to follow the Pit Guard.

"What's wrong?" Arnald heard Aamon Martano ask as the Sheriff of Northwell pulled alongside him.

"The man-wolf is having a moment," Wallace replied quietly, but loud enough for all to hear.

Martano and the two men from Mountainfall turned to look along the line of infantrymen to Heilig, only to be met by the steely stare of Runolffson.

"If any of you have a problem with my brothers," he growled, "you will need to get through me first."

The three men pivoted their heads to the road ahead.

"Let's move on, shall we?" Steigauf called.

That night, Arnald and Kysha huddled close together sideways, her back to his front, beneath their bedding covers. His arm rested lazily over her waist.

"Do you think Johaan is all right?" the she-elf whispered.

"I don't know," Arnald answered, his eyes growing heavy. "I hope so."

"I wonder what Wallace will do if he turns," she said, sounding sincerely worried. "I hope he doesn't try something silly."

Arnald smiled, tightening his arm around her waist.

"He'll need to get through me, five warriors, a Pit Guard, the Sheriff of Shiverwind and a wolf before he can get anywhere near Johaan," the boy replied. "Besides, Johaan can take care of himself. Both as a man and monster."

"You're referring to the bear?" she asked.

"Wallace is no bear," said Arnald.

"No, he is not," she returned, taking his hand, and holding it to her chest.

Arnald felt her beating heart thudding rhythmically through his fingertips and found it soothing. He closed his eyes and drifted to sleep.

Chapter Nine

ARNALD PUSHED THE TENT flap open and clambered out, looking over his shoulder in the hope he hadn't stirred Kysha awake. His heart skipped a beat as she rolled from one side of the bedding to the other. A small smile crept upon his face as he considered how gracefully she moved, even in her sleep.

Closing the flap behind him, he quickly peered about to see no one by the fire. The flames danced high, as if somebody had recently poked at the embers or placed new kindling on the coals. It appeared as if all the others remained in their tents; even those supposed to be on watch.

He couldn't blame them. A faint indigo glow stretched along the mountaintops to the east, signalling that the sun still had some distance to travel before it raised its bright head into the sky.

Turning his head, he found Heilig standing in the middle of the road with the wolf by his side. Both stared towards the south steadfastly. Unmoving.

Cautiously, quietly, he made his way towards them. He focused his efforts on stepping silently through the snow, trying not to wake any sleeping in the tents he passed by. Peering down the dark, empty road to a place where it turned gradually before vanishing into the forest, his curiosity built as he drew nearer to the man and the wolf.

"What are you looking at?" he whispered.

Heilig met his query with a sharp, "Shhh!"

Heilig and the wolf remained motionless, like statues. Arnald followed their gaze again and saw nothing. Before long, the boy found himself staring fixedly at the road for no reason.

"Lads," a voice said, snapping Arnald back to the world of the living. He turned to see Steigauf approaching in full armour, his focus on tightening a vambrace strap. "What news have you?"

At that moment, the old man looked up to see the three of them standing in the middle of the road, watching the south.

"I don't know," Arnald replied. "Something has their attention. I can't see a thing out there."

"Not see," Heilig said. "Something on the wind. Something calling or screaming in pain."

"Something?" Steigauf asked, looking from the man to the wolf.

"I don't know," the soldier answered. "It's very faint."

Steigauf abruptly turned and stomped briskly to the tents, thumping his fist onto the canvas of each one noisily, shouting, "Everyone up. Get up. Let's go."

Squinting, sleepy faces emerged from the tents, some glaring angrily at the old man for disturbing their slumber, others bearing arms at the ready. Kysha burst from the tent with her sword gripped firmly in her hands. She turned her head this way and that, looking for the fight she obviously thought the Pit Guard woke her for.

"You," Steigauf barked, pointing his finger at Nichol Kent and Jaysh Shen-Jon. The two men from Mountainfall stepped back from the old man fearfully. "Get your bearings. Look at the mountains and the road. How far is it to your village?"

Nichol shook his head dumbly while Jaysh looked at the peaks.

"Perhaps a day's ride," he answered. "A little more, maybe."

"Right then." Steigauf stepped over to the fire and started kicking snow and dirt onto the flames.

"What are you doing?" Wallace inquired. "How do we cook breakfast without a fire?"

"We eat from our supplies as we ride," Steigauf called for all to hear. "Clear up. We move out as soon as we can."

Aralore tucked her knees up to her chest, pressing her hands against her ears as she cried profusely on her bed. The incessant din of screaming echoed from the woods, flooding the tiny township.

"I don't know how much more I can bear," she sobbed. "How can this continue for so long?"

Yaleni shook her head, peering through the window. She saw The Lazy Traveller across the way with its doors open, swinging in the breeze, thudding noisily against the walls with each powerful gust. The fire inside had burned out days ago, leaving thick darkness behind to leer back at the elves from the tavern's windows.

She pressed her forehead against the glass pane to look across the road to the forest, towards the source of the wailing. Her eyes darted this way and that as the cries of pain intensified.

Poor Anne, thought Yaleni. Just die. Please, stop fighting and just die.

She immediately cursed herself for thinking such thoughts. But, like her sister, she didn't know how long she could bear the sound of her friend's torture.

A track leading from the roadside into the forest twisted up a gentle rise before vanishing into the thick forest. Shallow furrows leading from the tavern into the woods, now partially covered by fresh snow, reminded Yaleni of the creature dragging Anne away to whatever she now faced out there, alone.

Sobbing turned to loud bawling as Aralore tried to make herself as small as she could, bringing her knees up higher and pressing her chin to her chest. Long, deep groans eventually escaped the blonde elf, drawing Yaleni's attention from the window. She turned just in time to watch her sister vomit all over herself.

"Aralore," she gasped, quickly stepping across the room to crouch beside the bed. She reached her hands out and embraced her sister, both crying uncontrollably.

After a short time, they pulled away from each other to assess the situation. Wet splotches of green and grey slop stuck to Aralore's crimson cloak, reminding Yaleni of porridge. She frowned, meeting her sister's sad gaze.

"What do we do?" the blonde elf asked. "I don't want to go out there to clean up."

"Neither do I," the silver elf replied. She pointed to a wardrobe positioned against the wall. "Let's just find you something else to wear and use this to clean you up." She lifted the hem of the cloak, rubbing the gold trimming with her fingers and thumb.

Aralore nodded, using her sleeve to wipe the spew from her lips. She froze midway and looked to the window.

"What is it?" Yaleni asked, noticing the sudden pause in her sister's movements.

"Listen," she whispered.

The silver elf stood to her feet and became rigid.

Silence.

Moving to the window, Yaleni peered outside.

The Lazy Traveller leered back with its blackened windows, doors yawning in the breeze.

Pressing her forehead to the glass, Yaleni looked to the forest, following the furrows with her eyes, along the track to the top of the rise where the forest waited.

From there, Anne Forde stared back.

With horror etched upon her face, mouth agape in a silent scream, the tavern keeper's wife watched the tiny township of Mountainfall as the sun made its way over the mountains behind her.

Blood trickled from the wound where it once attached to her neck, down the length of the pike and into the snow.

Yaleni covered her mouth as bile stung her throat and tears burst over her cheeks.

PART SIX

The Southerlands and Fancy Chairs

Chapter One

THE TROOP GALLOPED HARD for miles and miles. By mid-morning, the horses tired, all except Naran, Aamon Martano's Eluvian horse. As the others slowed to a canter, the stallion started past Steigauf at the head of the party.

"I can ride ahead," Martano offered. "Naran is more than able."

"No," the Pit Guard barked. "We don't know what lies ahead. We stay together."

Martano looked at Wallace for his approval to disregard the old man's instruction, but the Sheriff of Northwell shook his head and gestured with a nod for the rider to fall in line.

Steigauf signalled the team to pull to a halt.

"We should press on," Jaysh Shen-Jon pleaded. The urgent tone in his voice broke Arnald's heart. "Our people may be suffering."

"The horses will not last," Nichol Kent told him. "We must allow them time to rest."

"Don't you care what happens to them?" Jaysh questioned his friend, water welling in his eyes.

"Of course I do," the other answered, his cheeks already damp from tears.

Steigauf turned in his saddle to face the troop.

"Johaan," he called. "Come up here."

Heilig steered his horse out of the line and steadily moved towards his commander.

"Sir?" he growled, pulling alongside the old man. His eyes were a glaring yellow.

"What do you hear?"

Heilig cocked his head, directing his ear to the road ahead. The riders held their tongues, trying their best to remain as silent as they could as the soldier listened steadfastly. Arnald peered down at the wolf standing beside his horse. She looked back at him momentarily before turning her head to the trees on the side of the road. At that moment, he knew the answer to Steigauf's question.

"Nothing," said Heilig. He shook his head. "Absolutely nothing."

"We're too late," Jaysh Shen-Jon whispered as he wiped his eyes.

"We don't know what's going on down that road," Wallace put in. "It may be that your townsfolk are fine, and what that monster and the wolf heard was nothing but the wind."

Cocking an eyebrow, Heilig glared at the sheriff irritably before peering back along the line to Benten, who responded with a simple shake of his head. Wallace turned sheepishly to look anywhere else but into the soldier's yellow stare.

"We move on," Steigauf called, urging his dark steed forward, settling at a steady trot and the troop on his heels.

"That sheriff is a cunt," Arnald heard Benten mumble as Heilig slid back in line.

"He certainly is," Kysha muttered.

Continuing southward, Arnald felt as if the air surrounding him turned densely cold. To him, it made little sense. He thought the farther south one travelled, the warmer it should become. Understandably, he currently rode his white steed within the boundary of Kedielewen, a land perpetually trapped in an everlasting winter. But, as the party drew nearer to Mountainfall, resting on the border of Asalethwen, he expected the temperature to rise a little, not fall.

As the day drew on, the puffs of vapour emitting from both men and horses wafted like small, thick clouds that lingered longer and longer near their faces. Pulling his cloak tightly around his shoulders, Arnald peered across to Kysha, who rubbed her thighs with her gloved hands. Clearly, she felt it too.

"This isn't natural," he said to her softly.

"No," she agreed. "Something dark waits for us ahead."

Night approached quickly.

The sky turned from red to a deep purple the closer they drew to the mountains to the south. Gentle snow fell, drifting aimlessly about them, almost lingering in the air.

With just enough remaining light, Arnald fixed his gaze on the one place where the line of mountains broke, making a gap between The Dragon's Teeth and The Stone Curtain not too far away.

"That must be Mountainfall," he pointed out.

"Aye," Kysha replied, her voice shaking slightly as she pulled her hood tightly over her head.

He looked at her, concerned. "What is it?"

She shook her head, staring at the place where a mountain once stood. "I don't know," she answered. "I suddenly don't want to be here."

He watched her for a moment. "We're not just going to find raiders, are we?"

She frowned and shook her head again.

"What will we find?"

"I don't know," she said again.

Arnald glanced at Heilig, who was stuffing his face with dried meat. Benten, watching his friend closely, turned to the boy.

"He has been shovelling that stuff into his face non-stop," he said before returning his attention to the man riding to his side. "You should slow down."

"I don't feel good," Heilig growled, turning his face towards Benten. His eyes glared an intense yellow and his teeth appeared to have grown.

"No wonder," the other returned. "How much have you eaten?"

"I don't know," the soldier said, looking down at his saddle bag. "I'm almost out."

An icy chill ran along Arnald's spine. He wondered what might occur if Heilig ran out of meat, hoping he and the other riders didn't become a substitute.

Eventually, the riders saw the small township of Mountainfall.

The darkened windows and smokeless chimneys of the houses and tavern caused a knot to form in Arnald's belly. He scanned the area as Steigauf called for the troop to halt in place.

The tavern's door creaked as it swung carelessly, back and forth, on its hinges.

"Where is everyone?" Jaysh Shen-Jon queried, keeping his voice low as he peered along the road.

Nichol's breath increased, rapidly building as he frantically looked towards his house down the side road that ran past The Lazy Traveller. Seeing no light emitting from the window, he immediately urged his horse into a charge.

"Helena," he called, driving past the tavern.

"Wait," Arnald shouted.

Nichol didn't hear him and raced down the road.

"What is it, laddie?" Steigauf asked, turning in his saddle to face the boy.

"There," he answered, pointing to the rise across the road from The Lazy Traveller.

All heads turned to face what the boy gestured towards.

There, positioned along the tree line, the heads of Mountainfall's population glared lifelessly down at the village from atop pikes.

"No," Jaysh Shen-Jon wept before falling into a blubbering mess.

"By the gods," Wallace gasped.

Chapter Two

T HE TROOP GAPED AT the ten severed heads set in two even rows on the hillside with the thin winding path in their midst, five on one side and five on the other. The sound of racing hoof falls rushing away reverberated around them as Nichol Kent charged towards his hut. Jaysh Shen-Jon dropped from his horse and fell to his knees a blubbering mess. Wallace carefully climbed off his steed, keeping his gaze fixed on the display on the rise as he lowered himself to crouch by the distraught man. He placed a comforting hand on Jaysh's back but said no words.

"Do you see that?" Runolffson asked, breaking the silence. He pointed to the ten heads posted on pikes.

"Of course we do," Sigemaer replied with a hint of gall. "We're not fucking blind."

"No." The large Jomaandian sighed. "Look. Five men on one side of the path. Five women on the other."

Sigemaer squinted, leaned forward in his saddle and shook his head.

"How can you tell that from here?"

Runolffson turned his head slowly and bored his eyes into the other soldier.

"I'm not fucking blind," he answered.

Steigauf shifted in his seat and pointed at the large man.

"You and Kolfinn take a look inside that tavern," the Pit Guard

403

commanded. He then turned to Agdestein, "You and Ulfar take a ride along that road our friend went down. Knock on doors. Announce yourselves. See if there are any survivors."

The four men immediately went about their duties.

"What about us?" Heilig growled, eyes glaring yellow.

"I need you and Viktor here, watching that hill," the old man told him. "I need those ears and nose of yours searching for anyone who is not us. Understand?"

"Yes, sir," the two men replied.

Arnald lifted his leg over his steed, intending to dismount.

"No," Steigauf barked.

Arnald froze in place. He looked at the Pit Guard, perplexed.

"Where do you want us?" Kysha queried. "We can't stay on our horses forever."

"You're right," Steigauf said. "I want you to take the pack horses along with mine, Johaan's and Viktor's, to that stable over there." He gestured to a building set behind the tavern. "See what stock might be there and feed them. After that, prepare your weapons and meet me on the porch of the tavern."

Heilig and Benten dismounted and handed the lead ropes to the two younger riders.

"Call out if you need us," Benten said in a low voice.

Kysha nodded before she and the boy led the horses away.

———◆———

A warm, roaring fire in the stone hearth filled the room with a tawny glow, casting deep shadows against the wall where they danced. The silent, lifeless interior of the tavern sent chills down Sigemaer's spine. To him, the sight of an empty room with blazing flames seemed unnatural.

As he followed Runolffson deeper into the room, sword clutched tightly in his hands, he peered around at the chairs and tables waiting for patrons to come. Glass jugs filled with ale and empty mugs sat neatly together on the bar. A knot tightened in Sigemaer's stomach as he watched the other man lower his face close to a jug. Runolffson sniffed the contents.

"Freshly poured," he said, looking to the doorway behind the bar. A strong, tantalising scent drew both men to the door. Runolffson started towards the passageway with Sigemaer in tow, but not before stopping to inspect the jugs himself. "Don't drink that," the larger man ordered.

The two men entered a galley where buttered loaves waited on a bench, along with neatly stacked plates, bowls, spoons, and a ladle. On the stove nearby, a large pot of stew simmered and bubbled.

"That smells so good," Sigemaer observed. He stopped in his tracks and stared at the steam slowly rising from the pot. "What do you think is in that?"

"I don't know," the other answered emotionlessly. "But you're right. It smells good."

Sigemaer instinctively reached for the ladle, unable to tear his gaze away from the bubbling stew.

"Should probably give it a stir, at least," he said. "Just so it doesn't stick to the bottom."

"Just so it doesn't stick to the bottom," Runolffson repeated, agreeing with the sentiment, fixated on the pot.

Dipping the ladle into the pot, Sigemaer slowly turned the mixture. Carrots, potatoes, mushrooms, and meat came to the surface. Pillars of steam rose from the thick soup, sending an intoxicating aroma into both men's nostrils. They both breathed it in deeply.

"One taste wouldn't hurt," Sigemaer whispered.

Runolffson furrowed his brow and slowly shook his head.

"I don't know," he grumbled as Sigemaer carefully lifted the ladle from the pot. It carried a small portion of the stew towards the soldier's waiting lips.

—◆—

Agdestein and Wynneiros moved to a small house across the way from the tavern. Snow clung to its steep roof, which hung over a tiny wooden porch. Thick curtains drawn across the windows on either side of the door made it impossible for the men to determine whether there was anyone within.

The archer tapped softly on the door, not wanting to frighten the occupants, if any.

"Hello," he called. "My name is Fridmund. I am with the Dendadian infantry from the Shiverwind barracks. Is anyone home?" The sound of muffled movement rumbled from behind the door. "Hello?" Agdestein called again.

Wynneiros gripped the hilt of his sheathed sword, ready to act. The archer shook his head, signalling the other to relax.

"We don't know who is in there," the tall, broad-shouldered man said, keeping his hand on his weapon. "Or what?"

"We don't need to appear aggressive," the other replied. "What if there are children inside? Scared children?"

"How many are you?" a woman's voice called from inside.

"Ah," Agdestein started, thinking about how to answer. "There are two of us here. But more of us about."

"Are you raiders?" the woman asked. "Perhaps mercenaries?"

"We're infantrymen in the service of Dendadia," the archer said. "We came with the Sheriff of Northwell, along with two men who claim to be from here."

"Who?" another queried, also female.

"Who are the two men?" Agdestein asked for clarification.

"Yes," the second woman replied. "Who are they?"

"A Nichol something." Agdestein scratched at his beard, trying to remember the names of the two men.

"Kent," Wynneiros put in. "Nichol Kent and Jaysh Shen-Jon."

A small moment of silence passed. Agdestein and Wynneiros exchanged looks, wondering what might be happening behind the closed door.

"Where are they?" the first woman asked.

The two soldiers turned to look along the road.

"The one called Jaysh Shen-Jon is kneeling on the road, being consoled by the sheriff," Agdestein replied. "The other, Nichol, rode down this side road."

The latch on the door clicked, and the door swung inward with a long creak. Two elvish women in cloaks, one with silver hair dressed in green and the other blonde and clothed in crimson, stood inside aiming loaded bows at the men.

"Did any of your men go into the tavern?" a silver-haired elf asked.

"Two." Wynneiros nodded.

The blonde elf hastily stepped forward, passing through the door and by both men.

"We need to get them out of there," she said. "Get everyone back here where it's safe."

"Aralore," the other called with a hint of panic in her voice, lowering her bow before following the other.

"What is it?" the broad-shouldered man asked, stepping after them.

"She was in and out of there all day," the silver elf replied.

"Who?" Wynnerios questioned, gesturing to the blonde elf. "Her?"

"No," she answered, stopping in her tracks to point to the heads on the hill. "The one who did that."

Arnald used the flint to light a lantern hanging from a post by the side of the stable door. Finding a pitchfork leaning against the wall nearby, Arnald scooped some straw piled together in a stall and carried it to a timber trough in the middle of the stable. Kysha guided the six horses across the room, the spotted stallion the first to bury its muzzle into the trough. The others soon took the hint and started feeding.

Cackling laughter reverberated from the forest beyond the hillside, filling the air with an almost tangible sense of dread.

The boy paused, watching the horses eat but twisting his head towards the door as if drawn by something unseen.

"I could eat something, myself," the boy put in, returning to the stall to retrieve more straw.

"Something is cooking in the tavern," the elf told him. "I can smell it."

"Cooking?" Arnald shot her a curious glance. "Someone survived?"

"Maybe," she replied, returning to the door to peer out to the dark road.

"Who else would be cooking?" he asked, carrying another load of straw.

The horses lifted their heads, allowing him to drop the straw into the trough. "Should we take all this gear off them?"

"What?" Kysha turned, lost in thought, distracted.

"The packs and saddles," Arnald clarified. "Should we take them off?"

"No," she answered immediately. "We may not have time to pack them again if we need to leave in a hurry."

The boy nodded as he carried another load of straw. After returning the pitchfork to its place, he moved to his white steed and stroked its neck. The horse nickered softly as it continued to munch on the dried stalks.

"All right," he said. "Let's close the doors and find what's cooking."

"Arnald," she said, turning to give him a stern look.

"Mmm?" He looked at her, confused.

"Aren't you in the slightest bit concerned about any of this?"

"About what?"

"The empty town," she started. "Those heads posted on the hill. The smell of food coming from the tavern. Something isn't right and you're too smart to act like this."

"Acting like what? I'm hungry," he said, shaking his head and shrugging.

"This," she said as she waved her hand at the scene outside. "All of this is a trap."

"Then we get our weapons," the boy replied, returning to his horse to fetch his sword and bow. "Osman said to do as much anyway."

She shook her head in disbelief as she watched him strap his sword and quiver to his waist. He strode by her and back into the frosty night air. "Let's go."

She followed him out of the barn, turning to close the doors before running a little to catch up to him. She gave him a vexed scowl, but he ignored her, fixing his gaze on the tavern's back door.

"You could have waited for me to close the doors," she said.

"What?" he asked, turning his head momentarily to look at her before placing his attention back on the building before them. "Smells good."

Kysha's gaze found movement to their left. A blonde figure dressed in crimson, carrying a bow, raced across the ground towards them. The she-elf pulled her sword free of its sheath.

"Arnald," she called, trying to get his attention.

He turned to face her, looking annoyed. "What?"

"Behind you," she shouted.

He turned to see the woman approaching. Instinctively, he dropped his bow and raised his sword.

"No," a voice called from the darkness, farther along the side road, past the stable. The boy and she-elf turned to see Nichol returning on his horse. "I know her."

Arnald and Kysha lowered their swords.

The blonde woman drew closer and closer with Agdestein close behind.

At that moment, the back door of the tavern burst open. All heads turned to see Runolffson dragging Sigemaer through the doorway by the arms and into the snow. Sigemaer's legs kicked and twisted spasmodically in all directions. His head shook back and forth, up, and down uncontrollably.

"Help me," Runolffson called. He let go of Sigemaer and glanced around at all the watching faces. "He ate some stew and started doing this."

Sigemaer contorted unnaturally; twisting, turning, writhing, and shaking on the ground. Foam built on the corners of his mouth as his eyes rolled back in their sockets.

"By the gods," puffed Wynneiros, running behind the blonde woman and Agdestein. "What is this?"

The blonde woman raced past them all and into the open door of the tavern.

Sigemaer continued to shudder and jerk. His arms and legs flailed and twisted as he made loud, rapid grunting sounds.

The tantalising aroma of something enticing drew Arnald's attention from the man on the ground to the door of the tavern. The blonde woman emerged, carrying the pot of stew in her bare hands.

She winced and whined as she stepped across the snow a short distance before dropping the pot on the ground. It landed on its side, splashing the contents across the ground, and sending a thick plume of steam into the air.

A silver-haired woman raced to the other's side as the blonde woman fell to her knees, placing her palms flat on the snow. She made a sound that told Arnald she was in great pain.

"Aralore," the silver-haired woman said softly, falling to her knees and placing her arms around the blonde woman's shoulders. "Are you all right?"

"It burns," Aralore answered.

Sigemaer suddenly stopped moving. All heads turned to look at him again.

Runolffson crouched beside the fallen man and inspected him, placing his hand on Sigemaer's chest. After a moment, he shook his head.

A sinking feeling filled Arnald's heart as he looked from the dead soldier to the spilled stew steaming on the snow.

Chapter Three

AGDESTEIN, THE ARCHER, GAPED at Sigemaer's body and shook his head.

"We should report this to Osman and fetch Kolfinn's bedding so we can wrap him in it," the boy said. "We'll carry him to the stable and leave him there with the horses."

"What do we do?" he whispered.

The other infantrymen stood motionless, saying nothing.

Arnald watched the steam rising from the spilled stew, feeling pulled by the aroma, knowing the sensation to be unnatural.

"Ospak," the boy said, gaining the attention of the golden-haired Jomaandian. "Did Kolfinn eat anything else, or only this stew?"

"Just the stew," the soldier answered. "It was only a taste. Nothing more."

Only a taste, Arnald thought, moving his gaze to the body.

"Did you eat anything in there?" Arnald asked.

"No," said the Jomaandian.

Agdestein looked over to the open door of the tavern.

"What other delicacies await us in there?" the archer inquired.

Runolffson turned to follow the other's stare.

"Some buttered bread and jugs of ale."

Arnald started for the door with Agdestein in tow.

"Where are you going?" Kysha called after them.

"To destroy any edible thing we can find," the archer answered.

Kysha watched the two of them disappear inside and continued to watch the door for some time before noticing a pair of eyes locked onto her, scrutinising her every inch. The silver-haired woman dressed in green, crouching by the blonde lady, considered the Sheriff of Shiverwind cautiously.

"May I help you?" Kysha asked defensively.

The woman shook her head quickly and turned her face to the door.

"Yaleni," Nichol called, dismounting his horse, and moving to the woman. They embraced one another. "Good to see you."

"And you, Nichol," the silver-haired woman said.

"Nichol," the crimson-clothed woman said, rushing across the ground. She wrapped her arms around both Nichol and Yaleni. "I'm so happy you're back. Is Jaysh here with you?"

"He is on the road," Runolffson told her. "Forgive my intrusion. But we have many questions, and we must report this to our commander."

"Can it wait a moment?" Nichol asked, pulling away from the two women. "Aralore has hurt her hands. Can't we get her wounds looked to first?"

"No," the Jomaandian replied before placing his attention on Yaleni and Aralore. "I already know your names, but I don't know who you are."

"I am Yaleni, and this is my younger sister Aralore," the woman in green answered. "We live in that hut over there."

Aralore dug her hands into the cold snow, covering them.

"Gentlemen, please," Nichol said, gesturing to the blonde woman.

"We're elves of Olendabwyn," Yaleni added, shooting Kysha a sideways glance.

A brief silence ensued.

"Did either of you serve Amalith or his cause?" asked Runolffson.

Yaleni appeared repulsed by the idea, frowning hard and shaking her head.

"We were very young during the war," she stated. "My sister and I spend most of that time running and hiding."

"Why?" Wynneiros questioned.

"Sorry?" Yaleni looked at him, confused.

"Why were you running and hiding?"

The silver woman looked at her sister. She bore an expression of apprehension.

Aralore nodded, giving the other silent permission.

"Amalith's soldiers killed our parents because they didn't publicly declare their loyalty to the king," she explained. "Then they took turns having their way with us."

Kysha's chin quivered as she listened to the elf-woman's words.

"You said you were very young," she said.

"We were children then." Yaleni glared at Kysha with disdain.

"I'm so very sorry," Kysha replied, her voice trembling.

"Are you?" the elf-woman whispered, moving her gaze to the fallen soldier.

Nichol moved across the ground to where the pot and stew lay. He scanned it for some time before turning his attention to the sisters.

"Who poisoned this?" he asked. "Did you see?"

The elves exchanged looks.

"Perhaps," Aralore answered. "We saw an old crone sneaking in and out of The Lazy Traveller through the day."

"Was this Helena's stew?" Nichol queried, crouching beside the puddle.

Yaleni shrugged.

"Who can say?" she replied. "It could be the old woman we saw made it or she tampered with a pot Helena prepared."

Nichol rose to his feet and peered at the sisters.

"And Helena?" he pressed, tears streaming over his cheeks. "Did you see her? Is she one of those we saw on the hill?"

Aralore stood, holding her hands together, shaking her head.

"We don't know," Yaleni said, placing a hand on her sister's arm. "We only saw the old woman."

Arnald emerged through the doorway carrying a jug of ale, Agdestein followed with a jug in each hand. They tossed the pitchers onto the ground by the door, where the drink spilled onto the snow, leaving brown puddles.

"Did you question them?" the boy asked the Jomaandian.

"Indeed," Runolffson replied.

Arnald nodded slowly and turned his attention to Sigemaer.

"What should we do with him?" Wynneiros asked.

Arnald looked across to Runolffson, expecting a response. Instead, the big man stared silently at the body as if in deep thought. After a quick moment of silence, Arnald moved to the body and answered.

It wasn't long before the rest of the riders gathered in the stable with their horses. With Sigemaer wrapped tightly in a blanket, resting in the stall housing the supply of straw, the others collected their weapons and waited silently for Steigauf to give orders.

They watched as the Pit Guard crouched by the fallen soldier, examining his face by turning Sigemaer's head gently.

"Bloodshot eyes," the old man said, pulling a corner of the blanket over the soldier's head to cover him completely before rising. "Darkened blood vessels beneath the skin near the jowls. I'd say it was poison if it hadn't occurred so quickly."

"Witchcraft, then," Wallace put in.

"Aye," Steigauf agreed. "We heard the bitch laughing. It's as if she knew one of us fell. I'd say she was hoping we'd all eat the feast she left for us so that we'd end up like poor Kolfinn here." He turned to Aralore, who stood by the stable door. "Thank you for what you did. You may have saved all of us."

She nodded, flexing her hands, and stretching her fingers. Yaleni placed her hands on her sister's shoulders, embracing her from the side.

"I need to get her home," she said. "I should put salve on her hands."

Steigauf peered out into the darkness beyond the door.

"You won't go alone," he told her. "Take Nichol and Jaysh with you."

"We don't need guardians," the silver-haired elf retorted. "We're quite capable of taking care of ourselves."

"I'm not sending them to watch over you," the Pit Guard replied. "After what we saw on that hill, I thought they'd feel more at home in your house rather than here in the stable with us and our fallen comrade."

"There's no need to bother the ladies," Nichol interjected. "We could stay in one of our own houses, or in the tavern."

"No." Steigauf shook his head. "She knows the tavern. It has too many places for her to hide. And isolating yourselves, even in groups of two, is just too dangerous." He peered at Arnald and Kysha, standing with the she-wolf. "Take them, too."

"No," Yaleni said defiantly, shooting a contemptuous glare in Kysha's direction. "I'll take Nichol and Jaysh, but she and the boy will stay with you." With that, she steered her sister out the stable door and into the night, glancing back to catch the Mountainfall men with her eyes. "Come along, you two."

Kysha gawked at the silver-haired elf, mouth agape as Nichol Kent and Jaysh Shen-Jon fell into line.

"Why do you hate me?" the she-elf called after Yaleni. "You don't even know me."

Yaleni stopped in her tracks and turned to face Kysha.

"Don't," Aralore whispered, but her plea fell on deaf ears.

"I know exactly who you are," Yaleni replied, her voice filled with hatred. She bowed, feigning a curtsey. "Your Majesty."

A stunned Kysha stared at the silver-haired elf in confusion.

Arnald furrowed his brow. "Majesty? What's that supposed to mean?"

Yaleni sneered as she stood upright. "You should ask your sweetheart, there," the elf-woman answered. "She buries her secrets well from your sight, but I see. She cannot be trusted."

"Quiet," Kysha barked.

Yaleni pointed to the hill.

"If this witch turns out to be an agent of Kaamwyn, one of Akasha Miroslava's dogs," she snarled, turning her finger to the young she-elf, "there's every chance she is in league with this one. Granddaughter of Amalith. Queen of Legilawen."

Yaleni turned again, steering Aralore by the shoulders towards their hut, with Jaysh Shen-Jon and Nichol Kent close behind.

A sudden, thick silence filled the stable as all eyes fell upon the Sheriff of Shiverwind.

Chapter Four

K YSHA FELL TO HER knees, shaking all over and tears streaming over her cheeks.

"Is that true?" Wallace queried, placing his hand on the hilt of his sword.

"Shut the fuck up," Benten snapped, pointing at the man.

Heilig stepped in the path between Kysha and the Sheriff of Northwell, his eyes a glaring yellow, his teeth long.

Arnald dropped to Kysha's side and immediately wrapped his arms around her.

Runolffson, Agdestein and Wynneiros positioned themselves to block any move Martano might make. The rider from Northwell put his hands up in surrender, silently declaring he didn't wish to get involved.

"Best get your hand off that," Steigauf said, pointing at Wallace.

The she-wolf lowered her head, raised her hackles, and glared menacingly at the man from Northwell.

"She's the Queen of Legilawen," Wallace argued.

"She's the Sheriff of Shiverwind and one of my company," the Pit Guard told him. "And I trust her far more than I trust you."

Wallace glanced about the room, realising they outnumbered him. He lowered his hand from his sword and stepped away. "Let it be on your heads if something comes of this," he said.

"You sleep by the door," Steigauf said to Wallace. "If you go anywhere near her, I'll run you through myself." He strolled across the room to where Kysha and Arnald kneeled. "Are you all right, lassie?"

She sobbed, unable to give an intelligible answer.

Arnald read the expression on the old man's face. "You knew," he whispered.

"Aye," the Pit Guard replied. "And now, so do you. Does it change anything?"

"No," the boy answered, keeping his arms around the she-elf.

"What was that?" Jaysh asked, staring at Yaleni as he closed the door behind him. He leaned his sword against the wall, beside Nichol's blade and the elf sisters' bows.

Aralore slumped onto a cushioned settee by the window and peered back outside to the stable. Nichol moved to the side of the room to lean on the doorpost, folding his arms and peering at the silver elf. She, in turn, took a chunk of wood from a pile on the floor, opened the oven door with a cloth, and threw the timber inside.

"Tea?" she asked flatly, keeping her emotions buried.

"Yaleni?" Nichol put in. "Please, tell us what just happened."

She took in a deep breath, taking a small iron pot filled with water from the bench to place on the stovetop.

"That girl is the granddaughter of Amalith," she explained.

"Yes," Nichol replied. "That much we understand."

"She's dangerous," Yaleni continued. "Her grandfather was a tyrant and his blood runs through her veins. What more do I need to say?"

Jaysh shook his head. "You can't expect someone to behave like another just because they're related," he said. "Look at me. Do I act like the seafarers of the Shattered Isles? That's where my people originated. I've never been on a boat. I'm nothing like them. We travelled with her. There's nothing of Amalith in her."

"How do you know?" Yaleni asked, preparing a teapot.

"How do you?" Nichol queried.

The silver elf put her hands flat on the bench on either side of the teapot. She took another deep breath and closed her eyes.

"She carries a bow," Yaleni put in as she reached for a tin canister, removing its lid.

"That's not a sufficient argument," Aralore said, continuing to watch the stable. "Many carry bows. We carry bows. Are we of Amalith?"

"She also has a sword and other blades," the silver elf added, turning to face the two men. "I wager she knows how to use them. She's probably the best fighter among them. Is she not?"

Jaysh gave Nichol a sideways glance with a small shake of his head.

Nichol sighed, ignoring the silent warning. "She is the Sheriff of Shiverwind," he informed her.

"Sheriff?" The elf raised her brow before reaching for a teaspoon resting with others in a cup on the windowsill. "At such a young age? Such responsibility."

"Yaleni," Aralore said, "that doesn't..."

"A cunning fighter and hunter of men." The silver elf turned back to spoon some crumpled and dried tea leaves from a canister into the teapot. "A leader of sorts. Nothing like Amalith at all."

"She's here to help us," Jaysh countered.

"Is she?" Yaleni placed the lid back onto the canister. A long moment of silence ensued. "He hurt our people. His soldiers killed my parents and..." she looked at Aralore with glistening eyes. "To see a part of him alive is like living through it all again."

Nichol crossed the floor and sat on the settee beside Aralore. With his elbows on his knees and head in his hands, he studied the timber lines on the floorboards.

Jaysh found a chair by the table near the tiny kitchen area where Yaleni prepared the pot of tea.

In silence, they waited as the water in the pot on the stovetop first steamed, then boiled. The silver elf poured the hot liquid carefully into the teapot before placing the iron pot on the bench. After some time passed, she poured the brew into four teacups before carrying one to Jaysh.

"Thank you," he said, taking it from her and placing it on the table.

She then carried cups to her sister and to Nichol seated on the settee.

Both received the tea with gratitude, Nichol taking a sip and wincing a little from the heat.

Yaleni took the last cup for herself and sat in a seat next to the man at the table. She reached across to his hand, resting by his steaming cup, and took it in hers. He looked at her, surprised.

"I'm glad you're home," she told him.

He frowned a little, considering what the two sisters must have gone through since he and Nichol left to seek help.

"Me too," he replied.

Some more silence ensued as Yaleni interlaced her fingers with Jaysh Shen-Jon's. She leaned into him, placing her head on his shoulder.

Nichol returned his attention to the floor and tried the tea again. The heat subsided a little, enough to tolerate. The brew tasted sweet and held the aroma of leafy herbs and jasmine. For whatever the reason, it reminded him of her.

"What happened to Helena?" he asked, looking to Aralore first, then Yaleni. Both women glanced at each other before offering the man apologetic looks. "She isn't among those on the hill. She isn't in my house and she's not here." Nichol's pleading eyes welled with tears. "Did the witch take her? Did she go back to her hut and not return?"

Yaleni opened her mouth to speak, but no sound came.

"Yes," Aralore answered.

Nichol turned to face her.

"Yes?" he queried. "She was taken, or she returned to her hut?"

"Both," the blonde elf answered. "Helena returned to the woods, and we haven't seen her in days. A twisted old crone with hollow eyes showed up soon after."

"She killed my Helena?" Nichol asked.

Yaleni looked from Aralore to Nichol.

"We don't know," the silver elf told him. "Until tonight, we haven't left our house. We only saw the old one creeping about from there." She pointed to the window near the settee.

Nichol felt his hands shaking. He placed the cup on the floor by his feet as carefully as he could, spilling a few drops of tea before bursting into tears.

Aralore put her own cup on a table beside her before placing her hands on the man's shoulders.

"I am so sorry, Nichol," she whispered.

<hr />

Arnald collected some timber chocks piled against the back wall of the tavern and built a hearth a few feet outside from the stable's door. Using some dried straw and the flint, he ignited the timber and set to create a blazing fire.   "We can't leave," Steigauf told him with a slow shake of his head. "If we do, she'll move elsewhere and prey on others as she has here. Perhaps she'll go south to warmer lands, or north to Coldwolf, or to Northwell. Besides, that's not a warning," the Pit Guard continued. "It's an invitation."

Benten and Heilig collected more timber and made a small pile near the boy.

With a little prodding and poking with a stick, Arnald had a roaring fire within moments. The two men, accompanied by Agdestein, collected more wood, and stacked it high next to the stable door, within easy reach.

Before long, three men and the boy sat by the fire, staring at the flames as a gentle drift of snow fell around them. Kysha slowly made her way out of the stable, passing Wallace, who sat with his back against the doorpost. She ignored him as she walked slowly by. He was watching her, wearing a scowl. All the while, Steigauf and the she-wolf watched the Sheriff of Northwell cautiously until the elf lowered herself beside Arnald.

Kysha, hugging her cloak tightly around her, rested her head on the boy's shoulder. He noticed the stains on her cheeks from the many tears she cried. Reaching over, he gently wiped them away with his thumb and wrapped his arm around her shoulders.

Soon, Runolffson and Wynneiros joined the troop by the fire, positioning themselves on the ground near the Kysha. Steigauf and the wolf followed them, standing behind the boy and the elf.

"May I join you?" Aamon Martano asked sheepishly from the doorway.

The troop looked to Arnald for a response. The boy gestured for the rider from Northwell to sit with them.

"It's another good fire, Arnald," the Jomaandian commented.

Arnald simply nodded.

"The Firekeeper." Wynneiros smiled.

All of them watched the flames, staring aimlessly into the dancing light and sparkling embers.

All except the Pit Guard, who looked at the darkened hillside where ten severed heads resting on pikes stared back.

"She's watching, isn't she?" Heilig asked in a low growl.

"I think so," Steigauf answered.

"I know it," said the young soldier. "I can feel her calling me."

Keeping his gaze on the hill, the Pit Guard nodded.

"I thought as much," he said.

Benten measured the old man, studying his expression.

"You know who she is," he stated.

All heads turned to the Pit Guard, pursing his lips, and cocking his head a little.

"I think so," Steigauf said. "I think it may be Lycia, the necromancer."

Arnald felt a cold spike pierce his heart and a knot form in his stomach.

He suddenly found himself in his home far away, where his father told him and Jörgen, his little brother, a tale of two witches falling with a mountain into the ground.

"Neophytes," the boy whispered.

"What's that?" Kysha asked, pulling away to look at him.

"Can't be," Arnald said to the Pit Guard. "My father saw her fall with the mountain, right here."

"Aye," Steigauf crouched and scratched the wolf's ears. "Right there." The old man pointed to the wide gap where The Dragon's Teeth abruptly ended.

"How?" the boy furrowed his brow. "How could she survive that?"

"She's a witch, laddie," the old man answered. "They live longer and don't age like the rest of us, which makes her one of the oldest and probably one of the more cunning. From what I've heard, she appeared beyond ancient, like a walking corpse. Some have suggested that she, being a necromancer, kept herself alive by using the same magic she used to raise the dead during the war."

"You never saw her?" Martano inquired.

"No," the Pit Guard replied. "I fought farther to the south. The closest I came to here was Shadowfort."

Steigauf stood and returned his gaze to the hillside.

"We should return to Northwell," Wallace put in, sitting by the stable door. "We need more men." He pointed to the dark hill. "That's a warning, that is. We should get those people in that house over there, get on our horses, and leave."

Chapter Five

—◦◦◦—

THE AIR BECAME EERILY still as a faint glow built behind the eastern mountains, signalling the new day. Already, the Shiverwind men collected their weapons and gathered on the road in front of The Lazy Traveller. Agdestein checked Arnald's quiver, slung across the boy's body, to hang by his hip.

"Carry your bow," the archer advised. "If you find yourself in close combat, drop it and reach for your sword. You can always retrieve your bow later."

The boy nodded, absorbing the wise words, trying to dull the rapid beating of his heart thrumming loudly in his ears. The archer peered at Kysha, standing beside Arnald.

"You make sure to stay close to him," Agdestein told her. "Look after each other. We might not have the chance to protect you out there. If this witch is who the commander believes her to be, know she is a cunning fighter. Miroslava didn't send useless bitches into the world to fight on her behalf."

"Understood," the elf agreed, her chin quivering as she scanned the hillside, stopping on each of the ten heads staring back.

One of them blinked. Or she thought it did.

"By the gods," Arnald gasped.

"What is it?" Agdestein turned to face the hill.

"I thought I saw one of them move," the boy replied.

"A trick of the brain from lack of rest and the dull light," the archer surmised.

"I saw it, too," the elf put in.

Steigauf grunted and strode over to them.

"As did I," he added. "The necromancer beckons."

Feeling a lump form in his throat, Arnald scanned the faces on the hill. A tightness built in his chest as he realised all ten watched the gathering on the road.

"She sees us through them," he said, looking at the Pit Guard. "Doesn't she?"

"I presume so," the old man answered, turning his attention to the road leading away to the gap in the mountains. A veil of grey mist and drifting snow hindered the view, preventing any clear sight of the Southerlands. "This may be the closest I come to reaching my homelands again," Steigauf whispered, just loud enough for the boy, the elf and the archer to hear. "Fridmund told you to look after each other. Do so."

"You're afraid," Kysha murmured, her voice shaking.

"Yes," the Pit Guard replied, turning to face her. "I'm apprehensive about going forward. If she is who I think she is, we may not all return."

"You're a Pit Guard," she protested. "One of The First. You placed the rope around Amalith's neck. You can't be afraid."

"I'm old, lassie," he reminded, running his fingers slowly over the figures of the four cloaked women on his breastplate. "I'm not the man I was back then."

"But you *will* fight," she pressed, sternly glaring at him.

Arnald wasn't sure if she queried the Pit Guard or commanded him.

"I will fight." Steigauf smiled. "We can't allow her to do what she has done here to anyone else. We all fight until she is dead or none of us remains."

"Fight until we can fight no more," Agdestein said.

Steigauf peered around at his men, facing the hill, hands trembling from fear and anticipation, but ready for battle.

All too young, he thought as he turned back to face the boy and the elf. Much too young.

"Ready?"

Arnald nodded, lifting his bow to signal his preparedness. Kysha did the same.

"All right then," Steigauf said, loud enough for all to hear. He started for the little path, not much more than a shallow imprinted line blanketed with snow, on the side of the road. The troop casually manoeuvred into a line behind their commander with Runolffson second in line, followed by Heilig, Benten, Agdestein and the younglings carrying their bows, the she-wolf stepping beside the boy, and Wynneiros at the rear with his hand resting on the hilt of his sword strapped to his hip.

A knot tightened in Arnald's stomach as they started up the hill. The eyes of all ten heads, posted on spikes, turned in their sockets, coming to rest on the advancing men. A lump formed in the boy's throat, and he felt as if he might be sick.

"Hang in there, Firekeeper," Wynneiros muttered, placing his hand on the lad's shoulder. "Don't let them see your fear."

Arnald swallowed hard, pressing forward, drawing nearer and nearer to the ten on the hill.

"Wait," a woman's voice called from behind them.

The troop turned, Wynneiros pulling his sword from its sheath.

The elf sisters trotted from their house towards them. They both bore bows and quivers slung over their shoulders and carried two water bags and many strips of torn cloth in their hands. Arnald noticed fresh bandages wrapped around the blonde elf's hands, covering the burns sustained from carrying the hot pot of stew. The two Mountainfall men followed them, swords on their backs. The gap between the elves and men widened with each step they took.

"Wait," the silver-haired elf called again. Her voice reverberated through the still air. The sound must have aroused the rider and Sheriff of Northwell from slumber as both stumbled from the barn onto the side road, wiping their eyes.

"Wait," the elf called again, reaching the edge of the path, and climbing after the troop. "We're coming, too. Look, we've prepared something."

Steigauf backtracked, walking back down the track towards the four approaching from the tiny township.

"This," the Pit Guard started, gesturing to the woods behind him, "is dangerous. What we're about to do may see the end of us. You should stay in your home, where it's safe and warm."

"Safe?" Yaleni raised her brows. "There's no place safe from her. She took everyone." The elf pointed to the heads higher on the hill. "We're all that remains here. She'll come back for us."

Pursing his lips, Steigauf nodded, considering her words.

"What have you prepared?" he asked.

Yaleni turned excitedly to her sister, who just caught up, puffing and panting.

"These." The silver-haired elf held the water bags and strips of rags in her hands up for the Pit Guard to see before waving them towards the identical items the other elf carried.

"We have water," Runolffson put in, almost sounding sarcastic.

Wynneiros grinned.

"Not water," Aralore puffed, still trying to catch her breath. "Oil."

Steigauf furrowed his brow, shaking his head.

"I don't see the purpose of fragrances in this endeavour," Agdestein said.

"It's not perfume," Yaleni said, sounding a little irritated. "It's burnable."

Looking at the strips of cloth, and the arrows in their quivers, the Pit Guard understood.

"We prepare here," he told them. "We may not have a chance to do so once we enter the woods. But first, do you have more oil?"

"More?" the silver elf asked.

He looked at the watching heads on the hill.

"The only way to make sure the dead stay dead," he said.

"We have half a barrel inside," Aralore answered.

"Good." Steigauf took his waterskin from his belt and poured it out upon the snow. "Empty them out, boys."

The troop complied, squeezing, and squirting out every drop before Runolffson collected them as he passed by the men, handing them to their commander.

"Give what you have to Ospak. Leave your arrows. We'll start preparing them for you," the Pit Guard told the elves, nodding towards Runolffson.

He held the water skins out to the elf women. "Take these and fill them with as much oil as you can."

Yaleni nodded, taking the water skins, and turning to head down the hill, back to the house. She passed quickly by the two men who had just reached the path.

"Where are you going?" Jaysh Shen-Jon asked, huffing and puffing.

"To fetch more oil," she answered. Aralore offered an apologetic look as she shrugged, racing off behind her sister.

"To fetch more oil," he repeated. "All right. I'll stay here, then."

Nichol bent over, planting his hands on his knees, sucking in deep breaths of air.

"And you?" Aralore called.

He pointed to the ground he stood on, showing he intended to wait for them to return. The blonde elf giggled as she jogged away, passing Wallace and Martano who were strapping their weapons to their waists as they walked towards the hill.

Steigauf waited for the elf women to be out of sight before he took one of the water skins from Runolffson. He continued on up the hill towards the severed heads.

"Arnald," he called. "I need your help."

Instantly, the boy fell in line behind the Pit Guard.

All ten heads fixed their glares upon the two, their eyes slowly turning as the soldier and the boy drew nearer.

"Get the flint ready," Steigauf commanded.

Reaching deep into his pocket, Arnald felt cloth touch his fingers.

Gertrude.

The sudden memory of her on the dock, by the fishing boats, stabbed him in the belly. He remembered being happy with her there. Stealing kisses. Holding hands. Peering out to the clear waters of the Cove of Safekeeping.

Seeing a dot on the horizon.

That egregious dot.

A pain like a knife in his belly turned, bringing indescribable pain as the image of her burning body beside those of his family returned.

He pushed past her, the cloth, and found the flint.

"You were going to leave us?" Wallace called from the bottom of the hill.

Steigauf ignored him, pressing on towards the ten on the hill.

"What's he doing?" Nichol asked, standing upright to watch the Pit Guard.

"Answer me," Wallace called.

Runolffson and Wynneiros stepped up to the Sheriff of Northwell.

"Not now," the Jomaandian said.

The Pit Guard moved to the right, passing before the faces of four men, stopping at the last. Arnald glanced at each one as he walked by, each of them watching him intently, hungrily.

Opening the waterskin, Steigauf slowly drizzled oil over the last head in line and moved around to the back of the line to pour oil over the next, working his way back to the path.

"Light them up," the old man commanded.

Arnald felt uncomfortable standing face-to-face with the severed head, so he followed Steigauf's path, walking around to the back of the line. With one strike of flint against flint, a spray of sparks fell onto the dampened hair of the head, igniting instantly.

Bright orange flames quickly spread over the hair and skin.

"Durskka Zabei," Jaysh said, bowing his head. "He was a good drinker."

"Aye," Nichol frowned. "Even better than Ivan."

Jaysh nodded, scanning the line.

"He's up there, too."

Arnald ignited the next head in the line.

"Kain Drovo," Nichol said.

Shaking his head, Jaysh turned away and wiped his eyes.

"I can't watch," he said, starting back towards the township. "I think I'll help Yaleni and Aralore with that oil."

He turned back briefly, noticing the other wasn't accompanying him.

"I'll stay," Nichol told him, staring at the hill as the next head ignited. "I need to see this."

With a quick glance to the hill, seeing three of his townsfolk burning, Jaysh started back to the house across the way from The Lazy Traveller.

Arnald waited until he had walked back along the road and inside the elf sisters' home before striking the flint again.

With the ten heads engulfed in flames, the troop regathered and started for the forest, each of Steigauf's men reunited with their water skins. Tightly wrapped cloth, damp with oil, embraced the arrow tips that Agdestein, Kysha, Arnald and the sisters carried in their quivers.

As Arnald neared the tree line, he held his breath as the stench of burning flesh tore into his senses. His attention fell onto Heilig, walking ahead of him, who stumbled slightly as they passed by the first of the taller trees. He looked on the path for what might have caused the man to stagger but saw nothing. A quick glance over his shoulder informed him Kysha had also noticed.

The sheriff and rider from Northwell, along with the survivors of Mountainfall, had not. They kept their gaze on the path by their feet, watching where they stepped. Turning back to look ahead, Arnald watched Heilig for some time, soon dismissing any concerns he held as they continued to trudge deeper into the woods.

Snow drifted between the tall pines and spruce, randomly floating in all directions, landing on his shoulders and the crest of his hood. The wolf shook violently, removing the built-up frost on her back.

Heilig stopped, placing a steadying hand against a thick tree trunk, causing Arnald and those behind him to pause. The soldier lowered his head, touching his fingers to his forehead.

"Johaan?" the boy called softly.

"I'm all right," Heilig replied with a soft growl. He walked on, quickening his pace to catch up to Benten.

The wolf emitted a high-pitched whine, peering at the man momentarily before looking at the boy. Arnald knew that, like him, she held concerns for the soldier.

"Come on," the boy whispered with a nod. He started after Heilig, hearing footfalls behind him as Kysha, the survivors of Mountainfall, the two men from Northwell and Wynneiros, followed.

"What's wrong with him?" Wallace inquired, keeping his voice low. "Is he changing?"

"Get your hand away from your sword," Wynneiros said sternly.

Arnald stopped in his tracks and turned to see the Sheriff of Northwell gripping the hilt of his weapon. The boy instinctively touched his fingers to the fletching of an arrow in his quiver. Glancing quickly to his left, he noticed Kysha's bow already loaded and aimed steadily at Wallace.

"You'll have all of us to contend with," the elf said, pulling back on the bowstring tighter and tighter. "Lower your hand."

Wallace's chin trembled as he darted his eyes from the boy to the young she-elf.

"He'll kill us all," the Sheriff of Northwell told them. "Best we put an end to him quickly before he changes."

"No one will put an end to any of my friends," Arnald replied, slowly lifting an arrow from his quiver. "Not if I have anything to say about it."

By now, the troop had backtracked to gather at the standoff. The sisters and two men of Mountainfall moved cautiously to the side, out of the line of fire. Wynneiros positioned himself between them and the Sheriff of Northwell. Martano stepped away also, moving little by little towards Jaysh Shen-Jon.

"Where do you think you're going, Aamon?" Agdestein asked, levelling his bow upon the man.

Martano quickly raised his hands and dropped to his knees.

"I don't want to fight," he said, pleading with his eyes.

Wallace shook his head. His cheeks turned red with anger as a deep scowl fell upon his face.

"You fucking coward," he barked at the kneeling man, tightening his grip on his sword.

Arnald instantly thought of Gertrude, the inner voice that taunted him with that word.

Coward.

"It's our duty to protect the people from monsters like that." Wallace jutted his chin towards Heilig, who glared back with intense yellow eyes, baring enlarged teeth as drool spilled from the corners of his mouth.

"Be careful what you say, Sheriff," Steigauf snarled, stepping past Heilig to the boy's side, his hand resting on the hilt of his own weapon.

"You can't protect him from me," Wallace barked. "You can't protect yourselves from what he will become."

Heilig fell to his knees, pressing his palms to the sides of his head as he cried out in pain.

Wallace pulled his sword free and charged forward.

Suddenly, a shaft zipped through the air, planting deep in Wallace's throat.

The Sheriff of Northwell halted in place and touched the fletching jutting beneath his beard before reaching around the back of his neck to find the cloth-covered tip with his fingers.

Dropping his sword on the ground with a thud, he made a soft gurgling sound as his eyes came to rest on Arnald.

A knot in the boy's gut tightened as he moved his gaze from the staggering sheriff to his outstretched left arm holding his bow, the taut string still vibrating after being released. His jaw fell agape with shock as he lowered his right arm back to his side.

Chapter Six

WITH A LOUD WHUMP, Wallace fell onto his side, sputtering blood from his mouth.

"By the gods," Jaysh whispered.

Steigauf placed a hand on Arnald's shoulder.

"You did the right thing, laddie," the old man said. "You protected your brother."

Arnald frowned and stared at the pooling blood gathering around Wallace's face.

For Arnald, it didn't feel like the right thing.

Steigauf moved away to approach Martano, who remained on his knees. Kysha quickly darted to Arnald and wrapped her arms around him, embracing him tightly.

Heilig sat with his back against a tree. With his elbows resting on his knees, he pressed his hands to his ears.

"What is it?" Benten asked anxiously.

"I hear her," he snarled. "She calls me."

"By name?" the other asked, crouching beside him.

"No," Heilig shook his head. "She calls the wolf."

Benten looked at Runolffson, who joined the men by the tree.

"You need to fight her," the Jomaandian ordered. "Fight her with everything you have."

435

Heilig wept as he winced in agony.

"The sheriff may have been right about me," he said.

"Fuck that," Benten snapped. "Get up. Press on. We will kill the bitch and fight together in many battles, you and I."

Clenching his jaw, Heilig glared at his friend and nodded. He put his hands on the ground and pushed himself to his feet.

"We fight until we can fight no more," Runolffson said, remembering words spoken by Agdestein earlier.

"Until we can fight no more," Heilig said, looking thankfully at the boy held in the elf's embrace.

Bewildered, Arnald walked onwards, hand-in-hand with Kysha. He peered about, trying to recollect what had occurred, but his mind held no memory.

"Are you all right?" she asked quietly, keeping her voice low so that only he could hear.

He peered at her, perplexed. "I don't know," he managed.

She offered an understanding look. "You did what had to be done, Arnald," she told him.

He shook his head. "I don't remember doing it," he admitted, glancing about to see if anyone else had heard. No one returned a questioning glance in his direction.

"It was instinct, then," she replied. "You protected your friend from danger."

A frown crept over his face as he considered her words.

"There might have been another way," he said. "Did he have to die? Did I have to kill him?"

A look of recognition swept over her as she studied his countenance. "He was your first," she whispered.

Sadness filled his eyes as he stared into the distance, through the trees to more forest beyond.

"Does it get easier?" he asked.

She bowed her head and looked at her feet shuffling through the snow. "I don't know," she answered.

He turned his head to face her, puzzled.

She looked at him apologetically. "I've killed seven men," she stated. "Six because justice demanded it. Magistrate Demeara called me into service as an executioner for murderers he sentenced to death. I felt nothing for them as I pulled the lever that opened the trapdoor beneath the gallows or swung the axe on the chopping block. But the one I killed with my bare hands..."

She trailed off and walked in silence. Arnald waited patiently for her to resume, keeping his hand in hers and moving closer to her side.

"He had outstanding warrants and fled Dendadia on a ship laden with cargo, bound for the cove," she explained. "We got word from one crewman, so Magistrate Demeara sent me to an inn on the docks to find him and bring him in."

"On your own?" Arnald asked.

She nodded.

"But he didn't want to come in of his own accord," the elf continued. "So, I did my best to persuade him. Only, after he broke a bottle on the bar during the tussle to cut up two men who offered to assist me, I turned that bottle back on him and buried it in his face."

Arnald imagined the sickening sight and how Kysha must have felt. Perhaps not that dissimilar to his current state.

"Men with a few mugs of ale under their belt tend to forget how strong we elves are," she said, her eyes glistening. "I've fought men with my hands before. That was the first time... The only time I killed someone in a fight."

She sniffed deeply and wiped her face on her sleeve.

"So," she said, her voice feigning cheeriness. "You will tell me if it gets easier."

Pushing on, Steigauf followed the track until he reached a dry streambed. Smooth, rounded stones and protruding tree roots, snaking over the ground, stretched away to the north.

He stopped dead in his tracks and scanned the ground, following the wide, empty tributary with his eyes to an area where shrubbery and trees grew thick, swallowing the streambed.

"Where's the path?" Agdestein asked, looking across the dry stream to the other side. He saw no sign of the track's continuance.

"I think this is it," Steigauf replied, pulling his sword free and pointing with its blade. "That's the way ahead."

The archer turned to face the elvish sisters and two men of Mountainfall, still approaching as the rest of the line caught up.

"Is this the way?" he questioned them.

Nichol stared at the smooth stones and twisted tree roots. "It looks different," he answered. "The path is well worn all the way to the hut."

"And you know this how?" Benten quizzed.

"Helena and I... you know..."

"So, you've come this way many times to dip your sword?" the soldier pressed.

"Viktor!" Steigauf barked.

"Yes," Nichol answered. "Many times. The path was clear. The ground is open, not like this. There are too many trees. We must have taken a wrong turn."

"A wrong turn?" Wynneiros put in. "Where? There were no other paths to follow."

"The snow," Jaysh suggested. "Perhaps the snow covered the correct path."

Aralore shook her head and placed a hand on his arm. Her countenance bore apprehension and terror.

"No," she said, "There is only one path, and this is it. And there is no open ground. This is the way. When I've come out here to visit Helena, I followed a winding path which turned past some smooth knolls." She pointed to the place where the streambed disappeared into the thick growth. "Right there."

Nichol shook his head. "No," he said, frowning. "It *must* be the wrong way."

Yaleni stepped to her sister, furrowing her brow. "Aralore, are you certain?"

The blonde elf nodded.

"This is the way," she assured the others. "We'll find Helena's home in there. Not too far."

"No," Nichol protested, tears falling across his cheek, dropping to his knees as he continued to shake his head.

Steigauf looked at the man with compassion.

"I'm so sorry, laddie," he said. "I really am."

With that, the Pit Guard continued onwards, treading carefully across the smooth stones and tree roots, gradually drawing closer to the dark shadows ahead. The troop fell into line once again, each glancing at Nichol sympathetically as they passed him by.

Arnald took an arrow from his quiver, placed the shaft under his arm tightly into his armpit, so that the oil-soaked cloth jutted away, out in front of him. He then took the flint from his pocket and struck it, igniting the arrow tip. As he dropped the flint back into his pocket, Kysha reached across to light the tip of one of her own arrows.

"She's no witch," Nichol cried. "She can't be."

Jaysh crouched beside his friend, placing a comforting hand on his back.

"Stay here," Wynneiros told the survivors of Mountainfall. "There's no need for you to come any further."

Yaleni quietly watched Nichol for a moment before glancing at Wynneiros, who followed the three archers, holding flaming arrows high, into the darkened woods.

"I'm coming," she called after him.

Aralore didn't hesitate, following the soldiers into the dense forest.

"Why?" Nichol begged, staring at the silver elf.

Yaleni frowned, unable to look him in the eye.

"She deceived us all," the elf told him. "She used our trust against us. We all loved her. You most of all. All the while, when she laughed with us, cried with us, held our hands, and cooked her mushroom soup, she was preying upon us."

She turned away and started after her sister, leaving Nichol and Jaysh on the stream bed.

The drifting snow started falling more heavily and a chill wind whistled through the trees.

In the distance, a loon cried.

———————◄O►———————

Arnald held his flaming arrow high to cast light on the ground before him. He clenched his bow in his left hand, ready to load the shaft. His heart raced in his chest and thrummed in his ears. The knot in his stomach tightened and his knees trembled with each step.

He watched Agdestein pace quickly by the others in line with his own flaming arrow high above his head, catching up to Steigauf to light the way.

It wasn't a long trek. Within moments, Agdestein's arrow stopped moving and all eight members of Steigauf's troop, a rider from Northwell, the elf sisters and a wolf, stood before a dishevelled cottage built into the side of a mound.

Constructed of crude materials, the hut appeared malformed and grotesque. Moss and fungus covered the dark outer facade. Two windows, merely square portals framed by broken tree branches and nursing closed lopsided shutters, emitted a faint orange glow through tiny gaps. A small, primitive timber door, dirty and rotten on the edges, blocked the access to the hovel.

Above the structure stood a thick spruce tree and a twisted stone chimney trailing light smoke into the snow-filled air.

"This isn't the house I remember," Aralore said. "Everything is wrong."

Lifting his eyes upwards, following the trail of smoke drifting around the outstretched, gnarled limbs and fingers of tall oak trees, Arnald spied a grotesque scene that churned his stomach.

"Look," he said as he jutted his flaming arrow tip to the sky. All those gathered craned their necks to see the headless, naked bodies of the villagers hanging by their feet by thin ropes, high off the ground. With their bellies torn open, entrails remained attached and dangled like macabre vines from the cavities.

"Kurst," blurted Martano upon seeing the only body with its head still attached. His back had strips of flesh removed, exposing the white of his ribs, and backbone among the glaring red of tissue woven between.

From inside the hovel, a low cackle resounded.

"No need to knock," Benten said, pulling his sword from its sheath. "The lady is home."

"Let's introduce ourselves," Runolffson said, stepping forward to kick the door in with one swift blow.

"Wait," Steigauf hollered.

But it was too late.

Within a blink of an eye, something sucked the Jomaandian inside the hut, as if an invisible hand gripped him by his middle and wrenched him from where he stood.

The others watched on in horror, staring at the open door as the man's screams rang out through the small passageway.

Shadows danced inside, causing the orange light of a fire inside to flash and flicker intermittently, obstructing any chance of a clear view.

A loud crunch and sudden silence followed.

Suddenly, a bloodied mess was flung out through the doorway, skidding to a halt on the snow at Steigauf's feet.

The mangled, twitching mess was mostly unrecognisable, except for golden hair protruding from broken flesh and dark blood.

Legs shaking, arms trembling, Arnald looked around, instinctively trying to find a place to take Kysha and hide.

Coward; Gertrude shouted.

His jaw shook wildly, wanting to say something but unable to willingly speak or move.

Purposefully, he clenched his teeth, hearing a low grinding in his ears.

You fucking coward; she screamed.

"No," he whispered, squeezing his eyes shut tightly in the hope to silence her. "Not this time."

He loaded the flaming arrow into his bow with his trembling hands.

"Light it up," Steigauf bellowed, uncorking his waterskin and throwing it at the hut.

Without hesitation, Arnald fired. The arrow whistled through the air, resembling a shooting star. The flaming tip penetrated the waterskin in mid-flight and shot through the doorway, spraying ignited oil into the hovel. The flames instantly smeared the door, floor and rafters inside the structure.

The other men of the troop took the hint, unsealing their water skins and tossing them into the engulfed doorway, where they burst into flames.

The chimney began spewing dark smoke as the witch let out a high-pitched scream.

"Burn, you bitch," Yaleni cried, tears streaming down her face.

The flames built higher and higher, lapping at the outer moss-covered walls, and eating into the timber shutters.

The screaming from inside subsided, and the sound of burning timber resonated around the troop as they watched the hovel burn. Eventually, the spruce tree sitting above the hut caught light, sending drifting flames along its trunk and branches.

Silently, Steigauf's men watched. Arnald breathed a sigh of relief; thankful they didn't need to engage in battle. He reached over and took Kysha's hand in his, allowing the heat of the fire to warm his skin.

The sound of crackling flames and cracking timber filled his ears.

Crackling flames.

Cracking timber.

Crackling.

Cracking.

Cackling.

Cackling.

Cackling laughter.

A knot in his stomach built.

His senses became more acute, and he let Kysha's hand go to load his bow again.

An explosive burst of flames and debris through the roof of the hut signalled the fight had only just begun.

All eyes went to the trees. The sound of laughter echoed all around them.

Steigauf turned around, peering into the treetops, searching for a sign.

Nothing.

"Fuck!"

Chapter Seven

—◆—

"**B**ACKS TOGETHER," STEIGAUF CALLED. "Make a circle."

The men, under his command, along with Arnald, and Kysha, quickly assembled together. Standing shoulder to shoulder, peering out to the surrounding ground and up to the treetops, they searched for the witch.

"You as well," Heilig growled, spitting foam as he shouted at the elf sisters. "Get over here."

The looks on their faces showed they didn't grasp what was happening.

"Quickly," Benten added, urging the elves to snap to reality.

Aralore moved first, grabbing her sister by the elbow as she raced towards the circle.

"In the middle," Steigauf barked. "Both of you."

Arnald and Heilig stepped apart from each other, just enough to let the two women through before closing the gap again. The boy used the flint to light another arrow, offering the newly lit flame to Kysha and Agdestein so they could light their own. He then turned and held the arrow towards the sisters.

"Light your arrows," he told them.

Their delayed response made Arnald nervous. His stomach fluttered and his throat swelled.

With each archer, aiming their bows at the trees, they searched.

A loud crack from high above them, the sound of timber splintering, drew their attention to the area just left of the burning hut and spruce tree. The small inferno leaped to the surrounding pine trees, spreading slowly to the surrounding foliage.

A loud thud made Arnald turn his head just in time to see two headless bodies fall clumsily to the ground.

Then another.

And another.

Soon, eleven dead figures lay on the snow around the circle.

"Shah," the witch hissed. Her voice was unnaturally loud, reverberating through the air and resonating over the sound of the inferno. She repeated the word again. "Shah."

"What is that?" Benten asked, tightening his grip on his sword, and correcting his stance.

A headless woman got to her knees. Her intestines swept against her legs and feet as she stepped slowly towards the circle.

"She calls the dead," Yaleni answered, aiming her bow at a man rising to his feet on the other side of the circle.

Kysha fired a bolt into the chest of another fellow who stepped towards them. The headless form continued forward, unperturbed.

The elf tried again, as did Arnald, firing into another corpse. Still, they kept moving towards the troop, closing on the tiny circle. The witch laughed from somewhere high above them.

"Fire," Agdestein shouted. "Light your arrows."

Arnald dug the flint from his pocket and lit an arrow from his supply. He stuck it, fletching first, into the snow by his feet so that the flame pointed to the sky, before taking another arrow from his quiver. Loading it onto the bowstring, he directed the tip over the flame, igniting the covering oil-soaked cloth.

Within moments, he had three flaming arrows in the chest, hip, and thigh of the closest figure. The dead man continued towards the circle, moving within arm's reach. The flames were too slow to catch and cause any significant damage.

All the while, the witch cackled from her hiding place.

"Move," Aralore shouted, grabbing Arnald by the shoulder, and pulling him aside. Before he could protest, she tore the cork from her waterskin and squeezed the sides, squirting oil onto the figure.

Instantly, the dead man burst into flames.

"Hack its legs," Steigauf commanded. Benten complied, swiping his blade through the knee of the figure's left leg.

It fell onto its open belly and dragged its burning body across the snow with clawing hands, trailing its intestines behind.

Arnald and Kysha continued to fire flaming arrows at the other approaching dead.

"Give me that," Benten said, snatching the waterskin from the blonde elf's hand. She looked at him, confused, as he broke away from the circle to chop into the legs of a headless woman. She fell to the ground and reached for him with outstretched arms. The soldier splashed some oil along her spine before turning for another woman a few paces away.

"Light that up," Benten shouted, gesturing to the fallen figure before raising his blade to hack into the next.

Aralore didn't hesitate. She quickly lit the tip of an arrow and fired it into the back of the woman.

Arnald noticed tears welling in the elf's eyes as he turned to light another arrow tip. Doing what she did couldn't be easy for her, considering she knew these people well.

Time to console her would need to wait.

The dead rider from Northwell stumbled towards him, almost tripping on his intestines. His mouth opened and his eyes rolled aimlessly in his head as he stepped awkwardly, swaying this way and that.

The wolf growled and started racing for the rider just as Arnald took aim.

"No," the boy called after her. "Back."

But the wolf ignored the call and leaped for the man, knocking him to the ground. Instantly, the dead man grabbed the wolf's front paw tightly in his hand. She tried desperately to pull away, but he held her firm.

Steigauf turned and swiftly tore the flaming arrow from Arnald's bow and took the waterskin from the boy's belt. He raced across the ground, pulling the cork from the container with his teeth. He kicked at the dead man's hands, forcing the rider to let go through brute force before splashing oil over the body. The wolf raced back to Arnald as the Pit Guard plunged the flaming arrow into the dead man's chest.

Martano frowned and pursed his lips as he watched his friend writhing and flailing as flames spread over his body.

"I could use some help," Benten called, putting the body of an elderly man on the ground.

"We cut them down," Wynneiros said, looking at the archers. "You light them up."

Arnald looked to his quiver and saw three shafts sticking out.

"I'm almost out of arrows," the boy shouted.

"Have some of mine," Agdestein offered.

"No," Steigauf ordered, slicing through the shoulder of a thin woman, removing her reaching arm. "Get out here and cut these fuckers down!"

Dropping his bow and quiver, he pulled his sword free and followed Steigauf into the fray.

Before long, the six swordsmen and four archers had most of the bodies burning on the ground. Three remained.

A loud creak from a branch high above placed their attention on the witch again.

Clumps of snow fell to the ground with loud thuds, trailing around the burning house and flaming bodies to the path through the dense woods they had come from.

"She's trying to flee," Wynneiros called.

"There," Martano pointed to a tall tree, rocking back and forth from a sudden impact.

Bright embers fell from the branches and the fire spread into the treetops surrounding the house.

There, the hag clung to a trunk of a thick oak, her head beneath her inverted, twisted, naked form. She glared at the boy with hollow eyes.

Glaring.

Glaring.

A sickly feeling swept over him at the sight of the monster. She spread her lips wide into a deranged smile, exposing crooked, yellow teeth and blackened gums.

"What are you waiting for?" Arnald shouted to the archers.

Agdestein pivoted away from the three attackers and aimed squarely at the hag, letting his arrow fly. It struck her in the ankle.

She yelped and fell just as another arrow struck the tree.

Rolling on the ground, she broke the arrow shaft and doused the flame quickly before scurrying away on all fours like a deformed insect.

The Pit Guard glanced about to see who he could spare from the battle.

"Go after her, Ulfar," Steigauf barked, sweeping his sword through the thigh of a large man. "Take Johaan with you."

Already racing into the woods, the wolf and Heilig tore after Wynneiros, quickly overtaking him, grunting, and growling with each rapid stride.

Racing through the thick growth, beneath twisted limbs of dead oaks and outstretched arms of evergreens, Heilig turned to his sense of smell to track the escaping creature. The wound Arnald inflicted left a faint scent of blood for them to follow. Together, he and the she-wolf leaped over fallen logs and darted around the thick stems of pine and spruce trees.

Bursting onto the dry riverbed, Heilig skidded to a halt suddenly to survey what lay ahead. The two men from Mountainfall, seated on boulders where the others left them, stood up, and stared back, dumbfounded.

The wolf pulled to Heilig's side. Upon seeing the two men, she spun on the spot to scan the ground and trees where they had come from.

A crashing sound, breaking twigs, and rustling leaves, drew the attention of all three men to a spot near the dark portal the troop had passed through earlier. Jaysh Shen-Jon pulled his sword and prepared for a fight.

Wynneiros burst through the thick growth, sword in his hand and glancing about wildly.

"Where is she?" the broad-shouldered man asked, puffing and panting.

"Who?" Nichol queried.

"Not here," Heilig answered. "I followed her scent here. I can still smell her."

"Who?" Nichol asked again, looking to one man, then the other for answers.

"An old hag," Wynneiros replied, stepping into the clearing, cautiously peering about at the trees and shrubs surrounding them. "You didn't see her?"

"No," Jaysh answered. "No one came this way."

"You're certain?" the other pressed.

"I think I'd know what an old hag looks like if I saw one," responded Jaysh, nodding.

Wynneiros shook his head slowly and offered a quick glance to Heilig.

Heilig grunted as both men positioned themselves back-to-back.

"She must be in the trees," Wynneiros said, moving his gaze upward.

"Or she's able to make us see nothing where there is witch," Heilig replied. "You heard what the elf-woman said about the house? That wasn't the house she remembered."

"Everything is wrong," the other finished. "I heard. Then I saw what that bitch did to Ospak. Fuck!" Wynneiros shook his head and frowned.

The men of Mountainfall exchanged concerned looks.

"What happened to Ospak?" Nichol enquired.

"The bitch twisted his body like a rag," Wynneiros answered. "Like a fucking rag."

Concern turned to fear.

"Then she made the dead come back to life," Heilig added. "The others are back there finishing them."

Both Mountainfall men shot a quick glance at one another again before swiftly pushing their backs to the other men, forming a tiny circle of four.

The wolf growled, fixing her eyes on the dark portal that marked the way to the burning hovel.

Nichol followed her stare and waited for something to appear.

"Did you find anyone else there?" he asked after some time.

"Anyone else?" Heilig growled.

"Helena," the other clarified. "Did you find Helena?"

Heilig shook his head.

"How would we know?" Wynneiros replied. "They were missing their head."

"No one else but the hag," Heilig put in, focusing his attention on the dark woods.

Baring her teeth and raising her hackles, the wolf lowered her head, still watching the portal.

"The house burns," Wynneiros added. "If there was anyone else there, they didn't come out when they had the chance."

Nichol trembled and wept.

"What do you mean, the house burns?" Jaysh asked.

Both soldiers furrowed their brows and looked at the man questioningly.

"Smoke rises there," Wynneiros pointed to a dark cloud rising above the tree line with his sword. "The trees are burning. Can you not smell it? That's the scent of people burning."

"I smell nothing," the man replied, looking in the direction the soldier gestured towards. "And I see no smoke rising."

"She's here," Heilig growled, staring towards the portal.

All eyes moved to the location.

"Where?" Nichol questioned.

"Careful," whispered Wynneiros. "She makes you see only what she wants you to see. She could be right there, looking back at…"

A soft creak above them caused them all to peer skyward at an overhanging branch of an oak.

Too sudden to respond.

Too quick to defend themselves.

The deformed creature dropped upon Wynneiros. He fought to stay on his feet as she pushed her fingers into his mouth; her left hand wrapped around his bottom teeth, her right hand around his upper. Suddenly, she pried them apart, tearing his lower jaw away from his head.

Wynneiros let out a bloodcurdling scream as he dropped his sword with a loud clank against the smooth stones of the dried streambed.

The witch let the soldier loose and leaped upon Heilig, who was already swinging his sword towards her.

As Wynneiros hit the ground, she dodged Heilig's attack, twisting around the blade to shove the man in the chest. Heilig flew, smacking hard against a tree trunk, causing built-up snow on the limbs to come crashing down around and onto him.

Copious amounts of blood sprayed between Wynneiros' fingers as he

449

held his face, writhing in agony on the cold stones.

The witch turned from Heilig and put her attention on Jaysh Shen-Jon, leaping towards him as fast as lightning.

He raised his curved sword, striking her in the arm. She shrieked as the blade slid into her forearm, leaving a shallow gash halfway between her elbow and wrist.

It wasn't enough to deter her.

She brought her knee up to his face and sent him flying backwards.

His head struck a boulder, knocking him out cold before she turned her attention to Nichol.

He stood motionless, afraid, staring wide-eyed at the horrifying creature before him. His hands shook and his chin quivered.

Glaring back with empty sockets, her countenance suddenly changed. Her twisted form straightened slightly as she stood more upright. The wrinkled features of her skin softened slightly, and her eyes became a discernible, sorrowful green.

At that moment, Nichol recognised her.

"No," he whispered as a sharp pain built in his chest.

She opened her mouth to speak but said nothing.

"Why?" he asked, tears falling down his cheeks.

Looking at the treetops, she appeared as if she might cry.

But the chance to do so didn't come.

The she-wolf cut the moment short, leaping high and snapping her jaws around the witch's throat.

Hitting the ground hard, the creature tried to push the wolf away. The wolf reacted by tightening her hold, drawing blood.

Reaching her hand out towards Heilig, the witch muttered one quick audible phrase.

It was enough.

"Shah-fa, lukan."

The wolf noticed movement from the man lying against the tree. Like a flash, Heilig was on his feet, screaming in pain.

Buckling over, he grabbed his stomach as dark hair burst from his skin.

Stretching his arms out behind him, he roared as his fingernails stretched into long claws.

Heilig's clothing ripped as his body expanded and contorted.

Within moments, the soldier vanished, replaced by a monster.

The she-wolf let the witch go, focusing her attention on the man-wolf glaring menacingly back at her.

The witch crawled away frantically, pressing her back to a bolder as she held her hand to her bleeding throat.

The wolf and monster slowly stepped closer and closer to each other.

With teeth bared and hackles raised, both beasts prepared to fight.

"Destroy," the witch hissed, pointing at the she-wolf, her eyes reverting to empty sockets, her body converting to her twisted form again.

The man-wolf prepared to lunge at the she-wolf.

A sneer spread over the witch's face as she focused on the ensuing confrontation.

"Destroy," she said again, urging the monster to act.

It stepped forward, towards the she-wolf.

TWACK!

The witch let her smile fall away to a look of shock as she reached to her stomach. There, she found a shaft sticking from her torso.

Slowly, she pulled it free and dropped the arrow on the ground beside her, searching for the archer who had fired it.

At the edge of the portal leading into the darkened woods, Arnald stood with a loaded bow aimed steadily at the witch.

Chapter Eight

———◆———

THE HAG GLARED ANGRILY at Arnald as she opened her mouth wide and hissed like an angry cat, plucking the arrow from her flesh. A thick line of dark blood fell from the wound as she dropped the shaft on the ground and scurried backwards on all fours towards the tree line on the far side of the empty stream.

Turning, Arnald crouched by Steigauf's side. A deep frown formed on the boy's face as he noticed the old soldier's eyes staring lifelessly at the sky.

Arnald fired.

The witch rolled, dodging the shot before dashing away, out of sight.

Arnald ran to retrieve his ammunition, the only two arrows he had. He kept his eyes on the patch of shrubbery he saw the witch scamper into as he collected the arrow that penetrated her middle, now resting on the ground. His hand touched the warm blood smearing the shaft. Glancing down to the tip, he noticed the oil-soaked cloth, now damp with dark fluid.

In haste, he peeled the cloth away from the arrow's head, scanning the ground for the other. As he dropped the shaft into his quiver, and the thin cloth on the ground, he found the second arrow lying on the ground a few paces away, elevated slightly as it rested awkwardly on two smooth stones.

He started for it, but the she-wolf dashed in front of him, hackles raised and growling wildly, facing away from him.

At that moment, the large hind foot of the man-wolf came smashing down on the arrow, snapping the stick in two.

The beast snarled, long strings of saliva dangling from its jaws as it stared hungrily at the boy. Slowly, it lowered to all fours, darting its yellow eyes from Arnald to the wolf and back.

Keeping herself between the monster and the boy, the she-wolf snapped her jaws and lifted her head, appearing as menacing as she could. Arnald placed his bow and quiver on the ground and drew his sword.

"Johaan," he called softly. "It's me. Arnald. Your friend."

The beast locked onto him, cocking its head slightly as if it listened to the words spoken. The man-wolf stepped to the side, beginning to walk a wide circle around the boy and the she-wolf. But she wouldn't have it, mirroring his movement to keep the monster away from the boy.

"Do you remember?" Arnald continued. "We trained at Shiverwind and ate together."

The beast stopped growling, slowly closing its lips to hide its teeth, continuing to circle the boy and wolf.

"We stayed at The Maidservant Inn where the nice lady talked to you," Arnald said, hoping to spark some memory the man held inside. "Maybe more than just talked?"

The man-wolf stopped moving, tilting its head, and lifting an ear.

"And Viktor?" Arnald asked. "Do you remember Viktor?"

The creature lifted its head, as if recognising the name.

"You do," the boy gasped. "You remember."

The man-wolf stepped backwards, as if recoiling.

"It's all right, Johaan," said Arnald, relaxing his sword by his side. "We're friends."

A soft whine emitted from the beast as it turned its attention to the dark portal in the growth leading to the hovel in the woods.

Steigauf, Benten and Agdestein ran into the clearing, followed by Kysha, Martano and the elf sisters.

"Shit!" Martano spat as Agdestein rapidly loaded his bow.

The man-wolf backed away on all fours, afraid.

"Wait," Arnald called. "He remembers. I think."

"You think?" the archer returned.

The boy gave him Agdestein look as he pointed to the place he saw the witch run to.

"She went that way," he told them. "We've got this."

The she-wolf continued to look threatening, puffing her fur up to look bigger than she was, growling and baring her teeth as she kept herself between Heilig and Arnald.

"Let's go after her," Benten said enthusiastically. "We have her on the run."

Steigauf paused and shook his head.

"No," he said, looking at the trees with gnarled branches reaching over the dried streambed like closing fingers.

The man-wolf continued to slink away, twisting his head to the side to look at the sky. Arnald understood the beast wasn't cowering away from the men. The boy followed the beast's gaze and saw her clinging to the branch directly above him.

His heart seemed to stop as she let go with her fingers and feet.

Falling.

Falling.

She drew closer and closer.

Suddenly, fearing the worst, something lifted Arnald off his feet and carried him away from where he stood.

Two giant, hairy arms clutched him tightly before planting him hard on the ground.

With barely enough time to comprehend what happened, Arnald watched the man-wolf leap towards the hag.

The she-wolf and man-wolf attacked together, tackling the witch to the ground. A terrifying skirmish ensued, with fur flying, loud snapping of teeth and deep growls as a cloud of dirt and snow erupted around the three battlers.

Getting to his feet, clutching his sword in his hand, Arnald watched the beasts fight the old crone, pinning her to the stones as they used claws and teeth to strike her again and again. She flailed, legs and arms kicking and swinging wildly in all directions.

The snow and dirt cloud grew thicker and thicker, hindering the boy's view.

Suddenly, something burst from the disorder, shooting skyward in an arc before skidding across the stones with a yelp.

The she-wolf.

Soon after, Heilig was flung towards the edge of the streambed, where he tumbled over and over.

Both beasts remained still and silent, unmoving.

"Javanakhan," spat the witch.

Arnald felt his head swim momentarily. He glanced about, noticing perplexed looks on other's faces. Assuming they experienced the same sensation as he, and feeling fine now, he moved his gaze to the she-wolf lying on the ground. Fearing the worst, he sheathed his sword and retrieved his bow and quiver before starting for the animal.

"Don't move, laddie," Steigauf called, striding across the smooth stones towards the boy. "This isn't over yet."

The dust cloud slowly continued to spin around and around the hunched silhouette of the old hag; or was it the outline of a young woman? Arnald furrowed his brow, fixated by the spectacle.

The dust swirled around the witch slowly, obstructing a clear view of her. Arnald knew it was a trick, something she made them see. But how?

"How?" the boy asked softly. "How is she able to do this?"

Steigauf shook his head.

"Something in the house, perhaps," the old man answered. "A spice or something carried in the smoke affecting our senses. It doesn't matter. Time to find out who this bitch is," he said as the others followed him into the clearing.

"Who are you?" Steigauf asked, taking the direct approach, tightening his grip on his sword.

She cackled softly.

"I know you, Pit Guard," she croaked. "One of The First."

"Answer me," he growled. "If I am to battle with you, I deserve to know."

A vile laugh built from within the cloud.

"I know the heir of Amalith is with you," she said.

Kysha lowered her bow, staring wide-eyed at the figure within the dust.

"How could she kn—?"

"Quiet," Steigauf instructed the elf. He returned his attention to the witch, staring at her with steely eyes. "Are you Lycia, the necromancer?"

A long silence ensued. The figure swayed from side to side slowly. Steigauf opened his mouth to address the witch again.

"Are you..." he began.

"Yes," she answered. "And no."

The old man shook his head, quickly looking at the others for clarification.

"What does that..." He peered back at the witch. "Explain. What do you mean, *yes and no*?"

"We are two," she said. "And we are one."

"Two?" Steigauf shook his head.

Arnald's jaw dropped open.

"Two," he repeated. He looked over to Steigauf. "Two fell with the mountain."

Suddenly, a look of clarity swept over the soldier's face. "Elene the enchantress?"

"Yes," the witch answered. "And no."

"What's that mean?" Martano asked the Pit Guard.

"I think they bonded together somehow," he answered. "Perhaps they are something else now. I don't know."

"Clever little Pit Guard," the witch said.

Agdestein shook his head, lifting his loaded bow and drawing its string.

"Why are we toying with this bitch?" he offered before firing the arrow into the cloud.

A deafening shriek radiated from the swirling dust. The cloud thinned and dropped away to reveal the hag, holding her shoulder where a shaft stuck from both sides.

All who gathered in the clearing cringed at the sound the witch made, dropping their weapons to hold their hands to their ears.

Seizing the opportunity, the witch darted across the streambed, closing the gap between the troop and herself within the blink of an eye.

Agdestein pushed his hand to his throat, blood pouring through his fingers. Giving Steigauf and Arnald a silent, sad, and fearful look, the archer stumbled and fell face-first to the cold ground.

Standing a few feet away, the witch touched her crooked fingers to her twisted smile, appearing pleased with herself.

"Fucking bitch," Jaysh Shen-Jon roared, raising his sword, and charging for the necromancer.

"Wait," Nichol protested.

She lowered her hand to her side and peered towards the man from Mountainfall; her hollow eyes squinting a little, irritation on her face.

He brought his blade downward, arcing it towards her head.

She stepped to one side, turning to face him as he charged by with momentum. With one hand, she pushed him hard on the small of his back, sending him flying into a tree trunk at the edge of the woods. A thin trickle of blood spilled from his left ear as he slumped.

"No," Yaleni cried, loading her bow, and firing arrow after arrow at the witch, each shaft zipping wildly by the hag, who cackled with glee.

Nichol raced to Jaysh's side as Aralore joined her sister, carelessly shooting bolts towards the monster. Their tears blurred their vision, causing each arrow to shoot mere inches off target.

Kysha, however, took her time. She levelled her aim carefully at the hag and pulled back on the string, all the way to her jaw, hearing the creak of the cord and timber in her ear. As the sisters exhausted their ammunition, each firing their last arrows and missing their mark, she let the shaft loose.

With a whistle, the arrow zipped across the clearing and struck the witch in the stomach.

The witch screamed, wrapping her fingers around the bolt, and tearing it from her abdomen, leaving a matching wound next to the one Arnald gave her earlier. She then snapped the arrow's shaft sticking from her shoulder and flung it to the ground before reaching over to her back to pull the remaining piece free.

Kysha took another arrow from her supply, feeling only one other in her quiver. She loaded her bow and took aim, knowing she had to make each shot count.

Arnald felt intense fear as the elf let the bolt fly. It darted straight for the necromancer's head. His body tensed as it drew nearer and nearer, feeling a heightened sense of hope and dread at the same time.

The witch ducked, and the arrow planted harmlessly among the shrubbery at the edge of the forest. Standing upright, she laughed out loud, taunting the elf, not noticing the second arrow already speeding towards her.

Kysha dropped her bow and quiver, pulling her sword from its sheath as the arrow stuck hard in the hag's hip. The elf darted forwards, running for the witch who fell to the ground holding the protruding shaft near her skin.

"Come on," Steigauf hollered, running towards the fallen creature, with Benten and Martano close behind.

Arnald looked briefly past the witch into the woods. Fire spread along the treetops and ground towards the streambed.

The boy then peered at the one arrow remaining in his quiver and the waterskin on his belt. Glancing up, he saw Kysha as she reached the creature who held a defensive hand towards the oncoming blade. The elf's sword came down hard, chopping through fingers and a portion of the witch's hand.

Screaming, the hag stood up and struck Kysha with a wide swing of her arm, sending her toppling over the stones on the far side of the streambed.

Arnald felt his stomach tighten and bile sting his throat as the she-elf skidded to an awkward halt, resembling a tossed rag doll. As he focused on the elf, Martano started his attack.

The witch blocked his blows easily enough, eventually grabbing his sword arm with her good hand and twisting it violently, so it snapped at the elbow. Martano let out a bloodcurdling scream as his sword clanged against the stones at his feet.

Kysha moved and tried to get up, but clumsily slumped back to the ground. She pressed her hand to the back of her hand before holding it before her eyes.

Even from his position, Arnald saw blood on the elf's palm.

He felt some relief seeing her alive but wanted desperately to go to her. Returning his attention to the fight, he saw Steigauf engaging in battle.

Chopping, swinging, and swiping his blade, the old soldier drove the creature back towards the oncoming flames spreading through the woods.

The witch dodged and ducked each blow easily, baring her yellow teeth and blackened gums in a wry smile. She glanced over her shoulders at the wildfire building behind her and then back to the old warrior who continued to bombard her with his attack.

Suddenly, she lunged at him, knocking him onto his back. Steigauf's sword fell from his hand onto the ground beside him.

Like a flash, in one swift move, she darted for the weapon, took it in her grasp, and spun around on her feet to plunge the blade through the centre of the four women standing on the Pit Guard's breastplate. The scream of iron against iron rang throughout the clearing as the sword pinned the old man to the ground.

Arnald let out a chilling scream, drawing the attention of the witch. She leered at the boy, smiling ravenously.

Benten charged and tackled the woman to the ground.

"We're losing," Aralore sobbed. "We're losing."

"I think he's alive," Yaleni said, staring at Jaysh lying motionless on the ground, his head cradled in the other Mountainfall man's lap. Nichol, a blubbering mess, tears dripping from his chin, watched the battle. His mouth hung wide open in a silent scream.

"We're losing," Aralore repeated.

Arnald glanced at her and tried to focus his thoughts, trying to figure out a way to not only fight but defeat the witch.

He looked at the raging fire as he dug into his pocket, retrieving the flint and the bloodstained cloth from his long-discarded tunic's sleeve.

A sudden, deep sadness swept over him as he remembered her.

Gertrude.

Tears streamed down his cheeks as he wrapped her around the tip of his last arrow.

Pulling the cork of his waterskin with his teeth, he carefully poured oil over her, letting the liquid soak into the rag.

A quick glance at the battle told him Benten wouldn't last long. The witch stood back upon her feet, clawing her good hand towards the soldier, who stepped back to keep out of harm's reach. Doing so also kept him from attacking the creature. Arnald knew it was only a matter of time before Benten grew too tired to fight.

Carefully, the boy directed the bottle to his mouth, placing the cork back into the opening. Dropping the waterskin into his quiver, Arnald wiped his eyes on his sleeve and loaded the bow as he raced towards the fallen Pit Guard.

Arnald glanced at the skirmish, seeing Benten swipe his sword at the witch. She stepped backwards, avoiding being struck before the soldier stepped back and away again.

Leading her.

Leading her away from the others.

Crouching by Steigauf, Arnald stared at the sword sticking from the breastplate. A small amount of blood streamed between the four women and down the sides of the armour. A thick pool of dark liquid built beneath the soldier.

"He'll sacrifice himself to kill her," the old soldier whispered, his voice sounding hoarse.

Arnald moved his gaze to the Pit Guard's face to see him peering towards the battle.

"He's a good soldier, that one." Steigauf smiled before coughing, blood spattering over his lips. "You must save him, Arnald."

The boy nodded, fighting the urge to cry.

"Take your time," the old man murmured. "Steady your breathing."

Tightening his jaw, Arnald stood to his feet and placed the shaft of the arrow into his armpit, pointing the tip wrapped in the cloth bearing Gertrude's bloodstain away from him. He took the flint and held it in place, chin quivering as he looked at the bloodstained cloth one last time.

"Goodbye, Gertrude," he said softly before striking the stones, igniting the arrow's tip.

Carefully, he loaded the arrow and pulled the bowstring back to his jaw.

Take your time.

The witch raised her arms as she prepared to strike the soldier, her back towards the boy.

Benten looked past her to lock eyes with the boy momentarily.

Steady your breathing.

"Any time soon would be nice, Arnald," Benten shouted.

The witch turned to face the archer, tearing her attention away from the soldier. A cruel smile spread across her face.

"Go on, boy," she taunted.

Her face contorted suddenly as Benten shoved his sword through her back and out through her chest.

Nichol stood up and cried out a painful howl. He staggered towards the witch as she fell to her knees.

Her countenance slowly transformed. The misshapen form of a hag straightened, rejuvenating before their eyes.

Shock-filled, youthful, green eyes peered at Arnald. Blood spilled over her firm breasts.

As her hair turned from white to black, Nichol called to her.

"Helena."

She glanced at the man from Mountainfall, her eyes filled with sadness.

"I'm sorry," she whispered. "I'm so sorry."

"Why?" Nichol asked, dropping to his knees by Arnald's side. "Why, Helena?"

"Why?" she spat, a sardonic smile spreading over her face as she cried. "*I love you, Nichol. But you are *our* enemy. Always.*"

Benten plucked his sword from her as Nichol burst into tears, buckling over from the pain he felt.

Arnald continued to direct the flaming arrow at her chest.

"Go on, boy," she said again.

The bolt stuck in the bone just beneath her neck. As she fell onto her side, Arnald reached for the waterskin in his quiver, removed the cork and squeezed oil over her.

The flames spread quickly, engulfing her flesh in a fireball.

Chapter Nine

Early the next morning, Arnald and Benten prepared five pyres on the side of the road across from The Lazy Traveller while, inside the tavern, the sisters carefully prepared the bodies of Sheriff Clay Wallace, Kolfinn Sigemaer, Ulfar Wynneiros, Fridmund Agdestein and their commander, Osman Steigauf with wrappings and scented oils.

The cloudless sky, turning from a light rosy blush to blue as the sun struggled to climb over the mountains, promised a fine day ahead.

Heilig sat on the steps of the tavern, petting the she-wolf lying by his side as he observed the others stacking wood. His body bore countless bruises, bumps, lacerations, and scrapes from the skirmish. The natural green pigment of his eyes returned with flecks of yellow persisting around the outer edges of the iris.

"You know," he said, pointing to the woodpile that the boy and soldier worked on. "You should put more kindling on that side. That way, when you light it from there, the breeze will carry the flames to the rest of the pyre quickly."

"I think I know how to make a fire." Arnald smirked.

"You want to show us how to do this, daffodil?" Benten quipped.

"I'm really sorry, but I can't," Heilig replied, shaking his head, and smiling. "Too sore."

"Too sore," both the boy and soldier chorused.

"Such a shame your mouth wasn't injured when the witch beat the shit out of you," Benten added.

Heilig chuckled, instantly regretting it, touching a hand to his abdomen.

The door opened with a squeak as Kysha stepped onto the porch.

"We're ready?" she said.

Arnald gave a nod, his eyes focusing on a dark mark stretching across her forehead and a lump just above her left eye.

"We just need to place some small pieces here and there," he replied. "And then we'll come and help."

It wasn't long before all ten survivors of the battle stood on the porch, gazing at the bodies resting on top of the pyres.

"Does anyone have any words?" Arnald asked.

A deep scowl swept over Benten's face.

"I wish we could have brought Ospak back here," he said, looking at the body of Wallace. "I'd rather see him there than that bastard."

Martano held his tongue, shooting the soldier a sideways glance.

Heilig put his hand on his friend's shoulder.

"He got his send-off," he said, nodding towards the dark smoke still rising from the woods.

Benten shook his head.

"He deserved better," the soldier muttered, wiping his eyes on his sleeve.

Kysha held a torch out to Arnald, fashioned crudely from a broomstick and oil-drenched cloth tightly woven to the bristles. Using the flint, Arnald ignited the torch and took it from the elf.

He crossed the road with the wolf limping close behind him and started at one end of the line, lighting Wallace's pyre first. Next came Sigemaer, Wynneiros and Agdestein, leaving Steigauf last.

Here, Arnald paused, taking time to pay his respects to the Pit Guard.

"Thank you," he whispered, a lone tear streaking down his cheek as he touched the torch to the base of the pyre.

The wolf whined as the flames took hold.

"Come," Arnald said, tossing the torch on the ground beside the burning timber. He started back to The Lazy Traveller. The wolf hesitated, watching the old man for a moment before following the boy back to the porch.

Arnald took Kysha's hand and reached down to stroke the wolf's ear as the flames tore through the timber stacks, growing tall and hot.

"What happens now?" Kysha whispered.

Arnald considered her question, breathing a deep sigh as he peered to the south where the mountain once stood.

Sitting inside The Lazy Traveller, drinking hot tea around a large table, the survivors discussed what to do next. All except Yaleni, who disappeared to run an errand at Arnald's request.

"I will return to Northwell with Naran," Martano said, rubbing the shoulder of his broken arm, held close to his chest in a sling. "I hope Naril found her way home. But I don't like the odds of that."

Arnald stared at the table, believing the missing Eluvian horse to be dead; possibly, part of the stew Sigemaer tasted and, as a result, died from ingesting.

"Will you tell them of what happened to the sheriff?" Benten asked, concerned for Arnald.

The rider from Northwell looked over at the boy.

"I'll tell them he fell during battle," the other answered. "That's all I will tell them."

A deep frown formed on Arnald's face as he recalled the moment when he fired his arrow into Wallace's throat.

Jaysh Shen-Jon tapped the table with his fingers, his head wrapped in bandages.

"Well, I intend to stay here," he said, waving his hand around the room. "With luck, I can make something of this place."

"You mean here?" Heilig asked. "In this tavern?"

"Absolutely!" He smiled. "I think the former owners had a terrific idea. Humphrey and Anne always said it was the perfect place for those passing by. It wasn't, admittedly. But some of the best people I knew made up this community. It would be a dishonour to all of them to simply abandon it." He sipped from his cup and held up a finger.

"Besides, with the witch gone, and news of the *supposed* curse lifted," he said, silently hinting with a raised brow, "especially if someone was to spread that information, more people will come. This might be a thriving city to rival Dendadia, given time."

The boy smiled at Jaysh's optimism.

"What about you?" the man from Mountainfall asked, turning to Aralore seated across from him.

"Well," she said, lifting her brow as she turned her gaze to the tabletop. "My sister and I will also stay. Like you, we see potential here. Perhaps we can be a welcoming sight to other vagabonds in search of a place to call home."

"And make some coin selling scented oils and herbs to unsuspecting travellers and merchants," Benten suggested.

She nodded and raised her cup with a smile. "And make some coin selling scented oils and herbs to *deserving* travellers and merchants."

"How about you?" Benten asked Nichol, who stared out the window looking to the road where the pyres smouldered and the hill beyond. He almost jumped as his train of thought snapped back to the present.

"Sorry?" he asked, not hearing the conversation at all.

"What will you do now?" Benten rephrased.

Nichol shook his head, moving his mouth as if to speak as he searched for the words.

"I don't know," he said eventually, looking at Jaysh Shen-Jon and Aralore. "I can't stay."

"What?" The other Mountainfall man furrowed his brow.

"I can't," Nichol said, wiping a tear from his cheek. He returned his gaze to the window and let out a long sigh.

"Where will you go?" Kysha asked.

"I don't know," he answered, his voice trembling.

"You're welcome to join me," Arnald offered.

Nichol smiled. "Thank you, but no," he replied. "I think I need to find my own way. Perhaps to Vertdell or somewhere of the likes to try my hand at farming."

The group sat in silence for a while, allowing Nichol to return to his thoughts.

"I'll go with Arnald," Kysha put in.

"Surprise, surprise." Benten smiled.

Heilig chuckled softly.

"Will you become a Pit Guard, also?" Aralore asked.

Kysha shrugged. "We shall see. I haven't heard of any elf or lady Pit Guards before. I, being both, might not fit the requirements. Nevertheless, I will go with Arnald."

Arnald looked at Heilig and Benten.

"You two are welcome to join us," he told them.

"Thank you, laddie," Benten replied. "But we're posted at Shiverwind and need to return. Duty and all that. You know."

The boy felt taken aback by the response but understood.

"We could go to Dendadia together," Arnald suggested. "There, we could make an official request for you to join the Pit Guard."

"You'll need to refer to it as the Temple Guard when you get there," Heilig informed him. "*Pit Guard* is a colloquial term."

"I heard it was because the guards were the victors of the fighting pit tournaments in Dendadia," Jaysh put in.

Heilig shook his head.

"The commander was one of The First," he replied. "The fighting pits were outlawed nearly a hundred years ago. He was old, but not that old."

Arnald felt confused. He glanced at Kysha, who wore the same baffled expression as he.

"So, where did the name come from?" she asked.

Heilig shrugged, suddenly wincing in pain, reminding himself too late about the injuries he sustained.

"Don't know," he answered, rubbing his neck. "That might be something you can ask when you arrive."

At that moment, Yaleni entered the room through the door leading to the kitchen.

"Will this do?" she asked, holding a fat clay jar with a cork stopper, as tall as Arnald's forearm was long. "I have more than enough stored in our woodshed behind the house."

Arnald inspected the container as the elf-woman placed it on the table. He spun it around and nodded.

"Perfect," he said solemnly. "Thank you."

———◆———

By late afternoon, Arnald, Benten, Kysha, and Martano scooped the ashes of their fallen comrades into five clay jars with small spades and shovels found in tool sheds throughout the community. They then wrapped each jar in a blanket belonging to the one contained within.

After carrying the wrapped jars to the stables and placing them with the equipment belonging to the fallen, Arnald and Benten took to preparing and cleaning Steigauf's armour and sword under the watchful eyes of the she-wolf.

"Will you take this with you to Dendadia, or leave it with him?" Benten inquired, scraping a whetstone along the sword's blade.

Arnald dipped a rag in a pail of water before wiping it along the sides of the hole where the blade pierced the breastplate, separating the two centre figures of women brandishing swords.

"He said to take his armour," the boy answered. "I'll leave his sword with him."

Benten glanced at the wolf sitting close by.

"And her?"

"She's free to do as she will," Arnald replied.

"She'll go with you," the soldier said, returning his attention to the blade. "Who else would she follow?"

"She could return to the wild," the boy said, looking at the wolf.

Benten shook his head.

"She's not a wild animal," replied the soldier. "Not anymore. Someone needs to care for her. And she needs to care for someone. It should be you, Arnald."

Arnald considered Benten's words and knew them to be true.

"Then, she will come with me," he said, wiping more blood from the armour.

Chapter Ten

A FEW DAYS PASSED.

The skies remained clear, painted with crystal blue, carrying a warm sun through the day and countless bright stars each night.

Arnald and Benten took to hunting each morning, crossing the timber bridge just to the south of the village, venturing close to the gap where deer and elk gathered to feed upon fresh grass shoots on the open ground by the roadside and clearings in the forest. It was, therefore, a bitter moment when they prepared the horses for departure.

They loaded the clay jars containing the remains of each of the slain upon their horses, wrapped in their blankets and placed carefully in saddlebags. Jaysh and the sisters gathered on the porch of The Lazy Traveller to see the riders off.

Heilig and Benten split the steeds from Shiverwind between themselves, each trailing one pack horse and two belonging to soldiers behind their own. Martano rode on Naran, leading Clay Wallace's horse ahead of them.

"Good luck, Arnald," Heilig called, turning to wave. "Maybe we'll see one another again someday."

"Who can tell?" Arnald answered from atop the white horse Steigauf gave him. "Goodbye, Viktor."

"Farewell, laddie," the other called. "Farewell, Kysha Naberyn. Sheriff of

Shiverwind. Queen of Legilawen."

"Fuck off, Viktor." The elf smiled from her spotted stallion. The soldier chuckled, slapping his thigh. "Take care, both of you," she said, her smile falling away.

The men offered one last wave goodbye before turning their attention to the road ahead of them.

"You ready?" Arnald asked Kysha. She nodded, still watching the others riding away in the distance. The boy looked down at the wolf sitting beside his horse. "How about you?"

The wolf licked her lips and yawned.

"Will you go directly to Dendadia after you take Commander Steigauf's home?" Aralore asked. "Or will you search for those who raided your village?"

"We'll go to Dendadia so I can begin my training," Arnald answered. "I see no purpose chasing after something I may never find. Besides," he added as he looked at Kysha by his side. "I think my future holds something far more valuable than seeking revenge."

Kysha blushed.

"You know," Jaysh said from the porch. "You are welcome back anytime. When you return, we'll have to kick people out to make room."

Yaleni took his hand in hers and smiled. "May the gods guide you on your journey and keep you safe, Pit Guards."

"Thank you," Kysha replied.

Arnald offered a polite nod and urged his steed forward, pulling the line in his hand to encourage Steigauf's black steed to follow. On its back sat the Pit Guard's saddle, sword, and armour, bundled beneath canvas sheets with the small tent, to resemble a pack horse rather than a warrior's charger.

Riding through the gap between the mountains, they followed the road over knolls and dips, passing high cliffs and snow-spattered rises on both sides. The wolf looked to be in her element, jogging in the lead and sniffing the ground at intervals. Slowly, the way opened before them, presenting a vast expanse of grassland, open plains, and distant forests touched with white.

"Still winter here," Arnald said, looking about at the land ahead of them.

"We may need to venture a little farther south to escape the frost," Kysha told him.

Spying an old wooden signpost by the edge of the road before them, Arnald steered his horse closer to read the engraving on four timber planks nailed to the post. Two planks pointed north, positioned one above the other. The other two planks mirrored them, pointing south.

On one side, the top plank read: *Mountainfall*. Beneath it; *Northerlands*.

The other side bore a sign reading: *Shadowfort*. The lower; *Southerlands*.

"That's very helpful," Kysha jeered. "As if we couldn't figure that out ourselves."

Arnald grinned and looked at the road ahead.

"Shadowfort is on the way to Wyvernmont," he told her. "Perhaps there'll be more signs when we get there."

"I hope so," she replied as they started forward again. "Else, we might get lost."

"No, we won't," the boy assured her. "I have a map."

A look of surprise spread across her face.

"You have a map?" she questioned, looking at his saddlebags. "Where?"

Arnald placed his finger against his temple.

Her countenance changed, smiling with her eyes as she remembered the first time she met him in Magistrate Demeara's quarters.

"You're a walking map," she said.

He nodded.

"And you're beautiful," he said, grinning. "And dangerous."

She locked eyes with him and smiled.

Riding side-by-side, Arnald and Kysha talked about where to next, what their future might hold for them and how they could get there.

"Where do you see us in ten years?" the elf asked.

"Both of us Pit Guards," Arnald replied.

"*Temple* guards," she corrected him.

"Temple guards," he repeated. "Sorry. Perhaps we have a family together."

She smiled, blushing a little.

"How many younglings do we have?"

"I don't know," he said as he scratched his cheek. "A good round number. Twelve."

"Twelve?" she blurted.

"All boys!" he chortled.

"No." She shook her head, grinning from ear to ear. "I need girls to help with all the chores while you grow fat from all the food I make you."

"I'm not growing fat," he told her. "I'll be a Pit... Temple Guard with arms as big as tree trunks and I'll hunt all the meat we will devour in our big house in the city."

As both shared their dreams and aspirations, wanting to be as optimistic as Jaysh Shen-Jon, Arnald wondered where their path would truly lead.

Experience taught him things aren't that simple.

But simple things are worth fighting for.

"We'll hang silk drapes and eat with silver cutlery," she continued.

He smiled, not able to take his eyes away from her as she started talking about rugs and the finest settees and divans from Etiendia. She noticed him gawking at her.

"What?"

"I love you, Kysha Naberyn," he said, meaning it.

Her chin quivered as her eyes welled.

"I love you, Arnald Oberlin," she replied.

Pulling closer to her side, he took her hand in his.

"Now," he said, as they continued along the road, the wolf circling them contentedly. "Tell me more about those fancy chairs."

Acknowledgements

Special thanks to my father, Robert; to whom I've dedicated this book. His fatherly advice and encouragement have been paramount to my life and his influence definitely played a part in creating several characters in this book. Without his support, I don't think I would have tried my hand at anything. A genuinely giving person who would care for his children well into their adulthood. Sadly, we lost him in 2022 and so now he rests next to our mother, Suzanne, who passed away in 1992.

A big thank you to my sister, Lee, possibly my biggest fan and the only person to have signed copies of my books.

To my editor, Sally Odgers, for tolerating and correcting my woeful words, and for enduring the insanity my brain expels onto the page.

To Dee Dee, my cover designer, for the beautiful artwork displayed on my books. I am so grateful that I found you.

To the writing and reading community who take a chance on indie authors and new publishers. Your words of kindness in your social media comments and emails are inspiring.

Last, to everyone who has purchased one of my books. Thank you, thank you, thank you, thank you. Unless you are an author, you do not know how exhilarating it is to know that someone is reading your work. I really hope you like this one. I think you will.

Thanks, everyone.

All the best, and happy reading.

Robert E Kreig

About The Author

Robert E Kreig was born in Newcastle, Australia and grew up in its outer suburbs.

He has always had a love for books, particularly well-told stories involving action, adventure and fear.

Some of Robert's favourite authors as a young reader included J. R. R. Tolkien, Stephen King, Orson Scott Card, Ray Bradbury and Frank Herbert. As he grew into adulthood, the list continued to lengthen, adding more influential writers such as George R. R. Martin, Matthew Reilly, Nathan M. Farrugia, Dan Brown, James Patterson, Michael Connelly and Lee Child just to name a few.

Inspired by movies like Star Wars, King Kong, Jaws, Jason and the Argonauts and other great adventure pieces, Robert listened to the voices in his head and entertained the strange visions dancing through his mind to assist him with writing his fantasy series The Woodmyst Chronicles.

Robert has penned ten books for the series which follow the lives of many characters, particularly focussing on a family who must face many trials before the epic conclusion. Clashing swords, strange creatures, flying dragons and sorcery inhabit the world surrounding Woodmyst.

Robert has also written two standalone books, Long Valley and The

ROBERT E KREIG

Calm Voice.

Robert currently lives in Canberra, Australia, where he hopes to one day become a full-time writer.

Also By This Author

THE WOODMYST CHRONICLES
The Woodmyst Chronicles is the story of a small community that faces the
hardest of trials in a world filled with darkness, violence and magic.
Books In This Series...
THE WALLS OF WOODMYST
THE SONS OF WOODMYST
THE HEIR OF WOODMYST
THE WARLORDS OF WOODMYST
THE HUNTRESS OF WOODMYST
THE SHADOW OF WOODMYST
THE BRIDES OF WOODMYST
THE GODS OF WOODMYST
THE WEAPONS OF WOODMYST
A FAREWELL TO WOODMYST

LONG VALLEY

In the small community of Long Valley, nestled comfortably beneath snow-capped mountains, people quietly go about their business. Everybody knows everybody and there are no worries to give mind to.

But something has awakened.

A tragic accident near the valley's army base sparks a number of terrifying events, placing the local civilians in mortal danger.

A contagion is subsequently released into Long Valley, infecting pets, livestock, wildlife and people.

It's up to the local law enforcement and a small band of citizens to try to keep the town safe.

In the end, it becomes a struggle for survival as the people of Long Valley are overcome by the urge to feed.

THE CALM VOICE

No one in the remote town of Edwards Hill could have known that she was capable of such carnage.

Least of all her parents, the first to die.

Driven by the gentle words of The Calm Voice, she inflicts a barrage of carnage and death, leaving a trail of blood in her wake.

Her goal is to bring death to all who have hurt her.

All she needs to do is listen to The Calm Voice.

All she needs to do is just focus...

Just focus...

Focus...

The Calm Voice is a dark psychological novel surrounding the actions of one girl on a fateful morning in April 2017. Kirstin Matthews is fed up with her life, her oppressive parents, and her bullying schoolmates. A soothing voice thrumming in her head compels her to seek revenge on those who have wronged her. At the top of her list is a trio of girls who have taunted her to breaking point. After careful planning, she embarks on a deadly rampage through Edwards Hill State High School, bent on destroying all her pain one last time. What follows is a haunting description of the day's events, culminating in an ending no one will expect.

robertekreig.com

whitekeepbooks.com